THE HUNTER AND THE PREY

His skin tingled from the top of his head to the bottom of his feet. Stars appeared in front of his eyes as the room started to sway. He couldn't believe what he'd just done. It was so impulsive and unplanned. So unlike anything he'd ever done before. He'd had no idea it would even work. But now he'd claimed another victim in a new way, in his own house. This was too exciting.

He kneeled down next to her and carefully placed two fingers along her neck. He was shocked to feel a strong, steady pulse. He had no idea what damage he had caused, but it appeared that he had only knocked her unconscious. Perhaps breaking her neck or back, but not killing her.

So he simply wrapped his big hand over her mouth and nose and clamped it shut.

There was no thrashing, no twitching, and there was no oxygen getting into her bloodstream.

A minute later he released his hand and checked her pulse again.

Nothing . . .

Books by James Andrus

THE PERFECT WOMAN

THE PERFECT PREY

Published by Kensington Publishing Corporation

THE
PERFECT
PREY

JAMES ANDRUS

PINNACLE BOOKS
KENSINGTON PUBLISHING CORP.
www.kensingtonbooks.com

PINNACLE BOOKS are published by

Kensington Publishing Corp.
119 West 40th Street
New York, NY 10018

All Kensington titles, imprints, and distributed lines are available at special quantity discounts for bulk purchases for sales promotions, premiums, fund-raising, educational, or institutional use. Special book excerpts or customized printings can also be created to fit specific needs. For details, write or phone the office of the Kensington special sales manager: Kensington Publishing Corp., 119 West 40th Street, New York, NY 10018, attn: Special Sales Department; phone 1-800-221-2647.

ISBN-13: 978-0-7860-2216-8
ISBN-10: 0-7860-2216-7

First printing: January 2011

10 9 8 7 6 5 4 3 2 1

Printed in the United States of America

One

Detective John Stallings had seen plenty of homicide scenes in and around the city of Jacksonville. Each one ate at him, stealing a little of his own life no matter who lay dead behind the tape.

On this cool, spring evening he felt a stab of annoyance when the young patrolman securing the crime scene asked to see his sheriff's office ID. There was a time when Stallings knew every patrol officer, detective, and administrator employed by the Jacksonville Sheriff's Office, but now, after years in the detective bureau and the massive hiring pushes, he was reduced to proving his identity just to enter a homicide scene. Fucking great.

His partner, Patty Levine, gave the young uniformed officer a wink as she held up her detective's badge. The patrolman didn't even examine it and said, "I recognized you, Detective."

As they walked toward the herd of crime scene technicians and detectives in the center of the scene, Patty said, "That creeps me out. How is it that you caught The Bag Man, but he recognized *me?*"

Stallings stopped and faced the diminutive detective. Her blond hair whipped around her face in the strong March breeze, her bright eyes and white teeth on a pretty, all-American girl's face. "Gee, I wonder why the horny young cop knew you and not me?" He scratched his head and started to make another comment when he heard the unmistakable bark of the lead homicide detective, Tony Mazzetti.

"What're you two doing over here? This is my scene." Twenty years in Florida hadn't dulled his Brooklyn accent.

Stallings held up a hand. "Relax, Tony. Just swinging by to see if you need any help."

"Do I horn in on missing persons cases?"

"You're not assigned to both squads."

"As I recall the damn LT said if we got busy you'd be a good guy to help, and one suicide in the park isn't what I call busy." He turned to yell at a crime scene tech. "Jesus fucking Christ, Kenny, try not to get your chewing tobacco on the corpse." He shook his head, mumbling, "Bunch of rednecks."

Stallings said calmly, "It came out on the radio as a body in Brackridge Park. I didn't know it was a suicide." He started easing his way toward the scene to get a look for himself, pulling Patty and Mazzetti with him. He didn't really know why he liked pushing the homicide detective's buttons so much, but right now it was one of the few bright spots in his life.

Patty had been neutral in his ongoing feud with Mazzetti. She had, unfortunately, started dating the turd and was careful not to pick sides. To Mazzetti's credit, just because he was seeing Patty, he didn't treat her any differently at work. He insulted her right along with Stallings and everyone else, but she gave it back like the little fighter she was. Stallings admired that kind of commitment to sarcasm and strife.

Mazzetti said, "Stall, what're you, deaf? I said we got this shit handled. It's just a suicide."

Stallings looked over the shoulder of a crime scene photographer at the body of a very young blond woman with a white cord still looped around her discolored neck. She'd already been pulled down and now lay on a plastic sheet. The cord had worked its way into her skin, and the hours of deterioration had made it appear to be part of her body. She was dressed in jeans and a nice shirt, as if she was going out for the evening. She had that grimace on her distorted face Stallings had seen too many times. An expression that wasn't peaceful but scared. The look that caused parents to grieve and reporters to salivate. He saw the whole story unfolding now: beautiful girl unable to cope with—any problem could be inserted in the sentence—takes own life. He'd read that some kids think it's dramatic or even romantic. He'd seen too much to think any of that was true. His Catholic school education leaked from the back of his head about the sin of suicide, and he shuddered.

Patty peeked around him and let out the sigh of relief that he should have. As a cop he could view any scene professionally and start trying to piece together what happened, but as the parent of a missing daughter he tensed whenever he heard about a female body. After three years it had gotten no easier.

He asked Mazzetti, "Any ID?"

"What are you, the new boss? I know the new sergeant is coming soon, but I didn't see your name on the list."

Patty stepped up. "It's a simple question, shithead. Who is she?"

Stallings suppressed a smile. He saw Patty do the same. Mazzetti was the only one who didn't see the humor in it, but that was normal.

Mazzetti said, "Her purse was on the bench over there. Her DL is from South Carolina. My bet is she was down here on spring break. Her license says she's Kathleen Harding, and there's a student ID from the University of South Carolina."

"How old?"

"Twenty-one."

All Stallings could do was shake his head. *What a waste. What a shame.*

Mazzetti said, "Aren't you on spring break patrol?"

Patty said, "I thought you called it the 'runaway roundup'?"

He smiled, his neatly trimmed mustache spreading with his mouth. "This is a seasonal name. In a few months you'll be on the 'summertime student sweep.' I got a bunch of names to use."

Patty leveled a stare at him. "You got a nickname for masturbating? Because something tells me that's what you'll be doing for a while."

Mazzetti seemed hurt. "What happened to keeping work and personal lives completely separate?"

Stallings chimed in. "Yeah, I think I like that better too. Keeps things more interesting on the job."

Patty nodded her head and glared down Mazzetti. "Fine," she said through clinched teeth. "You better make sure your people do a good job here, because we don't want to have to clean up one of your messes again."

Stallings thought, *Wow, good one, partner.* But when he looked back toward the crime scene techs around the body all good humor drained out of him.

Two

Allie Marsh felt a wave of joy as she gazed out at the dark, choppy Atlantic Ocean from the hotel room crowded with suitcases and sleeping girls. She didn't care that a misty rain was falling or that it was only sixty-five degrees. She could swim in the Gulf off Biloxi or even a few hours east in Pensacola, but for six days she was free for the first time in her life. Her parents had agreed to fund the trip during the week off from her classes in elementary education at the University of Southern Mississippi. It was her first time away from home without another family member, and she intended to make the most of it. She liked some aspects of living at home and commuting forty-five minutes to Hattiesburg three times a week. It saved money, and she could never have afforded a place half as nice as her parents' house. The downside was her social life was still centered in the small town of Laurel, where everyone knew everything you did or didn't do.

She did things she shouldn't, but it was the things she didn't do that she wanted to try on this excursion to the big city of Jacksonville, or at least Atlantic Beach.

Her friends promised that they'd go to all the hot clubs in Jacksonville every night and that whatever happened wouldn't ever be spoken of inside the state of Mississippi. Last night the four young women had visited five different clubs. Most were crammed with students from across the Southeast. Allie knew enough students and wanted to meet someone a little older and more mature. Someone totally different. That's what Allie was looking forward to: meeting guys who didn't say things like, "I might could do that," or "You seen my new custom Camaro?" She'd only had one serious boyfriend, Tommy McLaughlin, and he'd moved away to go to LSU, then a week later had pictures of a new girlfriend up on Facebook. She didn't even bother to call him to find out what had happened. Allie did hook up with one nice boy from Louisville who was in the counseling psychology program at USM. He had a sweet smile and good, tight body and had come all the way to Laurel to meet her parents. They did it in his seven-year-old Volvo in the driveway and in the parking lot of the university admin building. She liked it but never felt as if she could let go when either her mom or some flunky security guard might find her naked with a man.

This week was her chance to just let go and see what life on TV was like. She knew why they never filmed any of those reality shows in Mississippi. People were too boring there. Here in Florida things would be a lot different.

This was his third night out in a row. He was afraid the unusually cold Jacksonville weather might affect the small but steady spring break crowd that settled for the city. Daytona and Fort Lauderdale, farther down the East

Coast, were both still more popular than dreary old Jacksonville, but this was his hunting ground for now. That's how he saw himself: a predator prowling the concrete plain for his next victim. He was a leopard looking for antelope. Why not? God had given him animal instincts, athletic grace, and the looks to attract his favorite prey. He could blend into his habitat until he was ready to be seen and strike silently. He was so beautiful that he rarely scared his prey. Even at the end.

He peered across the bar of the busy dance club and saw tall girls with pretty faces, a shapely Latin woman with dark eyes, and a group of apparent cheerleaders with brown ponytails swaying behind their heads like horsetails shooing flies. But none of them interested him. He had specific tastes. Light eyes and hair. Anything else was negotiable.

He liked this particular dance club because the cops didn't come around much and he wasn't known here. The only patrons this time of year were college kids, his meat and potatoes. Then he saw his prey. The one he'd noticed and started to approach last night. She was with her own little herd so he had to be patient to avoid possible identification. The hair on the back of his neck began to rise. So did his dick. He felt that uncontrollable smile stretch across his face and his nostrils flare. Just like a predator. He flexed under his tight shirt for confidence, a mating ritual and signal to others to stay away. He waited at his end of the bar as the four young women chatted and laughed, sipping their colorful drinks. Two of the girls were asked out on the dance floor by tall young black men.

The shorter, pudgy girl headed toward the bathroom with a slight wobble in her step.

He made his move.

As he approached her, she turned, blond hair flipping with the movement.

He smiled and said, "Hey."

The girl had healthy white teeth and full, soft lips. "Hey there," she said in her light Southern accent. "What're you doing here?"

"I hit a couple of clubs on my night off." He gazed into her clear blue eyes and wondered if this was the right time to strike. Ease her out of the club before her friends noticed him. He had several magic pills. Then he said, "Wanna come to a different club with me?" He held out his hand with the spotted hit of Ecstasy. The homemade white pill was the size of a baby aspirin. He had a source that supplied him all he needed. So far no one had turned down the offer.

"What's that?" The girl asked.

"X."

"What's X?"

"It'll make you lose a little control. It's fun. That's why it's called Ecstasy."

She hesitated, then plucked the pill from his palm, examined it and turned toward the bar and took a sip of her rumrunner.

He wasn't sure she'd taken it, but asked, "So how about we try another place? Maybe one with a live band."

She gave him a smile and said, "Do you even remember my name?"

He froze. She had darted like smart prey trying to throw off a predator. He remembered she was from Mississippi. He searched for her name. What was it?

She waited, now frowning slightly.

Then out of nowhere he said, "Allie."

Now she let loose with a broad smile.

This would be one sweet hunt.

Three

John Stallings squinted through the water-spotted windshield to make sure he'd read the right address on the clean older apartment building off Roosevelt in the trendy Avondale section of the city. The address was the same as the lead sheet the crimes/persons analyst had given him. This missing persons case was a little different from the usual missing college kid who turned up drunk in New Orleans or in the slammer in Savannah. This guy, Jason Ferrell, was thirty and professional. Some kind of engineer over at one of the supporting companies for Maxwell House. He knew the building near the Police Memorial Building, or PMB. Ferrell's mother in Chicago hadn't heard from him, and he'd missed work the last few days. This one might be a real mystery. Something to sink his teeth into. He needed the distraction about now. Even though it was his concentration on police work in the first place that put him in this position.

Patty made a few notes on the pad in her battered metal case and said, "Looks like the place."

He nodded.

Patty said, "If he's here I'm gonna smack him for scaring his mom like that."

"I'd think he was avoiding her except he hasn't been to work."

Patty nodded, looking closely at him. "Are you sleeping any, John?"

"Some?"

"I'm not trying to pry, but what's your status with Maria?"

"I talk to her a couple times a week. She's usually scarce when I visit the kids and help them with homework in the evenings."

"You seeing them enough?"

"Every day. Charlie seems to be adjusting because we still play games and I coach his soccer team. Lauren is harder to gauge. She's got that moody teenage thing and she's so mature. She's been spending a few evenings with some girls from school." He turned to her and said, "Older girls."

"Don't worry too much—older girls could be a good thing. Older smart girls are the best."

"All I see are older pretty girls."

Patty snickered. "All fathers are the same."

Stallings considered his own childhood and thought, *I wish that were true.*

Patty Levine let her partner knock on the doors of the neighbors on either side of Ferrell's apartment. Stallings had no idea the effect he had on most women. They'd take one look at that curly dark hair and kind eyes and tell him anything he wanted to know. That whole ruggedly handsome, intelligent look was hot right now, but she figured it was timeless and Stallings had always been charming.

Instead, Patty waited on the first floor. She needed a moment alone to pop one of her Xanax and swallow it dry. She'd been starting to control her prescription drug use until she'd gotten caught up in the massive Bag Man case, and the trauma she'd suffered at the end of it hadn't help wean her from her regular regimen of Xanax for her anxiety, Vicodin for joint and back pain, then Ambien to sleep at night. Dating Tony Mazzetti had affected her use a little. She had to plan things better and sometimes lay awake at night with her head on his shoulder, staring blankly up at the ceiling instead of downing twice the recommended dosage of the sleep aid. Even Tony had no idea that she used the drugs. No one did and no one would. Unless disaster struck. No single doctor realized she was taking any prescription other than what he had prescribed.

Patty knocked on the building manager's door. Then knocked again. Finally, as she was about to leave her card on the door, she heard someone inside say, "Hang on, hang on."

The door opened and a man about fifty stood looking down at her. Instantly she made a cop's assessment: *This is an annoyed redneck who had one too many beers at lunch.* The red face, sloppy comb-over, gut sticking out of his Dickies plaid shirt, and dirty jeans led her to this conclusion. When he said, "What's the po-po want?" before she even showed ID, she added *ex-con* to her assessment.

Patty stayed professional and took the time to show her credentials, badge first. "I'm trying to find one of your residents."

"Jason Ferrell?"

"How'd you know?"

"'Cause some other ol' boys were by here yesterday and a couple of really big colored boys were looking for him the day before."

"Really?"

"Do I look like I wanna waste time jawing with a cop when *Jerry Springer* is on and I got the couch just the way I like it?"

"Do I look like I want to smell your stale beer breath?" The guy smiled. "I like cute, feisty cops."

"Then we better get this over with because the next cop you'll see isn't nearly as friendly. What do you know about Ferrell?"

"Just a nerdy college boy. He pays on time and never has no problems. Smells funny in there once in a while, but he said it was just some project he was working on. The two that was just looking for him weren't from around here. They were from one of the western counties, I could tell."

"How could you tell?"

"John Deere caps, work boots. These were country boys. They wanted in his apartment, but I wouldn't let 'em. Even with the fifty bucks they offered."

"Got a key?"

"Ain't supposed to use it unless I think it's an emergency."

She looked at him. "What'd you do time for?"

He was about to ask how she knew, but it was obvious. "Beat up my ex-wife pretty good."

"How long you do?"

"Two years."

"And what else?"

"Five years federal time for off-loading coke back in the eighties."

"So you don't think me asking nice is enough to borrow the key?"

"Like I said, it has to be an emergency."

"Is a broken arm an emergency?"

"Not really. What makes you think Ferrell is in there with a broken arm?"

"Not his, yours."

Allie Marsh woke up to the sun slicing through the narrow opening of the motel drapes. She turned on her side and found her little Timex Ironman runner's watch. Ten-fifteen. That was something new for her. At home, if she slept past eight she had her mom yelling for her to get moving. This trip was turning into an adventure.

She heard Susan say, "Hey, Allie."

They were the only two in the room for the night. When Susan started feeling ill she asked Allie to come back to the room with her. What kind of friend would've let her leave alone? The other girls said they had rides and kept dancing with the cute young men from Holland. Allie was a little sorry to leave the guy she'd seen two nights in a row, but she'd see him again. She had pretended to take the little speckled pill he gave her, but had stuffed it into her jeans pocket instead. The slight headache from the rumrunner was a small price for her to pay for partying until midnight.

Allie stretched in bed, then leaned up and stood, pulling her long T-shirt down as she did. She opened the curtains slowly, letting the sunshine fill the room.

This was the first day since they had arrived that the clouds had broken. In the other queen bed Susan still lay under the covers. Allie knew she was sensitive about her shape—wide hips and pretty but tiny boobs. Her face had a cute quality like a chipmunk's, but so far the boys they'd met preferred the lithe bodies of Cici and Karen to a cute smile and wide hips.

Susan said, "I'm sorry I ruined your fun last night."

Allie smiled. "Sweetie, you didn't ruin anything. I'm out of Mississippi for a few days, and not one club has caught my fake ID. I'm having a wonderful time." She crossed the room and sat at the edge of Susan's bed. "Are you feeling okay today?"

"Yeah, but I want to get wild too. Cici and Karen are still with their dates, and I don't want to be bored."

Allie thought hard how she might be able to cheer her friend up. Then she remembered the pill. Without a word she popped up and found her jeans draped over a chair. She dug into her front pocket and found the small, funny-looking pill. She held it up. "We could try splitting this and see what happens."

Susan's smile gave her the answer.

Four

John Stallings spoke to three neighbors, but no one had seen Ferrell. No one really knew him. He had a few people over to his apartment now and then. He left for work most days or was just dead silent during the day. Not much to go on.

Patty came through the stairwell door dangling a key from a short chain.

"Ferrell's?"

"Yep."

"How'd you manage that?"

"I did my John Stallings impersonation, and the guy saw the light." She stepped to the door and unlocked it instantly. No inside chain caught, so his concern that the guy was dead inside lessened.

Stallings waited before entering and murmured his affirmation. "Is this the day that changes my life?" It was a little trick he'd been taught in the academy to make sure he never took any assignment too lightly and stayed sharp. It had probably saved him professionally a couple of times, but he'd recently learned it didn't do shit for his personal life.

The entrance was a short hallway where they both paused. Stallings noticed the open curtains and sun filling the room. No specific smell attacked his nose the way a body decomposing would have. He called out, "Mr. Ferrell? Jason Ferrell? Hello, anyone here? This is John Stallings from the Jacksonville Sheriff's Office." He waited, listening and watching for any movement beyond the hallway.

They split up and made sure the two-bedroom condo was actually empty. Then they settled down to see what they could find.

Patty pointed to a framed diploma. "Northwestern, not bad."

There was a framed photograph of Ferrell and a cute, young woman with long dark hair hanging on the wall next to the diploma. At the bottom of the photograph a small caption read, *Jason and Alyssa forever.*

Stallings said, "No messages on his machine." He rummaged through some kitchen drawers until he found the one drawer every home has. Crammed with odd pieces of paper and pens, loose change, and errant business cards, it was a chaos pit of possible leads. He pulled it out and dumped it on the counter. Patty joined him to start going through the pile of crap.

They found a few phone numbers that Patty copied down on a sheet from her notepad, two tangled sets of stereo earbuds, a business card from a car detailing place, Jason Ferrell's own business card that read *Chemical Engineer, Commercial Waste Inc,* and a hard, clear plastic bottle that held an ounce of light yellow fluid.

Patty held it up to the light and shook it gently.

"What's it look like to you?"

Patty kept staring up into it and said, "I thought it was clean urine until I shook it. It's thick like an oil."

"Let's check the rest of the house." He didn't say anything when Patty stuffed the bottle into the front pocket of her jeans. She was so curious that she couldn't let something so simple go unanswered. He knew she'd talk some chemist at the SO into analyzing it. Before he'd finished checking the drawers in Ferrell's bedroom his cell phone rang.

"John Stallings," he said in his usual professional phone greeting.

"Stall, Lieutenant Hester says for you and Patty to come back to the Land That Time Forgot by three for some kind of squad meeting." Stallings recognized the secretary's voice. A lot of the staff referred to the detective bureau on the second floor of the PMB as the Land That Time Forgot because of the lag time in new equipment and nice furnishings. Even though the unit had made strides under the guidance of Lieutenant Rita Hester, it fit a cop's natural tendency to bitch to call the office by its nickname. All Stallings said to the secretary was, "See you then."

Administrators always found a way to screw up real police work.

Allie and Susan giggled uncontrollably at the Tiki Bar of the Hide-a-Way motel. The cold wind had chased everyone away from the outdoor bar, but they still insisted on getting margaritas outside, then joining the other visiting students inside the room overlooking the closed swimming pool. The little pill they'd split had relaxed Allie, but it positively transformed Susan. Wearing a skirt to hide her butt and bikini top, inside and out in the freezing gale, she had already kissed a University of Georgia marching band drummer, danced on an empty space in front of the bar by herself, and downed about six bottles of water.

Susan said, "Whatever that pill was, I like it."

Allie grinned. "I know. I hope he has one if I see him tonight."

"You like him?"

"Yeah, I guess, but I wanna keep my options open. If we go to the Wildside again I'm gonna dance with at least five different guys. That's a promise."

"Wish I could be that confident."

Allie put her arm around the shorter, plump girl. "Are you kidding me? Girl, you can have any man you want."

Susan looked up at her. "Really, any man at all?"

"I guarantee it."

"Good, I got one in mind."

"Who is it?"

"The guy who gave you the pill."

He finished a set of thirty push-ups, then hopped up and rattled off six pull-ups on the bar set into his bedroom doorframe. He had a few more sets, then a thirty-minute run before he would cool down, catch a nap, then clean up for his evening out hunting. This was his version of baiting the field. He knew that with his body and face it was almost too easy to attract women. That was one of the reasons he liked to focus on blue eyes and blond hair. It gave him a goal.

His job helped him stalk his prey too. He had the chance to meet a lot of people and talk with them. No one would worry about him if they saw him working; it was too natural. He made enough money to live comfortably and still maintain the two different places to live even if one was a cheap apartment and one was shared, so no one would ever know he had two lives. It was a sweet setup.

He had a talent of dealing with people, and he made the most of it.

On the wall behind him was a corkboard framed in wood with photos of most of the girls he'd met in the last five years. A two-foot-square montage of light hair, big smiles, and him, the silent predator with an arm around one or on the dance floor with another. Most made it back to their hometowns, but some he had claimed for himself. Claimed forever. They were part of him now. Psychologically as well as physically. That's what drove him. He never hinted about his needs. No ordinary person would ever understand. He'd be considered a monster. That made sense because the antelope viewed the lion as a monster. No, this was a solitary task, and he liked it that way.

On this blustery afternoon he couldn't get cute Allie from Mississippi out of his head. She had that look. Bright, wide smile, pleasant Southern accent, and healthy naturally blond hair. He would've had her last night if the little chubby one hadn't needed her. But he'd be ready tonight. If she came to him at the Wildside, then he knew she was his. Just like all the others before.

He let out a whoop as he flopped back onto the ground to do some crunches.

Five

The Police Memorial Building, or PMB, sat on Bay Street looking out toward the St. Johns with ugly new condos blocking what was once a good view. John Stallings and Patty Levine trudged up the inside stairs to the second floor where the Land That Time Forgot, or the detective bureau, was located.

Stallings marveled at how fast Patty could walk with her petite frame. Without ever telling him, Patty had conveyed that if he ever slowed down for her or showed her any preference because she happened to be female, she'd beat his ass. As far as he was concerned, she never had to prove anything to anyone. He'd seen her use good judgment, be decisive, and be brutal when needed. She backed him up and kept her mouth shut about their own business. That made her a great partner. He dreaded the day she made sergeant and they moved her to the road on midnights in some lonely section of Duval County. For now he was happy things were going so well at work.

His mother used to say, "It's always something," and now it was his family life that had gone to shit. It felt as if he couldn't have both work and home life going well at the same time. He hadn't accepted it either, and that's what hurt. He spent as little time as possible alone at night in the little duplex he had rented a few miles from his family. He tended to stay at the house as if he still lived there, helping the kids with homework and practicing soccer with Charlie until he felt Maria had seen enough of him. Then he'd excuse himself and dread the rest of the evening watching baseball on the Sun Channel or *NFL Replay* on the NFL network.

As they crossed the threshold between crimes/property and crimes/persons he heard Lieutenant Rita Hester's voice from across the squad bay.

"I'll be damned, John Stallings is early for a meeting. I should play the lotto tonight."

He had a long history with the tall, large-framed lieutenant. She'd been another good partner on the road and now did a decent job as an administrator. He was pretty sure that once they had a permanent sergeant she'd be like every other lieutenant in the agency and feel like a ghost. She'd show up when you didn't expect her, but no one would able to find her most of the time.

Stallings smiled as he walked toward her. His eyes scanned the immediate area so he knew who was around. Just before he was about to address her by her former nickname, the Brown Bomber, he noticed a staff assistant working at the end of the conference table behind her. He just nodded and said, "I hate to hold things up."

The lieutenant smiled. "What's the spring break patrol look like?"

"Dammit, that name is catching on."

"What can you do, even Mazzetti comes up with a good one once in a while."

"We cleared three of the missing college kids. The kid from Boston College is in the can for possession of alcohol by a minor, then taking a swing at a cop."

Lieutenant Hester shook her head. "Bad judgment."

"The young man from Auburn found true love with a forty-year-old secretary from Fernandina Beach until her husband came home early from a fishing trip."

"Any casualties?"

"Nope. He called his parents, who had the sense to call us. He's not even coming back through J-Ville." He thought about the other student and lost any good humor he had talking with an old friend. "The last missing kid was the girl Mazzetti is working over in Brackridge Park."

The lieutenant looked down. "The suicide. That's a tough one to tell the family about. The Columbia, South Carolina, cops are going to make the notification. Still gonna be tough. The report of her missing came in before we found the body. I'd hate to hear news like that."

Stallings knew that was true. Even worse than him hearing that there were no leads on his missing daughter three years ago. He still hadn't recovered from it.

He remembered that Friday afternoon. It was one of those days that stood out in his life. Everyone had those days. Most adults have four or five days that stick out in their minds and maybe affect how they live the rest of their lives. Some are good, like hitting your first home run or your first serious kiss. Some are traumatic, like a car accident or a parent's death. Those days fuel most people. But Stallings's day, the day his life took a serious turn off the path he'd been traveling, ground down his heart and soul every day. It was about three years ago, coming home after a long day stuck on a drug homicide with no witnesses who were talking and no administrator who really cared if he solved it or not, finding Maria passed out on the couch and Charlie playing quietly in his room completely unsupervised. All of that wasn't even the problem. It hadn't even dawned on him that Jeanie was missing.

It wasn't till later, much later, that he noticed his oldest daughter had not made contact with the family in any way for almost a whole day. Then it took time to check with everyone from his mother to all of her friends before he sounded the alarm. He still remembered it as if it was just yesterday. That shocking fear. The terror that your baby, no matter how old, was gone. Then the anger at Jeanie for being gone, the cops for not finding her, and Maria for distracting him. It was still an issue he'd never resolved. Anger. It boiled out of him at the most inappropriate times, when he wanted to remain calm or appear professional. It seemed as if Jacksonville was awash in broken noses and black eyes from Stallings's anger issues.

Then the sorrow and despair sank in along with the realization that Jeanie might not ever come back. One of the hardest things was sitting down with Lauren and a very young Charlie to explain to them what happened. Why Mommy fell into such a deep sleep, why the police are around the house, and why Jeanie was gone. Nothing he told them was exactly true. Lauren had figured some of it out.

He felt the familiar lump in his throat as the LT brought him back to reality.

The lieutenant said, "What about the guy who works for Maxwell House?"

"He might be a real mystery. We went by his apartment, and there's nothing suspicious there. I'll drop by his work after the meeting. It's not really Maxwell

House, but some kind of waste-removal company that they subcontract. I'd like to spend some time on this one."

She nodded. "Good, I'd like to see it resolved." She paused for a moment, then, in a completely different tone, said, "What's new at home?"

He shrugged. The universal sign for cops who are separated from their wives. The lieutenant knew not to delve any further.

Other detectives filed in, every one of them keenly aware that they'd been without a sergeant for more than five months due to personnel shifts and retirements. The right sergeant could make everyone work together well and get a lot accomplished. The wrong one could get a cop killed. The sergeant was probably the most important position in a police agency. A squad seemed to take on the personality of its leader. A cautious sergeant made for a slow, deliberate squad. A hyper one usually pushed everyone else into a frantic rush of activity. But the rare, even-tempered, fair, intelligent sergeant could positively transform any squad. From detectives to road patrol, a good sergeant made everyone shine.

Stallings waited for Patty to pad over from her desk, then take a seat around the long conference table with the other detectives. Mazzetti and his crew were still finishing up at the medical examiner's with the body of the Brackridge Park suicide.

The lieutenant never had to raise her voice to get anyone's attention; her physical presence and reputation were enough to quiet down any group of JSO cops.

Luis Martinez, one of the hardest-working cops in the bureau, said, "What's the scoop, LT? We got a new sergeant on the way?"

"We do."

"Who is it?"

The lieutenant just smiled.

Tony Mazzetti had a headache. He'd missed lunch, and the goddamn ME blabbed his ear off about a nephew who is a starting nose tackle at FSU. Southerners and their football. Growing up in Brooklyn, all he cared about in football were the Jets. He did like that a Jersey school like Rutgers was starting to field a decent football unit, but the rednecks down here lived and breathed football. His headache was proof of that.

His headache was exacerbated by thinking about Kathleen Harding from Columbia, South Carolina. He still hoped to find some of her friends to talk to and maybe attach a reason for her suicide. That usually shut the family up. At least it was cleared, and he didn't have to worry about an unexplained death hanging over his head like a weight. If he wanted to stay as the lead detective in homicide he needed to keep his clearance rate high. Administration had overlooked what his desire to clear cases had done in the Bag Man case. He had been credited, along with Patty and John Stallings, with capturing the crazy shit. No way anyone in command staff would punish him for clearing the first victim as an overdose when the media was so positive right now.

In the squad bay he saw the looks on a couple of detectives' faces. What was it? Had someone died? Were they cutting back the D-bureau and sending guys back out on patrol? He glanced over and saw Patty quietly working at her computer. He purposely avoided too much conversation with her at work so it wouldn't draw any attention. He hated gossip. But this was an exception.

Mazzetti stepped over to her and kneeled so he could look her in the eye. He always took a second to appreciate just how pretty she was with blond hair framing a cute, cheerleader face and those magnificent blue eyes. He wondered how she ended up with a name like Levine, but hadn't asked about it yet. He didn't even know if she was Jewish.

For her part she never made a fuss about him in front of the others. She turned and said, "What's up?"

"Why's everyone seem so down?"

"You haven't heard yet?"

"Heard what?"

"We're getting a new sergeant?"

"Really? Who is it? Morris from traffic? O'Connor from the courthouse?"

"Yvonne Zuni."

He swallowed hard. "Yvonne the Terrible?"

"She's leaving narcotics and should start here anytime."

"Holy crap, she's a ball breaker."

Patty smiled. "Guess I'll be okay then."

"Funny. I heard she doesn't care if you got a dick or not, she'll chew it off if she's in a bad mood."

"If she were a man you'd say she was just tough."

"I heard she used to be a man." He held his smile, but knew Patty got his humor. That was one of her strengths.

She shoved him and said, "Get back to work, you moron."

* * *

John Stallings and Patty Levine followed the nervous little man through a string of corridors and staircases inside the Maxwell House coffee factory on Bay Street near downtown Jacksonville. Stallings had been raised in Jacksonville, but had never seen the inside of the factory. Of course it was rare for his father to take the family on any kind of outing. The career Navy man and amateur drunk spent most of his time either out at Mayport or in a bar called the Blue Marlin off Blanding Boulevard. Stallings hated that place so much that he drove his patrol car over to it a few years after starting at the Jacksonville Sheriff's Office just to see the place knocked down to make way for a new shopping center. His stomach still tightened when he drove past the little strip mall.

The man turned his head on what appeared to be very little neck at all and said, "You have to understand that since we're contractors we don't get the nicest or most convenient offices."

Patty said, "What exactly does your company do?"

"We ensure that the factory disposes of waste properly and efficiently. Sometimes we design systems to eliminate the waste, and sometimes it's as easy as contracting with a collection service." The man stopped and opened a door with a hazy glass pane and a smeared sign that was unreadable. Inside were four offices and a lobby. A large, surly-looking woman at the reception desk barely glanced up at the visitors.

The manager offered them the only two chairs; he leaned on his ancient, nicked-up wooden desk.

Stallings said, "We're looking for Jason Ferrell. He's not in trouble, just missing. His mother's worried, and he doesn't appear to have been home recently."

The manager nodded. "He strolled in here last week for one or two days, but I haven't seen him since. We're processing his termination now."

"What if he's been hurt or has a reason?"

The manager shook his head. "He'd be gone anyway. He's been sliding downhill for months now."

"How do you mean, like depressed? Suicidal?"

"I'm not sure what I can say." He looked at each detective, then over their shoulders to the reception area. "There are confidentiality issues, I'm sure."

Patty set down her gray metal case and held up a hand. "Mr. Ferrell isn't in trouble. He's missing."

"I know, but I don't want to say something that could get me sued later."

"Would a subpoena make you feel better? You know, legally speaking."

The man relaxed and smiled and said, "Yes, it would."

Patty immediately stood up and said, "Let me make a quick call and I'll be right back." Stallings caught her quick look at him.

Once she had left, he stood and stepped over to the man. "While we wait, tell me why you think Jason was on a slide."

The man leaned in and said, "I think it was drugs. He got paranoid and then started coming in later and later. He was forgetful and barely completed any of the chemical work he was supposed to."

"Chemical work?"

"He was our chemist. Quite smart actually. Went to Northwestern."

"He have any friends here?"

The manager shook his head.

"You have his file out already, right?"

The manager turned and plucked it off the top of his messy desk. "I was just going through it."

"Can I take a look?"

The manager handed it to Stallings, who thumbed through the few pages. He noted a couple of past addresses and several phone numbers. He didn't want to scribble them down in front of the man, so he locked them in his head as best he could.

Stallings said, "Thanks very much." He stood and got ready to leave.

"But I thought the lady detective was getting a subpoena to cover me?"

"I think you might have read too much into that. She said, 'Would you feel more comfortable?' Then she asked to make a call. The statements weren't connected." Stallings loved doing things like this. It made him feel smart once in a while. It also saved time because he knew he'd never have to deal with this squirrelly little man again.

He grabbed Patty's notecase and wrote down some addresses as he left. The manager had given them a few leads to work.

Six

Allie Marsh used all her powers of persuasion, some learned in rhetoric class, some developed during her two-week stint on her high school debate team and some of it from her gut, to convince the other three girls to go back to the Wildside and stay there a while. She knew the loud, crowded dance club was her best bet to meet up with him. She'd already decided that tonight was the night. Allie couldn't go back to Mississippi if her only experience of note was trying half a speckled pill one afternoon. She'd felt jittery as an aftereffect of the pill, but a two-hour nap and decent dinner had convinced her the little pills held no real danger.

Susan had just gotten back to the room after spending the entire afternoon up in the UGA student's room. Her broad smile told Allie that her friend didn't mind the half a pill either. The other two girls had been snoring in separate beds, still in their clothes from the night before when Allie had returned from the downstairs bar.

Now they were all on the same sheet of music. Dressed nicely but casually in jeans and each of them in a different kind of blouse. That was part of Allie's brilliant plan. A couple of the places didn't let you inside with jeans. She was narrowing the field. Karen's Chrysler 300 was headed west toward downtown with the other girls quietly taking in the scrub brush and occasional house. This wasn't a crowd ready to party; this was a crowd who already had. Except Allie, and she was anxious. She remembered the odd feeling that had crept through her after she had taken half the speckled pill. It was warm and electric, and it made her think that no one would judge her or care what she did. It made her want to dance, and that was in the relative calm of the hotel bar in the middle of the afternoon. What would she do tonight?

Her cell phone chimed to the University of Southern Mississippi fight song. It made her realize just how few calls she'd received this week. The small Verizon screen showed her mom's number. She hesitated, then decided to let the call go directly to voice mail. She didn't want to talk to her mom while she was thinking of what the night held for her.

As she stuck the phone back in her small purse, a broad smile spread across her face. Tonight was all about her.

John Stallings waited in his county-issued Impala outside the house he'd lived in for fourteen years, wondering if he had the guts to say to his wife, "Where are we going?" It might be the catalyst to move back or more likely, at least for the moment, Maria telling him she was filing for divorce. This thought occupied his mind more and more as the days stretched into weeks, then months, of living in a one-bedroom duplex over in

Lakewood. He had yet to miss a day of visiting the kids. Thankfully it had been slow around the office and he'd made use of the easier schedule to show up most days in the afternoon and really try to connect with the kids. He thought he'd been doing that for years, but it took Maria pointing out his obsession with police work, and his justification that if he worked hard he might somehow help find Jeanie, to make him realize he hadn't.

His oldest daughter had disappeared three years earlier at sixteen, and to this day no one was certain if she ran away, was dead, or had any number of other things happen to her. It had eaten at Stallings day and night, and not until Maria showed him so clearly had he realized how working in missing persons had soothed the ache of a missing daughter.

His own sister, Helen, who now lived in the house with his wife and kids, had disappeared when she was a teenager. Everyone knew she'd run away. The way his father had bullied and beaten them as children, it was probably a smart move. Then Helen showed back up a couple of years later and barely acknowledged her absence. She still lived with their mother most of the time. He thought she liked feeling needed and helping out around his house. He just wished he was experiencing the same thing.

He slipped out of the car and slowly made his way up the walkway, then paused at the front door. It didn't feel right to just barge in, and it felt equally awkward to knock at his own front door. He had this debate with himself every day. Today he turned the knob as he knocked, announcing himself as he stepped into the foyer that led to either the family room or a small formal dining room. He turned to see his daughter Lauren at the end of the couch, engrossed in a thick hardcover book. She glanced up and mumbled, "Hey, Dad."

He was struck by how mature she seemed with her dark hair straight down and a casual, long-sleeved shirt over a T-shirt. There was something else he couldn't quite grasp. Oh shit, she was wearing makeup. He wasn't a conservative dictator that outlawed makeup and dancing, but he was a father, and the first time your daughter is involved in either of those things it rattles you. He'd seen her dress up for nighttime school functions, but not just for reading in the house.

Before he could comment, which was perhaps for the best, Charlie came barreling down the stairs, using his left hand to hook his momentum and send him into a wide arc directly into Stallings's arms.

From the instant hug the boy said, "Ready to kick?"

"You bet." Kicking the soccer ball with the seven-year-old was about the best exercise he got right now. How had he slipped from a potential pro baseball player to a cop who stayed in shape with a half an hour of kicking a youth-sized soccer ball everyday?

Stallings looked over to Lauren. "Where's your mom?"

She shrugged.

"Aunt Helen?"

"In the kitchen."

He was about to ask her if everything was all right, a dangerous question for a teenager, when he heard a car horn outside and Lauren popped up off the couch and said, "Gotta go, my ride is here."

"Where are you going?"

"To study."

He peeked over her shoulder as she opened the front door and was only slightly relieved to see two girls in the front seat of a new Nissan Altima. They appeared to be a little older than Lauren, maybe seventeen.

He said, "Good-bye," even though he knew he wouldn't get an answer and it broke his heart just a little every time it happened.

Patty Levine slid into the booth across from Tony Mazzetti. She was ten minutes late, had just popped half of a Vicodin to ease the throbbing in her lower back, and knew what his first comment would be.

Mazzetti shook his head and said, "Yvonne the Terrible is gonna screw up my whole caseload."

Patty smiled and said, "Hello, Tony, I've been looking forward to our date too."

"Sorry," he mumbled. "I've just been wound up about it all day."

"You're always wound up."

He smiled and said, "Yeah, but usually it's about nothing. I like my assignment, and now that you're working so close, the squad is great. We all learned to work together with no sergeant around to interfere."

"Maybe things won't change. Too much."

"Are you kidding me? Yvonne completely revamped narcotics. They make half the arrests they did a year ago. She had community policing for two years and those guys griped all the time. You don't get a nickname without a reason."

"Your nickname is the King of Homicide."

"That's a compliment."

"You really think other cops would give you a complimentary nickname?"

"You mean that's a joke?"

She took a moment and sighed. "Tony, to people

who don't know you or haven't taken the time to get to know the person you are, you come off as a little pompous."

He took a swig of water from the dirty glass in front of him.

Patty smiled and said, "Hey, what about our rule not to talk work outside the office?"

He looked up at her. "Pompous? Really?"

Seven

Allie Marsh let the music rattle her teeth as the live band on the center stage cranked out Nirvana's "Smells Like Teen Spirit" for the older people in the crowd. And tonight it was a crowd. In addition to throngs of students from across the South, there were a lot of nice-looking, clean-cut men who were obviously out of school and a few women too. But not nearly as many.

Immediately Allie noticed that Susan had hooked up with the drummer from the UGA marching band. She must've tipped him off to where they were going. She smiled at her friend's excitement. Cici started talking to a tall black guy who looked like he should play basketball. Karen settled in with two of the Dutch exchange students she had met the night before. As Allie scanned the place to see if her guy was there, Karen pulled her toward the group of young Dutch men.

She made small talk, surprised at how little accent the Dutch boys had. Two of them went to Florida State and one to Tulane, but they all liked to meet at a different city during spring break. This was their third break together.

The best built of the Dutch boys, with his shirt opened way down his chest, said, "We went to New Orleans last year to help out their economy. Too many criminals there. You can't let down your guard. Know what I mean?"

Allie nodded absently. She liked his wide face and broad shoulders, but he had what her daddy used to call "European teeth." She never really understood until she attended USM and met a lot of exchange students. It wasn't the norm, but she picked up on bad teeth very quickly. This guy's were yellow and had big gaps between each upper tooth. Then his slender, better-dressed friend smiled and said, "Would you care to dance?" When he smiled his bright teeth lit up the room. She took his hand and let him pull her gently onto the crowded dance floor.

She stayed on the floor with him for two songs; then they retreated to a table by themselves. He leaned in close and said, "My name is Yan."

Allie had to shout in his ear. "Yan?"

"No, with a *J*, but it's pronounced 'Yan.' " He had blue eyes and a cute shell necklace tight around his neck. "Wanna have some fun with your new friend Jan?"

"What kind of fun?" She knew to smile at those kinds of offers now.

He held up a small speckled pill.

It was a little differently shaped from and darker than the one she had tried earlier. Allie didn't want to risk missing her good time tonight and took the pill from his large hand and slipped it onto her tongue.

From the corner of the cavernous room, crammed with people, he watched Allie mingle near the main bar. Then she did the unexpected. He saw his little prize from Mississippi ask other men to dance. The first two appeared to be his age. She was on the prowl and grinding so hard he wondered if she'd scored more X. Then she started to down water. She picked up other people's bottles and poured it down her throat as if a fire was in her stomach. He knew she had Ecstasy in her system. Half the girls on the floor did, but it was really hitting Allie. Her tight body moved to every beat of the band. Then, when the band took a break, she still bopped to the piped-in rock anthems. Her fire fueled his.

He could sit and watch her all night, but that might draw as much attention as talking directly to her. He knew where they could talk and where inside the giant club he needed to stay away from her.

After a few minutes she ended up with one of the slightly older guys at the bar. He had a hard, almost military look to him with short black hair and an angular face. Something about him said he wasn't a Navy man, but he still had that kind of look. He knew that look, even had it himself, but he was patient like any predator. He'd wait for her to come to him.

After more than an hour of intermittent surveillance of cute, wild Allie, she seemed to tire of her new boyfriends and noticed him, way at the end of the bar. Her smile grew as she approached with a certain sway in her hips. This was not the quiet little girl he'd met at the beginning of the week.

He said, "Looks like you're having fun."

She fanned herself and accepted a bottle of water with a smile and nod. "I can't believe I'm seeing some of the same guys I met over the weekend. I guess Jacksonville isn't as big a town as I thought it was."

"It's big, but only a few people go to places like this."

Allie swigged some more water. "I was hoping you'd be here."

"I was hoping you'd come by."

"Are you busy later?"

He smiled. He'd snared his little prize. "I hope so." She tittered at his old joke, and he felt a rush of excitement at his conquest. And now he could imagine the fun they might have later.

John Stallings watched his sister yawn and contained his smile. Her whole life she'd been a night owl, watching TV or reading until early in the morning. She'd never really held a job, hiding behind the need to care for their mother and living in the little house near the St. Johns River. Her mom had gotten the house in the divorce and then inherited some money from her own mother. It was blessing to Stallings that he didn't have to worry about his mother or sister. Helen was smart, really smart, and could do anything she wanted, but when she returned from her youthful two-year disappearance she never seemed to want to leave the house much. Once his father split and it was just her and his mom, they fed off one another and found a peaceful life in the quiet neighborhood.

Now he wondered if Helen wasn't seeing how much good she could do in the world if she got out. She had single-handedly saved Maria, and the kids seemed pretty well adjusted to her presence.

Helen said, "It's a weird situation."

"Weird how?"

"It's like I took your place. The kids look to me for day-to-day decisions, and Maria counts on me to keep her on track. I don't think I'm helping the chances of you and her getting back together."

"As long as you aren't sleeping with her it's not too weird."

Helen gave him a flat stare. "I'm serious. I don't want to screw up my little brother's life."

"I did that on my own. You're just helping out until Maria and I can set things right."

Helen smiled. She was a nice woman, and as her brother, Stallings never really noticed how attractive she was. What had caused her to withdraw from the world so completely? He'd never known her to even have a date. Maybe it was a family trait, because, in a way, he had withdrawn too. He just called it working hard, but even he had to admit it had given him a reason to stay separate from people, especially his family. The hell of it was that he had no idea how to correct it. Sure, he was around the house more, but had he really connected with anyone under this roof? Maria wasn't speaking to him, Jeanie had left, he barely got a grunt out of Lauren anymore, and Charlie liked to see him because he would play soccer with the boy until they both dropped.

Helen said, "Look, John, you can't just fix things overnight. You have time. I like it here. Let's see what happens."

He heard the lock on the front door turn. Lauren stepped in on high heels. He hadn't seen them when she left to supposedly study.

"Where have you been?"

"Out?"

"Past eleven on a school night?"

"Mom said it was okay."

He hesitated because he hated overriding Maria, but sometimes she agreed to things she shouldn't.

Lauren didn't finish the discussion; instead she stomped up the stairs.

Allie watched the scenery rush by as she felt the effects of the drug wash through her. This was all a big adventure to her, and she didn't want to miss one thing. Jacksonville had seemed like a giant city to her, and it was hard to believe even after ten minutes on this road, that they were still in Jacksonville. The was nothing but fields with the thick underbrush and tightly packed pine trees interrupted by the entrance to some fancy housing development every half mile or so. She was excited. And scared. She talked a good game, but in reality she really didn't know much about sex. Her first boyfriend, Tommy, knew less about sex than she did, so she didn't feel self-conscious. The best experience she'd had was in the Volvo parked in her parent's driveway. But that had serious drawbacks, like the bruise the gearshift had left on her thigh, and she'd never been able to relax fully with her family only a few yards away inside the house. This was different.

In a way she'd put the pressure on herself to go through with it. She told herself that meeting a guy and having sex in a distant city was part of the spring break experience. She had to be honest and admit she'd turned this into a more romantic adventure than it really was. She attributed some of that to just being a kid and scared of something new. It'd be fine. It wasn't like she was a virgin. But it still scared her.

She looked over at him, so confident and handsome

behind the wheel of his Jeep. He turned and smiled back at her. He was so good looking it almost seemed fake, like a mask. His muscular arms and handsome face would have been right at home on the big screen. But even in that nice package she wasn't sure she felt enough emotionally to justify having sex with him. She thought about what she'd tell the girls when she got back to the hotel and decided she couldn't back out now.

Allie took a deep breath, trying to relax. She couldn't deny that she was attracted to him and that this was something that she'd decided to do. Allie reached across and placed her hand on the back of his head, running her fingers through his short, neat hair.

This would be her fling for the week. Maybe for the whole semester. And she'd be able to look at the other girls on the ride back to Hattiesburg and tell them how romantic and exciting the whole encounter was.

She hoped she wouldn't be lying, but if she had to she would.

His heart beat with a rhythm only felt when he had his prey. These were the moments he lived for. The sex was incidental; he could have sex any time he wanted. It was the power he needed. He needed it to live as much as air or water. That was why he was so careful. He'd taken great care to learn about Allie's companions and not let them see him with her. He also had talked with Allie about what she'd told them about him. She had shared the Ecstasy hit with her chubby little friend but never said exactly who had supplied it. He'd spent a small fortune buying the quality homemade Ecstasy that couldn't be traced. And it packed a wallop.

He relaxed and enjoyed the feeling as it consumed him here in the wide-open field near a small private airport east of downtown. The clouds over the moon had made the night a deep black void. But this was a tactile experience. Her bare, muscular back rubbed against his chest as he dropped his hands to play with her swaying breasts. He felt her breathing increase. She had a shitload of Ecstasy in her. She'd taken one hit from someone else; he had given her one more and then slipped another into a bottle of water. This girl was on fire. A chemical fire that burned inside her as he pushed her farther and farther, ramming deeper and deeper inside her.

The first set of screams were of encouragement, even if they were enhanced by the drug. Then, as he picked up the pace and more of the drugs worked their way into her bloodstream, the screams changed in tone. Now, as he pounded harder, the screaming and squirming were not sexual. At least not on Allie's part. The X had raised her body temperature to the point that now her skin was soaked with sweat and was hot to the touch. He straightened up and let just the cheeks of her shapely butt touch his pelvis.

She panted, "Please, stop." She gulped some air. "I need a break."

He reached around and placed his palm on her chest. Her heart hammered at almost two hundred beats a minute.

Her legs gave out, and he let his weight fall on top of her, still thrusting.

Allie raised her head once more to breathe or scream, but she just let out a groan and collapsed.

He kept pumping, feeling her entire body go limp. The feeling of excitement and power flooded over him, making him come so hard he was afraid he'd shoot the condom off right into her.

He fell on top of her sizzling hot body, panting himself and his limbs weak. He wanted to absorb her dissipating energy. She made no movement beneath him. No breathing, not a flutter from what had to be an exploded heart, not even a settling of gases. So much better than the slow choking he used a few nights earlier. This would be the easiest death to hide yet.

He rolled off the quiet, lifeless Allie Marsh and admired his handiwork. He moved her onto the grass and started to pull on her clothes. He still had a little work to do.

Eight

Patty Levine peered across the squad bay at John Stallings behind his bare old wooden desk, crammed over next to the unused holding cell. They had both been moved into this squad bay for a big-deal homicide a few months ago and had decided they liked being in close with crimes/persons, which included any violent crimes, homicides, and robberies. Most of the other detectives that had been brought over for the Bag Man case had gone back to their own offices in auto theft, fraud, and computer crimes. A few, like Luis Martinez and Rod Morris, stayed. No one mentioned that the squad was now four detectives bigger; it just sort of happened like a slow, unstoppable evolution. That's the way a lot things happen around police departments. No real orders are cut, just one day you look around and there are new people or you're in a new office.

Patty wasn't worried things might change with a new sergeant on the way. Everyone had heard rumors about Yvonne Zuni, but Patty knew how rumors about women in public service tended to be overblown. She thought it was cool to have a female sergeant and lieutenant. It was the only unit in the SO like that. Maybe one of the only police units in Florida.

Patty crossed the cramped room and settled into the hard, wooden, straight-back chair next to Stallings's desk.

He looked up from some notes but didn't say anything. Typical.

"What're you working on?"

"Jason Ferrell. We're gonna find that guy today."

"You make him sound like a fugitive. He's not even wanted."

"Except by his mother."

"He's thirty years old."

"Tell that to a parent missing her child." He sighed. "She called me first thing this morning, anxious for any news. I told her we'd do everything we could to find him." He looked around the room. "There's nothing else cooking. I've screwed up too many promises lately to let down this lady."

Patty smiled at her partner. The guy didn't have a fault as far as she was concerned. "I'm with you. What's the game plan?"

"If the landlord says other guys are looking for him we might want to sit on the apartment and see if they show up. If we know what he was into, we might figure out where he's laying up." He looked through some notes, then back to Patty. "Did you drop off the yellow liquid we found at the lab?"

"Yeah, but it'll be a little while. They don't see the urgency we do."

"Let's save our battles for when we know who we're fighting."

She was about to suggest checking the local surveillance video feeds in stores and other places Ferrell might have frequented, when the lieutenant stepped in through the rear door and said, "Listen up, people. I want to introduce you to your new boss."

Patty stared as Yvonne Zuni stepped up next to Rita Hester.

John Stallings heard someone behind him mutter, "Holy shit, I don't remember her looking like that." Stallings wasn't sure he had ever met the woman standing by the door, but he'd seen her around. He felt a pang of guilt that he had assumed she was an analyst or maybe someone's executive assistant. It was a chauvinistic prejudice that he hadn't thought he held. But Stallings had to look at this beautiful woman with tropical dark skin and bright green eyes and wonder, *How on earth did you ever get the name Yvonne the Terrible?*

She stepped up next to the lieutenant and said in a clear voice, "First I'd like to see each set of partners privately in the conference room to get a handle on what you're working on. Second, I want a written summary of each case on a single sheet of paper on my desk by noon. And finally, I'm glad to be here." Without another word she turned and stepped into the conference room. Within twenty seconds she called out, "Well, who's gonna be first?"

Stallings and Patty exchanged glances; then both stood at the same time. He knew putting off something unpleasant didn't make it any more tolerable. They marched together into the conference room.

"I'm John Stallings."

"I'm Patty Levine."

Yvonne the Terrible stood up. She held out a delicate hand and shook his hand firmly. "I know both of you. Patty, we worked the snatch-and-run bandits a couple of years ago."

"Good memory."

The sergeant said, "I was just a detective then."

Patty nodded. "But you ran that case."

Yvonne Zuni looked toward Stallings. "And everyone knows you, John." She motioned them to sit down. "You guys are our missing persons team, right?"

Patty added, "And backup homicide."

"We'll see. What are you working on?"

Stallings and Patty took turns going through their cases. Stallings finished with a detailed view and plan on finding Jason Ferrell.

Sergeant Zuni closed her notebook in which she had scribbled several comments, then looked up at Stallings. "Instead of finding this middle-aged loser, we have a new missing persons report on a student from Mississippi named Allison Marsh. I don't want a big media drama over a missing student. Drop what you're doing and track her down."

Stallings said, "I didn't even see anything on it yet."

"I know. Consider this your assignment. The call came in upstairs."

"That's a little odd. Usually . . ."

The sergeant cut him off. "Usually there was no sergeant here. Usually hotshots like you and Tony Mazzetti did whatever you wanted to. Now, as of this minute, you better get out and find this girl." She smiled, but somehow she'd gone from beautiful to scary. "Any questions?"

Stallings didn't have one.

Nine

John Stallings, like any seasoned cop, knew his strengths and weaknesses. He could read people and interview well. Some would say there was a large element of fear that made people talk to him, but he got results. He also was willing to work ungodly hours to find a missing kid or solve a homicide. His greatest weakness was not using all the available sources of information from computer databases and intelligence files. Patty understood the physics of such work and seemed to like it, so he let her run with it.

An hour after Yvonne Zuni had ordered them to find the missing Allison Marsh, Patty had her metal notecase crammed with printouts, photographs, and information on the case. They were about to head over to Atlantic Beach to catch the travel mates of the missing girl. Allison Marsh's mother had reached the girls and had started the chain of panic even though Allie hadn't been missing long.

As he pulled onto Edgewood Avenue, Patty said, "Where are you going?"

"Just a quick run by Jason Ferrell's apartment. See if anyone is around."

Patty started to sift through her notes.

Stallings smiled and said, "Worried Yvonne the Terrible is gonna catch us veering off our assignment? Should we call her when we want to stop and get lunch?"

"It's not like you to ignore a missing girl, or to mock a boss. You usually follow orders."

"I am following orders and doing a little extra. Just because Jason Ferrell is a little older doesn't mean his mother isn't any less worried. I promise we'll be talking to Allison Marsh's friends within an hour."

As Stallings pulled his Impala to the curb right in front of the main door to the apartment complex, two men walked out and froze at the entrance.

Stallings said to Patty, "Do those two look like the guys the manager described to you?"

"Exactly how he described them."

Stallings knew to get out quickly. Something about these two made him lift his shirt to show his gun and badge on his hip. These weren't city people; they'd come from the farther reaches of the south. Maybe South Georgia or the center of North Florida.

The taller of the two men, in jeans, a dirty white T-shirt, and John Deere hat, said, "Oh shit, five-O." He turned and started to walk quickly down the sidewalk with his pudgy, bald friend behind him.

"Hang on, fellas," called out Stallings.

The men slowed.

Patty stepped out, but used the car as cover. She saw the pair as a threat too.

Stallings kept his voice loud and firm. "Turn around and walk back this way."

The big man turned. "Why?"

"You said it before. Because we're cops and we want to talk to you."

"I don't think we have to consent to that demand."

Stallings turned to Patty. "Fucking *Law and Order*." Then he called out, "You do have to consent."

"Why?"

"Because if you make me come over to you boys, I'll kick your asses."

The men exchanged glances and then, without warning, started to run hard down the sidewalk.

The move surprised Stallings so much that he hesitated between jumping in his car or chasing them on foot. He and Patty slipped back into the unmarked police car and pulled from the curb in time to see a blue Ford F-150 rumble over a chain-link fence at the far end of the apartment's side parking lot. They pulled onto the next block as Stallings hit the gas and cut through the lot. He pulled up short of following the raised truck over the crushed fence. The low clearance of his Impala would never make it over the fence.

As the car squealed to a stop at the edge of the parking lot, Stallings slammed the steering wheel. "Shit." He could see the truck speeding away. He had no reason to jump on the radio and call out a pursuit. He just wanted to talk to the men.

He looked over at Patty. "What are you grinning about?"

"I got the tag."

Less than thirty minutes after the rednecks had given them the slip, Patty Levine and John Stallings had crossed the wasteland between J-Ville and the beach towns. Patty liked to see how well her tough, street-smart partner could talk to young people. In his years assigned to missing persons, he had developed a reputation for being able to deal with Jacksonville's large homeless population. One of the reasons, Patty could clearly tell, was because he treated everyone with respect until they didn't deserve respect. He also had a good rapport with younger people.

Now he sat on a couch next to Susan Meyers in the lobby of a little family-run motel off the ocean. The girl was worried about her missing friend and scared, but Stallings had a way of reassuring people without being condescending or fake.

He had established that none of the girls traveling with Allison Marsh, whom everyone called Allie, had seen whom she left with the night before. They had all gone to a popular dance club called the Wildside, which was known as being easy on underage drinkers, especially pretty girls. It was so easy that the bar also attracted an unsavory older male clientele as well.

Susan was round and dowdy in the bright lights of the motel. She'd been crying and now was down to just a sniffle.

"The way Allie's mom yelled at me for allowing her to leave without us just got to me. She's very strong."

Stallings said, "It's not your fault—we just need to find her. Now tell me anything else I might've forgotten to ask you. You're sure you didn't see her with a specific guy?"

Susan shook her head and blew her nose into a wadded-up Kleenex. "She danced with a bunch of guys. I think she wanted to hook up with one, but I don't know who he was." She blew her nose again. "Her mom started calling about one in the morning and said she couldn't get ahold of Allie. When I told her I was already at the motel she freaked. I guess that's when she called you guys."

"Did Allie meet anyone this week she talked about?"

Susan hesitated, and Patty saw that she was hiding something. Patty cut in. "C'mon, you're not in trouble. Did Allie meet someone?"

"Well, she did meet a guy who gave her this little pill."

"What kind of pill?"

"A speckled one. She kept saying he was a nice guy even if he was a little older than us. I never saw him."

"Did she take the pill?"

Susan waited, looked at both detectives, and said, "We both did. We split it."

"What happened?"

"It made me sort of breezy. I just coasted through the afternoon." She snapped her fingers. "And thirsty too."

At the same time both Stallings and Patty said, "Ecstasy."

Ten

Stallings had used his contacts at one of the local cell phone companies to get the records for Allie Marsh's phone. There'd been no calls made since 8:20 P.M. the night before when she called Susan's phone. Susan had confirmed that she called just after they entered the Wildside because they'd gotten separated. The lack of activity made it difficult to see if there was a pattern of calls going through cell towers in different areas.

Now, as he sat in his Impala and Patty grabbed a sandwich, he tried to think of whom he could harass about Ecstasy and maybe see if Allie fell in with one of the local dealers or if a dealer knew someone passing some X around.

Patty hopped back into the car and offered him half her tuna sandwich. He waved her off as he stared at the sheet of phone records.

Patty shook her head. "It would've taken most of us three days to get records like that."

"It was an emergency. This girl still hasn't shown up, and the idea that she had a source of X makes me nervous."

"What about the rednecks in the truck from this morning?"

"You said it was registered to someone in Sanderson."

"Leonard Walsh."

"I'd like to talk to him about Jason Ferrell, but this is more urgent."

"When's the last time anyone tried to call Allie?"

He shrugged, looked at the number on the top of the page, and dialed. What did he have to lose? The phone rang once, twice, a third time; then, to his surprise someone answered.

"Hello." It was a man's gravelly voice.

Stallings hesitated a moment and said, "Is Allie close by?"

"No. No one here but me." Then the line went dead.

Stallings turned to Patty and said, "This ain't good."

John Stallings felt his face flush red as he approached Yvonne the Terrible in the detective bureau. They'd been called back to the SO just after the strange man had answered Allie Marsh's phone and he had the cell company scrambling to see which cell tower it pinged off of. It was a long shot, but it was a lead. A lead he couldn't follow up if he was wasting time in the office.

Even Patty noticed his anger and said, "Take a minute to calm down, John."

"We don't have a minute now. This went from a missing party girl to a suspicious disappearance in a matter of minutes. We need to get out there and look for her."

As they approached the sergeant's office, which had been vacant for many months, Yvonne Zuni stepped out and turned casually toward them. She smiled and nodded.

Stallings fought the urge to yell. He respected the chain of command even when command staff was wrong. He said evenly, "We have a hot lead. Do you really need us here right now?"

Sergeant Zuni matched his even tone. "I wouldn't have called you if I didn't."

"Then what's the emergency?"

"I didn't say it was an emergency. I just said come back to the office. If you're gonna be outraged know why you're outraged."

"What's that supposed to mean?"

"It means you should consider who you're barking at and if it will do any good."

Stallings realized she had just told him to shut up in a decent, boss kind of way.

Then the sergeant said, "I want you two to meet someone." She turned and started walking toward the conference room, pulling Patty and Stallings along silently.

In the room, at the far end of the long table, sat a pretty blond woman who appeared to be in her late thirties. She sat straight with a manner that, coupled with her clothes, suggested she had money. The woman looked up at them with bright blue eyes that seemed familiar to him.

The sergeant said, "Detectives Stallings and Levine, this is Diane Marsh, Allison's mom."

Now Stallings felt like an ass.

Daytime had never been his best time to function. He was a creature of the night. But the thrill of his little adventure with Allie Marsh had kept him from sleeping, and now he hustled around the small cottage he rented, cleaning out any dust and wiping down the kitchen with Clorox. His refrigerator was nearly bare, not because he hadn't been shopping but because he hated garbage. Most things he ate were self-contained and easy to wrap up and dispose of in his kitchen can with two heavy-duty plastic bags. He took his bags to his landlord's large outdoor cans because he hated to be around any kind of decomposing garbage. There were no remnants of meat or other food on his kitchen counters and few odors in the small house other than cleaners.

That was why he took his prey anywhere but in his own lair. Not only did it keep him safe from any possible suspicion, if there ever was any, but it kept potentially disgusting remnants away from his house.

He found himself smiling at the thought of Allie's tight body under his, the thick, sticky film of perspiration between them. Those screams of hers right near the end echoed in his ears and gave him a feeling of euphoria. This was his idea of a vacation. Just dreaming about his past exploits.

He knew he'd have to get back on the prowl tonight to keep the feeling going.

Twenty minutes into the interview of Diane Marsh, Stallings started to realize how this case had gotten spun up so quickly. Diane Marsh was a strong woman with a husband who had a lot of cash from a small fishing-boat-manufacturing business in Laurel, Mississippi. Mrs. Marsh, who had asked to be called Diane, said that they'd never worried about their children in their quiet hometown and that this was Allie's first trip to a big city.

Stallings almost snickered at the idea of Jacksonville being a big city. Although it was the biggest city in square miles in the United States, that was more of an administrative move than a growth issue. The county and city had combined governments in the sixties. But the city and its management still had a chip on its shoulder for not being a big city. Despite its slogan, "Bold new city of the south," J-Ville was eclipsed by Atlanta a few hours northwest and Miami due south. Aside from the stray Super Bowl or decent college game, no one took much notice of the bold new city of the south.

Overall, Diane Marsh offered little help in the case. She had not been able to reach Allie for a couple of days and panicked. When she talked to Susan and learned Allie had not come home she contacted the Mississippi attorney general, who was a personal friend, and he contacted someone in JSO command, who had apparently lit Yvonne Zuni's ass on fire.

When Diane Marsh started to cry, Stallings reached across the table to take her hand. "I know it's hard, but we're doing all we can." He'd heard the same words and they hadn't made him feel any better three years ago.

The three years seemed like a lifetime to him. Sometimes all he could think about was how he'd wasted precious hours trying to figure out what Maria was using, where she got it, and how long it had been going on without his knowledge. In hindsight they were all useless questions. By the time he'd brought in JSO on what he thought was his own personal problem, his world and especially the house was in chaos. He was still dizzy from just how fucked up things could get so quickly. Dizzy was the only way to explain it. He physically felt as if the room were spinning and he was going to be sick. The realization that Jeanie was missing had left a hole that nothing could fill. He fended off questions from his mother and his sister and his friends that meant nothing. They weren't contributing; they were only distracting. He had to focus. He had to do something. Anything.

Then the first cop showed up. A nice kid in uniform who gave him the fucking company line. Same bullshit he was laying down for Diane Marsh right now. God forgive him, but he didn't have enough sense to find something new to say.

Diane said, "You can't know what this feels like."

"Yes, I can."

She looked up at him, and he instantly saw the recognition shared by parents who had lost children. Diane Marsh started to weep uncontrollably.

Tony Mazzetti held Patty tight to his chest as she drifted off to sleep. He knew her routine after sex; she got up, took some kind of vitamin, brushed her teeth, and came right back to bed. Once she was out, she was out. It took him longer to fall asleep because he ran through the problems of the day and what he had to accomplish the next day. He'd done the same thing for the entire fourteen years he'd been with the Jacksonville Sheriff's Office. In the long years without a girlfriend, while he lay in bed alone, he'd rough out some of the history articles he liked to write. Sometimes he read. Now he liked just holding Patty's small, perfect body as she drifted off. Even if it was early.

She expended a lot of energy. Especially in bed. He wouldn't admit it, but he had to adjust his gym workouts around their dates because he couldn't perform adequately at both in one day. But with their schedules and Patty's independence, they rarely spent more than two nights a week together and sometimes they went two weeks with only a dinner or two shared. She seemed happy with this arrangement, but after years of almost no relationships he wanted more. He just didn't know how to express that to her and not scare her away.

He worried about things he never used to care about. He wondered if his years without sex because of his massive use of muscle supplements had screwed up his technique. If he was completely honest, he'd have to admit that no woman ever really complimented his ability even before his quest to gain huge muscle mass.

The frustration of the day caused him to sigh and shift his body. A lump in his throat had not dissipated since the afternoon.

Patty reached across his chest and mumbled, "What's wrong, Tony?"

He groaned. "Nothing."

Patty propped herself up and looked at him in the dim light. "We'll waive the 'not talking about work' rule. Now what's wrong?"

"You shoulda heard how she talked to me today."

"Who? The sarge?"

"Yeah, the goddamn new sergeant."

"What did big bad, one-hundred-and-five-pound Yvonne the Terrible say to my meek, little, two-hundred-pound boyfriend?"

He could see her perfect smile even in this light. "She talked to me like a kid."

"Tony, sometimes you act like a kid."

"She said my clearance rates are too good and wants more care taken with each death investigation. She wants a new analysis of each of the last ten deaths." He waited for a comment, but the silence said it all. "You think I miss things?"

More silence.

Mazzetti said, "You're going back to the OD case. I admit I screwed up on that one. How was I supposed to know that was the Bag Man's first victim?"

"You said it, not me."

Mazzetti groaned. "Now the new sarge thinks the same thing. What a waste of time to go back through the cases."

Patty's continued silence told him she didn't necessarily think it was a waste of time.

It was after ten, and John Stallings was still driving around the area where the cell tower for Allie Marsh's phone last pinged, thinking of all the terrible things that could've happened. Meeting Diane Marsh had ratcheted up his concern, and now he found himself trapped too deep into a case again. The fact that he hadn't visited the kids today was a sign of the obsession he developed on certain cases.

It didn't take a psychiatrist to figure out what drew him to these cases. He always hoped that some detective in some city might piece together what had happened to his own daughter after she disappeared. By working these kinds of cases hard he was somehow helping and nurturing that hope. The hollow spot inside him had never healed. The thought of Diane Marsh suffering the same pain pushed him to keep thinking up scenarios of how the phone was taken from Allie.

On one hand he liked when he was busy, but it was

only a temporary fix to his restlessness and hurt him in other areas, like family. But he knew himself well and resolved to go with it for now.

Stallings cruised east on the Arlington Expressway near a residential area that also held some apartments and homeless people; then he pulled his Impala into a nearby gas station and got out on foot. He knew everyone would make him for a cop, but that's how he had gotten by on this job: honestly. Sometimes that meant he had beaten someone or at least scared them, but no one seemed to resent him for any of his actions. He was occasionally reminded of that when the lieutenant asked him to do her a special favor and use his "own methods" to find out something. She knew he could be rough, but that he always said or did something that smoothed it over afterward. He'd never had an official complaint filed against him. At least not for violence.

He headed into the park, keeping his head moving so he wouldn't be surprised. He nodded to a pair of old men, tattoos covering their forearms, sharing a bottle. At the far end of the park were low-rent apartments. Every officer with JSO had been there at some point to break up a fight or check on a sexual predator. It held a lot of recovering addicts and more than a few released prisoners.

He kept walking around to the front of the apartments, keeping his eyes open for one person in particular. It only took a moment before he almost bumped into him.

Stallings froze and looked into the old man's cloudy brown eyes. Gray stubble covered his cheeks. The man held a basket of clean laundry. Old military habits died hard.

The old man said, "Look what the tide washed in."

Stallings said, "Hey, Stan."

"What brings you by the drunks' ghetto?"

"I need some info."

"You think that just because I'm sober now I'll cooperate with the cops?"

"I think you'll help out because I took a knife in the side for you."

Eleven

John Stallings sat on a dryer in the dank laundry room of the old apartment building while Stan finished another load. The old man didn't want to be seen in public with any form of law enforcement officer. It was an unwritten code at this refuge for derelicts that anyone from a lowly probation officer to a JSO detective was only here to mess with the residents. Stan was making an exception because, whether he liked to admit it or not, Stallings had shown him compassion and tracked down his attackers when no one else seemed to care.

Years ago, when Stallings was assigned to crime/persons, he responded to Shands Hospital to interview Stan, who was homeless and had been beaten and left for dead by a gang of thugs in Arlington. Stan, as well as everyone else, thought the cops would just take a cursory report and dismiss it as they did almost every crime against the voiceless homeless. Stallings, following his usual obsessive pattern, had found the four men responsible and while talking to one of them was attacked with a knife by another. Even with the wound in his side from a three-inch Buck knife blade he managed to wound two of them with his duty pistol, knock one of them unconscious with a solid elbow to his chin, and then chase down the last one with his police car and break both of his legs with a not entirely unintentional late stop with the car. The impact had sent the man twenty feet through the air off Stallings's bumper.

Stan couldn't believe it at the time and used the incident to clean up his life, sober up, get a job at the VA as a maintenance man, and reestablish contact with his estranged family. Stallings knew all that because he kept up with many of the people he had helped over the years. He hated to ask him for help, but when a young girl was missing there were no rules or etiquette. Stan understood that.

The old man shook his head at Allie Marsh's photo. "I don't get out much anymore, Stall. I lead a prayer group over at the pavilion in the park behind the building here and see those guys most everyday, but I'd remember a pretty woman around here."

"Her phone was used by a man, and it pinged off a cell tower near by."

"What kind of phone?"

"A cell phone, small . . ."

Before Stallings could say it, Stan added, "Red?"

Stallings perked up. "How'd you know?"

"Because I know who had a phone like that."

Ten minutes later, John Stallings was on the move. He didn't like marching through the brush on the far side of the apartment building at night without backup, but he liked the idea of leaving a lead like this hanging until morning even less. The path was pretty obvious even in the ambient light from the street and a quarter moon rising over the Atlantic.

He had seen no one since he started walking into the thick scrub, but knew that this was a popular homeless hangout. Not the younger runaways who tended to hang out near downtown and had a chance to turn it around, but the older, burned-out, alcoholic homeless that tended to be men in their fifties, some of them veterans of the Vietnam War who were never able to fully integrate back into society. Some were convicted felons who couldn't find a job and decided to turn their backs on the rest of the world, and some were just mentally unbalanced and were turned out into the world by a system that often couldn't afford to care for them.

There was no real bond among most of the men. They talked a good game about looking out for one another, but Stallings knew they constantly stole from one another, beat each other, and sold each other out when it was convenient. Stallings knew Stan wasn't selling anyone out. He was concerned about the missing girl and had told Stallings that the man he saw with the phone was not the violent predatory type. But he knew the violent predatory types were usually not too obvious; that's how so many were able to operate without detection.

Stallings had seen several different studies on serial killers. The newest ones had revised the number of murders committed by serial killers in the United States from about 200 a year to as many as 2,000 a year. That was an astonishing number to a cop. Yet the threat from a serial killer was never mentioned until the media got ahold of a story and played it up.

He continued on his slow trek through the scrub and pine. Up ahead he heard voices, and the flickering light of a campfire bled through the trees. He eased up and tried to figure how many men were in the small camp. He could hear two voices, but could see at least four bodies through the bushes.

Stallings cleared his throat loudly, then made sure he didn't surprise anyone as he crashed through branches into the clearing. He'd misjudged. There were ten men in the clearing, and they all jumped at the sight of him. He hoped this wasn't going to be a problem. But that hope faded as he ducked a board swung at his head.

He tapped his heel to the beat of the "You Found Me" by The Fray. Heel tapping was more alluring than toe tapping. Not that it made a difference with him. He peered out over the dance floor, disappointed in tonight's offering. It was a little soon since his last capture, but he'd found that he waited less and less time after every kill. His memory of Allie was fresh and so was her scent on him. He didn't shower, because he loved the musty smell of sex mixed with a woman's perfume.

He'd posted her photograph up on his collage at his east apartment. It was one he'd taken with his cell phone and printed on his good Epson photo-quality printer. She held the top right edge of the collage of blue eyes and blond hair. Some might have been too thin or too short, but they all had that clean, European look.

He'd also kept a memento. This was a new trick, but he'd found he wanted something from every prize he brought down with a swift foot and extended claw. In Allie's case it was her belly-button ring. A little gold number with a loop of fine chain that drooped down her tight stomach. He'd plucked it out after she was dressed and tucked away in the corner of the park. Now it was in a wooden box he'd made in seventh grade along with a couple of earrings, a ring, and a silver ball that was part of a tongue stud.

He knew keeping photos and trinkets wasn't a smart move, but they were subtle. If his landlord wandered in, he wouldn't think anything about it. The girls were from other cities or listed as suicides so they wouldn't have been in the news much. It had taken him a few times before he realized that suicides or just plain missing girls raised a lot less fuss than a murder victim. Man, he remembered the stink in Daytona a few years ago. Luckily no one ever tied it back to him. Cops generally didn't stay hot on the trail of cases once the media died down.

Even the mementos weren't alarming. Everyone had the odd piece of jewelry. It wasn't like the crazy-assed killer here in Jacksonville a few years ago named Carl Cernick. He'd been caught because he had a finger from one of his victims. Crazy people caused all kinds of shit.

Now he looked across the floor and saw a blond head with hair that hung straight down a beautiful back with strong shoulders. Immediately his penis stiffened at the thought of finding more prey so quickly. He'd still have to cut her loose from the herd, but that usually wasn't a problem. Especially since here, where no one knew him, he didn't have to be quite so careful.

He eased along the edge of the floor to get a look at her and see whom she was with. She had a long, lithe body and swayed to the beat unlike a lot of girls. He liked that. He'd already seen an emerald ear stud that would make a great memento. His heart began to beat faster, sharpening all his animal instincts. He edged closer, realizing that the girl was here with a couple of friends. The easiest possible target.

Then she turned and saw him. He paused to let her take in his full image. She smiled as he expected, but then his heart sank. In the light he could see she had brown eyes. Dark brown eyes.

He turned, deflated enough to simply leave alone.

Stallings ducked the two-by-four that would've cracked his skull, then dodged a brick from another direction. He stayed low and dove behind a thick pine tree and called out, "Not very friendly of you."

Another brick bounced off the tree trunk.

Stallings yelled. "I'm a cop, and the next mother-fucker that chucks something at me is gonna get his ass kicked. Is that clear?" He raised his voice and took off the friendly edge.

There was silence and an absence of projectiles.

He peeked from behind the tree, showing his badge as he did. He took another look, accounting for all ten men. Then he stepped out and said, "That's better."

No one spoke at first. Then an older man in the back said, "What are you hassling us for all the way out here?"

"Hassling you! You're the ones who tried to take my head off."

"This is our camp. We don't bother no one." The others nodded in agreement.

"I heard one of you might have something I need."

"What?" asked a couple of them at the same time.

"A cell phone. A red cell phone." He searched the faces in the group to see if anyone flinched or gave it away.

Everyone stayed calm.

"I expected this kind of response and was ready." Stallings already had Allie's number in his phone and pressed send. In a few seconds he heard the beat to a song that was also a ring tone. All the heads started turning until one man was the focus of the entire crowd.

The heavy, older white man rolled onto his knees in an attempt to spring up and flee, but Stallings was standing next to him and had to help him up to his feet.

Stallings said, "Looks like we need to talk."

Twelve

Jacksonville Sheriff's Office Detective John Stallings sat with the old man from the woods, drinking stale 7-11 coffee and munching on hard, dry donuts. For his part, the old man appreciated the way Stallings had dealt with him and seemed to be enjoying not only the refreshments but the show as well.

They watched two JSO crime scene techs recover and process Allie Marsh's purse and a shirt that may or may not have belonged to the girl. The old man, after taking a few minutes to decide if he could trust the JSO detective, had told Stallings he had heard the phone ringing as he passed the Dumpster, reached in, and retrieved it. He hadn't used it because he really didn't have anyone to call and only answered once, which was when Stallings had called. The story had checked out, and Stallings didn't believe the old man had anything to do with Allie's disappearance, but he couldn't let him wander off just yet. He made the man believe staying and watching the law enforcement spectacle was his idea. Truthfully, now that Stallings had been on duty for almost twenty hours, he didn't mind the company.

As the sun rose and cast a pleasant light over a possibly nasty situation, he saw Patty Levine pull up in her county, unmarked Ford Freestyle with Tony Mazzetti right behind her in his big Crown Vic. Another police-looking unmarked car, a Dodge Charger, rumbled in behind them. He was surprised to see the slim, attractive form of Yvonne Zuni pop out of the Charger and start marching his way. She had a certain sway in her hips that said she was not all business, all the time.

She smiled, as she got closer. "This is impressive, Stall." She stopped short when she saw the old man next to him.

"Who's this?"

"He found the phone."

"He's the one that answered it when you called?"

Stallings nodded.

"Did he turn himself in?"

"Sort of."

"What's that mean?"

"When I found him, he explained the whole situation and led me here."

"Then he's a suspect."

"Barely."

"Why isn't he in cuffs?"

Stallings looked at her with a cocked head, wondering if she was serious. "Handcuffs? Why? He's not technically in custody."

"Then why is he here?"

"I'm holding him in case I have more questions. It's consensual."

"Have you Mirandized him?"

"I don't have to. He's not in custody."

"Is he free to go?"

Stallings hesitated. "What are you, his attorney?"

"No, I'm your sergeant and I want things run properly. Now, you need to shit or get off the pot. Charge him and cuff him or tell him he can go. I don't want a complaint the first week I'm in a new job."

Stallings started to answer, then realized she wasn't making a personal attack. She was doing what she thought was right. Even if it was all fucked up. He nodded and walked away, motioning the old homeless guy to follow him. Stallings said, "I don't need you anymore. You have my phone number—I want you to call me tomorrow at noon."

The old man nodded.

"And I'll be able to find you at your little camp?" ·

"That's where I stay unless it rains. Then I use the back of the Regency Square Mall a little east of here. I don't want to ruin it so I go by myself and only stay there every once in a while."

Stallings nodded, understanding, like few others, the plight of homeless people. He reached in his front pocket and checked the little brown alligator money clip Charlie had given him at Christmas. He had three twenties and four singles and a five-dollar bill. He yanked out the three twenties and handed them to the old man.

The man took it and nodded his thanks. Then he said, "I'll probably watch from the front of the 7-11. I don't want you in trouble with your pretty sergeant." He smiled, showing as many gaps as teeth.

Stallings let out a laugh, realizing how sharp the old man was to hear and understand what was going on. He watched the old man walk away and wondered about his own father, who had ended his career as a bully and shitty father by rolling out onto the streets himself. Stallings had seen him once in the last few years but kept tabs on him though different sources. He used to live downtown in a cheap, pay-by-the-week motel, his Navy pension keeping him safe, but alcohol slowly rotting him from the inside out. Stallings knew he had moved in the last year and hadn't looked for him.

He'd thought that his father had at least provided him with a negative role model so he wouldn't screw up his own marriage or kids. Now, separated and still mourning his missing Jeanie, he didn't think his father had provided him with anything, either negative or positive.

He heard Patty say, "You need a hand with anything, John?"

He turned to see her with Mazzetti standing next to her.

Mazzetti said, "Yeah, the real cops are here now, Stall."

"Well, Mr. Real Cop, this case just got kicked up a notch. What do you suggest we do now?"

Mazzetti just stared at him.

Stallings was sincere when he asked for investigative recommendations, but somewhere inside he hated to admit he enjoyed seeing the homicide detective baffled with such a direct inquiry.

Patty said, "I'll see if we can get any more information off the cell towers and then check to see if there are any security cameras for businesses along the road for a couple of miles in each direction. Maybe the 7-11 had some traffic and somebody saw something?"

From off to the side, Yvonne Zuni spoke up. "That's the first decent plan I've heard on a case since I came into crimes/persons. Go ahead with all of that, Detective Levine." She looked at Mazzetti. "What are you doing here? Waiting to see if we find a body? Detective

Mazzetti, if you don't have enough to do in homicide I'm certain I could find something for you to work on."

Mazzetti nodded and said, "Yes ma'am," turned, and scurried to his car.

Stallings and Patty exchanged glances, but neither laughed out loud.

John Stallings stood at the rear of his Impala with a large, detailed map of the county spread out across the trunk. Patty was on the other leads with two analysts assigned by the new sergeant. They had all the high-tech avenues covered. The leads were viable, and Patty was running down more detailed cell records, checking video cameras, and staying on top of any lab developments.

Stallings was different. He had learned the basic skills of a cop before the world of high-tech had changed so many things. He knew how to talk to people or scare them if necessary. He knew luck was involved in so much of police work and he knew how to reason things out. It didn't always work, but sometimes he surprised himself as well as others. Right now he studied the map and drew a blue circle downtown where the Wildside dance club was. He knew she'd been there at some point. He marked the Dumpster, which was where he was standing right now, on the map. Then he let his cop eyes roam up and down the map, thinking about the possible scenarios that had led to Allie Marsh's purse being discarded in the Dumpster.

First he had to assume the person who threw it in there didn't expect it to be found. That person thought either no one would look in a nasty Dumpster or it would be emptied soon. Next he thought of the reasons Allie left the bar with someone. He didn't like to dwell on any of it. Finally, he searched the map for the kind of open, but private, area someone could park a car and not be bothered. Places like parks, green spaces, canals, or tributaries with wetlands around them. It was as if he was up in one of the sheriff's office's helicopters without the use of time or the inevitable airsickness.

He used his finger to trace the main road, starting at the Wildside and slowly moving it along the map, keeping track of the mile legend and then following it east, over the river, across the marshes and residential neighborhoods, past the municipal airport, then all the way to the ocean. He could check the beaches. Every would-be Romeo in Florida tried to impress tourists with the ocean. Many of the beaches even had webcams to show what the waves were like for surfers. That was one of the breaks he'd gotten in the last big homicide case he had worked on. But something told him they didn't drive as far as the ocean. The couple of parks off the road were small and tended to get a lot of walkers and runners cutting through them.

Then he started tracing back from the beach, and his finger lingered on the outer edges of the municipal airport. There were trails back in there and it was secluded. He packed up the car and waited for the last crime scene tech to leave before he headed east the 2.3 miles to the airport. He drove past the main fields and found one of the dirt paths that led behind the small airport. He had purposely not mentioned his plan to Yvonne Zuni. While it was amusing to see her cut Tony Mazzetti down to size, he had no interest in experiencing it today. She must have failed to notice that he'd been on duty almost twenty-two hours now or she definitely would've said something. He planned a long afternoon of sleep as soon as he checked his one theory.

He found a field with mowed grass and a tree line set back fifty yards. Low-hanging branches of wide scrub brush formed a thick, green wall with the occasional southern pine that towered near the runways of the small airport. He got out and started walking the perimeter of the field, letting his eyes scan wherever something caught his attention. Stumps in the grass, unusual piles of leaves, anything that broke the straight lines of the field.

Then he noticed something all the way over in the tree line and started walking that way. He tried to continue scanning as he came closer, but whatever was on the edge of the scrub brush had captured his attention fully and he couldn't take his eyes off it. He saw a splash of red and blue and knew whatever it was it wasn't something from nature.

Then he slowed as a form started taking shape. He saw the blond hair and one arm splayed out to the side, and his heart sank. He slowed and noticed the shoe missing off one foot; her face was turned away from him.

He carefully stopped and eased to the side through the brush about ten feet away from her so as not to disturb the crime scene in any way. He could see her blue, bloating face and recognized it as Allie Marsh's formerly pretty face. He stepped back out of the brush, his hand already reaching for his cell phone when he had to stop, look up at the sky, and scream as loud as he had ever screamed. "Fuck!"

Thirteen

As soon as Patty Levine had gotten the call from John Stallings telling her he'd found the body she'd dropped her inquiry into cell tower hits and security cameras and raced to meet him. At some point she would have to resume that kind of work, but right now her partner had called. He sounded a little shaken. She knew it had as much to do with his own daughter as with the case itself.

She stepped into the ladies' room at the sheriff's office and popped a Xanax to steady herself before the ride back east to the municipal airport. As she swallowed the pill with a palm full of water from the sink, the door opened. Patty turned her head quickly, perhaps with a tinge of guilt for having almost been caught and was surprised to see her new sergeant, Yvonne Zuni, standing there.

Sergeant Zuni said, "I need to make a quick stop before heading out to the scene. How did he find her?"

Patty finished swallowing and shrugged. "That's just John. He figures out stuff the rest of us don't even know is important."

"I've heard he has his own methods of getting information."

Patty knew to keep her mouth shut.

Sergeant Zuni said, "I believe in letting cops work, but there are rules. Some of law, some of conduct, but I want everyone to follow the rules."

"Don't you think some rules are stupid?"

"Like the one about not dating someone who has the same supervisor as you?"

Patty just stared at the new boss.

Then Sergeant Zuni said, "Get your stuff together. No matter how he did it, your partner found the girl's body. Now we all have to pitch in and help."

Tony Mazzetti rolled up at the old municipal airport before the crime scene van. He was lucky his girlfriend was in the loop and had dropped him a line before Sergeant Zuni called to order him over to the scene. He felt a real satisfaction in telling his sergeant he was already on the way. He'd even stopped to pick up his usual partner, Christina Hogrebe, from her little house in Dames Point, then shot across the Dames Point Bridge, cutting south to the airport.

Christina was a rising star at the sheriff's office. The youngest full-time homicide detective ever, she had the instincts of an old-time street cop wrapped up in a package few men could ignore. There was a rumor a year back that Mazzetti and she were an item. He let it slide because it kept people from guessing why he hadn't had a date in a while. Christina heard it and didn't care. If information wasn't being used to put someone's ass in jail, she barely acknowledged it. He finally had to step up and deny it because someone asked how he and

Christina could date and still work in the same squad. It made him wonder if anyone would care if he went public with Patty. He doubted it. He was homicide and she was missing persons. Usually.

They were screaming south on St. John's Bluff Road when Christina said, "Tony, either slow it down or put on the lights, but I don't want to buy it because you've got a hard-on to beat the new sergeant to the scene."

"Who says I care about shit like that?"

"Hello, I think I just did. C'mon, admit it, big guy—working for a woman intimidates you."

"What're you talking about? I worked for Rita Hester and still do."

"But I hardly think of her as a woman."

"What's that mean?"

"Not that she's not attractive, but she's been a boss a long time. And you'd have to admit she could kick your ass if she wanted to."

Mazzetti just nodded at that. Lieutenant Rita Hester could kick just about anybody's ass.

Christina said, "But the new sarge is a little different. She's like a china doll, all small and beautiful. And she's hands-on. She even corrected one of my reports in red ink yesterday."

"Sounds like you're the one with a problem."

Christina shook her head. "I don't mind correction or criticism if it makes me a better cop."

"You saying I *do* mind it?"

"You tell me."

"I listen to your suggestions all the time."

"But you're still senior partner. The sarge can order us around all day and doesn't have to ask about opinions. She takes 'em or leaves 'em as she sees fit."

"What's your point?"

"That the sarge has you spooked." She smiled as she chomped on the bubble gum that was always wedged in her molars.

It was tough to get upset with anyone who looked like her and had that kind of delivery.

Yvonne Zuni took a minute to survey the scene before she got out of her nice new Dodge Charger. Being new to the unit she was still trying to get a feel for how everyone worked and interacted with each other. She knew Mazzetti's type: brash, arrogant, efficient. And Patty Levine was smart, professional, and insecure. It was John Stallings who gave her a hard time. She couldn't get a decent read on him to save her life. She'd heard all the rumors. He was tough, resourceful, and he paid little or no attention to the SO policies. That was something they might butt heads over. The new sergeant was smart enough to realize that Stallings was an old friend of the lieutenant's. That could be tricky too. She also knew his personal story. He wasn't living at home right now, even though he didn't broadcast it. She'd listened to two of the secretaries gossip about it, each with her own plans to scoop him up if he stayed on the market much longer. The sergeant figured that the split was a delayed result of his daughter's disappearance. Marital problems were a well-known side effect of family tragedy. She knew it from personal experience.

She watched as Stallings directed the crime scene people toward the body of the young woman. He also seemed to deal well with that loudmouth Mazzetti. The two exchanged a few words, but she noticed that Stallings had enough sense to let Mazzetti walk toward the scene alone.

The sergeant wanted to see if she could have the two men work together. As long as her detectives followed the rules they'd all get along like a big happy family. And she was the mother. She missed being a mother.

Fourteen

Stallings's last major case had been a serial killer who had murdered one of the runaway girls he'd returned home several times over the years. That case was so big that a task force had been formed to stop the killer. No one would be forming a task force for this poor girl. It would be Mazzetti and Christina Hogrebe all the way. Unless Stallings could find a good enough reason for Sergeant Zuni to assign more detectives.

He realized this was a quirk with him. He got so entangled in cases involving young women that he couldn't think about anything else. He knew it had to do with Jeanie. He didn't care. This was one impulse he didn't intend to fight.

He and Patty stood straighter as the sergeant walked their way and talked into her cell phone at the same time. No detective sergeant alive could go thirty seconds without getting a phone call. It was one of the rules of police work.

Finally she closed the small cell and looked up at the two detectives. "You did a great job of finding her, Stall. I'm just sorry it turned out this way."

Stallings nodded.

"Anything obvious around the body?"

He shook his head. "She's clothed, no obvious signs of trauma. But I didn't get too near."

The sergeant looked up at him but said nothing.

Stallings was struck by her clear green eyes and high cheekbones. She could be a runway model if she wanted and was a few inches taller.

Mazzetti stomped over, muttering about the crime scene techs. The homicide detective always built up an excuse in case he couldn't clear a case. Sometimes he'd claim the crime scene techs screwed up the scene. Other times he'd blame the arriving unit for trampling a scene. In the past he'd said the media coverage inhibited his investigation. There was always something that derailed an unsuccessful investigation. Stallings knew a lot of every case was fate. To find a minute piece of evidence had an element of luck in it. To find the right person to interview and to have them tell the truth was incredibly lucky. He used the term "luck," but in the last few years he knew there more to it than luck. He'd come back to his early Catholic school roots and realized there were higher forces at work in the universe. Maybe it was all the A.A. meetings with Maria or his need to feel that someone was watching over his Jeanie, but he had come to the conclusion that there was, in fact, a God. He also felt, much like the old saying, that God favors those who are prepared, so he left as little to chance as possible. But it was always that last tip or piece of fiber evidence or security video that solved a case. Those things were in God's hands.

Mazzetti briefed the sergeant, but he didn't know anything yet either. Like any decent homicide detective he had a list of things he was going to do right away and most of those, at least for right now, concerned the crime scene and subsequent autopsy.

Mazzetti said, "Who knows, this girl might've died of alcohol poisoning. Happens all the time with these wild-assed spring breakers."

Sergeant Zuni turned her head slowly and said, "Is that what you want to tell her mother? She's staying at the Marriott downtown."

Mazzetti didn't answer.

"Maybe we could hold off on the conjecture until we have some kind of evidence to support theories."

Mazzetti nodded.

The sergeant turned to Stallings. "Have you found anything in your interviews or the victim's background to indicate drug use or heavy drinking?"

Stallings hesitated to mention that one of Allie's traveling companions had admitted to them trying Ecstasy. He didn't want the death dismissed so easily. But he had to be open in a case like this. "One of her friends said someone had given them X."

"Did she know the supplier?"

"No, she'd never met him. It was someone Allie had met. Maybe more than once during the week."

"That could be important. Do we know where she was last seen?"

"Probably the Wildside the night before last. That's our best information now."

The sergeant nodded as she considered this information. She turned to Mazzetti. "Finish the scene and autopsy. Stall and Patty will determine if anyone saw her at the Wildside and talk to the bartenders and staff there."

Mazzetti said, "You want us to treat this like a homicide? It's probably an overdose. It's like natural causes for spring breakers. If we investigated every overdose we'd never have time to work the real homicides and we'd have a shitload of open cases."

The sergeant said, "There may be extenuating circumstances in this case. You don't know all the facts or all the issues. This could end up being a high-profile case."

Mazzetti got that glazed look on his face like he did when he was about to go before the cameras, then said, "But Christina and I are the lead, right?"

The sergeant said, "For now."

He ran hard, invigorated by his recent kill. Like any predator, he had to keep his skills up, and a run like this along Neptune Beach in the middle of spring break did two things: it kept him in tip-top shape, and it offered him a look at all the blond prey hanging around. He knew that the first sunny, relatively warm day in a week would bring the crowds out to the beach, and he needed a little sun. He had his shirt off to show his pecs and wore the smallest pair of shorts he had.

His eyes scanned the crowds as he raced by. This was a fitness lap and a chance to let the young girls see him. In ten minutes he'd jog at a reasonable pace to inspect the prey more closely.

He preferred to meet his prey in bars. It seemed more anonymous and safer in a dark, crowded club. That wasn't a strict rule. He'd met Kathleen from South Carolina in a café. But the more he thought about it, the beach was a good choice too. As long as he found a girl away from her group. Anything to make his identification more difficult.

He made the wide loop of the parking lot and street, then ran back down onto the hard packed sand of the beach. He kept a measured pace, his eyes sifting through the throngs of women on the beach. The ones with dark hair were easy to pass by, but the blondes made him slow down. On this pass he saw five good possibilities. All blond hair and blue eyes. Size and shape were secondary. On his next pass he'd assess possible witnesses. Were they with groups or boyfriends? Were they with one or two girlfriends? He had his prey picked out for the next loop.

He was breathing hard by the time he reached the north end of the beach again. He slowed to a near walk as he approached the first girl he'd singled out on his last pass-through. She was sprawled on a bright green blanket and turned on her side as he approached. She had bright blue eyes, short blond hair, a fairly serious acne problem, and cellulite on her hips. But the reason he kept running was her boyfriend on the towel next to her. The boyfriend placed a hand on her back, and he could tell they weren't in a platonic relationship.

The next three girls were all surrounded by hordes of sorority sisters or cheerleaders or some other chattering, perky group.

Finally, he spied one girl reading a paperback book about three quarters of the way down the beach. She appeared to be alone on a single towel. She wore cute black-framed glasses that seemed to accentuate her blue eyes, and she absently fingered her wavy blond hair draped over her right shoulder. She wore a one-piece bathing suit, but she had a muscular body. Something a predator like himself could admire. He slowed to a trot, then a walk, making a show out of checking his pulse by placing two fingers on his neck and looking at his watch, carefully stopping well before his intended target.

He continued to check the immediate vicinity to make sure she was alone and no one was paying any attention. It seemed clear as he eased up the beach slightly from the waterline.

He stopped a few yards from her and sat down to stretch in the sand. As he turned toward her, she looked up and smiled. It filled him with excitement. She had a great smile, and he knew he'd taken the first step.

"Whatcha reading?"

She glanced down at the cover as if she couldn't remember. "Patricia Cornwell." She made a face, but he wasn't sure if she liked the book or it was a little gross.

He said, "I read a lot of history."

"Like who?"

In fact he'd only read one book recently and it was about Iwo Jima. He remembered the author. "James Bradley."

"*Flags of our Fathers.*"

"I'm impressed."

"I'm a little bit of a bookworm."

He cut loose with a big smile. She had a cute silver nose stud. "What's your name?"

"Holly."

"Where are you from?"

"Right here. I go to North Florida." The University of North Florida sat in the southeast section of the city of Jacksonville.

He started to focus on the tiny nose stud, thinking what a great memento it would make. Then he said, "You don't have to come far for spring break."

"But it's more fun to travel."

"Do bookworms like to travel?"

She had a sly smile when she said, "Bookworms like a lot of things."

He had found his prey.

Fifteen

John Stallings knew this was a big deal because the meeting was held in the lieutenant's plush office. Although Rita Hester supervised the detective bureau, among other things, her office was not in the Land That Time Forgot. She did not have a shitty linoleum floor or scuffed beige walls, nor did she have thin, industrial carpet.

Today she sat at the head of the conference table opposite her wide oak desk. The sergeant sat immediately to her right and Mazzetti to her left with Stallings, Christina Hogrebe, Patty Levine, and an assistant to the sheriff filling the rest of the table. This was either something big or someone had fucked up in a big way.

The lieutenant looked down the long table at the sheriff's assistant, then cast a broader glance across the table and said, "This comes from the colonel, who got it from the sheriff, who got an earful from the state attorney. We will treat the overdose of the girl from Mississippi"—she looked down at the notepad in front of her—"Allie Marsh, as a homicide. We will find out who gave her the Ecstasy and what led to her death. And even though we're flooded with robberies, shootings, fatal domestics, and all other kinds of fire-and-brimstone shit, we'll work this overdose until we have found her supplier." Lieutenant Rita Hester was never particularly good at hiding her true feelings about certain things. She was political as anyone else in a command position at the sheriff's office, but at heart she was still a street cop who wanted to put people in jail. She stared down the sheriff's assistant until the thin man nodded his approval.

Of course no one was going to argue with her, but she continued. "We don't need the negative media about any deaths, accidental or otherwise, while Jacksonville is trying to build a reputation as a spring break destination. Daytona and Fort Lauderdale can handle the occasional jumping off a balcony, but we can't risk even a simple overdose. This girl's family has money and clout and so we will treat this like it's the fucking Lindbergh kidnapping case." She glared up and down the table, then said, "Are there any questions or comments?"

Every detective at the table knew that meant, "Shut up and get to work."

And that was just fine with John Stallings. He had already decided he'd find out who would leave a girl like that in the field without even a call to fire rescue. He didn't think he'd ever get away from being drawn into cases like this.

Tony Mazzetti fidgeted during the final minutes of the autopsy. The procedure didn't bother him—he'd seen hundreds performed on everyone from shot-up drug dealers to babies that had been shaken too hard.

At this point it was just business. It had to be. If he looked at each body that rolled through these doors as a person with family and hopes, he'd have gone crazy years ago. Instead he observed and provided any pertinent information the medical examiner wanted, like surroundings where the body was found, theory of how the victim died, and history that might have contributed to the death. It was this kind of relationship between a veteran homicide detective and a good ME that led to the quick, successful clearance of most deaths.

He liked the young assistant medical examiner who was currently examining the remains of Allison Marsh. Mazzetti hated to think of the names attached to the bodies while they were on the table because once again that made them more real to him. It felt like an invasion of privacy. He not only saw the dead people naked, but past that into their innermost places. Physically. As layers of skin were peeled back and organs removed and examined, he learned things that no one knew about themselves, like the weight of their livers, the degree of plaque built up in their arteries, and if tumors were growing deep inside their seemingly healthy bodies.

The assistant ME said, "Look at this."

Mazzetti didn't see anything unusual; he never did at these things. Sometimes he felt as if these pathologists were just showing off. He said, "What are you looking at?"

"She had a belly-button ring." He pointed at her pale stomach. "See the discoloration around the edges?"

Mazzetti looked closely and nodded. He made a note in the file.

The young assistant ME looked up from the body and said, "Tony, she seemed pretty healthy except her heart is shredded. Just blown out."

"Ecstasy?"

"We have to wait for toxicology, but that would be my guess."

"We have a witness who said she had a source and had recently tried it."

"What spring breaker doesn't?"

Mazzetti nodded, making a few notes.

The assistant ME said, "She had sexual intercourse with someone using a condom. I took a sample of the residue when she came in and already sent it to the lab."

"Did you do any preliminary checks?"

The ME nodded.

Mazzetti knew the drill here. "What was the chemical residue?"

"We still have to do analysis, and it's not an officially accepted form of detection yet."

"I know, I know, but you've helped me before with it. What does the preliminary analysis look like?"

"Polyethylene glycol."

He knew what brand used the chemical. "Durex." The brand of condoms had played a role in a recent case.

"That would be a decent guess at this point. The only reason I could make the call so quick was the suicide earlier in the week had it in her as well."

Mazzetti nodded.

"That girl also had some X in her system."

He stopped writing and looked up at the assistant medical examiner. "You saying the deaths are connected?"

"That's not my call. I'm giving you all the relevant information. I'm gonna take another gander at the report on the other girl from South Carolina. My guess is that it's a coincidence. Different methods of death, every one of the kids uses X during spring break, and Durex condoms are not exactly rare."

Mazzetti nodded as he breathed a little easier. It was probably the X that killed her. The drug was technically known as MDMA, or a variation, and was a man-made stimulant with hallucinogenic properties. It usually came in tablet form and could resemble anything from a commercial aspirin to something a kid made in his basement. The Dutch were big on it and sometimes seemed to have an endless supply for the willing students both in the United States and Europe.

Finally Mazzetti worked up the nerve to ask, "So what about this girl? What precisely are you saying killed her?"

"Pending toxicology, I'd say an overdose of Ecstasy and related effects. You know, extreme dehydration, overheating, and stress on her heart."

His clearance rate was still good.

Sixteen

John Stallings and Patty Levine had been at the Wildside all afternoon and evening. Patty had caught on immediately as the young corporate manager had explained the digital video surveillance system inside the club. The cameras each recorded a night's activity and stored it as a file on a main computer. Patty had sat in front of the computer and printed out images of Allie Marsh and the men she talked to during the evening. Stallings spoke with a lot of the staff, finally narrowing his focus to a couple of bartenders and waitresses.

Stallings conferred with Patty, and she showed him some of the more interesting video she had found. It was hard to see Allie unless she was close to one of several cameras. One showed the center part of the main bar, and after a few minutes of fast-forwarding and scanning different angles, Patty found her twice. Each time talking to a different man. Both a little older with dark hair and nice clothes. Another clip showed her laughing with a scraggily-looking young man near the small stage. The camera got a clear view of him, and Patty printed out each of the men's faces so they were easily identifiable.

During a slack time on the dance floor they saw her again talking with a funky-looking kid with long hair. This was also the first time they noticed a bottle of water in her hand. Did that mean she had already started on the X by then? They printed out the frame of the long-haired young man talking to her.

Patty had searched and searched but could not find footage of her leaving with anyone. Patty took the counter up to midnight and could still see Allie hovering on the left side of the club near the small bar on the side. But after that there was no sign of her in the club, exiting the doors, or in the parking lot. As the club emptied, it became easier to spot individuals, and Allie clearly was no longer there.

The manager breezed back in a couple of hours later, surprised to see them still working at the computer with a short stack of frames printed out on the high-quality laser printer.

He smiled, "Find anything useful?"

"Yeah, a few things," started Stallings, wondering how much to trust the sharp-dressed man. "We're gonna need to talk to two of the bartenders on the floor now and look at some credit card receipts as a way to identify a few suspects." Stallings handed him the printed photos Patty had retrieved, and the manager thumbed through each one, studying it carefully, shaking his head, then moving on to the next one. He stopped at the last one and stared. He looked up at the detectives and held the photo for them to see it. "I know this guy."

Stallings said, "Who is it?"

"He's the drummer for the band. His name is Donnie Eliot."

* * *

He waited with a nervous and giddy chill running through him. Holly was supposed to meet him at a little deli by ten. It was less than ten minutes away, so he could handle what he had to do now and still make it in time. He never gave out his cell number or tried to get a girl's because that was a link he just didn't need. This hunt had been an easy one with the cute young junior at UNF offering to meet him. The fact that it had been so easy had taken a little of the fun out of it. The element that had changed was the frequency of his hunts. Holly would be the third one in a week. He usually went months, a few times more than a year, between hunts, but this was his season. He'd never bagged prey outside the traditional spring break period of roughly March through mid-April. One year he'd given up hunting for Lent. He'd learned that was something he didn't want to do again. To make up for it the following year, he'd singled out a girl at Mardi Gras and hunted and bagged her in the same day. He hadn't even tried to make it look like a suicide.

He felt an erection bloom as he recalled Fat Tuesday the year after Katrina had hit. He saw her on the corner of Bourbon and Conti Street in jeans and a tight midriff shirt. He could tell by the way her head hung down and long, blond hair floated in the breeze that she was alone and sad about something. It started with a simple lunch of a muffuletta and then an afternoon of hearing how she was visiting in town with her family from Oklahoma City and was bored. Her younger brother and sister were out on the town with her parents, but she had brooded until she was allowed to stay at the hotel alone for the day.

He took the young woman on a tour of the city,

which he knew pretty well, leading her farther and farther from the more crowded tourist area with each stop. He bought a couple of hurricanes and let the alcohol work its way though her system until she swayed when she walked. He cut her off before she got sick. He'd seen too many college students barf in the street to buy her a third rum-infused red monster.

They crossed Rampart into Louis Armstrong Park and enjoyed the quiet outdoors as the sun began to set. He knew he had to make his move quickly before her parents made a fuss. That became obvious when she dropped the bombshell that she was only seventeen. In the recesses of the park, near one of the ponds formed by the running brook, they started a hot session of kissing and petting. When he realized she didn't want to go past a certain point he became much more excited and let his predatory instincts run wild. God, it was glorious and liberating as he ripped her shirt from her, exposing small, firm breasts, then yanked her jeans and panties off at the same time. He'd always remember the look on her face when she saw the size of his dick. Because of the situation he knew he didn't have time for a condom, but he'd already planned her disposal and didn't think leaving evidence on her was going to be a problem.

He entered her despite her pleas to stop and after a very, very short time felt himself starting to lose all control. He was on her back, mounting her like an animal should when he popped the blade on his nice Browning knife and ran the razor-sharp edge across her exposed neck. The move silenced her to a slight gurgle, and he felt the life run out of her as he came into her. It was the best of his kills so far.

But he had been lucky that day and he knew it. No

one saw him with her. Few people wandered into the park, and no one heard her cries. He used a length of nylon rope some homeless person used for a clothesline and two loose cinder blocks to weigh the dead girl down and send her to the bottom of an impossibly small pond. It was so small no one would think to search for a body there.

Two days later he read a tiny article about the missing girl that implied she had run away. That was the only story ever printed about her. Now she held a place near the center of his prey collage.

He sipped a bottle of water and was glancing out at the near-empty dance floor when he felt a tap on his shoulder. He turned and saw the smiling face of pretty Holly.

He used his tongue to check the inside of his mouth. His fangs were ready for the hunt. He smiled, feeling the surge of wildness pulse through his body.

Even if it was nearly nine o'clock at night, John Stallings had analysts at the sheriff's office running Donnie Eliot's name through every possible criminal index. While they waited for information on their first suspect, they talked to waitresses and bartenders in the spacious administrative offices of the club. Photos of Allie Marsh and the three unidentified men who had talked to her sat on the table. Credit card receipts were laid out next to the photos to help anyone with a cloudy memory.

The father in Stallings had a nagging feeling that there was more to Allie's death than a simple overdose. He couldn't explain it, but maybe it had to do with the connection he felt with her mother. Diane Marsh had elected to stay in town, at least for a few days, while information was still being sorted out by the detectives. Stallings knew he was hooked and couldn't let things drop now.

The door to the office opened, and a lean, muscular man of about thirty poked his head in.

Stallings looked down at a sheet of paper and said, "Larry Kinard?"

"Yes, sir."

Stallings motioned the bartender in and to a seat. "Thanks for taking a break to talk to us."

"I'm not on break, I'm off today."

"Why were you in the building?"

"Picking up my check and seeing if anything was happening. You know how it is. Work at night, you can never just sit at home."

Stallings knew exactly what he meant. He looked at the younger man and said, "We're hoping you might be able to identify a couple of photos for us from the other night."

The lean man nodded his head and smiled at Patty. "I heard it had to do with a girl who died."

"That's right. From an overdose of X. You see much of that in the club?"

"I see signs of it, you know, the sweating and heavy water use. The flaky behavior. But truthfully this place hops so hard that I'm usually just slinging drinks and collecting money."

Stallings set down Allie Marsh's photograph. "Recognize her?"

The bartender nodded. "Yeah. Real cutie. I saw her a couple times recently. Probably in the last week."

Stallings nodded and laid down the first photograph of one of the men Allie had chatted with.

The bartender studied it carefully. "He was at the bar. I served him. He's been here before. Not a flat breaker."

"A what?"

"A spring break student who's flat broke and orders three cheap beers for the whole night." The bartender looked at the photo again and said, "More likely a break runner."

"Excuse me?"

"Break runner. A guy who slips into spring break crowds and tries to hook up with younger students. See 'em all the time. Not too old. Fit and with more cash than the students. Girls love these kind of guys."

"So they'd go for an older guy?"

"Like a Cajun for crawfish."

Stallings smiled, then said, "If you saw the credit card receipts could you remember his name?" He slid over a stack of receipts.

Larry the bartender started at the top and within a minute pulled a slip and said, "This is him. Chad Palmer. I remember because he tipped me twenty bucks on a fifty-five-dollar tab. See." He pointed to the tip line.

Patty said, "Now we're getting somewhere."

Stallings shoved the next photo of a fit, dark-haired man in his early thirties. The photo wasn't that clear.

"Oh, I know him." Larry the bartender looked up at the two detectives. "What is this, a test?"

"Why do you say that?"

"Because this guy is a cop."

Seventeen

Holly's bright smile accentuated her beautiful and nodding blond head when she agreed to leave the deli with him. It had happened so fast he had to plan things on the fly. First of all she wanted to leave her car there and ride with him. That'd be too much of a hint to anyone looking for her. He told her the little Toyota wouldn't be safe there and had her follow him to a parking garage near the Modis Tower. Then she jumped in with him as he considered all the places they could go to be alone. So far his predatory instincts had been perfect. No one had noticed them together. She'd told him about her wild experiences with other drugs, so he knew that she wouldn't turn her nose up at the X when he offered it to her. All that was left was the location.

The thrill he knew so well rushed through him like a drug. Like some kind of super Viagra that kept him hard and dangerous as a predator should be.

As he navigated the straight streets of downtown Jacksonville, Holly turned in her seat and said, "Let's go to my old sorority house. It's quiet and we can be alone."

"What about your sorority sisters?"

"Oh, we don't use it anymore. It got condemned. But it's really cool."

He smiled and said, "Sounds like a plan."

It was hard to describe what she was feeling right now. Almost like electricity making the tiny hairs on her arm stand on end. She'd searched for a long time for someone just like him. It'd taken a while for her to learn exactly what she was supposed to look for, but he had it. The most obvious thing was his looks and athletic ability, but there was something deeper—or nothing deeper, depending on how you look at. He had a cocky, self-confident manner that was difficult to fake. He really did feel as if he was the king of Jacksonville and she was just one of his subjects. She knew that was the perfect attitude.

She had to do something to make up for her last effort to find a man. Billy was his name, and he was a little young at the time, fifteen, but he had a tight, muscular body and a sweet face. She'd taken him to the same empty house and done things the young man had never imagined possible. But in the end he hadn't handled it well and his immaturity came through. It turned out to be embarrassing, with a lot of crying and begging.

She hadn't liked the role of older, more experienced lover. She liked this role of bookworm much better. It was almost as if she was an actress in a role, wearing her reading glasses even if she didn't need them, putting her hair up in a ponytail. She just liked the idea of being someone she really wasn't. She liked hiding her muscular arms and covering her washboard abs under heavy clothing only to surprise someone later. She doubted she'd surprise him much because the first time he saw her she was at the beach, but it was still a fun façade. Sweet, smart, and safe.

She was pretty confident she'd lulled him into a false sense of security and his expectations were low. He'd be in for the surprise of his life once he knew the real her.

Suddenly she was so excited her lungs couldn't keep up with the oxygen her body needed.

This was gonna be one wild, fun night.

Since her marriage had broken up and the life she loved had completely ceased to exist, Yvonne Zuni had viewed the detectives who worked for her as her family. Sometimes family members clicked and laughed and all was well. Sometimes family members fought. She knew enough about the history of crimes/persons to know that Tony Mazzetti was the star homicide investigator and viewed John Stallings as a threat. This was something that could be a problem or something she might be able to use for motivation.

At times like this, all alone in her three-bedroom house, in the evening, she sometimes felt a panic at facing the long night alone and being so many hours from going back to the office. She remembered when her evenings were busy with feedings and cleaning, sharing a TV show or quiet conversation with her husband. Back then she had considered giving up her career to spend more time with her family. She really had it all.

She looked down at the roasted chicken she picked at while she read over a few reports, making corrections and suggestions in the margins. Her TV had not been on for anything other than the local news in at least three months, and the house seemed unnaturally quiet with the thick carpet and insulated walls. A sliding glass door allowed the cool night air into the house, but there was no sound from outside.

It was in this silence that the sound of her phone beeping made her jump. She grabbed it off the table in front of her.

"Sergeant Zuni."

"Sarge, we got a shooting near the stadium."

It was a JSO dispatcher.

The sergeant said, "Who's rolling?"

"Mazzetti and Hogrebe."

"Good. Tell them I'm on my way."

She closed the phone and smiled. At least she could avoid spending this night alone.

"This is an old sorority house?"

She nodded from the front seat of his Jeep.

"Isn't it kinda far from the UNF campus?"

She hesitated, then said, "The sorority had to draw from other local schools too, like the University of Jacksonville."

"I thought sororities and fraternities all came from the same school."

She just shrugged those cute shoulders.

He parked the car in the rear of the giant old house, then followed Holly's instructions to pull it into a carport so it'd be safe. The old carport appeared unused, but the idea of a safe, deserted house where he could spend some time with innocent little Holly excited him to the point of explosion. His hunter's instincts came out as he scanned for other people.

Holly said, "We still get to use the house and no one will be around. We'll have this grand old place all to ourselves." She spread her arms like a display model at a car show.

Her smile alone was enough to attract predators, but that cute, athletic body, blond hair, and blue eyes were irresistible to him. He followed her up the cement steps in the back of the house into a dark kitchen. She produced a flashlight from a kitchen cabinet.

"What happened to the lights?"

"We haven't paid the bill in a while, so we keep the flashlights handy."

He wondered why she brought him to an empty, abandoned house, but those thoughts faded as she took his hand and led him into the wide living room. There were three couches and a table that made it feel like the main lobby to a sorority house. She pulled him to the longest of the three couches and shoved him playfully, then plopped into his lap and started to kiss him. She wasn't as innocent as she played.

He decided to let this go on for a while before figuring out how to claim this kill. He could just picture the surprised expression on her face as he did whatever he was going to do. He had a knife with him, but he could also try something new. It was secluded here and quiet. Now might be a good time to be innovative.

His first two questions were the same that everyone else who'd ever visited the house had. The first was, "What about your sorority sisters?" The second was about the lights. Both were easily explained, and if she played it right it could be more exciting. She stopped in front of the back door and made a show out of adjusting her glasses and pulling her blouse tight, then held her hands up like a model to show off the house. Just like everyone else, all he did was shrug and willingly walk inside. This always reminded her of the old Dracula movies in which the ancient vampire instructed people, "Enter freely, of your own will." Everyone came in. As he stepped through the door and into the kitchen her excitement grew to the point she had to pause to grab hold of one of the old wooden chairs left in the kitchen. He didn't notice. He seemed distracted as if he was thinking about what was going to happen instead of what was happening now. She never understood why guys idealized sex before it happened but discounted the woman after it happened. It seemed like he was working on a scientific formula in his head, considering all the variables and outcomes. She stepped up behind him after she recovered her senses and placed her hand on his broad shoulder.

She gently led him into the living room with its two comfortable couches. She'd worked hard not to come on too strong yet. She wanted this to last. She wished she could bottle this feeling and save it whenever she was down. If it could last all night it still wouldn't be long enough. She didn't want tonight's adventure to end up like Billy, the teenager. Abrupt and awkward. She'd liked the way his fresh young skin felt under her hands and how he looked as he quivered. Somehow she didn't get the sense that this guy would quiver much. She saw him more as a strutting, football-star type. He'd think that no matter what he did, women loved it. He was probably right. Holly was already thrilled at the idea of him inside her.

She smiled as she thought about the first time she'd brought someone to the old abandoned house. Had it only been two years ago? It seemed as if she'd been doing it for a lifetime. That guy was a little older, maybe thirty-eight, and it hadn't been that much fun. He was drunk and sluggish and tended to doze off. He didn't appreciate her natural ability. He never realized she was playing a role. That time she was the dull-witted barista who turned into a sexual tiger. But the drunken idiot didn't catch the subtleties and change of personality. He'd been damn near catatonic through the rest of the night. She had high hopes for tonight

Eighteen

John Stallings secretly enjoyed pissing off any of the detectives from Internal Affairs—most cops did. The hell of it was that IA really didn't go after cops all the time; they cleared them of allegations too. It was just a deep-seated, almost police-DNA-level distrust that kept Stallings taking the extra steps to annoy some of the investigators in the unit.

These prima donnas were used to fairly steady hours, usually dayshift Monday through Friday. That's why tonight, at ten, he had called the emergency contact for IA to get one of them down to the office to let him look through some personnel files. During the day, Stallings would have had to deal with some sour, civilian personnel manager, but now, after hours, a sworn IA investigator had to come down to the PMB and let him have access to the records. Stallings had certified it was an emergency over the phone and now waited just outside the personnel office to see which IA detective had gotten the call at home.

He smiled, then laughed when he saw the normally dapper Ronald Bell pad out of the elevator dressed uncharacteristically in jeans and a T-shirt. He was the best possible IA detective to annoy.

"Hey, Ron," said Stallings, not bothering to conceal his delight.

Bell just glared at him. Usually he corrected people because he liked to be called Ronald.

"You look like a bear that was just stirred out of hibernation."

"When I heard it was you who needed to get into records I wondered if you somehow figured out I was the duty detective. I guess I don't even have to ask if this could've waited until the morning."

Stallings just stood silently as Bell unlocked the solid wooden door, then led Stallings through two more until they reached a long, narrow room crammed with file cabinets and cardboard boxes of paper jammed on top of every one.

Bell gave him a tired sigh and said, "Who are we looking for?"

"A motorman named Gary Lauer."

Bell didn't move, his poker face giving away a slight twitch.

"You know him?" Stallings had a personal dislike for Ronald Bell that went back three years, but he knew the creep well enough to listen.

The IA detective said, "I shouldn't say anything."

"C'mon, Ron, this has to do with a girl's OD."

"You think Lauer gave her the drugs?"

"I didn't. He was just a witness. Why, what do you know?"

The older, red-faced detective took in a breath, then sighed. "He's had a few IA cases. The usual bullshit about use of force we had to clear. No problem there."

"But?"

"He had a domestic that was a little ugly."

"What happened to him?"

"Nothing."

"What do you mean 'nothing'?"

"I mean his girlfriend at the time clammed up, then changed her story. There were other factors, so we had to shit-can the investigation."

"But you remember this guy from that?"

He leveled his brown, bloodshot eyes at Stallings and said, "Stall, think about it. If I remember this guy, the incident was ugly."

He felt his erection stiffen as Holly wiggled in his lap, kissing him and nibbling his ear. The flashlight cast an errant beam against a bare wall. He was as excited at the prospect of what he was going to do to claim his kill as he was by the sexual activity. The longer this went on, the more he considered using the knife just as he had in New Orleans a few years ago. This time he decided he wanted to face her, looking into the beautiful blue eyes when he jammed the blade into her soft neck. He wondered if her eyes would pop open or slam shut when he did it. But first he had to slip his dick into her.

He twisted and laid her down on the couch, so he could be on top of her. He slid one hand under her blouse and felt her small breast with an erect nipple in the palm of his hand.

Holly giggled and slid away from him, then sat up on the arm of the couch. "You've got naughty thoughts." Her smile was broad and inviting.

He said, "You have no idea." His eyes kept staring at the nose stud he wanted for his souvenir case. The tiny, clear stone picking up the beam of the flashlight.

Holly said, "Oh, yeah? What do you want to do to me?"

"Get wild. What about you? What do you want to do to me?"

She paused, placed her small hand on his sleeve, and said, "You know what I'd really like to do?"

"No, what?" He felt for the knife in his pocket.

"I would love to eat you." Then she let out a laugh, jumped up, and darted to the far side of the room. "But first you have to catch me."

He started to stand, wondering if he might try killing her first.

Holly said, "Count to three, then chase me. But my advantage is that I know this old house a lot better than you."

He said, "One, two, three," in a blur, then sprang up after her as she sprinted off in a wild fit of laughter. She had no idea how short her future was.

It was time to take the evening up a notch. In the blink of an eye, Holly shed her bookworm persona and decided it was time to be a stripper. In her mind she felt like a superhero as she whipped off her glasses and shook out her hair. She added a subtle, sexy sway to her walk and then slid into his lap like a stripper getting paid for a lap dance. She immediately felt his reaction and transferred it to her as excitement. It was like electricity, and she couldn't keep from kissing him deep and hard. She felt her tongue up against his and let it explore his mouth. It was almost as if she was tasting his essence from the outside.

She felt his erection grow, as well as the pace of his petting and rubbing. The intensity of his kisses grew as he used his tongue to taste her as well. She had to be careful or this would be over too soon. She didn't want to put the brakes on too hard and break the mood. She liked the effect she was having and decided to add the role of stripper to her repertoire. It was certainly a lot more fun than the bookworm. She'd never been to a strip club and only seen the idealized versions of dancers in movies where they all had big boobs and rhythm and aspired to be showgirls in Las Vegas. She suspected that was a lie. The strip clubs she saw in Jacksonville were not nearly as glamorous and the girls not nearly as talented. Still it wouldn't hurt to go to one and hone her own ability. That would give her five distinct personalities she could use: bookworm, stupid barista, stripper, underage babysitter, and track star at the University of North Florida. She had the body for it and was fast for short distances. She doubted anyone would ever test her beyond that.

As much fun as grinding on his lap was that she had to put an end to this and find another way to keep him interested. Then she thought of the rabbit and the fox. She'd run and see if he could chase her. The only question was who was the rabbit and who was the fox?

Tony Mazzetti felt his body sag as a breeze kicked in from the eastern part of the county. The quieter zone, closer to the ocean. Right now he was near the stadium outside a small house with three bodies and about fifty bullet holes in it. He and his partner, Christina Hogrebe, had been called out an hour ago when reports of gunfire started rolling into the communications center and responding patrol officers found the bodies. It took Mazzetti about thirty seconds to figure out it was a drug rip. The three bodies were all members of a street gang called Street Cred that dealt crack in this area of the city. Someone had entered the house, shot them each in the head, then sprayed the house with nine-millimeter bullets on the way out. The way the victims were close together and didn't defend themselves made it seem as if they knew the killer.

Now the trick would be finding whom they owed money to, had crossed in a deal, or were fighting for territory. Not the most complicated whodunit in the world, but certainly one he'd be able to clear to keep his record looking good. In these drug rip-offs someone always bragged about it and wanted people to know who did it so they would get the message and no one else would have to be killed. The problem with that theory was that the cops found out at the same time. With snitches in every neighborhood and rewards coaxing residents out of silence, nothing said on the street stayed quiet for very long. Not in Jacksonville or any other city in the country.

A teenage girl had been in the house at the time of the shooting. The mother and another daughter were only a couple of houses away, visiting a family member. One of the victims was her twenty-two-year-old son. The older daughter, Tosha, had seen a car drive by, but she had already changed her story from black males to Hispanic males. He didn't know if she was naturally a little flaky or stoned, but she was a mess. No one would admit there were guns in the house. He made a quick search and couldn't find any. But the three victims were all known dealers and all had a history of gun violence. Had the killers taken the guns?

He finished up some notes on who needed to be interviewed immediately when the new sergeant, Yvonne Zuni, strolled over from the edge of the scene.

She said, "You gonna need some extra detectives?"

"I think me and Hoagie can handle it."

"What about your other cases?"

"We're still waiting on the lab results on the suicide and the girl that overdosed on X, Allie Marsh. The files are on my desk, and they can sit till we sort this shit out."

The sergeant shook her head. "We'll leave Marsh open. There are other considerations there. I'll let Stall and Patty run with it. They're already trying to find who gave her the X."

Normally Mazzetti would've raised hell about losing one of his cases to anyone, especially Stallings. But this shooting would be all over the news and a major case. No one but her mother cared much about the Marsh girl.

The sergeant focused those beautiful eyes on him and said, "I want this solved with arrests as soon as possible. Am I understood?"

"Yes, ma'am." He could see where she got the nickname Yvonne the Terrible. She'd just scared the crap out of him.

He watched as Holly scampered up the old, creaky, wooden stairs and smiled as he followed at a slower pace. He liked her little game because the longer it went on, the more excited he became. Like a drug, he had found he needed more stimuli to reach the same level of satisfaction. That was one of the reasons he'd picked up the pace of his hunts recently.

At the top of the stairs he caught her cute butt, in tight shorts, as it disappeared into a room at the end of a long hallway. The solid wooden door slammed shut behind her, cutting off a squeal. She was enjoying this as much as he was.

He paused outside the door, confident that there was no other exit and figuring that she intended him to come into this room because it had a bed or maybe a window for some fresh night air. He thought about pulling his knife now, but decided to leave it in his pocket and wait until he had a few more minutes of fun with her before he got down to serious business.

He opened the door and jumped into the room with an exaggerated grunt, then froze.

There were candles already lit around the room, and Holly stood behind a tall bench, still smiling.

The door swung shut behind him, and then he noticed the other people in the room. He scanned and counted six figures besides Holly: five men and one tall, dark-skinned woman.

He said, "What in the hell is this?"

A tall man with broad shoulders next to Holly slowly drew a long knife that reflected the candlelight.

Now he wondered who the hunter really was.

Nineteen

Stallings searched through the bland personnel file and saw that Gary Lauer had been with the Jacksonville Sheriff's Office for six years. He'd been in the motorcycle traffic unit for three years and a member of the department's SWAT team for two years. He was twenty-nine, very fit, and, based on his evaluations, a good, aggressive cop. There were several complaints of use of force, but that was normal. Anyone who was arrested wanted to cry foul and blame others. Stallings saw a one-page memo that said an allegation of domestic battery had been investigated and dropped due to "lack of evidence and witnesses." That was a different finding from "unfounded" or "false accusation."

Ronald Bell waited silently near the door to the file room. Stallings hated to admit it, but the IA detective had provided him valuable information. It was something to keep in mind when Stallings interviewed Lauer in the morning.

Stallings made a few notes and walked past Bell at the door.

The IA detective said, "This something we're gonna have to take over?"

"I'll let you know. My new sergeant will make that call."

"Yvonne the Terrible."

Stallings nodded, still worried about that nickname.

Bell said, "Ask her about Lauer."

"Why, what would she know?"

"She had to straighten him out once. You'll know by the scar on his left eyebrow."

"How'd you know that?"

"C'mon, Stall, I'm IA. I know everything."

All Stallings knew was that this guy was still an asshole.

He stared at the knife and the other men standing around him. No one made a move or threatened him, but he knew the situation. It was as if he were a leopard trapped by a herd of water buffalo. Numbers counted for something.

Holly, still cheerful, patted the table and said, "It'd make this so much easier if you climbed up onto the altar for us. Would ya, please?"

He was careful not to telegraph his intentions. "You guys are a cult. I think you might want to try and bag someone else."

One of the men said, "Holly says you're exactly who we need. Lean and athletic, your essence will live on in us for years to come. It's the best way to go."

He nodded slowly. "I doubt that, and I doubt you'll be able to succeed tonight." Then he kicked the man to his right hard in the knee, knocking him back and making him howl at the same time. He didn't hesitate to grab the doorknob and yank, striking the man on his left with the edge of the wooden door. He turned and threw an elbow into the man's face for good measure and darted out the door as he heard confusion erupt in the room.

Instead of fleeing down the stairs he paused outside the room and struck the first man out in the face with a solid back fist. That made the rest hesitate.

He ran as quietly as possible down the stairs, through the kitchen, and out to his car. He had his own knife out for defense as he backed the car out quickly, hoping one of these morons would wander out the door behind him.

No one did.

His tires squealed briefly as he tore away from the house, wondering how he would get his revenge, but certain he would.

John Stallings stood between his and Patty's cars outside the Police Memorial Building. She seemed tired to him, but he fought his big-brother urge to tell her to get some sleep. Instead he tried to be subtle.

"Don't screw up your personal life like I did. As much as I hate to say it, you have a boyfriend now."

She smiled. "Why do you hate to say it?"

"I'm glad you have a boyfriend, but your choice in men is not exactly comforting to me."

"C'mon, John, Tony is a good guy. No one gives him a chance."

"Because they're usually pissed off at him."

"I'm working on that."

Stallings laughed and said, "Women always want to fix men."

"Because most of you are severely damaged."

"You really should get some rest."

Patty sighed. "Tony's out on the triple drug shooting. I won't see much of him for a few days."

"We got a lot to do too. Now that we have leads and people to talk to. I'm hoping the cop, Gary Lauer, noticed someone talking to Allie."

"Why would a cop hang out in that place?" Patty made a face to show her disgust at a twenty-nine-year-old officer mixing with college kids.

"Ron Bell said he could be trouble."

"I've seen him around. Kind of a gung-ho, motorman type. Superfit pretty boy who likes to show off a little."

"Isn't that most young men?"

Patty laughed. "Let's see what we find out about Lauer before we bumble in and talk to him."

"You want to treat him like a suspect?" That hadn't really occurred to Stallings.

"Don't you always say, 'Is this the day that changes my life?' "

"How does that apply here?"

"I thought the whole point of the mantra was to keep you alert and keep your mind open."

"I guess we can score one for the junior partner. That's exactly what it's for." But the idea that a cop could be handing out a drug to college girls lodged in his head and started to bug him. This case was turning into so much more than the simple missing college girl it started as.

Twenty

The sun smacked him in the face, making his eyes snap open to a startling sight. Staring back at him were deep blue eyes and a bright row of teeth. He breathed deeply, adjusting to his surroundings. The blinds were up and at an odd angle, letting the mid-morning sun flood the small bedroom.

He cleared his throat and said, "Hey."

The steady smile didn't waver.

"What time is it?"

Still no movement, just a smile.

He reached out and grabbed the smiling face and pulled the small boy onto his bed.

The boy giggled loudly as he started to tickle him and said "Why did you open my blinds?"

The boy lay back, gasping between laughs and said one of the eight words he knew. "Uncle."

"What do you need, you little creep? More tickling?"

The boy shook his head.

He rolled out of bed and got dressed while the boy stayed on the rumpled bed. In the small, adjoining bathroom, he brushed his perfect teeth, slapped on a splash of Pierre Cardin, calling out to the boy, "Where's your mom?" It was rhetorical—he knew the cute little boy would never answer him.

As he wandered through the small house the boy followed him. Then he heard, "Man, this is late for you."

He followed the voice into the kitchen.

"I'd still be snoozing if master-pooper hadn't opened my blinds."

The woman turned and gave a look at the boy. "Why'd you wake up your uncle? You know he works late."

He said, "That's okay. I got a lot to do today."

She turned and smiled. "Oh yeah, what's her name?"

"Holly."

John Stallings knew how to play this first interview with Gary Lauer. He'd been under the microscope himself, and he didn't want to be the cause of someone else going through the wringer if it wasn't deserved.

He and Patty waited outside the PMB for motorcycle patrol officer Gary Lauer to finish the pre-shift roll call, the ritual for all major police departments that gave sergeants a chance to go over a few procedures or bulletins with their patrol officers right before they hit the streets. Stallings knew the motorman would have to cut through the side door to get his heavy Harley-Davidson Electra Glide from the parking lot. He saw an angular, dark-haired man about thirty strutting through the garage. He wore a tailored uniform that showed off his biceps. He looked more like a marine than a cop.

Patty said, "That's him," and nodded toward the young man.

As Lauer came closer, Stallings noticed the straight

scar across his dark left eyebrow that Ronald Bell had mentioned. It intrigued him that tiny Yvonne Zuni hurt a guy like this.

Lauer smiled and nodded as he approached, his brown eyes scanning the JSO IDs around Stallings's and Patty's necks.

Stallings stepped away from the patrol car he'd been leaning on and said, "Gary Lauer, right?" He held out his hand.

The younger man shook his hand and said, "You got him." His eyes flicked over to Patty for a quick appraisal.

"I'm John Stallings, and this is Patty Levine from crimes/persons."

"Everyone knows you, Detective."

Stallings cleared his throat and said, "That's not completely accurate, but I appreciate it." He focused back on the sharp young man in uniform. "I have a couple of questions and think you might be able to help me."

"Sure, anything."

He knew not to hesitate. "Were you over at the Wildside Monday night?"

Lauer paused as if he was thinking about it. That made Stallings's radar ping instantly. Why deny it? Why think about it? It was only three nights ago.

Finally Lauer said, "Why?"

"Were you there?"

"Yeah, I think I stopped by for a beer."

"That really the kind of place you stop by for a beer?"

The young man kept quiet and shifted his gaze from Stallings to Patty. "What's this about?"

"Just one of our cases. We're looking for witnesses."

"How'd you know I was there?"

"Then you were at the Wildside?"

Now he had regained his composure and said, "Yeah, I was there, but I wasn't in cop mode."

Stallings didn't think this guy would ever be out of cop mode.

Patty said, "What kind of mode were you in?"

He looked at her with a smirk and said, "Pussy mode." He held her cold glare.

Stallings thought about Lauren running into a creep like this and felt his face flush red.

Patty said, "How'd you do?"

"I'm afraid I went home all alone." He winked at Patty.

Did this asshole really think he was charming? Or was he playing a game to piss them off? At least Stallings understood the scar on his eyebrow.

Stallings said, "You know any of the staff there?"

"A few."

"Any band members?"

"Sometimes."

"What about the drummer from the other night, Donnie?"

"Donnie Eliot? Yeah, he's okay."

"Know where he lives?"

Lauer shook his head. "We're not close or anything. He's just a good drummer. He usually plays downtown at the Bamboo Hut."

Stallings made a note.

Patty pulled a photo of Allie Marsh from her battered notecase and held it up. "Ring a bell?"

He glanced up at it. "Maybe. Lotta tail running around that place."

"Why is a cop your age running around that place?"

He gave Patty a flat, steady scowl. "Why's a chick that looks like you a cop?"

Stallings realized things had gotten personal and out of hand. He tried to turn the interview back. "Look, Gary, we're just wondering if you saw or heard anything that might help us."

"Help you what? I don't even know what you're working."

"It's a death investigation. Looks like she overdosed on X, and we'd like to know her source."

"Shit, everyone in that place has X in their system."

Patty said, "What about you?"

"I'll take a pee test right now."

Stallings held up his hands. "Relax, Gary, we're all cops here."

"You're not treating me like a cop. You're treating me like a goddamn scumbag."

Patty didn't have to say anything. She just shrugged.

Stallings could see the anger in Lauer's face as he turned away from Patty. He looked at Stallings and said, "I can't think of anything right now. But if she keeps talking to me like that I'll call PBA." PBA stood for Patrolmen's Benevolent Association, the police union.

Stallings had reached his limit. "Call anyone you fucking want. She's right, it's weird that you hang out in a place like that. You can call PBA and maybe I'll call IA."

The two men locked their eyes, and no one looked like they were going to back off.

Patty Levine wasn't used to driving John Stallings around, but he'd asked her to pick him up at the little house he was renting over in Lakewood. It was eight in the evening, and they were on their way to the place where Gary Lauer had told them they could find Donnie Eliot. The Bamboo Hut had nothing to do with bamboo and little to do with huts other than being small and dingy. She looked across at her partner and wondered what was going through Stallings's mind as he silently stared out the window at the passing Jacksonville streets.

The tiny club sat on the first floor of a rundown office building and was known for its music. The weekends saw kids jammed into the stuffy room, but weeknights were a different story. Patty knew Stallings was on a mission and right now all he wanted was to find out who gave Allie the Ecstasy and the circumstances of her death.

A large black man standing next to the door said, "Five bucks each."

Patty was about to pull her JSO credentials when the large man looked past her and said, "Oh shit, I didn't see you there, Detective Stallings. Come right in." He opened the door and even performed a slight bow as if Stallings were royalty.

Patty smiled, not bothering to ask what Stallings had done to deserve such treatment. She had learned in her time as his partner that it was just as likely that he had scared the man with physical violence as it was that he had paid the rent on the man's apartment.

Stallings smiled and nodded. "Thanks, Curtis."

Inside, the bar stretched from front to back with tables sprinkled across the dirty linoleum floor. It was way early by bar standards. In a couple of hours this place would be pulling in a decent crowd.

The stage had instruments on it but no performers.

She hoped their information was right and Donnie Eliot was here. They had a lot to talk about.

Stallings said, "Let's find the manager. He'll point us to Donnie."

"Think he'll mind talking to the po-po?"

"Not really my concern." He looked up and his expression changed immediately.

Patty said, "What's wrong?"

He just pointed.

Patty followed his finger to a group of girls sitting at the table closest to the bar. At first she didn't see the problem; then, after a moment of study, she understood his attitude.

Sitting in the middle of the girls was his daughter, Lauren, dressed like a college student and sipping a drink.

Twenty-one

John Stallings was at a loss while he waited outside the little bar with Lauren. He checked his watch every twenty seconds as he waited for his sister, Helen, to swing into the lot and pick up the precocious girl. He didn't like leaving Patty inside alone, but they still had a job to do.

Patty had confronted Lauren and her friends and then led the girl out to her father.

Outside, when they were alone, Lauren said, "Dad, stop treating me like a little kid."

He shook his head. "I'm treating you like a fourteen-year-old. A fourteen-year-old who should not be at a bar. Not for another seven years."

"Patty checked my drink. It was just Diet Pepsi."

Thank God for small favors. He'd had plenty of practice with her mother, checking to make sure a drink wasn't alcoholic.

Lauren said, "What are *you* doing here at eight o'clock?"

He turned, red faced. "I'm working. I'm where I'm supposed to be."

"Really? I thought you were supposed to be at home, with us." Her angelic face held no scorn, which made the impact that much more brutal on him.

He couldn't think of an answer and stared silently at his wayward daughter as he spied his sister Helen's little Honda CRV racing down the street. She probably thought she was saving her niece from certain death.

Stallings realized Helen was saving him.

He'd spent the day thinking of something clever to say. Holly had surprised him, and that was a fact. Who would've thought that cute little towhead was a member of some kind of cannibal cult? He never would've imagined there was any such thing in Jacksonville. Maybe that was their first attempt, because they sure didn't seem to know what they were doing.

His effort to keep distance between his victims and himself had backfired because after last night he had no way of finding Holly again. No cell, no address, nothing. But now he realized she had played the same game and kept her information from him. She didn't want any links either. It was a little spooky.

He'd been by the old "sorority" house. It was just an abandoned building on a block with a lot of abandoned buildings. It was late in the day when he had the idea that he thought might work. He'd driven to the garage where they'd left her little Toyota the night before, when they were on a date, before she tried to eat him or he attempted to kill her. It was still up on the third floor of the garage near the Modis Tower.

He sat back in an unlocked Mustang, two rows over and a few spaces down. There was no trace he had entered the parking garage. The lone camera on this floor pointed only at the elevator. If she came from that direction all the cops would have is a time she arrived. No one had seen him. Like any good predator he was stealthy as well as deadly.

It was dark now, and he didn't know how long he'd have to wait. But the idea of surprising this girl excited him enough to give him patience and stamina. When he felt like this, he didn't get tired or hungry. He could sometimes go for days just on this kind of thrill.

He didn't have to wait for days. About an hour later he saw the door to the outer stairwell open, and to his surprise out walked little Holly all by herself. She wore a yellow sundress as if she had been used as bait in some other area. She had a small leather purse and looked older and more sophisticated in high heels.

Slipping out of the Mustang he stayed low behind the few cars that were still there. She whistled a song he recognized. It was an airy whistle with a weak sound but cute coming from Holly. As he crept along he drew the long knife he had been saving for an occasion just like this. It was solid with a nine-inch blade and solid hilt like a medieval dagger. It felt like his claw instead of a tool.

He made it all the way to the rear of Holly's little blue Toyota before she even turned. Her bright eyes widened at the sight of him, and her song trailed off uneasily.

He didn't say a word. Just stepped up to her and thrust the knife straight up, catching her under her chin and driving the steel pike up into her brain. The entire blade disappeared into her soft flesh, and he felt the tip of it ping off bones and cavities inside her skull.

Her eyes remained open as a short breath of air

spurted out of her. Then her legs just gave out and she started to fall.

He reached up with two fingers and managed to grasp the edges of her tiny nose stud as she started to drop. The miniscule diamond came out, and he had his coveted souvenir that easy. A broad smile spread across his face. This was the harshest, quickest kill he had ever made.

And he liked it.

Twenty-two

John Stallings felt as if he had an open wound in his chest as he tried to regain a professional perspective after watching his daughter leave with his sister. Her friend, Angie, who had driven, said that her parents didn't mind the seventeen-year-old coming to a bar as long as she didn't drink alcohol. What were parents thinking these days?

Patty looked over and said, "Do you need to go? I can handle this."

He shook his head. "I don't think it's a good idea to check on Lauren just now."

"Helen has her safe for the night. I'd tell most fathers not to worry about it, but with you I'll advise you to calm down for the evening and talk to her in the light of day. We can look for this mope tomorrow if you want."

"Let's grab him tonight. If he knows something or supplied Allie Marsh the X, then we can take it from there. We might have a hard time finding him tomorrow."

Outside the club they could hear the band play, with bass pulsing through the walls. Stallings rolled his eyes at Patty.

She reached over and patted his arm. "It's okay, grandpa. I'll go in and tell those kids to keep the racket down."

"Funny," he muttered and stepped out of the car.

Curtis the doorman was nowhere in sight. Inside the low-ceilinged, musty club, bright lights shined on the three-piece band crammed on the tiny stage at the front of the club. Maybe twenty people listened as they pounded out a heavy-metal anthem. All Stallings cared about was the drummer stuck in the rear between a bassist and a tall guitarist. The drummer's long, dirty hair, matted from sweat and sticking to his bare shoulders, dipped onto a stained white undershirt. A "wife beater" shirt is what everyone called them now because it seemed as if every mope in a domestic dispute walked out to meet the cops wearing one of the Walmart specials. The TV show *Cops* was an advertisement for the simple, white undershirt.

No one approached to see if they wanted a drink, but he realized every person in the place knew two cops had walked in the front door. They might have assumed he had come in earlier just to get an underage drinker, not realizing Lauren wasn't drinking and was his daughter. A few furtive glances and hurried movements told Stallings that this place was like most little bars where all kinds of shit went down. The JSO could spend every night just in places like this and make plenty of arrests. It still wouldn't put a dent in the crime rate or drug use. He knew all cops did anymore was keep a lid on a pressure cooker. Any little incident could be blown out of proportion, and any group of thugs could push a crime spree and turn it into a new media focus that would terrify the city.

But for right now all he wanted to do was focus on the asshole who gave Allie Marsh the drugs that killed her.

The band finished to a round of mild applause. Then, without consulting with his bandmates, the drummer stood up and stepped behind a thick, velvet curtain surrounding the stage.

Patty immediately stepped forward, and Stallings took the route to the opposite side of the curtain. As they stepped behind it at the same time a man in the small room looked up and said, "Employees only back here."

"Where'd the drummer go?"

The man ignored the question. Then Stallings stepped up to him and growled, "Where'd the drummer go?"

The man nodded toward the rear of the building. "Think he stepped out for a smoke or something. Can I help you?"

But Stallings and Patty knew when they had been given the slip and headed for the rear door. It opened into a narrow alley crammed with overflowing garbage cans and old pallets stacked next to each door. They caught a glimpse of the fast drummer as he skittered around the corner onto the next street.

Stallings looked at his partner. "Why do you think he did that?"

"No idea, but I know he'll come back."

"How'd you know something like that?"

"His drums are still inside."

* * *

Tony Mazzetti couldn't even get a name from this guy.

"C'mon, just a street name so I can call you something."

The black man had a deep yellow tinge to his eyes and a vacant gaze. He turned his wide head stacked on a wider, flabby body and scowled at Mazzetti, who was sitting on the edge of a low wall, his jacket off and gun exposed on his hip.

"Some of the folks down here call me"—he paused for dramatic effect—"Pudge."

Mazzetti nodded. "Now there's a shocker. Why would people call you Pudge?"

"Because I am somewhat corpulent."

Mazzetti just stared at him.

"Because I eat and drink a little too much."

Mazzetti was still quiet.

"So, rather like Friar Tuck from the beloved Robin Hood fable, I am a portly prophet in this land of constant dismay."

"You're not from around here, are you?"

"I am a wandering prophet who has nested here in this lovely jewel of the South for almost six years."

"Have you seen anyone shot in those six years?"

"I have."

"Any of them in the last three hours?"

"Perhaps, but I would be a stupid prophet to admit it."

"We could protect you."

"Like Germans protected the Jews."

"Look, I can see you're a smart man. Don't you want to help clean up the streets?"

"I would if I could do it at a cost less than a painful death."

"So whoever did this was tough?"

"I have no idea who did it, but the victims are bad-asses. I'd hate to get on the wrong side of the killers."

Mazzetti scribbled a few notes, wondering if pulling this guy in as a witness and throwing him in front of a grand jury would do any good. Would they compel him to testify? Could they? Mazzetti didn't even have his real name yet. Did he know anything of value?

Pudge leaned in and said, "Might could give you the name of a witness who may not be as invested in the local neighborhood and therefore feel free to speak."

"Who?"

"A white man who is currently shacked up with the lovely Miss Brison in the yellow house across the street."

Mazzetti followed the man's crooked finger to a small yellow house, built up on blocks to avoid flooding and leaning ever so slightly to the left. The windows all had curtains, but one was pulled to the side. It flopped closed as soon as Mazzetti's eyes scanned the house.

Maybe there was someone inside who could help.

Twenty-three

Stallings kept the binoculars on the front door of the Bamboo Hut from almost four blocks away. This was Police Work 101. They needed to talk to the drummer. He ran from them. A common occurrence on the streets of Jacksonville. The difference was that this wiry drummer was more important to them than the average crack dealer hoping to evade arrest until he can sell off enough of his stock to make bail.

Patty said, "What do you think?"

Stallings didn't lower his field glasses. "He'll be back pretty soon. That's the beauty of cell phones and dumbasses in the same room." He had purposely said to Patty, as they walked back through the club after losing the drummer, that they would get him another night and that it was late. He knew a couple of the staff had heard his supposedly offhand remark and that the cell phones would start to burn up before too long.

Patty said, "How long you figure? Couple hours?"

"Not that long. He wants his drums. He'll be back in less than an hour." Before he could say anything else, a figure hustled down the sidewalk to the front door of the club and paused, then ducked inside. Stallings said, "Make that less than a minute. It's showtime."

A minute later Stallings pulled open the door to the little club, only to have someone stand up and block his way. It was the tall guitarist he'd seen earlier.

The young man with long, spindly arms said, "Sorry, dude, we're closed."

Stallings held up his ID and said, "JSO." He started to step around the guitarist.

The man stepped to the side and blocked him. "Got a warrant, dude?"

"Don't need one, dude. I'm in pursuit. But nice try." He stepped the other way, but the man matched him. That was a mistake. Stallings shoved him to one side and had started marching to the rear of the club when he felt a strong hand on his shoulder.

Without hesitation, Stallings's training took over and he reached up and grabbed the fingers of the strong hand and squeezed. He spun, pulling the man close to him with the hand firmly in his grasp.

Stallings said, "Wrong move there, dude."

The guitarist swung his free fist at Stallings's face.

Stallings cranked down on the attacker's fingers, feeling the small bones crunch. "I tried to be nice." He released the man's hand and let him crumple, whimpering, onto the ground. No one else dared step forward.

Stallings raced to the back of the club. Nothing. He hit the back door hard, then froze as a smile spread across his face.

Patty stood over the bleeding drummer. She was ready to kneel down and slap on a pair of handcuffs.

"You were right. He'd have run right into me if I waited by the back door."

Stallings shook his head and mumbled, "Dumb-ass."

Mazzetti had let Pudge slink away with that funny, half-leaning gait. He almost looked like one of the assistants to a mad scientist in an old horror movie. He eyed the yellow house and considered who was holed up there. No one had come out since the po-po had been on the scene, and that was a little odd, because the rest of the neighborhood couldn't wait to see all the commotion. They may not have been talking to the police about the shooting that left three dead on their block, but they were certainly out and about, gawking at all the emergency workers.

He waited as Christina Hogrebe eased over from the other corner.

"Got anything, Tony?"

"Maybe." He cut his eyes to the yellow house. "In a second, take a glance over there and see if there's any movement. Just had someone tell me a white man is inside with a Miss Brison."

"You think he might've been some kind of lookout or spy?"

"It's just weird that a white guy is right in the middle of this neighborhood and a shooting occurs within viewing distance."

Christina shrugged as they walked over toward the yellow house's front door. He'd worked with the young detective long enough for her to know when to argue and when to just back him up. He liked the arrangement.

He paused on the poured-cement porch of the house. Deep fissures ran from one side of the porch to the other, and it felt unsteady in a way he couldn't quite pinpoint. The door rattled as he knocked. He heard someone inside and glanced over his shoulder to see Christina standing to the side of the window but still looking in as much as she could. He stepped to the side of the door and brought his hand up to the Glock on his right hip. Someone paused on the other side of the door, the door handle moving just enough for him to notice.

Mazzetti's heart rate picked up as he sensed something odd about the house and its occupants. Suddenly he wondered if the shots could've come from here. No one in the neighborhood had actually said they saw a car.

As he was about to call out to Christina, the door handle twisted and someone fought with the door, jiggling it to come open. He turned his full attention to the door.

Patty liked that Stallings let her conduct interviews without any interference. Sometimes a senior partner wanted to handle everything. Some male cops wanted to do everything, but Stallings had never shown any kind of prejudice against a female coworker. He treated everyone exactly how he felt they needed to be treated based on their behavior. If they were asses he treated them like asses. If they tried, but weren't too sharp, he tried to help and support them. If you'd proven yourself, he trusted you completely.

They had the drummer, Donnie Eliot, in the backseat of her car with his hands cuffed behind him. A small pile of money, assorted baggies, a toothpick, and nail clippers that had come from his pockets sat inside a clear plastic evidence bag next to her in the front seat.

She turned around to face the scared young man. A trickle of blood still seeped from his nose where she had cracked him with a palm-heel strike as he ran right at her from the rear of the club.

Patty said, "Why'd you run in the first place, Donnie?"

"You know why." He kept his eyes down on the seat.

"Why don't you tell us?"

"I'm holding," he mumbled.

She held up the evidence bag. "Something in here? That's not why we were looking for you."

"Then I'm free to go?"

"Not a chance."

Mazzetti let his hand slip off his gun when he saw the young black woman who opened the door. Her green, oval eyes and perfect complexion and white, frilly nightgown gave her an angelic appearance. Until he glanced farther down and realized her white nightgown was some kind of incredible Victoria's Secret special, cut for maximum exposure of her tight stomach, firm round breasts, and shapely hips.

She focused those lovely eyes on Mazzetti, who took a second to bring his up. "Hi," was all she said.

"Hi, ma'am. I, um, I'm Tony Mazzetti from Jacksonville Sheriff's Office, and this is Christina Hogrebe. Can we come in a talk to you for a second?"

The woman gawked at Christina and said, "She's pretty." The listlessness to her voice and the way her eyes tracked slowly told them she was high.

Mazzetti took a closer look and noticed her pupils were barely pinpricks.

Christina said, "What's your name, dear?" She sounded like a mother, even though she was about the same age as this woman. Christina had a way of talking to certain people.

"Miss Brison," the woman mumbled. "But you can call me Miss Brison."

"Can we talk to you inside, Miss Brison?" Christina was already at the door, pulling Miss Brison along.

As soon as he crossed the threshold, Mazzetti sensed someone else was in the house. He turned and said, "Who's here, Miss Brison?"

"Jus' me and my cat."

He heard a thump in the rear of the house and rushed down a narrow hallway to see an open window. He stuck his head out just enough to see a flash of a man's face as he disappeared around the next house. There was no reason to chase the man, especially in this neighborhood. But he made note of his face. A thin white man with dark hair.

He had a few questions to ask Miss Brison.

Twenty-four

Patty Levine had never used this interview technique before. She had heard some of the older detectives talk about it in the past, but none of them ever made it sound like anything other than a practical joke. But now that she and Stallings were alone in the Land That Time Forgot, on the second floor of the PMB, with the drummer in handcuffs sitting quietly at Stallings's desk she realized her partner was serious and thought this might work.

Donnie had been quiet, courteous, but not particularly helpful since they had arrested him outside the Bamboo Hut. They were on their way to book him in jail on a minor possession charge. Although there was always a great uproar about the number of people that went to jail for seemingly minor marijuana and other drug charges, in fact, the only time anyone was arrested in Jacksonville for marijuana was in connection with a more serious crime or if they gave the cops shit. Donnie had some meth and about half an ounce of weed. Normally that wouldn't warrant much attention from a cop, but they needed him and wanted him a little frightened right now.

Stallings sat with him as the drummer said for the tenth time, "I swear to God I am telling the truth."

Stallings said, "What's the most time you ever spent in jail?"

Donnie looked down at the grimy floor and said, "I did four months at a juvenile facility and a couple nights here and there for stupid things. Never anything worse than smoking pot."

Stallings stared at him. The hard cold stare he usually saved for the predators they caught with young girls. He didn't say a word, make a fist, or even look angry. It was just those cold blue eyes and the sense that he was past the point in his career where he wanted to hear nonsense.

Donnie quickly added, "Well, smoking pot and breaking into cars. But I always made sure they were tourists and not local people."

"Why is that important?"

"I wouldn't want to hurt the hardworking people who live here." The young man seemed sincere. He had an odd, earnest, goofy appearance, his wavy brown hair flying out in wild directions. He managed a smile, showing his crooked teeth with a huge corner taken out of one of his upper front teeth.

Stallings continued to stare without a word.

"And the tourists tend to have more money and leave it stashed in a car."

Stallings said, "All I really want is information about Allie Marsh. You already admitted that you'd been talking to her."

"That's not a crime."

"No, it's not. But she had a lot of Ecstasy in her system, and you don't seem like a guy who would shy away from giving someone Ecstasy. I have a way we might be able to make sure you're telling the truth."

"Anything you want. Anything. I'll do anything."

Stallings turned to Patty and said, "Should we set up the polygraph?"

"Polygraph? You mean a lie-detector test?" Donnie said.

Stallings just nodded.

Patty heard the anxiety in Donnie's voice and could see how nervous he'd gotten. Maybe this idea wasn't as crazy as it seemed.

After almost a minute Donnie finally said, "Okay, I'll take a polygraph."

Stallings just looked over at Patty, who immediately turned to a gray metal box that sat in the far corner of the squad bay. It usually was just a place to stack all the files, but the detectives had kept it for sentimental reasons. It was not a polygraph. JSO rarely used polygraphs, and polygraph results weren't admissible in any court in the United States. At best they were a tool for a good interviewer to scare someone into giving a more accurate account of events. The old polygraph schools were months long, and the equipment was expensive and constantly in need of updates. Years ago there was always a polygrapher in any big-city detective bureau, but those days had passed and most departments didn't bother. Patty tied wires to the back of the large gray box, which was actually an old telephone trap-and-trace device that no one had used in twenty years. It was a way, before modern computers and software, to determine who was calling a telephone. All it provided was a number that called in, and then more subpoenas were required to determine who subscribed to that number. It was tedious and usually unproductive because most phones got a number of calls that had nothing to do with criminal activity. But the gray box had dials and meters that appeared important, and if they sat the suspect in the right place and he had no experience with polygraphs, it was a way to scare someone into telling the truth without actually going to the trouble of using a polygraph. Many people would argue it was just as accurate.

Patty sat by the fake polygraph and motioned for Stallings to bring their suspect over. He uncuffed the young man, grabbed a few wires connected to pads that had been used for physical fitness evaluations and some smart-ass had saved. He made a show out of placing the pads on Donnie's temples, inside of his upper arms, and then one around his middle and index finger of his left hand.

Patty could see the sweat building on the young man's forehead already. It was difficult not to chuckle. She started out slowly and let him answer his name, date of birth, and profession. He told them he'd flunked out of Jacksonville University and now all he wanted to do was play in a rock 'n' roll band.

Then Patty had the first test of her impromptu polygraph. "How do you make enough money to live?" She knew his answer would determine how truthful he would be, believing he was hooked up to a polygraph.

He mumbled something.

Patty used a sharp voice to say, "Speak up."

"I sell grass to spring breakers and to the waitstaff at almost every bar downtown."

Patty looked over at Stallings and nodded, indicating that she felt Donnie was being truthful and the little ploy was working. It also reinforced that Donnie should tell the truth because he caught the little nod too.

After a few more innocuous questions, Patty finally said, "Did you give Allie Marsh any Ecstasy?"

There was no hesitation. "No, I didn't give her anything. I just talked to her that night."

Stallings, who wasn't supposed to say anything during the fake test, said, "Did you see any break runners talking to her?"

"Any what?"

"Break runner. You know, an older guy with money who hits on the spring break girls."

Donnie shook his head. "I've never heard that term before. But I see those kind of guys around the Wildside."

Stallings laid down the two photographs of Chad Palmer and Gary Lauer.

Donnie studied the photographs and said, "Yeah, I seen both of those guys around the club. The one guy might even be a cop or something. He comes to hear me play at the Bamboo Hut sometimes."

Patty cut her eyes up to Stallings and could read that he believed the drummer too. But she knew they still had to book him until things were cleared up.

It was late and he was tired. He had his apartment dark except one dim desk light to illuminate the small box full of his mementos. He could play with each loose piece of jewelry and remember the girl and how he took it with crystal clarity. And it was times like this that he sat and gazed at them. He was a little down. Sort of a post-activity dip in enthusiasm. Holly had been an unexpected pleasure, but he couldn't count her as one of his normal spring break kills. In fact, if he hadn't been quick, it would've been the other way around.

Now he had the small emerald earring that had belonged to Kathleen, the cute girl from South Carolina who was studying English literature. He had met her at a small café in the trendy part of southern Jacksonville. He had enjoyed listening to her light Southern accent and her cute giggle. She was the first one of the season, and she was also the safest he had ever taken. He'd met her once at the café and convinced her to meet him for a drink late. None of the friends she'd come down from South Carolina with had seen him and Kathleen had told him she had a boyfriend and that they had to keep things secret. That was fine with him.

They had ended up at Brackridge Park after he'd slipped her one of his Ecstasy tabs. She never suspected anything other than a strong rumrunner had made her feel so loopy. She'd been wild on the park bench, and when he was close to a climax, he leaned her over the bench, and mounted her like a real animal until he was about to come. Then he looped a rope around her neck, just as he'd planned. She offered surprisingly little resistance.

From there it was easy to hoist her body into the tree and make it look as if she jumped with a rope around her neck. Just another depressed college student away from home and disappointed in life.

Sometimes he wondered how he'd slipped into this lifestyle. He knew that he'd been promoted to the top of the food chain by God himself, but he still remembered his mother's reaction to his behavior as a child. Even before his father had split there had been issues. In fact, he was pretty certain his dad left because there was nothing he could do to change what his son really was.

He remembered overhearing a psychiatrist talking to his mother after he'd been sent for in an evaluation when he was seven. He'd been teased at school and retaliated by laying sharpened sticks in the ground. He lured the bigger boy into a confrontation and then shoved the bully backward onto the sticks. The bully only suffered minor scrapes and punctures, but the story had taken on epic proportions by the time it reached the principal and he'd been called in to the office.

His mother had taken him to a county psychiatrist, who had asked him stupid questions and treated them as if they were morons during most of the evaluation. The psychiatrist had left him in the small room next to his office. It was easy to lay his ear against the wall and hear the psychiatrist explaining to his mother the difference between a psychopath, who had no conscience, and a sociopath, who had a conscience but still acted out. But the psychiatrist was quick to say he didn't like to label kids that young, and all he would write in the file was that he had severe behavioral problems with aggressive overtones.

He knew he had shown little reaction to most of the discipline his parents had laid down. He could sit out groundings quietly in his own room, pretending to be a tiger or a leopard with his sister's stuffed animals as his victims. He could withstand any beating his father would dish out. Something inside always told him that in time everything got better. It was this calm reaction to discipline that had spooked his mother in the first place.

This psychiatrist said he couldn't comprehend the consequences of his actions and that he had no empathy toward other people. That he was cool and calculating and lived in a very rich fantasy world. That was all just more bullshit. But it was valuable to hear. Because after that he concealed his efforts much better and faked emotional reactions to punishment. He could command tears at the mention of groundings and squeal like a wounded pig at a spanking. That relieved a lot of the concerns of his mother, and to this day he didn't think she had a clue of what he was really like.

Tony Mazzetti was so tired he could hardly focus. That was one of the reasons he hadn't chased the man who had jumped out the window. He knew it was more likely a marital infidelity than anything to do with crime. But Pudge was probably right: A guy like that might not be afraid of retaliation, but he would be afraid of his wife.

Now, sitting on the edge of the couch with Miss Brison in a conservative bathrobe Christina had found, he got out his notepad.

"You don't want to tell us who jumped out your window?"

She shook her head. "Just some dude I like."

"What's his name?" Mazzetti found himself speaking slowly and loudly.

Miss Brison turned her pretty face up to his and said, "I call him Chuck."

"Chuck what?"

She shook her head. "His name isn't even Chuck. That's just what I call him."

"Why?"

"Because he looks like a Chuck to me." As she spoke, she leaned forward and the robe opened, exposing the sexy white nightgown, only now her right breast had fallen loose.

Christina reached over and closed up the bathrobe and tied the belt in a tight bow. "There you go, dear." She waited until Miss Brison slowly turned her way.

"Did you or Chuck see the shooters?"

"What shooters?"

"The ones that shot up the house across the street."

"The house across the street was shot up?"

"You didn't hear it?"

She shook her head. "We was in the back, and we didn't hear nothing."

Christina said, "What are you using, Miss Brison?"

"What'd you mean?"

"Please, we've been polite and you're not in trouble, but I'm worried about you. What drugs are you on?"

Miss Brison smiled and reached up to touch Christina's face softly. "You're nice. I like you."

"What are you using?"

"I took a tab."

"A tab of what?"

She just pointed to a little dish on a bookshelf.

Mazzetti stood up and checked in the dish. There were a dozen little speckled pills that seemed familiar. "What is it?"

"I don't know. Chuck gave 'em to me. I like them."

He looked at Christina, who shrugged. He took the

dish and stepped into the bathroom. He took one tablet as a sample but dumped the rest down the toilet. He wasn't about to arrest this woman, no cop would, but he didn't want her to overdose, and they were clearly contraband. Toilets served as the biggest evidence receptacles in the whole city.

Twenty-five

Patty Levine was not only exhausted, she had just taken two Ambien, knowing that this big lump that was her boyfriend, Tony Mazzetti, would either slide off her couch and trudge to bed or slide off the couch and drive home to sleep. She realized soon after they met that after long days at work neither of them was in any mood to make love. She also knew she was in no mood to stare up at the ceiling of her bedroom wishing she could fall asleep. The Ambien was her insurance against that.

She liked just sitting there on the couch with Tony's head in her lap, fiddling with his hair. It seemed normal for a couple to do something like that. She wasn't used to normal. Her life had been interesting, exciting, tiring, and unconventional, but never too normal. Meeting so late for a quick meal was one measure of her odd hours.

She said, "What are you thinking about?"

"Nothing."

"You have to be thinking about something."

He sighed.

"You're thinking about work, right?"

"I'm sorry, baby, but that's years of habit. I think about work every night. It might take a while to change."

She smiled. "Don't sweat it, Tony. I think about work too. I just don't want us to only talk about work at night."

He sat up to look at her. "I know, and I agree."

"How's your triple shooting going?"

"If not for your invitation for a late dinner and my biological need for food and sleep, I'd be out there right now. No way can I have a triple murder unsolved on my watch."

"You'll find a way to clear it."

"What's that supposed to mean?"

"It means you'll catch the shooters."

"Hope so, but a witness or two would be helpful."

"Anyone talking?"

"No one. Even had one guy run from me."

"Why'd he run?"

"Who knows. Married, at a girlfriend's. Drug dealer. White guy in that neighborhood."

"It's not against the law."

"No, but it's suspicious."

Patty sighed and changed the subject. "Anything I should know about the two files John and I took from you?"

He paused.

Patty said, "What, you worried about Stall trying to steal something?"

"No, not at all. I'm worried about him turning a simple suicide or OD into some wild-ass conspiracy."

"What are you talking about, Tony?"

"The lab results aren't in yet, but there are a couple of links between the two girls."

"Like what?"

"The X in their systems and polyethylene glycol."

"What's polyethylene glycol?

"The chemical on Durex condoms."

"So spring breakers had sex and did drugs."

"Exactly."

"But something made you notice it, so we can't ignore it."

Mazzetti said, "I'd like a better idea about the X. If it was from the same source."

"We don't have any of the actual tabs, do we?"

Mazzetti mumbled. "We might."

"What's that mean?"

"The suicide, Kathleen Harding, had a couple of unidentified pills in her purse."

Patty said, "Please tell me you didn't toss them out."

"Oh, hell no."

She relaxed slightly. "What did the lab say they were?"

"I didn't turn them over to the lab. She was a suicide. I didn't see the point. I just stuck them in evidence."

"The lab would be the smart move."

"But the fucking lab takes forever."

She smiled. "I have a way to speed things up sometimes."

"How?"

"Sweetheart, you don't want to know." She ruffled his thinning black hair and shoved him off the couch.

The sun had just popped over the horizon. John Stallings had several files he'd grabbed off Mazzetti's desk stacked on the front seat of his county-issued Impala. He was still troubled by the idea that a cop could be shady enough to give drugs to anyone. Gary Lauer had some issues, but Stallings hoped this wasn't one of them.

The Impala was parked in the driveway of his house. Or at least the house his wife and kids lived in. He tried to clear his head of all the work clutter before he went inside. Even when she was using, Maria was an early riser, and sometimes this time of the morning was the only chance he had at a few lucid moments with her. He knocked and waited for someone to answer. After a moment the door cracked open and Maria's dark, haunting eyes looked up at him. She stepped back and silently let him in.

Stallings didn't say anything either. She looked good. Beyond good. Almost forty, his wife could pass for her late twenties with a firm, curvy body, lush skin, and eyes that showed her intelligence. She didn't seem much different from the first day he had seen her on the campus of the University of South Florida.

Finally he said, "Is Lauren upset?"

"About what?"

"About me catching her at a bar?"

"Oh, that. She said she wouldn't drink. I'm not sure what the big deal is."

He paused, thinking he had misunderstood her. "You don't think our fourteen-year-old daughter hanging out at a bar is a big deal?" He kept his tone steady and even, but she knew him well enough to realize how hard he was trying to maintain a calm façade.

"She was with friends, not drinking, and it was only eight o'clock."

He stared at her silently, hoping it wasn't a glare.

Maria sat down on the couch in the living room. "I

understand what you're saying, and I'm trying to tell you my view of it. I don't seem to be getting past your initial anger. I don't want to come down too hard on her for little things. I don't want to drive her away."

And there it was. He didn't speak as a lump swelled in his throat at the insinuation that he had driven Jeanie away.

The whole situation had happened mainly because he'd always thought of Lauren as a little girl. He knew that she was a beautiful fourteen-year-old who could dress up and look much older. But in his head she would always be the younger sister to Jeanie, and she had always been so quiet and obedient that this incident had knocked him numb. But he shied away from harsh punishment. That was a common side effect for parents who lost a child. It wasn't just an effort to make the remaining children happy. He knew that in the back of his mind he wanted to make sure he gave her no reason to run away. It made disciplining children very difficult and stressful.

Lauren always had been very much a little girl, whereas Jeanie had been more like his little buddy. She had come almost five years before the other kids, and like any father, he wanted someone to play sports with and roughhouse around the house with. That was Jeanie. Even when she was older, she chose a sport like lacrosse instead of something more feminine. She could throw a football as well as any boy and never shied away from delivering a block or knocking someone down when she had the ball.

She looked like a perfect girl with lighter hair than the other two kids and beautiful creamy skin. But she had the attitude of a cocky, athletic boy, and Stallings always loved that. He could take her to any sporting event, and she'd stay interested and ask the right questions. She'd even ride her bike with him while he jogged. She'd been easy to deal with until she wasn't.

He had to look rationally at the last year she was still at the house, during which she'd rebelled and seemed uninterested in anything to do with the family. It was a slow evolution but one that had troubled him then and haunted him now. It was his first time dealing with a teenager in the house, and although he had heard all the horror stories about the crazy things teenagers said and did, he wasn't prepared when he had to confront it himself. At the time he wondered how Maria had handled it so quietly and comfortably. It wasn't till later that he realized she was too stoned most of the time to give a shit. Then he had asked himself a hard question: Were his punishments too harsh? Had something he'd said or done drove her from the house? Or had something else happened? Had she been kidnapped or fallen in with the wrong crowd? These were all questions that ran through his head on a daily basis and right now were hammering his brain like a machine gun.

Finally Maria sighed and said, "John, we've been through a lot together, and I haven't handled it well."

"That mean you want me back?"

"I wish we had our whole lives back."

In her tone and words he felt the blow of how much they had lost. Maybe that was what was making him crazy about Lauren, but he didn't think so.

His cell phone rang, and out of habit he quickly dug it out of his pocket. The analyst from the detective bureau was on the line and said, "Stall, you said to call you if I found anything on Donnie Eliot."

"Yeah."

"We got him listed in our intel database as dealing in prescription narcotics but no arrests. Want me to start checking some of the other cities with local databases?"

"No, Faith, that's okay. I know detectives in Daytona and Gainesville. I'll give 'em a shout and see if they know this knucklehead. Thanks." He shut the phone and absently returned it to his pocket.

Maria looked up and said, "See? Even when you're at home, work comes first."

Stallings knew when he'd been dismissed, and this time he had been dismissed physically as well as emotionally. He kept his mouth shut, turned silently, and started for the door. But something made him look up over his right shoulder. That's when he saw her. Lauren was sitting on the landing of the landing with a Kleenex in her hand and her eyes red and puffy from crying. He looked back over to the family room, where Maria continued to sit on the long couch, staring straight ahead. With just a flick of his head he motioned Lauren to follow as he opened the front door and like a ghost she appeared next to him on the porch.

He closed the door and sat on the edge of the wooden porch with his foot on the steps leading up from the sidewalk. Lauren slid in right next to him, still not making a sound. He didn't feel the need to talk either. He looked each way down the empty street, appreciating the old-style streetlights mounted on wooden telephone poles in the relatively quiet neighborhood, even though they weren't that far from downtown Jacksonville. The temperature had dropped and felt nice out in the night air.

The sky was clear, and a half moon cast a gentle light across the yard. He sat there in silence with Lauren, just appreciating the fact that she was next to him.

After a few minutes she sniffled, cleared her throat, and said, "I never thought I'd run into you in a place like that. It just surprised me. I don't think I've ever even seen you drink a beer."

"I wasn't there to drink, sweetheart. I was looking for someone. I was working."

"Is he dangerous?"

"Is who dangerous?"

"The guy you were looking for. Sometimes I forget how dangerous your job is."

"No. He wasn't dangerous." When Stallings turned, she was staring him down like a veteran detective trying to make him tell the truth. It was such a good, intense stare he had to add, "Really, sweetheart, it was a fairly routine interview."

"But not everyone you interview is routine. I saw the news coverage of that guy William Dremmel you caught last year. Your job is dangerous. You're paid to take risks. It scares me. A lot. The way mom is, I have no idea how we'd make it without you. I already miss Jeanie so much it's hard to comprehend what it'd be like if something happened to mom or Charlie or you. And you're the only one who has to be dealing with dangerous people."

It had never occurred to Stallings that his kids looked at things in those terms. Certainly Lauren had never given any indication that she was worried about him. In the last couple of years she'd barely acknowledged him, let alone shown any concern. He was so touched he felt his own eyes start to water.

Lauren wrapped her arm around his back and said, "You know that Mom really needs you. I think she's just a little confused right now."

He was so choked up he couldn't say a word. Instead, he wrapped both arms around his daughter and squeezed her tight, thanking God for little moments like this. The sad thing was he knew a half a dozen cops who would feel the same way if only they could have a moment like this.

Twenty-six

Patty Levine felt a pang of guilt at the sight of the lab tech's cheerful face as he greeted her.

"Hey, Patty, how're you?" His brown eyes big with excitement and face flushed enough to hide some of his acne.

"Good, Lee. Sorry I'm so early."

"Are you kidding? When you texted me last night I was thrilled to be able to start my day by seeing you."

"That's sweet, Lee. Did you have any luck?"

The tall young man in casual clothes was the only one in the wide, clean lab deep inside the Police Memorial Building. She didn't expect anyone else to be there at seven-thirty in the morning. Even Patty was dragging at that hour, the effects of the late-night Ambien hanging on a little longer than usual.

Lee scurried around, collecting files and reports for Patty. She knew his efforts were based on her looks and flirting more than anything else. All she heard from most of the detectives was how long it took for lab results to come back, but she'd befriended this young man with a degree in forensic science from the University of Central Florida, and he'd been remarkably helpful for the past two years. She tried not to lead him on but worried about the day when he finally screwed up enough courage to ask her out for lunch. Until that day she gladly accepted the fact that she could work a little more efficiently than others. It made up a little for her not being part of the good old boys network that often cut through bureaucratic bullshit and got reports or other kinds of help for the seasoned male detectives. She didn't begrudge them the shortcut. Patty was in favor of anything that sped along justice and helped people. She just wished everyone had access to it. At least that was the justification she used to get her lab results much faster than anyone else.

In this case, Mazzetti had submitted the request as part of the autopsies of the two spring breakers. The idea that there would be links between them set off an alarm in Patty's head and made her push the limits of her flirting to find out the answers fast. Patty had added to the young lab tech's workload by providing him the three pills found in Kathleen Harding's purse. Two were obviously prescription pills, but the third was a curious speckled pill she thought had to be X.

He photographed each pill through a magnifying glass and gave her a good copy of each. The speckled pill had *J2A* stamped into it.

Lee stepped back to her as he studied the pages. "What exactly are you looking for?"

"There was a chemical residue found on both bodies that indicated the possibility of sex with a condom before death."

Lee nodded. "Polyethylene glycol. I see the note here."

"What about drugs?"

"Ecstasy. Looks like at least some of it was from the same source."

"What'd you mean?"

"There're a couple of ways to make X. No recipe is quite the same. Both these girls took some of the same batch, but the second one, Allie Marsh, also had some other X in her. Probably what killed her."

"Could it have been intentional?"

"You mean did she know she was taking it?"

Patty said, "I mean if someone wanted to kill her, he could keep giving her the drug."

"I suppose."

Patty looked at him and said, "Okay, Lee, why the big, shit-eating grin?"

"I got the results of the yellow liquid you submitted."

"From our missing persons case?"

"The same."

"And?"

"Safrole oil."

"What's that?"

He just kept grinning.

John Stallings sat across from Sergeant Yvonne Zuni in the conference room. He was a little uncomfortable without Patty next to him, and he'd expected her. Since her run-in with the serial killer known as the Bag Man a few months back, Stallings had become a little over-protective of his partner and started to panic if he couldn't reach her. But this morning she had sent him a text message, which he hated, that said she was busy in the building and would be up shortly.

He looked at the new sergeant, trying to get a fix on her. Despite her reputation as a tough veteran, he didn't think she could be much older than thirty. But there was nothing soft in that pretty face. She didn't shy away from his gaze.

"Stall, you and Patty will have to handle the death investigations Mazzetti and Hoagie had before they caught the triple."

"Anything new on the triple?"

"Just that it was gang related. Rumor is that it might have a racial undertone, and that means there's gonna be retaliation. You know how when someone starts saying they saw a carload of white kids it morphs into being a truckload of Klansmen. Just like a lone black kid in a white neighborhood gets called in as a gang. I swear street rumors waste more of our time than anything else. That's why the administration wants every effort put into it." She paused and added, "Every effort that doesn't require a lot of overtime."

Stallings nodded, knowing that meant virtually every other victim in the city would be ignored for a while until the news media backed off the triple murder near the stadium.

"I have Allie's mother calling me every hour about the case." The sergeant started to say something, then looked at Stallings and stifled it. Cops often made callous comments to vent their frustration. Stallings sometimes overheard cops make comments about runaways or young female deaths, then realize his situation and get embarrassed. He was getting used to it, but the new sergeant obviously wasn't. She just said, "Anything new on her?"

He looked down, unsatisfied with their progress.

"The drummer we chased is still in the can. We talked to the cop, Gary Lauer, and he was less than helpful, but I still wouldn't call him a suspect. Just an asshole."

He caught an odd expression on the sergeant's face.

"Am I missing something?"

Sergeant Zuni hesitated, then said, "This is not official. Just you and me."

He nodded.

"I know Lauer pretty well."

Stallings still kept quiet.

"I don't want to go into detail, but he's got issues."

"You think he could be a suspect?"

"I'm saying that with a young pretty girl in the mix and knowing him, I wouldn't rule anything out."

He finished his Chick-Fil-A sandwich in the food court of the small mall. After a brief post-activity let-down he had found his groove and his predatory instincts returned. He had real power. He hadn't stopped smiling since he'd placed Holly's nose stud in his souvenir box. The surprise on her face for that instant after he shoved the knife into her brainpan had been the sweetest surprise of his whole life. He'd thought that Allie from Mississippi squealing under him as her heart exploded was one of the most exciting things he had experienced. But now he had to put Holly's expression at the top of the list.

He leaned back, satisfied. No one could connect him to anything here in Jacksonville. He was originally reticent to hunt in his own valley. In the past, he liked to travel and carve the occasional weak one out of the spring break herd in other cities but not here where people knew him.

His hunting season would draw to a close soon. The girls of the cheaper southeastern schools would start heading back home in beat-up cars with bad sunburns and lasting hangovers. He felt confident he could score a few more kills. Just something to last him until next year. He had no idea where to hunt for the moment. The beach made him a little skittish after Holly. The Wildside was done, at least for a while. He had to work this problem out in his head.

His eyes drifted up until they caught the blue eyes of a young woman sitting with two friends, eating a salad. She smiled and flipped her blond hair.

He smiled back, realizing his problem had just been solved.

John Stallings gawked at the lab results spread over Patty's desk.

He said, "You believe these two girls got their X from the same source."

She nodded.

"You think there could be more to the girls' deaths?"

Patty was cautious. "Could be."

"Then we need to investigate it, Detective Levine," he said in a mock-formal tone. He glanced over the notes and added, "I wish we had a lead that was common to the girls."

"We might."

Stallings just stared at her.

Patty said, "And this might be a long shot."

"What is it?"

"You know that yellow liquid we found at Jason Ferrell's apartment?"

He thought about their search for the missing chemical engineer, then nodded.

"It's safrole oil."

"And you'll explain what this is to me."

"It's the precursor and main ingredient in homemade Ecstasy."

Twenty-seven

John Stallings hit the accelerator on his Impala a little hard as he tore west on Interstate 10. He knew the logical move was to find the next suspect on the list provided by Larry, the bartender at the Wildside. Patty had determined that Chad Palmer was a married pharmaceutical rep with a house west of Jacksonville in a little area called Normandy. But Stallings zipped past the exit for Normandy on his way to Sanderson and Leonard Walsh.

The redneck and his friend had given him the slip at Jason Ferrell's apartment, and it had bugged him ever since. Now that Mr. Walsh might have information that could help on the case, he was happy to pay him a visit.

Patty seemed a little anxious, and based on his history she had reason. But all he really wanted was to solve the mystery of what these morons were doing at Ferrell's. If the guy was making bathroom X, then Stallings wouldn't be as bothered about his disappearance. It was a karma thing. If you worked in the drug business you got what you deserved. He'd still feel bad about Ferrell's mother. If he was an amateur pill maker he could be hiding from any number of lowlifes or one of them could have found him.

Twenty-five minutes later they pulled off the interstate onto the maze of state and county roads crisscrossing North Florida. The edge of the Osceola National Forest bordered the north side of the road, and what seemed like endless, empty cow pastures spread out to the south. One dirt road cut east into a field in desperate need of some maintenance. Stallings took it as if he'd been down the rocky road a thousand times.

He slowed the Impala as they approached a broken-down wooden gate permanently propped open.

Stallings said, "Getting a little lax on security."

"Who'd want to come back here to steal anything?"

A double-wide trailer, up on blocks, sat near the rear of the cleared section of the field. A smaller travel trailer in terrible disrepair was parked about fifty yards from the double-wide with a new Ford F-150 parked in between.

"That's the truck that ran from us," said Patty.

Stallings took another second to scan the entire open area and especially the corners of the trailers and truck. He said quietly, "Is this the day that changes my life?"

He parked right in front of the double-wide and didn't waste any time pounding on the thin door. He stepped to the side and appreciated that Patty stood at the corner of the big trailer so she could see anyone coming from the rear.

After a few seconds the front door opened, and the man that had run from him, in the same green John Deere hat, poked out his head and looked down at Stallings standing at the base of the three metal stairs that led into the trailer.

Stallings said, "Thought you could run from us, didn't you?"

"Goddamn, you're the five-O from J-Ville." He started to ease back inside, but Stallings jumped onto the landing to block the man from closing the door.

Stallings said, "You Leonard Walsh?"

"Yeah, so?"

"Jacksonville Sheriff's Office, we need to talk."

"I got nothin' to say to you. This here is Baker County, not Duvall. You got no juice here."

Stallings smiled. "And the local cops don't know me either. I think that might be worse for you."

He stared, open mouthed, trying to figure out exactly what Stallings meant. He stepped back all the way into the double-wide, and Stallings followed.

Stallings said, "Why'd you run from us, Leonard?"

"I don't want no trouble."

"Neither do I. All I want is answers. If you tell me what I need to know, then we'll be gone in a few minutes. But if you don't . . ." Stallings knew to leave the threat open. Imagination was worse than anything he could've said. He watched Leonard Walsh's face closely, knowing he'd sufficiently scared the man when he saw his Adam's apple bob in a deep swallow.

Leonard bowed his head. "What do you want to know?"

"Why were you at Jason Ferrell's apartment?"

"How'd you know that's who we were going to see?"

"Lucky guess."

Leonard hesitated, then said, "He was doin' some work for me."

"C'mon, Leonard, speed this along. Get to the point. What kind of work?"

"He said he could find a new way to make meth without using the ingredients that are on the watch list so we don't have to show no driver's license just to get cold medicine."

"That's why you have the small trailer, isn't it? That's your cook shack."

Leonard nodded.

"All I really need to know is where Jason is now."

Leonard shrugged.

"Why were you at his apartment?"

"We owed him some cash."

"He come up with the recipe?"

Leonard remained silent.

Stallings said, "I think I'll take a look around the property."

"You can't do that. You got no warrant. You don't even got jurisdiction."

Stallings looked over to Patty at the door in a signal to get ready in case this guy did something stupid.

Then he turned and stepped back out into the yard.

It was early, but he enjoyed getting out to someplace different. No one knew him here and no one knew he liked to come here. Closer to the University of North Florida in the southeast part of town, this little club featured a live band later in the evening but cheap beer early. That meant it was crowded. Really crowded.

Lisa, the girl he had met in the food court at the mall, grinded her hips up against him. She wasn't technically a spring break visitor because she had flunked out of a junior college in north Georgia, but she had a great smile, blue eyes, and straight, long blond hair. Her hips were strong enough to bump him over a few inches.

He had agreed to meet her in the little club but now

was sorry because of all the blond heads he saw. He could go wild in a place like this. He wondered what would happen if he did something really crazy like use a gun to kill five or six of the blondes. Would the cops think all the blond victims were a fluke? The thought made him chuckle.

Lisa said, "What's so funny?"

"Nothing." He liked her big, curvy frame in perfect time to the music. This chick could dance.

"What's on your mind?"

"I could never tell."

"Maybe I can figure it out later. At your place." Then she winked.

Was he wrong or were the hunts getting easier?

Lisa was glad she'd seen him in the club. Even though it was much less of an accident than he suspected. She had scanned the giant club with kids crammed into it like chickens at a commercial chicken farm. She didn't much care for the stuck-up college girls, and it had nothing to do with her having flunked out of community college. Who cared if she knew who wrote the *Odyssey* or how to figure out the outside distance of a circle? She could never remember if it was called the radius or the circumcision or maybe it was the circumference. She got a lot of worse things confused. She felt that she was basically a decent person and always tried to do the right thing. And the right thing in this case was letting this good-looking guy know that she was interested and he couldn't ignore her.

Ever since her first boyfriend, Lucas Martin, had started to ignore her until he finally ended up sleeping with that bitch Peggy Lynn, she'd made it a point to keep a man's attention. It usually didn't work out that well, and she had two restraining orders to prove it. That didn't mean she couldn't keep trying. And that meant using the assets and talents that God had given her. That's what the pastor had said at the Hahira Baptist Church. He had a whole sermon about using God's gifts in the best possible way. God had given her a big, beautiful butt. It was so perfect it was a legend in Hahira, Georgia. In fact, there was no black man under the age of thirty who didn't dream about her ass on a regular basis, and she knew it. Right now she was using the great ass God had given her by grinding it against this guy's crotch on the dance floor of the giant club.

She'd taken the X tab that he'd given her, and between dancing with this guy's tight, hot body next to hers and the drug, her heart felt as if it were about to jump out of her chest. Sweat had made her hair dampen and hang down into her eyes, but she kept grinding and moving to the beat. This was why she'd come with her friends on spring break even though she wasn't really on spring break. This was more fun because she didn't have to worry about getting back to some dreary class on writing or mathematics. She wished she could stay longer than a week, and if she had her way, that's exactly what this guy would ask her.

Leonard Walsh trailed Stallings, yammering in his ear, "Wait, I'll talk, I'll talk."

"I know you will."

"Then why don't you stop walking around?"

"Because now I want to know what kind of setup you have. Might be dangerous, and I don't want to risk you getting hurt by substandard lab practices." He stopped just short of the small trailer. He'd already made sure Patty was well back, ready to respond if he had to tussle with Leonard and far enough back to be safe if the little trailer blew for some reason. Meth production was a tricky, dangerous business, and more than one redneck had bought the farm trying to get rich in the competitive meth market.

He placed his hand on the trailer's flimsy doorknob.

Leonard said, "Wait."

Stallings paused.

"You don't need to look in there."

Stallings jerked open the door, and the smell, like rotten fruit, almost knocked him over. The trailer had four huge tubs and a barrel in one corner. The rear windows, open to the wide, empty field, provided rudimentary ventilation.

"Damn, Leonard, I'm impressed. This is a good setup"

The rangy redneck smiled, showing his yellowed teeth. "Thanks."

"You don't have any matches, do you?"

Leonard pulled out a frayed book. "Why?"

"Can't have any possibility of an open flame."

"Yeah right, good idea."

Stallings turned and pushed him back outside, taking the matches out of Leonard's hand as he did.

"Now, did Jason give you the new recipe?"

"Not yet. We were paying on installment. I still owe him sixty-five hundred bucks."

"Do you know how to find him right now?"

Leonard shook his head. "It's not like he owes me money. I owe him. He should be easy to find, but he ain't."

"Any ideas where he might be?"

"Nah. The manager of his apartment told me some black fellas was looking for him. I think he might have promised too many people things, and now he's laying low."

"He ever make anything else for you, like Ecstasy?"

Leonard nodded, digging into his pocket. He pulled out a small vial with three speckled tablets in it. "He tried to convince me that these were more profitable than meth. He said this X was cheap to make and easy to sell. I think that dumb-ass college boy didn't understand that out here there ain't no spring break partiers. Out here we need meth."

"No idea where he might be?" Stallings said, casually collecting the vial from Leonard.

Leonard shook his head. "Said he had a girlfriend, but never said where."

"Mention a name?"

"Called her Miss something. Baxter or Barnes. Hell, I can't remember. All I cared about was our meth recipe."

Stallings turned to Leonard and said, "Okay, you've been helpful. Now run."

"What?"

"Run, Leonard, run."

"Why?"

Stallings struck a match from the pack Leonard had provided. He looked over his shoulder at the meth trailer and smiled.

Leonard yelled "No!" but turned and started loping away toward his double-wide.

Stallings tossed the match inside the door, watching it ignite the cheap synthetic rug.

He jogged away; then the first of the tubs ignited.

* * *

On the ride back toward Jacksonville, Patty Levine looked across at her partner. "Why'd you light the trailer on fire?"

"Couldn't leave an active meth lab intact."

"But it's Baker County. We had no jurisdiction."

"Even if we did, we had no PC."

"Aren't you the least bit concerned he might make a complaint?"

"What's he gonna do? Call in and complain someone blew up his illegal meth lab?"

Patty grunted and focused on the road.

Twenty-eight

On the drive back from blowing up the meth lab, Stallings stopped in a subdivision near Jacksonville called Normandy. He hoped to catch one of the other men in the Wildside video at home. Chad Palmer was a pharmaceutical rep who looked as if he made a lot of money. He was twenty-nine years old, appeared to be in good shape, was good looking, and shouldn't have been hanging out at a bar that catered to college kids. That was enough to make Stallings want to talk to this guy.

The one-story, ranch-style house, with a perfectly manicured lawn and a load of plastic toys sitting on the front porch, wasn't showy but seemed comfortable. He let Patty take the lead, knowing that the sight of her often set people at ease. The idea that a cop like Gary Lauer could be involved in giving drugs to young college girls gnawed at him. Stallings hoped someone like this guy Palmer might be their man.

Patty mashed the doorbell and waited. That detail demonstrated the difference between her and Stallings. He would've pounded on the door as he had a thousand times before. He stepped to one side and muttered his little mantra to himself, "Is this the day that changes my life?" Patty rarely even reacted to it anymore.

The door opened a crack, and a pretty young woman with green eyes peered out at them. She was in her mid-twenties, wearing just shorts and a T-shirt. A boy, about five, peeked around one of her shapely legs, but didn't say a word.

"Yes?" the young woman said.

Patty knew to take this one. "Mrs. Palmer, is your husband around?"

"I'm not Mrs. Palmer."

"I'm sorry. Does a Chad Palmer live here?"

The young woman smiled. "Can I ask what this is about?"

Stallings, feeling a little impatient, said, "Ma'am, we're with the Jacksonville Sheriff's Office. And we need to talk to Chad Palmer."

"Oh. I'm his sister, Debbie. He actually lives over near the beach."

Patty said in her usual calm tone, "This house is listed as one of his addresses."

Debbie smiled. "Technically he owns this house, but I'm the only one who's ever lived here. Well, me and the rug rat here." She ruffled the silent little boy's hair.

"That sounds like a good brother."

"Yeah. He's a pretty good guy. What's this all about?"

"He may be a witness to something, and we need to talk to him. No big deal."

"Where? He travels all over with his job."

"Where's he travel?"

"From Miami to Atlanta."

"This has to do with Jacksonville."

"He spends a lot of time in Daytona, but he has an office in Jacksonville too. What did he witness?"

Patty hesitated, then said, "Just a routine investigation. I'm sure we'll get hold of him soon."

"What kind of investigation?"

Patty looked over to Stallings, who nodded. "It's about a Mississippi college student who died from an apparent drug overdose."

"What kind of drug?"

"Ecstasy."

Stallings noticed the woman relax a little, as if the fact that it wasn't a pharmaceutical drug relieved her.

As they walked back to the car, Stallings looked over his shoulder at the cute boy staring through the window at them.

Stallings said, "A pharmaceutical rep has access to a lot of drugs."

"So why would he need to make his own?"

"That, my young partner, is a very good question. I hope we can get an answer from Mr. Palmer in the very near future."

Since the uncomfortable incident with Holly he'd been a little more careful. He hadn't told Lisa where he'd be tonight because he wasn't ready to make his move. Still, the music, the crowd, and the girls were giving him an erection that drew so much blood from his head it was making him dizzy. He knew he had to be more careful and that people were looking at Allie Marsh's death. He didn't know why the cute girl from Mississippi deserved so much attention, but he didn't want to do anything stupid now.

He knew that moving too quickly with Lisa, no matter how exciting her blond hair and blue eyes were, could get him in trouble in the long run. Besides, he liked the thrill of the hunt. He almost wished she weren't so accessible. It had been hard convincing her he couldn't give her his cell phone number. She'd been all too quick to give up hers, but he mumbled some half-assed excuse. Now she was convinced that he was married. But she didn't seem bothered by the excitement of an older, married man. Somehow the prospect of a guy who might have a little money, was in pretty good shape, and could dance blinded her to the problems that arose from him not giving her his phone number.

To be on the safe side, he'd called her in the afternoon and told her that he was busy tonight, but that he'd make sure that they got together tomorrow. That would give him the whole night to dream about her and what he might do to her. The image of Holly with the steel knife stuck in her head was still in his brain. The excitement and enjoyment he'd gotten out of that was on a whole new level. He wondered if that was going to be his new standard: quick, bloody, devastating. Perhaps it was a kind of evolution he was undergoing. The problem was it was so much easier for the police to detect those kinds of crimes. Another issue was that he was getting low on Ecstasy tablets. Usually his source would come by and he could pick up a couple of tablets quietly, with no one asking any questions, and usually no money changing hands. There were things he could barter. Favors, friendship, drinks. Ecstasy was a fluid currency, as well as the best hunting tool around. He paid a lot for the first, large batch, but it had proven to be worth the investment.

Lost in his thoughts, he didn't notice as the young woman approached him. She said, "Excuse me."

He gazed up into perfectly clear, blue eyes. A wisp of blond hair hung over a cute face. His heart raced as he tried to answer her.

As far as he was concerned it would be spring break for another couple of weeks. And he had at least two targets to focus on. Lisa and this girl.

He straightened up and smiled. "Hey, what's your name?"

She focused her blue eyes on his and said, "Ann— why?"

"Because I want to ask you out on a date, Ann."

The hunt was on.

Twenty-nine

It was Saturday morning, and John Stallings was alone in the crimes/persons office. Budget cutbacks and tax shortfalls had reduced the detectives' overtime budget to almost nothing. That wasn't why Stallings sat here alone; this case had started to eat at him. And he had nothing else to do. Maria had taken Charlie and Lauren to visit her sister in Orlando for the day. Stallings had scheduled an outing with them in the morning. It was almost as if he and Maria had already gotten a divorce.

In front of him, he held the glass tube with three Ecstasy tablets that Leonard Walsh had given him. Somehow he felt Jason Ferrell could be a link in this case, but he had to consider the suspects for now. Gary Lauer and Chad Palmer were high on his list. Donnie Eliot had all but convinced him that he had no part in Allie Marsh's death. It seemed prudent to let him rot in jail a while longer and focus on suspects he thought were viable. One thing he wanted to do was make certain the goofy drummer wasn't known in other spring break towns as a serious troublemaker who distributed Ecstasy

on a large scale. There were hundreds of different police databases, but the best way to find out things like
this was through contacts. Usually cops from local juris-
dictions who could talk to people and know what the
word on the street was.

Stallings picked up his desktop phone and dialed the
Daytona Beach Police Department. His friend, Detective Hugh O'Connor, often worked on Saturdays, so he
would have more time in the evenings to coach his
daughter's softball team.

The phone in the Daytona Detective Bureau rang
once, and then he smiled as he recognized his friend's
voice.

"Detective Bureau, Hugh O'Connor."

"Hugh, John Stallings, at JSO."

"Stall, how's life in Missing Persons?"

"Not bad, not bad. Working a couple different things
right now. I was wondering if I could run a name past
you. A musician."

"Fire away."

"A drummer named Donnie Eliot."

O'Connor laughed. "A drummer? I thought you said
he was a musician."

"Do you have anything in your local database?" Stallings searched through a few notes as his friend worked
the computer on the other end of the phone line. The
usual curse words that every cop who's ever had to type
away on an ancient computer mutters came over the
phone. He checked back with Stallings twice to make
sure he had the right spelling. Finally he said no, there
was nothing in the computer about a drummer named
Donnie Eliot.

Stallings said, "I just wanted to see if he's been passing Ecstasy out at any of your clubs."

"Is he a spring break guy? Does he follow the crowd from city to city and hang out with the young girls? Or is he more like one of the flat breakers?"

"I even know what a flat breaker is now."

O'Connor laughed. "Welcome to my world. Five weeks every year, everything gets put on hold while we have to deal with all this bullshit. We had three deaths last year during spring break. One drowning, one suicide, and one still listed as open, all with X in their systems."

"What about this year?"

"We were lucky this year. No deaths. It seems to run in spurts. A few years ago, we had an out-and-out murder. Someone choked the shit out of a girl. We never did solve it. But the Ecstasy, that never goes away. Kids find a way to mix it up, buy it—there's even a bunch of Dutch kids that seem to have an endless supply."

"We have two dead up here in Jacksonville. One suicide and one OD. It's a shame."

O'Connor said, "Yeah. All three of the girls last year were cute blond things. Made me think of my own daughter and what I would do if some knucklehead gave her some X."

Stallings thought for a minute about what his friend just told him. Both his deaths were blond too. For no obvious reason he said, "Hugh, you think you could send me up what you have on those deaths?"

"Sure, Stall, whatever you need. Is there something I need to know about?"

"No, just trying to be thorough. You know how it is when you're an old cop. You can't let anything go easy."

"Stall, you never let anything go easy. Even when you were young."

Even as the two men laughed, Stallings had an uneasy feeling. He had a lot of work to do.

He was satisfied with the situation. There were a couple of weeks left in the spring break season, and he had two possibilities on his plate. The last girl he'd seen, Ann, had a cool demeanor but perfectly straight, natural blond hair that fell across her shoulders like a golden blanket. She had light blue eyes and high cheekbones that accentuated her classic beauty. But she always had friends around, and that was a drawback. He'd get his chance if he was patient.

But now he was dancing with Lisa, the girl he'd met in the food court. She had more meat on her bones, real Southern curves. And he liked it. Most men did, even if the image of a supermodel was rail thin with hollow cheeks. He liked the way she showed off her form and swayed to the music. He did the usual male shuffle, just providing a backdrop for her to dance. But then she moved closer and wrapped an arm around his back, pulling in tight. It made him uncomfortable on a number of levels. He didn't want people to remember the two of them together even if no one in here knew him. And this wasn't the way that prey acted. He was the aggressor. He was the predator.

He wandered back to the bar as soon as the music stopped, and she fell in line with him, taking the stool to his right. She started to lean over to kiss him, but he held up his left hand to hold her in place. She giggled, leaned around the hand, and tickled his ear with her tongue.

He snapped, "Don't do that."

"Most guys love that." Her words were slurring from too many cheap beers and a hit of X.

"I'm sorry—I'm just not a big fan of public displays of affection."

"That's okay. I know a lot of guys who don't like PDA."

He stared at her, trying to figure out what PDA meant.

She wasn't that drunk, because she caught on and said, "Public displays of affection." Lisa smiled at him, looking deep into his eyes, and said, "So do you want to go back to your place?"

He hadn't expected things to move this quickly. He hadn't planned it as clearly as he wanted to, not even knowing how she was going to die. But they were at a bar in central Jacksonville, and no one would notice him slip out with her. He could always move her car to another lot too.

Finally he said, "Why don't we go down to the beach? I know a nice quiet, private beach where we could have a lot of fun."

"You want to fuck in the sand? Do you have any idea how uncomfortable that could be?" She shook her head as if it was on a wobbly pole. "What's wrong, do you still live with your parents or something?"

He shook his head, realizing how little he liked this girl as a person.

"Then why can't we just go back to your place?"

He was about to answer her when he noticed a blond head a little taller than everyone around her. He took a closer look and realized it was Ann. Immediately he knew he wouldn't be taking either of them home tonight.

*   *   *

Lisa had been putting on the drunk act so she'd have some cover if she did something embarrassing. It was weird because he didn't like her kissing on him and sticking her tongue in his ears like most guys did. She was frustrated because all she wanted was a quiet room where she could do this guy and then sleep peacefully without five college girls screaming and giggling in the next bed. This was all minor. There was only one thing she could never tolerate—not being the center of someone's attention—and right now he was not paying enough attention to her. Then she saw him look over her shoulder, so she followed his eyes to see the pretty blond girl at the end of the bar staring back.

She sat up straight, resisting the urge to slap him hard across his face.

Lisa said, "Who the hell is that?"

"Just a girl I talked to one night."

Lisa looked over and saw the girl smiling at him. That tore it. It was bad enough he wasn't paying complete attention to her but to look up at that whore right in front of her—she couldn't let it slide. If she was back home in Georgia, she'd have that bitch by her dyed hair and would be jerking her ass out the door right now. But in a fancy city like Jacksonville, she had to act a little more carefully.

She noticed other girls around her at the bar and calculated how many of them she might have to take out before she could deal with this bitch. She left her bar stool and started to march to the other side of the bar.

He reached out and grabbed her by the arm, saying, "What are you doing?"

"Protecting my territory."

"Are you insane? Don't draw any attention to us."

She was surprised how panicked he sounded. It was the first real emotion she'd sensed in him. And it was as close to pleading as she thought she'd ever hear from a guy like this. But she still ripped her arm out of his grip and continued on her single-minded mission. When she was only a couple steps away the girl from the bar looked up and their eyes met.

Lisa said, "Just what do you think you're doin' flirting with my man?"

The girl said, "You'd know if I was flirting with him because he would've left your fat ass at the bar."

The guy ran over from the dance floor and said, "Lisa, would you cut this shit out?" Then his eyes shifted to the girl, and he said, "I'm sorry, Ann. She's had a little too much to drink."

So that was his bitch's name: Ann. Lisa didn't bother to look back at him; instead she focused her full fury on Ann standing so calmly and quietly at the bar as if there wasn't a girl from Georgia about to whip her ass. "Don't be too sure I'm drunk, Ann. I've done a lot of things a lot more drunk. Now you back off or we're gonna have a big problem."

Ann did the worst thing she could do. She ignored Lisa. She stepped away from the bar and took a wide step around Lisa, then said to the guy, "Not very impressive. I thought you'd aim higher." She continued on a slow, steady trek across the dance floor and right out the door.

Lisa felt that she'd won this round. Then she felt as if there was a fish or something swimming in her belly. She looked up to see the guy checking around the bar to make sure no one had noticed the confrontation. But it was too late. The fish in her belly had kicked up the tacos she ate for lunch, and now they wanted to come up.

She raced out of the club in time to throw up all over the bouncer.

Thirty

It was humid and hot even though it wasn't yet nine o'clock on Sunday morning. Patty Levine may have been shorter than her boyfriend, Tony Mazzetti, but she was a much more efficient runner. She had an easy stride and years of aerobic training behind her. Mazzetti, for all his time in the gym, had not spent a lot of time on the treadmill. And it showed. All she could think about was an African rhino chugging along the plains. He kept up with her, but it was out of sheer will. He held his side, he coughed, he hacked, and his thick legs moved his wide shoulders and broad chest like a ship coming into port. But she appreciated his effort, and it showed he wanted to do things with her. She ran every Sunday morning. Sometimes up to fifteen miles, but today, she was going to take it easy on her boyfriend and only do about five.

At first she couldn't believe that he'd take a day off during the middle of an investigation like the triple shooting. It was only after talking with Mazzetti's partner, Christina Hogrebe, that she realized they'd both been told to take the day off and let the weekend detectives cover any leads that came in. Patty didn't care that it was a cost-cutting measure; she was just glad to spend a few hours with her boyfriend away from work.

She liked being in command during the run and peppered him with questions. All the effort he needed just to stay up with her kept him from coming up with his usual mantra of bullshit that he tended to hide behind. She got a little more insight into his childhood. How his mother raised him and was overprotective. How he still felt insecure about his physical fitness. Why he always dressed as if he was going to be on TV. All the little things that made him who he was. Then she said, "You'd rather be out on a homicide right now, wouldn't you?"

"No, baby, this is exactly where I want to be." He gulped some air. "And this is exactly what I want to be doing."

She rolled her eyes and mumbled, "Bullshit"

"No, baby, I swear."

She picked up the pace and pulled away from him. It'd do him some good to get a dose of humility. She put about one hundred yards between them, enough distance down the winding path in the park near Atlantic Beach that she couldn't hear him wheeze or breathe hard anymore. She passed several walkers, a couple of joggers, and one older man with his granddaughter on a bicycle and then took a turn onto a path that climbed toward the beach.

She saw a runner cross the path in front of her. Shirtless and sleek and very, very fast, he looked like an agile animal. But there was something familiar about him. She just couldn't put her finger on it. She sped up and took the same path as the fleet runner, but he'd already turned another corner and was moving too fast to catch.

She had an odd urge to chase him down and see who he was. It wasn't that she thought he was cute, even though she thought he probably was. It was something else. Something she couldn't form clearly in her head.

Instead she slowed, taking a second to stretch her legs as her pet rhino slowly rumbled up behind her.

The idea of two of his targets meeting at first struck him as dangerous; then an element of excitement crept into the equation. He would have worked something out with Lisa last night had Ann not walked into the bar. Conversely, had he not been with Lisa, he would've approached Ann. Instead it'd been a quiet night, relatively speaking.

He'd started out on a hard run to clear his head. The park near Atlantic Beach was one of his favorite places to run. He occasionally discovered prey in the park. But today, with the image of both of his new girls floating in his head, prey was the last thing he wanted to bump into. He just wanted his heart to beat hard and the sun to bake him and make him sweat. In running shorts and new ASICS shoes, he felt efficient, loose, and good.

He still couldn't help turning his head and looking at the cute blond woman with the graceful stride coming toward him on another trail. He didn't get a good look at her face, but some instinct told him to keep running. When she took the same trail, he decided to really turn it on and put some distance between them.

Maybe it was his animal instincts that made him want to escape the woman. Or maybe it was something else. But with Ann and Lisa already on his plate, he didn't want to risk finding another target. It seemed easier to run fast and get on with his day. He was supposed to call

Lisa but hadn't had time yet. She'd wait. He thought about asking her out to dinner. And as long as she showed up alone and didn't expect him to be part of the main course, she was a big step up from Holly.

John Stallings sat in the small booth with his kids on either side of him. A half-eaten pepperoni pizza sat on the table, along with three gigantic cokes. He'd taken the kids to an early movie and was relaxed for the first time in several weeks. Charlie and Lauren debated the merits of the movie. Lauren discussing the length, acting, and special effects, while Charlie was more interested in the possibility that humans really could mutate into new life-forms. The normally quiet boy seemed exceptionally boisterous, talking about everything from sports to school.

Stallings was worried it was a side effect of the separation, even though he saw the boy most days. It felt as if they were trying to catch up. It wasn't the same as when he lived at the house. He listened to Charlie go on and on about his week as class supervisor. The young man had assured his father that he had not let the power go to his head.

"Yeah, Dad, it's tough. Kids think they can get by with anything. If I showed one person attention, everyone else got mad at me."

Stallings said, "Tough to be in charge, sport."

"I sure did learn that, Dad."

The conviction in Charlie's voice and the simple statement made Stallings think about his new supervisor, Yvonne Zuni. Maybe she wasn't as bad as he'd initially thought. With his interest in finding who had given Allie Marsh the Ecstasy, it could be an interesting week ahead of him. He'd see what kind of support the new sergeant gave him.

Charlie said, "I'm not sure I'm cut out to be in management. I'm like you, Dad, I'm an action kind of guy."

Stallings and Lauren both laughed at Charlie's sincerity. As much as he loved hearing Charlie's stories, seeing his teenage daughter smile made him feel just as good. There was so much the young lady had taken on in the past few years. From trying to be the lady of the house while Maria recovered, to her concern for her father's long hours and dangerous work. It felt as if the concern he'd had for her earlier in the week when he caught her at the Bamboo Hut had just melted away. Who would've thought you could miss a sullen teenager this much?

As the kids continued to debate about the movie and mutants, Stallings couldn't get his conversation with the Daytona detective out of his head. He knew kids did stupid things during spring break, but no one should have to die for it. Maybe the same person was handing out too much Ecstasy. Maybe there was a connection between them. He had a lot of work to do to try and figure that out.

Stallings glanced up from his pizza, laughing absently at something one of the kids said; then he saw him in the front door. Instantly he recognized the older man, and it felt like a punch in the stomach. He couldn't take his eyes off his ruddy face and pitted nose. His face was more wrinkled, but still the same. His gauzy eyes scanned the small restaurant and fell on Stallings and the kids.

It was obvious the old man recognized him. He hesitated at the front door, and, like Stallings, appeared uncertain what to do. Would he simply turn and step back out onto the street? Would he stay and ignore them? The questions ran through Stallings's mind.

The old man started toward them. Stallings didn't know what to do. The kids didn't even notice him. It took about five seconds for the man to shuffle across the floor to their booth.

"Hello, Johnny."

The kids both looked up with no recognition whatsoever on their faces. There was an awkward silence as Stallings stared at the old man. The flood of feelings: fear, resentment, nausea, and even some love, kept him from saying anything at all. The old man stood there staring in awkward silence.

Stallings felt Lauren nudge him under the table. She'd never met the old man. And only caught the mildest of stories about him. Charlie had no clue at all. Finally, Stallings managed to nod a curt greeting.

The old man's eyes flicked to each child. He wiped his face with a shaking hand and finally said, "Maybe you should come by and say hello when you have time. I'm over near Market Street." He laid down a Post-it note with an address scribbled on it. "Bring these two with you if you think it's been long enough." With that, the old man turned quickly and with surprising speed shuffled out of the restaurant, onto the street, and out of sight.

Lauren said slowly, "Who was that?"

Stallings swallowed hard and said, "My father."

Thirty-one

It was late Sunday afternoon, and the sun reflected off the St. Johns River in the back of the Yvonne Zuni's parents' suburban Jacksonville house. Yvonne sat at the end of the long table with her three sisters on one side and their respective husbands on the other. Yvonne's father sat at the other end of the table, and her mother, as usual, scurried around with giant plates of food. Jerk chicken, black beans and rice, fried plantains, and a Caesar salad sat across the long table on the covered patio.

Yvonne had missed very few Sunday dinners with her family in the past seven years. She even had her own husband sit across from her for almost three years, but that was the past, and now she was the only Zuni girl who had no husband. But no one here judged her or treated her any differently. They loved her, and she loved them. They felt the sorrow she felt, and her mother had cried with her when her one-year-old son, Jason, had died from a rare blood disease he'd had since birth. Her sisters had felt the same anger that she had when her husband had sought to ease his own sorrow with another woman, or more accurately, with other women.

These dinners with the family helped her keep things in perspective and keep her mind off work, if only for a few hours. It was hard to keep a gung-ho detective off an investigation because of budget cutbacks. She didn't like sending Tony Mazzetti home, even on a Sunday, because there was no overtime. But it was tough being the boss. Anyone who had ever supervised people knew how hard the job was. That was the joke when she went to the one-week supervisory training at the sheriff's office. The instructors used to say, "Management is great. It's telling people what to do that sucks."

She'd be curious to see what progress her detectives had made on their investigations this week. Pride pushed Mazzetti to make sure every homicide was cleared, and conscience pushed Stallings to make sure he'd find an answer to Allie Marsh's death. But the sergeant knew she had to count on both of their partners to keep them from doing anything stupid. That was the way things worked in a police department.

Her father tapped her on the shoulder, and she looked over at his smiling face.

He said, with his quiet Trinidad accent, "So sweetheart, how's the new job in the detective bureau?"

She shook her head. "It seems like no matter what you do someone's not happy."

He laughed and said, "That's why I spent my life as a veterinarian with only family working at the practice. Your mom was the closest thing to a supervisor we ever had."

Hearing her dad say it made her realize she did have two families. But this one had much better food.

* * *

It had been a busy day for him—the workout, a good run, cleaning up his Jeep, visiting his sister and nephew. He spent over an hour at the grocery store buying organic and healthy food. As he pulled into the driveway of his apartment that sat behind the main house, he froze. A gray Mazda was parked directly in front of his carport.

He cautiously stepped out onto the weed-and-gravel driveway. He didn't bother to shut off the Jeep as his eyes scanned from one side of his apartment to another. Then he saw someone move inside the dark tinted Mazda. The gray car's door opened, and a thick female leg stepped out onto the gravel driveway. As the figure emerged from the car his stomach tightened.

All he could say was, "How did you know where I live?"

She smiled and brushed her blond hair from her face. "Why? Am I not supposed to know where you live?"

"No, I just don't remember giving you the address."

"Or your phone number, or any other important information. Am I supposed to wait for you to call me whenever you want to? I have rights too."

He leaned back into his car and shut off the engine. This had never happened to him before. None of his prey had ever figured out where his lair was. He'd intended to call Lisa tonight. Now he wasn't sure what to do. He looked around hoping no one had noticed her come to the house. He couldn't have any connection with her and didn't want her to be able to find him. This was freaking him out almost as bad as Holly and her crazy cult friends.

Lisa stepped away from her car and slammed the door. "Are you going to invite me inside?"

"You didn't answer my question. How did you find out where I live?"

She gave him a sly smile. "I followed you home from the club last night. I knew you were all alone, but I thought it would be better if I came by to see you today."

He walked toward her, and she rushed at him and wrapped her arms around him, kissing him hard on the lips. It wasn't the aggressive action that aroused him; it was the idea of what he could do to her. The power he had over her. She was a simple antelope, and all he had to do was use his powerful jaws on her neck and she would be his forever. Before he knew what he was doing, he said, "Let me grab the groceries from my car and we'll go inside."

This was dangerous territory. He wasn't sure he was in control of his own actions, and that's what could get him in trouble. It was nearly dark. His landlord, Lester, was away for the weekend, and the front house was empty. This might be the best opportunity he ever had to hunt in his home field.

Lisa felt a little like a detective. All she'd done was find her man and then follow him home last night. But she didn't think that it was right to scare him late at night, so she waited until this bright sunny afternoon. What man wouldn't want a booty call in the middle of a Sunday afternoon? She just hoped he wouldn't even mention her confrontation with the skinny little college bitch at the club the other night. There was no way she was going to let him just walk out of her life. She was so much better for him than that bitch Ann. She'd let too many men slip out of her life. Hahira, Georgia, had very few places to hide, but somehow men seemed to find them. But now she was older and wiser. There'd be no more incidents like Lucas. She had given everything to him and let him do anything he wanted to her, and then he just walked away. He found out it wasn't that easy to walk away, but he tried it anyway. She wasn't even sure she was done with Lucas yet. She'd thought about going up to Athens to see him at the University of Georgia. But right now all she wanted to focus on was her Jacksonville hunk. He had it all: looks, the moves, and the car. She even liked his little bungalow not far from the beach, where he wasn't living with his parents and it didn't look as if he had a wife lying around anywhere.

Now that she was older and wiser at twenty-two, she felt a certain satisfaction at finding him and forcing him to show her some attention. Those days of being shy and not aggressive enough were over now that she knew what she wanted and she was going after it. She'd earned it. Her daddy may not have ever noticed her no matter what she did. And her boyfriend had treated her like a big soft sex toy and then lost interest, but this time it would be different. She planned to go inside and make him a nice dinner and show him there was more to her than just a couple of available holes. Well, first she'd get his attention with her special female ways. Then she'd make him dinner and maybe even breakfast tomorrow morning.

This was so exciting she felt her crotch start to tingle.

Stallings didn't need additional complications in his life. The kids peppered him with a thousand questions about his father. They knew their grandfather was alive and that there had been a falling-out in the family. They saw their grandmother several times a week and loved their aunt who lived with them now. But somehow, no one had ever explained to them what had happened to Grandpa.

He struggled with how much to tell them. It was easier to leave most of it out. The beatings, the drunken rantings, the abuse, and Helen running away from it all. The fact that his children's grandfather was a mean drunk who lived in a boardinghouse in Jacksonville was one thing he really hadn't thought he'd ever have to tell them. But fate had decided that assessment was incorrect.

He decided to keep everything vague. He said that he and his father had had many disagreements and hadn't seen each other in years.

Charlie couldn't comprehend this and said, "Why?"

All Stallings could say was that for reasons he really didn't want go into right now, they had not spoken in years. He also said he was surprised to see his father today and hadn't known what to do. He apologized to the kids for not making it clearer that their grandfather lived relatively close by.

Maria was astonished when the kids told her excitedly about meeting their grandfather. She had some questions of her own.

Maria said, "How'd he look?"

Stallings shook his head, "I don't know. I guess he looked like an old man. He didn't seem pissed off at all, if that's what you mean. That's what threw me. The last time we spoke his face was all red and he was screaming at me. He just kinda looked tired. Somehow the word *resigned* comes to mind."

"Are you okay?"

"I wish I knew." He looked into Maria's clear, dark eyes. "I'm separated from my wife, overwhelmed at work, worried about my kids, and now the man that made my childhood a living hell shows up out of nowhere and says he'd like me to drop by sometime. You tell me, Maria, am I okay?"

They stared at each other in silence.

Inside the small apartment Lisa's eyes immediately fell on the large collage of beautiful blond girls on the wall.

"Are they your girlfriends?"

"What if I said yes?" The urge to act was overwhelming, but he didn't know what to do. No one had ever been inside his apartment before. Especially not an antelope like this. He felt sweat bead across his forehead. He had a slight tremor in his right hand. His eyes were glued on her long, beautiful blond hair falling across her tan, beefy shoulders. The sundress she wore showed off her curvy shape, but he couldn't get a sense of how she was feeling. He didn't know if she was pissed off, turned on, or just plain crazy. She'd gone to a lot of trouble to find him, and obviously had spent some time waiting for him. She knew way too much.

"Did you tell anyone you were coming over?"

"Why, are you married?"

He laughed and shook his head.

"Then why are you so secretive?"

"I like my privacy. Is that a crime?"

She slowly shook her head and said, "I guess not. I'm sorry—I didn't mean to be needy. I just felt like we'd made a connection on the dance floor the other night."

"We did. I mean, we have a connection." He stepped

closer, reached up, and caressed her pretty, sculpted cheekbones. "And I'd like to explore it more closely." He kissed her softly on the neck, lingering for a minute, letting his tongue make a little swirl. Then he stepped back and assessed her. "Does anyone know you're here?"

She shook her head, and said with a little laugh, "I try to keep my stalking quiet. My girlfriends think that I can be too aggressive sometimes. I hope that doesn't scare you." She reached behind her and undid the tie on her dress, then let it drop down her tan body to the hardwood floor. She pushed her panties down her legs, stepping on them with her left foot so she stood completely naked in front of him.

The blood seemed to race to both his brain and his dick at the same time. It made him a little unsteady on his feet. She stepped back toward the desk against the wall. The collage of photos was directly behind her. She sat on the desk, her legs spread, and pulled him toward her, embracing him with both her arms and legs. She reached up to give him a long, slow kiss. He responded without reservation and felt his body react.

She used her feet to tug off his shorts as he unbuttoned them and let them slide to the floor with her pile of clothes. He felt himself pulled toward her and hesitated.

"What's wrong? What is it?" She whispered into his ear.

"I need a condom."

"It's all right. I'm on the pill."

"I always practice safe sex." He stepped away from her and opened a small top drawer on the desk, scooting her legs gently out of the way. He looked down in the drawer and saw his pack of Durex condoms. He froze for a moment because next to the condoms was a long, sharpened letter opener. It looked sinister in this setting. He could imagine it plunging into her soft skin.

He really couldn't decide what he wanted to do more.

The more Lisa thought about it, the more she realized she could never tell her girlfriends exactly what she did. She'd make up some fabulous story about how he'd swept her off her feet. Somehow she was certain no matter how she told the story, the word "stalking" would never come up. A couple of girls had been with her through her restraining-order days and knew that she was prone to following guys a little closely, but she didn't want to have to tell them exactly how closely she'd followed this one. Even the word "stalking" made her sound creepy. She used to use it as sort of a joke and it would make people laugh, but afterward it always embarrassed her no matter how much attention it got her at a party.

But now she was pretty sure he noticed her as she sat up on the little table and spread her legs, guiding him inside her. A little attention, that's all she ever wanted. She wasn't crazy about the feel of the condom, and it was awkward helping him slide it on. She never made guys wear condoms. She was on the pill and stayed pretty clean even though she had to visit her doctor a couple times because of not using a condom. Actually, because of sleeping with a guy who had a venereal disease. She wished she hadn't known the doctor since she was a little girl, but he'd stuck to his oath and not told her mom about it. Both times.

She made her little passion face and let out a couple of moans now and then. She knew that's what men like. Every time she had sex, she thought about the very first time with Lucas by the little pond west of town. He was sixteen and she was seventeen, and he seemed as if he had such a little dick at the time. But she sure found ways to make him grow bigger. It wasn't till later that she learned that it wasn't really all that big in comparison to other guys. But Lucas with a sweet smile and blue eyes always made her a little sad. And every time she had sex she thought about him and sometimes almost cried. But this guy wasn't giving her time to cry. He was throwing it at her hard and heavy. It even felt kinda good knowing that a guy like him could focus so hard on nothing but her. He had his own passion face and let loose with some odd sounds like an animal. But somehow she liked it.

She wanted to keep this one and knew she had to show him a good time. A great time. She started wiggling her legs to make her butt jiggle on the little table. Even though she didn't like to feel a condom, she increased her grunts and moans and reached over and gently brought her fingernails along his back. Then she nuzzled his neck. Just a little nibble at first. He seemed to like it. It certainly made things more exciting for her, tasting the salt of his perspiration and feeling the muscles strain under her teeth and tongue. Then she decided to go a little further, and she bit him. She didn't bite really hard and was surprised when a little blood trickled out. But she wasn't sorry.

It sure seemed as if he was. He looked at her, shocked.

She didn't care; at least he was looking at her. He'd probably leave her soon anyway.

Thirty-two

John Stallings thought about how his father ambushed him in the restaurant and was curious what he had meant when he said to stop by and talk to him sometime. It was Sunday evening, and he'd wrestled with his emotions all afternoon. He went from angry that the old man thought he could just show back up in his life, to sad that he had lost so many years. But that didn't compare to the years he'd spent being scared of the tyrant and wishing someone else was raising him. Now he was just tired enough to confront the old man without fear of getting physical or even too vocal.

He was on North Liberty Street looking for the address his father had given him. It turned out to be a boardinghouse that had ten rooms for rent. It was west of the stadium where the Jacksonville Jaguars played in an odd part of town with houses, businesses, industrial buildings, and apartment buildings all mixed together. It was, in fact, the kind of area where he would've expected to find his father.

He parked in the front of the old two-story Spanish-style house, and paused after he got out of his car. He looked up at the mostly dark windows and tried to think of reasons to wait until tomorrow. Or next week. It'd been so long since he talked to the old man. So long since he even thought about him—or at least that's what he told himself—that he wondered if this was even worth the effort. There was also the issue of bothering the other residents. He eased up the uneven walkway toward the porch, which held an old couch and three unmatched chairs. As he was about to climb the four wooden stairs, the porch light came on and the front door started to open.

A heavyset elderly woman in a thick bathrobe leaned out of the door and said, "Who you looking for, officer?"

Stallings froze, looked at her in surprise, and said, "How did you know I was a cop?"

"Son, you run a place like this for long enough and you can spot a cop and a social worker from a mile away. Something tells me you're no social worker. Who you looking for?"

"James Stallings."

"Now, what did Jimmy do that would attract the attention of the police?"

Stallings was about to make up some story, something he would feel guilty about later. He didn't want to lie to an old lady. Then the woman clapped her hands and let out a short squeal of laughter.

"You're Johnny, his son, aren't you?"

Stallings had no idea his father had ever mentioned him to anyone.

The woman said, "You look just like your photo in the newspaper. Your father has made me read stories about you for hours on end. How're Lauren and Charlie doing?"

"They are, um, fine." He gazed at her for a moment while he gathered his thoughts. Then he said, "So·my dad is here?"

"Not right this second. I think he went down the street to help one of the boys who had too much to drink. He might be a while. He likes to avoid confrontation with the drunks and let them wear out before he drives them back here."

He wondered if somehow she had gotten his father confused with someone else.

He liked the feel of her strong legs wrapped around him. Even the short, awkward pause to slip on a condom had not ruined the moment. He was also glad Lester was not in the front house because, if nothing else, this chick was loud. It may have been just that her mouth was so close to his ear, as she screamed and grunted and squealed to every thrust that he made. This was almost as hard a workout as his run had been that morning.

Even as he grasped her and kissed her and felt himself deep inside her, his eyes kept looking down into the open drawer with the long, sharp letter opener. He could picture it in his hand, driving into her neck or her chest. The image of her shocked face while he was still inside her was thrilling. It was almost as if the letter opener had its own personality and was forcing him to pick it up and use it.

She started to kiss his neck, then nibble, until she finally bit him.

He jerked back. "What the fuck?" Reaching up with his right hand, he felt the blood running from his neck. He was bleeding. She was the prey. The prey didn't bite the predator. He looked at her face, a smear of blood above her upper lip, sweat running down her forehead, still swaying to every thrust he made. She liked it. So he pretended to like it too. He rubbed more blood off his neck and then smeared it across her breasts. She grinned, the light from outside making her teeth glow an eerie shade of white. He started to thrust harder and faster.

"Oh yes," she gasped, three times in a row.

Now all he could think about was the letter opener in the drawer. It screamed at him. It taunted him. His right hand slipped off the desk and into the drawer as Lisa continued to pull him tighter and tighter to her naked body.

But somewhere in his brain, a rational thought popped out. How would he ever clean up the mess made by a sharp implement stuck in this girl's throat? The blood and pieces of flesh. It was too much like leaving food around the house. It bothered him. He pulled his hand from the drawer and felt like he was about to come. He still wanted to be the hunter. He leaned back slightly, letting Lisa look up in his eyes. His left hand came up to caress her chin, and his right hand held the back of her head as he felt himself about to explode, his intensity pulling her along with him. She took quick, shallow breaths, trying to keep up with the energy she was expending.

He said in a soft voice, "Just relax. Let everything go for a moment." He felt her shoulders and neck relax, but her legs were still wrapped around him. He tightened his grip on her chin and her hair, then twisted his hands in opposite directions. He used all of his strength and leverage to make the motion quick, violent and exact. A crackling sound rippled up from her back and neck, and she went limp as he exploded inside her.

He was good for a few more thrusts as her legs slowly slipped off him and dangled from the desk. Even with the condom on, he could feel her warmth. She slumped against the wall, her head bumping the framed cork-board collage of all the other prey. He slipped out of her and let her slide right off the desk and onto the floor with a thump.

His skin tingled from the top of his head to the bottom of his feet. Stars appeared in front of his eyes as the room started to sway. He couldn't believe what he'd just done. It was so impulsive and unplanned. So unlike anything he'd ever done before. He'd had no idea it would even work. But now he'd claimed another victim in a new way, in his own house. This was too exciting.

He kneeled down next to her and carefully placed two fingers along her neck. He was shocked to feel a strong, steady pulse. He'd had no idea what damage he had caused, but it appeared that he had only knocked her unconscious. Perhaps breaking her neck or back, but not killing her. So he simply wrapped his big hand over her mouth and nose and clamped shut. There was no thrashing, no twitching, and there was no oxygen getting into her bloodstream.

A minute later he released his hand and checked her pulse again. Nothing. He'd brought down another antelope.

Thirty-three

Stallings had driven slowly down a couple of the streets with bars where all the rummies hung out. His father's landlady had told him more about his father in a few minutes than he'd learned on his own in almost a whole lifetime. Apparently the old man did keep track of his children and had some pride for his son's accomplishments. That was one of the reasons that Stallings was looking for him now in a bad part of town late on a Sunday night. It was close to the scene of the triple shooting that Tony Mazzetti and Christina Hogrebe had been working on. Anything could happen in this part of town.

He slowed the car several times thinking he'd seen his father, only to attract the attention of other older men wandering the streets. He pulled into the parking lot of a pool hall near the Expressway. As he was about to get out of his car a blue Mustang rumbled in right next to him. He noticed a younger man behind the wheel of the Mustang.

Stallings and the man both stepped out of their cars at the same time. They looked at each other, and each man held the other's gaze for just a moment. Immediately Stallings realized he knew this young man, but he couldn't think of his name or where he'd met him. Most experienced cops immediately ran through their arrest logs in their heads. The last thing anyone wanted to do was be surprised by a criminal who still held a grudge. This man didn't look anything like a criminal, and Stallings had the idea that he'd never arrested him.

While they were still staring at each other it hit Stallings where he knew this man from. He couldn't keep his eyes from widening as he blurted out, "You're Jason Ferrell."

Without hesitation, Ferrell slipped back into his car, cranked it, and was backing out of the lot before Stallings could react.

The thrill of Lisa's death had not worn off, but sitting naked on his hard, cold wooden floor, he turned his head, looked through his screen door, saw Lisa's Mazda in the driveway, and realized he had a problem. He'd never had to dispose of anything like a car before. He didn't know enough about forensics or crime scenes to eliminate all the evidence that could implicate him. All he knew was the TV show *CSI* was complete and total bullshit. He gazed down at Lisa's naked body. She looked as if she were sleeping. There was no blood, and in the dim light he couldn't tell if her neck had bruised at all. It didn't really matter. If he got caught with her in the car, lack of blood or bruising still would not explain what he was doing with a naked dead girl.

He thought back over his career and what he'd done to cover his tracks so successfully. In most cases he'd learned to just make the death look like something other than murder. Then he recalled New Orleans and the girl he'd dumped in the pond in Louis Armstrong Park. No one had ever found her, and little had ever really been written about her. As far as anyone knew she'd just disappeared. That was the next best thing to making the death appear to be an accident. Jacksonville was full of lakes and canals deep enough to cover the dinged-up gray Mazda in his driveway now.

Stallings wanted to grab Jason Ferrell, but he'd been so stunned at seeing the young man that he'd allowed him to get a big lead in his Mustang. He had no real reason to risk lives in a high-speed pursuit. Besides, he wasn't even certain which street the young chemist had driven down. There was no question that Ferrell didn't want to be found.

Stallings drove the streets in a rundown area west of the river and stadium not only looking for Ferrell and his father but thinking about what he needed to do to get this case rolling.

As much as he wanted to talk to his father tonight, finding out who gave Allie Marsh the Ecstasy and was responsible for her death was more important. He felt that if he could clear this up then maybe he could focus on his own family problems.

After an hour of aimless driving and feeling the exhaustion sweep through his body, Stallings finally decided to head home.

He'd spent more than an hour checking out several bodies of water he'd found on Google Earth. The detailed satellite images had not shown certain trees, curbs, and other impediments to driving a car directly into the water.

Lisa was still naked and curled up in the trunk of the little Mazda. There was very little traffic on the road at this time of the night. He had yet to see any police cruisers and didn't think he would draw much attention in the plain car as long as he didn't venture into some of the areas known for selling crack.

Two of the parks that had decent bodies of water also had signs that said they closed at sunset when the gates were locked. One of the canals that he wanted to use had a very steep embankment, and he wasn't sure he could get the car into the water by himself. Now he was at the edge of a park near an offshoot of the St. Johns River. He had a simple plan. There was a seawall here, and he knew the water immediately dropped down to at least twenty feet. He was going to shove the car off the side of the seawall and hope the murky water kept it hidden for a good, long time.

There was no moon, and the little bit of light from the city cast a haze over the open fields of the park and the trees surrounding it. He positioned the car near the seawall and was getting ready to push it when he heard a noise and noticed a funny odor. It only took a second for him to realize it was marijuana. He spun quickly toward the swing sets on one side. There, in the dim light, he saw a figure swaying slowly on one of the swings.

He called out, "Who's there?"

"No one here but a fellow criminal." The figure stood from the swing and walked slowly toward him. When the man had gotten within a few feet he stopped and said, "The government says I'm a criminal because I smoke weed. Why are you out here in the middle of the night about to push your car into the water?"

He didn't know what to do. He wanted to reach back into the car and find something sharp to ram into this young man's head. This was exactly what he didn't need. A witness. His options ran through his head. But he didn't answer the young man's question.

The young man took another toke off a small roach, held the smoke in his lungs, then, in a long exhalation, looked up as the cloud of smoke drifted away. He said, "Insurance?"

He just stared at the young man. "What?"

"You got to get rid of the car for insurance money?"

It took a second; then he realized what the young man was saying. "You got me. I can't afford the repairs on this old piece a shit. Do you mind giving me a hand?"

Without another word the young man stepped to the rear of the Mazda and shoved until the car tipped over the side of the seawall and flipped, roof first, into the water. It drifted away from the wall for several seconds and then after several loud bubbles, dropped beneath the surface. He couldn't have planned it any better.

He turned toward the young stoner. "Thanks, dude."

"No sweat. Now what are you gonna give me to keep quiet?"

He made a quick assessment of how hard it would be to kill the stoner with nothing but his bare hands.

Thirty-four

Tony Mazzetti felt a little embarrassed creeping out of Patty's condo before the sun came up. But she was sleeping so soundly, that cute little combination of a snore and a wheeze keeping a steady rhythm, and he didn't want to wake her up. He had a ton to do, and it was technically Monday morning even if it was only four hours into it.

This time of night it was only a ten-minute ride to his house on the river. But he couldn't resist swinging past the stadium toward North Market Street to see if there was any activity around the house where the triple murder had occurred. It wasn't like he was scratching for overtime. It was just an impulse to see if anything popped up at him. It was a little out of the way, but he couldn't stop himself.

There was still crime scene tape draped across the porch of the empty house. The state's attorney had used witness protection money to move the three residents from the house to a hotel on the other side of town. Only one of the residents had seen anything at all, and her story had changed a couple of times. Typical. Even though they weren't helping the case, they were still witnesses to a crime, and it appeared to have some elements related to gang activity. That was enough for the state's attorney to spring for a safe place to sleep.

The house was dark and silent, not a soul on the street, and only a few houses had lights on. He turned the corner and saw the mysterious Miss Brison's house. There were no lights on there either. A dark blue Mustang was parked on the street between Miss Brison's house and the rundown apartment building next door. He wondered briefly whom the Mustang belonged to but realized he needed to get home and grab another couple of hours of sleep and then hit this case hard in the morning.

The stoner's face was a little clearer in the single beam of light that came from across the water. "I asked you how you were gonna pay me to keep me quiet?" His voice cracked a little.

He kept his anger in check as he considered twisting this boy's neck just like he had Lisa's. The stoner was in his late teens, tall and skeletal, with long, greasy brown hair. On first blush, he doubted anyone would miss the youth if he were to disappear. He patted the pockets of his cargo pants as if he was looking for his wallet. He was really just buying time before he decided on a course of action.

Then he felt something in his pocket that just might save this boy's life. He reached deep into the left-side cargo pocket and pulled out a green plastic container. He held it up next to his face, smiled, and shook it.

The stoner said, "What's that?"

"Something a man like you might appreciate."

"I'm listening."

"Ecstasy hits."

"How many?"

"About twenty." Even in the dim light he could see a broad smile spread across the boy's acne-scarred face.

"I could get laid almost every night for a month with that."

"Then we have a deal?"

"Just for helping you push the car in the water?"

"And I need a ride."

Twenty minutes later he hopped out of the stoner's battered Saturn. He couldn't risk going to his regular apartment so he had the young man drive to Cleveland Street near his sister's house. He didn't think it really mattered as high as the guy was. And the stoner seemed excited about finding a girl to share the Ecstasy with as fast as possible. He made it a point not to say much on the ride home. There was nothing really to worry about unless the car was found by some stroke of luck. Even if it was, the stoner would have to remember the evening and some details. He doubted that was possible.

It was about five o'clock when he slipped his spare key into the front door and padded through the house to the back bedroom. He popped his head in to check on his nephew, who snored softly on the small bed built in a race car kit. Shaking his head he backed out of the boy's bedroom and walked down the hall and into his own room. He hoped no one would wake him up too early this morning.

As soon as he hit the bed his mind drifted back to the feeling of Lisa wrapping her legs around him and her neck cracking in his hands. He didn't think he could ever fall asleep with such an intense erection.

Patty Levine looked across at her partner in the bright lights of the plush office of the small pharmaceutical company where Chad Palmer worked. She said, "You're dressed awfully sharp today in that nice shirt and tie."

"You dress for the job you're doing."

He seemed distant, not his usual laid-back self. She couldn't put her finger on it, and it bothered her. Patty said, "You look tired. Everything go all right with the kids yesterday?"

"The kids weren't the problem."

Patty nodded, saying, "I can't believe you found Jason Ferrell so late. What were you doing near Market Street in the middle of the night?"

"It's a long story. I'll tell you about it later." He glanced down the hallway. "Here comes our man."

She saw a tall, impressive man in an expensive Brooks Brothers suit. She'd seen his photo from the driver's license database. He reeked of self-confidence. A graduate of the University of Florida School of Business, Palmer was the senior sales rep for a company that sold pharmaceuticals from six different manufacturers. As he came closer, he also reminded her of Gary Lauer. That same sort of swagger and belief that women found him irresistible. His precise haircut, manicured nails, white teeth, and fake smile made him the perfect lounge lizard.

They had already spoken to the receptionist, so he knew who they were. The real question was did he know why? His first interaction would tell them a lot.

He stopped right in front of them, raised his hands, and said, "You got the wrong man, officers." Then laughed at his little joke.

Patty and Stallings introduced themselves and showed their IDs so there was no mistake they were here on official business.

Palmer said, "My sister said you'd been by her house. I knew we'd run into each other today if it was that important. I must confess that I am curious what this is all about."

Patty held up a photo of Allie Marsh and said, "Do you recognize this girl?"

Palmer showed no emotion as he studied the photograph, then finally said, "She looks familiar. But I have to confess I meet a whole lot of women."

Just the comment and the way he grinned reminded Patty of Gary Lauer again.

Palmer looked at Stallings and said, "Why, is there a problem?"

Stallings simply said, "She's dead." His tone and manner left little doubt who he thought was responsible.

Palmer still didn't react.

Patty did the follow-up. "Is there anything you'd like to tell us?" It was an old detective trick, but sometimes it worked. This guy obviously wasn't used to criminal investigations. He might start to blab without thinking.

Instead Palmer calmly said, "Do I need to contact my attorney?"

Thirty-five

Stallings plopped into his office chair. He'd evaded most of Patty's questions about his personal life on the short ride back to the PMB. The interview had been a bust; at least if they were looking for a confession, it was a bust. But it was never that easy in cases like this. Especially with smart, rich guys who knew the threat of an attorney would shut most cops down.

Patty slid over from her desk. "Why were you so rough on Palmer? He's a suspect, just like Lauer. I don't see a big difference between the two except Palmer is a little more polished."

"Lauer is a cop."

"He's still an asshole, just like Palmer."

The pharmaceutical rep had loosened up and not called his attorney. He admitted that he liked to hang out at dance clubs and he flirted with a lot of women. It was as if he had practiced the word "flirt" and never used any other phrase. The shocked expression on his face seemed almost genuine when Stallings asked him about giving X to any of the girls.

Stallings said, "I'm trying to be objective with all the

suspects. But Palmer's whole career won't be marred by rumors and innuendo just because we talked to him. Lauer doesn't have that same luxury. I want to believe that a guy who worked hard to get through the police academy wouldn't do something like this."

Patty was about to say something else when Stallings picked up an envelope that had been sent by overnight mail. He didn't even check the return address as he ripped it open to pull out several photographs and reports from the Daytona Beach Police Department.

Patty said, "Who are they?"

"Daytona's spring break deaths last year."

"Are there any dark-haired girls that go on spring break anymore? Those three look just like the two we have."

"You know what else is interesting?"

"What's that?" Patty said as she pulled the photos from Stallings's hand and eyeballed them.

"All three of these girls had Ecstasy in their systems too."

Patty said, "I hope this is just a coincidence."

"Me too. But we better show these to the sarge just in case." Stallings had an uneasy feeling he'd stumbled onto something he didn't want to consider.

Sergeant Yvonne Zuni sat in her office in the back of the Land That Time Forgot. She still hadn't had time to hang some photos and certificates. Her favorite photo showed the governor handing her a medal for stopping a bank robbery in downtown Jacksonville. She'd been a little embarrassed by the accolades because all she'd been doing was cashing her check at lunchtime when a man walked up next to her and stuck a gun in the teller's face. She simply stepped back to her left and pulled her Glock from her purse, stuck it in the man's ear, and said, "Police, don't move."

The newspapers had said that her quick action had saved countless lives. In reality the robber's gun was a C02 pellet pistol that wasn't even loaded. The captain of narcotics, the unit she worked in at the time, told her if she tried to correct anyone who said she was a hero he'd make sure he loaded his real pistol before he dealt with her. His rationale was narcotics agents get no credit for most of the hard work they do and that she, and the unit, would benefit from some positive media attention.

Now she was going over some schedules and overtime budgets, figuring out which cases merited closer investigation and which cases needed to be pushed to the side. She'd been in the office since seven and hadn't stopped staring at either a computer screen or paperwork in the three and half hours since. God did she miss working the streets.

A gentle rap on her open door frame made her look up to see Patty Levine and John Stallings standing there.

She said, "Whatcha got?"

Patty stepped in, laying three photographs on her desk. "These are the spring break deaths from Daytona last year."

She studied the three pretty blond girls and said, "So?"

Patty said, "All three of them had X in their system."

The sergeant said, "There could be a connection, but it seems like a real long shot to me. Still, we might want to figure out where the suspects were during spring break last year."

Now Stallings said, "Already working on it. We have a subpoena for Chad Palmer's credit card records. I'm headed down to personnel to check on when Lauer took vacations over the last couple of years."

The sergeant nodded, appreciating self-starters like this. A motivated detective could get a lot done, even in times of cutbacks like this. She noticed how tired Stallings looked even after the day off and wondered if his home life had taken an even worse turn. After only a week in the unit, Yvonne wasn't sure it was her place to ask him any questions as long as the work was getting done, but that didn't mean she wasn't concerned. Instead the sergeant looked up at them. She handed back the photos and said, "You two really don't need much supervision, do you?"

She appreciated the smiles she got back from both the detectives.

It was almost eleven o'clock when he woke up, and he still felt a little tired. He got out of bed, washed his face, slipped on the same clothes he wore the night before, and ventured out to the kitchen. A note on the refrigerator said his sister had taken his nephew to the doctor and would be back around one.

He didn't mind a little quiet time in the empty house. It gave him a chance to reflect on his wild night. He had lingering images of Lisa wrapping her legs around him, lying still on his floor, curled up in the back of the Mazda, and the stoner helping him push the car into the water. It made for an interesting life. And he still had time left to hunt.

He'd find a way to casually run into Ann and start

back on his slow, methodical stalking. Surprises were great, but the idea of circling the prey gave him something to look forward to.

He had the stoner's name and had managed to copy down his license plate in case he needed to deal with him at a future date. He knew the stoner was a regular at some of the clubs that hosted the spring breakers, lived at home with his parents, and worked at Wendy's.

But paying off the young man had virtually depleted his Ecstasy supply. So it was convenient that he found himself at this house. He was careful never to leave anything at his little apartment at the beach. He didn't know if his landlord, Lester, ever peeked in the apartment. Since he had one room to himself here, he made use of the closet and had it packed with his stuff. Wedged up in the corner, up high where his nephew couldn't reach it, was a Tupperware container that held his Ecstasy and a few other pills he'd acquired. He stood up on a stool and reached way back into the crowded closet and found the plastic container behind a bag of old T-shirts. He sat back on the bed and opened the container. He only had two Ecstasy tablets left.

That meant he'd have to visit his Ecstasy source very soon.

Tony Mazzetti had two anonymous tipsters that said the triple shooting he was investigating was done by a rival gang that sold meth on the outskirts of Jacksonville. The shooters were not only a gang, they were a white supremacist group called the Hess Party. The fact that someone called them something other than a street gang and associated them with a fringe group like racists meant that a special unit in the sheriff's office probably had been keeping tabs on them over the years.

Now Mazzetti found himself in the third floor office of the intel unit, better known as the "rubber gun squad." Members of the rubber gun squad didn't have to make arrests or go to court to prove that they were working. They collected information on groups that most cops had no idea even existed. From radical Muslims who attended mosques in the area, to the few members of the Klan who rambled through North Florida, the intel squad knew what they were doing and what they intended to do. Groups like that always had informants moving in and out. They found that out the hard way about ten years ago, when it was discovered that sixteen of the eighteen attendees of a Klan rally were all informants of various state, federal, or local police agencies.

Mazzetti looked across the table at the stern and serious face of Lonnie Freed, a detective for the last nine years in the rubber gun squad. Mazzetti and Freed had worked as road patrolmen soon after he graduated from the academy. Freed had been wound too tight for the road, going by the book on every possible infraction. A ticket for speeding had to have an extra sheet just for his narrative details. He drove sergeants crazy with probable-cause affidavits that were six pages long. But he found a home here in intel, where they honored straitlaced, hardworking, meticulous cops who viewed every group from the B'nai Brith to the Taliban as a dangerous threat to U.S. national security.

Mazzetti said, "What about this Hess Party?"

The thin detective with the thick glasses spoke in a fast, clear tone. "The Hess Party is named after Rudolf Hess, the deputy Führer under Hitler who fled to

England during the war. He was also the last prisoner of Spandau Prison. He died at ninety-three in 1987. Hess was considered—"

Mazzetti had to cut him off. "Come on, Lonnie, get to the fucking point. Do you think these assholes that live right here in South Jacksonville are good for the shooting?"

Lonnie nodded his head. "Oh yeah, they're badasses. They're not even true racists. They use it as a marketing tool to scare people so they can sell more meth and make money."

"Why would they shoot up a drug house on Market Street?"

"Like I said, they're not crazy—it's got to be a business matter. Maybe the Street Cred boys were trying to move in on the meth field. Or maybe they just owed them money. The Hess Party is not the kind of group to shoot someone just for running their mouths."

"Would they be smart enough to use a spy shacked up across the street?"

"Why do you ask?"

"Because there was a white dude in the house across the street. But when I tried to talk to him he gave me the slip."

"I hope they're not that sophisticated."

Then Mazzetti remembered the speckled pill marked *J2A* that he'd taken from the house and left on his desk. "Does the Hess Party ever deal in X?"

"Not that I've ever heard of."

"Thanks, Lonnie, you were just as helpful as you used to be on the road."

The intel detective grinned and said, "Sure, anytime, Tony."

Mazzetti thought, *What a dweeb.*

* * *

It had taken Stallings fifteen minutes to convince Patty to take the evening off and have dinner with Tony Mazzetti. It wasn't that he didn't want her with him, but he didn't want her to screw up her life like he already done to his own. Although having dinner with Tony Mazzetti seemed like a mistake in itself.

Stallings decided to go by the Wildside and see if Larry, the bartender, had any new information for him. He found the athletic bartender at the far end of the club, at a secondary bar that seemed to be more for VIPs than the general crowd. For a Monday night the place was on the loud side with groups of young college girls and hungry-looking fraternity nerds setting up camps at various places around the dance floor.

Larry gave him a broad smile and said, "Hello, Detective. What brings you around here?"

"Just wondering if anything was new on your end."

The bartender shook his head. "I haven't seen Donnie Eliot in here since last week."

"He's still in the can."

"No shit? What for?"

"Possession."

"So you don't think he's the one that gave a girl the X?"

"No, it doesn't look like it. What about the other guys in the videos? Have you seen either of them?"

Larry shook his head. He reached in his shirt pocket and pulled out Stallings's business card. "I told you I'd call if I saw them. The one cop hasn't been back in here. Neither has the guy who gave me a big tip. I'd know them if I saw them again."

"You guys been busy?"

"Spring break is winding down. About half the schools

are back in session—that means about half our bartenders are gonna be laid off soon."

"You won't be asked to leave, will you? You've been here quite a while, right?" Stallings had noticed the other bartenders and staff all had T-shirts with the Wildside logo on them, but Larry wore a white, oxford button-down shirt. There were no logos, nothing to indicate he worked at the bar, and it had a collar.

"I work here in the season and then float around from time to time, but I think it's gonna be my choice."

Stallings said, "So you'll still call me if you see any of the guys I've been looking for?"

Larry absently filled a glass from the Diet Coke fountain spigot and handed it to a busty waitress, who didn't even notice Stallings. Larry looked behind Stallings, smiled, and said, "It looks like someone wants to talk to you."

Stallings turned around, and for the first time in quite a while was truly surprised.

The voice said, "I bet we're here for the same reason."

Stallings's stomach did a little flip.

Thirty-six

It was a little after six in the evening when Yvonne Zuni walked out the front door of the Police Memorial Building. She wanted to make it to the gym and then by her sister's house before she even could think about eating. Her usual fast gait carried her through the lobby and down the stairs quickly until she heard some-one call out, "Hey, Vonnie." She turned to see who was calling her by her nickname. There was no one by the front door except one young man in jeans and a casual pullover. She paused for a second, then realized who stood there.

"Look what the cat dragged in," she said as Gary Lauer stepped from the shadow of the pillar and walked toward her.

He smiled that charming smile of his and said, "Still the last one out of the bureau every night, huh?"

"There's always plenty going on, and a good sergeant has to be on top of everything." She checked him out from his perfect haircut, perfect ass, and perfect legs to his beat-up Top-Siders. She paused for just a second at the scar through his left eyebrow and leveled a flat stare at him. "What do you want, Gary?"

"I wanted to tell you that I know your man Stallings has been looking through my records."

"All part of an official investigation."

"I never had any doubt that you were all business. I just wanted to tell you I never gave a girl any kind of drug and I don't know why you guys are even looking at me. I think it's because your detectives think I have some kind of negative attitude about chicks. I haven't broken any laws."

Yvonne started to turn away, saying, "If you did nothing wrong, then you have nothing to worry about."

"I've heard that one before, and we both know how that turned out. I'm just asking you as a friend to give me some consideration."

"First of all, this is Stallings's case and I'm letting him run with it, and second of all, we're not friends." She bumped open the door and headed to the gym.

It had only taken Stallings a few seconds to regain his composure and know enough to get Diane Marsh out of the last place her daughter had been seen alive. Now a few blocks away at a little mom-and-pop coffee shop, they sat across a small table as she sipped the huge latte, then dabbed her eyes with a tissue. In jeans and a casual top she didn't seem as formal or intimidating as she had at the sheriff's office. She also looked too young to have college-age kids. Her blond hair spread over her shoulders, and her blue eyes gazed at Stallings through intermittent tears.

She said, "I've gone into the Wildside a couple of times since we found Allie's body. I really couldn't tell you why I've gone in there other than to find some kind of connection with Allie. We lost our connection a long time ago. She was a good girl. I knew what she was up to most of the time. But we hadn't been close like we had been most of her life. I think any parent would do anything they had to do to establish that connection with their child. You know I mean?"

Stallings nodded. Words couldn't express how much he understood what she was talking about.

Diane Marsh said, "My husband and I are not close. The boys always seemed to gravitate toward him. Going out on the boat, camping, all the sports that men like to play. But Allie was mine. Since she'd been at Southern Miss, we drifted apart. Nothing blatant or overt. No big fights or drama. We just hadn't talked like we used to. And it took her disappearance to make me realize it." She put both elbows on the small table and started to cry with her hands over her face.

Stallings let her go for as long as she wanted. He reflected on his own life and the connection he'd lost with Jeanie. There had been fights and drama before she disappeared. And a lot since she disappeared. But he missed interaction with his oldest daughter. Missed her more than he could express. He wished he could talk about it as Diane Marsh talked about her own anguish right now. Maybe that would've made things easier on Maria and the kids. Maybe he'd even still be at home if he'd talked about things instead of burying himself in work.

Finally, Diane Marsh looked up, her eyes ringed in red, and said, "Have you ever known any parent that didn't search for some way to connect with her kid?"

Stallings thought about his own father and remembered, just barely, how they would play catch in the tiny front yard of the Jacksonville home. It was a memory he hadn't recalled in decades. His father coaching and encouraging him with every toss. Telling the young boy he had a gift and he'd be able to do anything he wanted with it.

Stallings shook his head, saying, "No, I really can't think of a parent that didn't want to connect with their kid."

Patty Levine had told Stallings she was going to have dinner with Tony Mazzetti tonight. The only reason she said that was because Stallings insisted that she not go with him to the Wildside. He used some bullshit excuse that he didn't want her to make the same mistakes in her personal life that he'd made in his. But Tony was busy on his own triple homicide and she knew there was a lot to do on their case, so she had gone for a run earlier in the afternoon than usual, then cleaned up and come back to the office just after seven.

There was a lot more to this case than anyone wanted to admit. On one hand, if a cop like Gary Lauer had handed out Ecstasy, there was a huge problem. On the other hand, if someone else was systematically handing out Ecstasy to spring breakers, that was another huge problem. This was not a simple case of a girl who overdosed on drugs. The case may have initially gotten so much of their attention because the family was wealthy and the mother insistent, but now there were other elements that overshadowed all that.

Now Patty had records in front of her, solid evidence of the suspect's activity. It was the sort of thing that she was good at, and everyone knew it. Some detectives interviewed endless numbers of suspects. Some detectives sat on surveillance for days on end. Some detectives were so lucky that they just rode whatever lead came along. But Patty Levine was meticulous and had the sharpest memory of any detective in the unit. She remembered names and dates from cases that were long closed. She could make sense of bank records, phone calls, class rolls, and even convoluted Jacksonville Sheriff's Office personnel records.

She had two piles of records in front of her right now. One of the stacks contained American Express records she had subpoenaed for Chad Palmer. The other, copies of everything from Gary Lauer's JSO personnel file including assignments, complaints, and vacations.

The personnel records were easy to get once they had classified Lauer as a "person of interest." At Stallings's request, they had not called in Internal Affairs. Stallings said it was because he didn't want to ruin Lauer's career if there was nothing to the allegation. But Patty knew it had just as much to do with Stallings's dislike for Ronald Bell, one of the chief investigators in IA.

Usually subpoenas for financial records took weeks or even months to arrive. But as usual, Stallings knew someone, and now she had eight inches of detailed American Express records in only two days.

The office was empty and quiet, but she was far from lonely. This was exactly the kind of police work she enjoyed, and this was exactly the kind the case that she wanted solved.

She got to work.

*   *   *

John Stallings sat in his issued Impala watching the dark rooming house west of the stadium. He'd been there about an hour and hoped he might see his father stroll in or out of the two-story house. There had been almost no traffic on the street since he arrived, and only two lights in the house had been on.

He couldn't explain what had driven him to come all the way over here after speaking with Diane Marsh, but it was an urge he couldn't resist. Maybe somewhere in the back of his head, he hoped that there was a connection strong enough between him and his father to create an opportunity.

He had always liked the solitude of surveillance in his county car. That's what this felt like. Waiting quietly, watching the door to a house. It used to make him anxious because it meant he didn't know when he was getting home to his family. But now they didn't seem to need him nearly as much, and on surveillance he felt needed. He also knew that they were going to have to get much more active on this case. Talking with Diane Marsh had intensified his fire to resolve the case. And that could mean long hours of surveillance.

He waited until just after three. He never saw his dad that night.

He liked the atmosphere of this club on the southeastern side of the city, near the University of North Florida. He could appreciate how hard it was to maintain the beach theme in a dingy little warehouse ten miles from the ocean with the interstate virtually overhead. The staff was very professional as well.

He had already danced once with Ann, but he didn't want to be seen with her too much because she had four friends in the club. It would've been easy to ask her to leave with him, and he thought she'd say yes. But he couldn't risk being identified later. So the stalking of his cute little antelope would continue, and he didn't mind that one bit.

He sat at the end of the bar and sipped a beer as he watched Ann and her friends laugh around the high top near the dance floor. It was an odd position to be in because she knew he was interested in her and she had made it clear she was interested in him, but he couldn't make a move right now. He couldn't even hang out chatting with her and her friends. It was too big of a risk.

These were all tactics he'd developed over the last few years. Two years ago, in Panama City, he'd been questioned by a detective who was looking into the suicide of a coed. It was a very informal and casual interview, but the reason they even knew to talk to him was because he had spent too much time with her in public the night before. When they had sneaked out onto the roof of the nine-story hotel, using an old maintenance ladder that hung down near the window of the girl's hotel room, he knew exactly how things would end up. The one hit of Ecstasy had loosened her up, but she'd refused to take off her pants. It didn't really bother him as he watched her blond head bob up and down on him. When she was finished she tried to kiss him, but he fended her off, as most men would. She had started to get a little loud when he eased her to the side of the building and then, without any warning, said, "I wonder if that X can make you fly?" And shoved her off, watching her float for just a second, then plummet like an iron pole, falling straight through the roof of a Suburban parked below.

He told the detective that while he was dancing with

her she seemed perfectly all right. He didn't know where she had gone when she left the club. But if he'd been smart no one would've known to look for him in the first place. And now he put those kind of lessons to use.

A scruffy-looking kid with a hint of a beard shuffled over and asked her to dance. This was the perfect time to slip out the door. Next time he saw her, he'd make his move.

Thirty-seven

John Stallings walked into the Land That Time Forgot at eight o'clock sharp. The first thing he noticed were two large dry-erase boards covered with figures and dates behind Patty Levine's desk. He stopped and stared at the incomprehensible data, then looked down at Patty, who was examining a credit card statement with great care.

"Somebody's been a busy beaver."

"Because somebody didn't want me to come with him to the Wildside last night."

"I thought you were gonna have dinner with Tony."

"In case you hadn't noticed, Tony has his own case to worry about. I just had some free time and knew this had to be done. What'd you find out at the Wildside?"

From across the squad bay, Yvonne Zuni said, "Why don't you both come fill me in on what you've been doing?"

The sergeant started with her own bombshell. "Guess who pulled me aside last night?"

Neither detective answered.

"Gary Lauer tried to convince me he had done nothing wrong and that we were harassing him for no reason."

Patty said, "He really said there was no reason?"

The sergeant smiled and said, "Actually he said the only reason you were harassing him was because you didn't like his attitude toward women."

Patty didn't say anything.

The sergeant said, "He does have a shitty attitude toward women. I've seen it firsthand. Where are we on this thing? Is there a connection to Daytona or any other town? I want to know if this is this a real homicide investigation or a narcotics investigation."

Stallings cleared his throat and said, "I spoke with Diane Marsh last night."

"Where did you see her?"

"I went by the Wildside to talk to the bartender there. She's been going in as a way to find a connection between her and Allie. It was just chance that I saw her."

"Did she add anything to the investigation?"

"No, but she didn't screw anything up either."

The sergeant moved her dark eyes over to Patty and without saying a word was able to convey that she wanted to hear what Patty had turned up.

Patty said, "The drummer, Donnie Eliot, was in rehab last year during spring break. He gave his counselor in Delray Beach permission to speak to me. That doesn't eliminate him from suspicion in the Allie Marsh case but clears him in any Daytona cases that could be connected."

"Have you looked at Lauer and the other suspect's travel yet?"

"Palmer's credit card receipts show him all over the state all the time. I have five different days where he made purchases in Daytona in March and April of last year."

"What do you have on Gary Lauer?"

"Lauer's personnel records show he took vacation last year for three weeks in March. The year before that he took two weeks in March. But of course there's no way to tell where he went while he was on leave."

Stallings said, "I'm afraid if we approach him, he might be smart enough to get an attorney. He'd connect the two investigations in a heartbeat."

Yvonne Zuni let a sly smile spread across her pretty face. "I think I have a way to figure out where Gary Lauer was during vacation the last couple of years."

Tony Mazzetti sat at his desk considering all the leads to his triple homicide that had turned into dead ends. He held the little speckled tablet with the *J2A* marking that he'd taken from Miss Brison's house. The spacey bitch was the only open avenue he had right now. He really wanted to talk to the white guy who'd given him the slip the night of the shooting. He'd done a full background on Miss Brison and discovered her first name was Marie, she apparently owned the house near Market Street, there was no record of her employment in the wage-and-hour database, and her only arrest had been six years ago at the age of twenty for shoplifting. He wondered how she made a living but decided she probably didn't need much money for a month-to-month existence in that neighborhood.

Christina Hogrebe had been nearly as frustrated as

he was with a lack of witnesses from the area. She was now running backgrounds on some of the Hess Party's miscreant turds.

Patty Levine startled him as she popped up out of nowhere. Instinctively he hid the speckled tablet in the palm of his hand. She didn't appreciate his lax evidence-handling methods, and he didn't feel like a lecture right now.

"Whatcha doin'?" asked Patty.

"Looking for witnesses."

"How can you do that sitting in the office?"

He turned his head to look up into her pretty face. "Did Stall send you over here to break my balls?"

She smiled. "No, I can do that all on my own."

He grunted a short laugh and said, "How are you guys doing on the overdose case?"

"It's slow. Stall doesn't want to admit that a cop could be involved."

"Who would?"

"I hadn't thought of it that way. I just hate Lauer's attitude so much, I didn't see the bigger picture."

Tony said, "It happens to us all sometime."

"I always try to be a check and balance to John on any cases involving young women. He can get tunnel vision."

"He does get focused on crimes against young women."

"Can you blame him?"

He shook his head, glanced around the room quickly, twisted, and gave Patty a quick peck on the cheek.

Patty returned a quick hug and then lingered, pinching his midsection, saying, "You're getting a little pudgy there, Detective." She winked and was on her way.

Mazzetti poked at his stomach with his index finger

and realized he had not been hitting the gym as he usually did because his hours had been all screwy. Then he stopped at that thought and realized there was someone worth talking to from the Market Street neighborhood: Pudge, the street prophet. He grabbed his Windbreaker and rushed out the door.

John Stallings had contacts with virtually every missing persons detective in the Southeastern United States. One call to the Panama City Police Department got him the best man to answer the sensitive questions that had come up in the case.

After one ring a cheerful voice came on. "Doug McKay, Missing Persons."

"Well, Detective McKay, you sound awfully chipper for the end of spring break. This is John Stallings over at JSO."

"Stall, how goes it in the rectum of the state?"

Stallings had to give the detective a minute to chuckle at his own joke. "You know we're developing a little bit of a spring break crowd too."

"In Jacksonville? Why?"

"Very funny. Are you done yet?"

"Seriously, is it a lot cheaper to stay over there now? Because on my last visit it seemed like the hotels were expensive, it rained all the time, and your beach communities weren't set up to handle big spring break crowds."

"You know how it is, Doug—our city commission is looking for their share of tourist dollars."

"Sometimes I wonder if the money these kids bring in is worth the hassle. You get a group of flat breakers in here and they cram six into one room, each eat one giant meal at Golden Corral, and buy two beers at night. By my calculations that's about fifteen bucks a day into the local economy. I don't think they're worth the trouble."

"You sound like you're a little tired of the spring break crowd."

"That's like saying black people are little tired of the Klan. I wish they'd just wipe out the whole idea of a vacation in the middle of the semester."

"Are you guys at least making a little overtime?" Stallings knew by the silence it was time to push on. "For a change this isn't about Jeanie or any of my personal problems. I was just wondering how closely you guys watched drug use during spring break."

"Hell, Stall, I watch it all the time. I watch it on the beach, I watch it at the clubs, and I even have to watch it at the movie theater with my kids sometimes. Watching it is no problem. Being able to do something about it in times like this is what is hard."

"Do you have a lot of overdoses?"

"Not many, that's why it's not a priority for us to stop the drug use. I think we had one heroin overdose this year and one cocaine overdose last year. We also had a drowning this year, but drugs weren't a factor. The boy was from Kansas State, and I guess there's no reason to learn how to swim out there."

"Any Ecstasy overdoses that were deaths?"

There was silence on the line for a moment, and then detective McKay said, "Now that you mention it, not for a couple years. Two years ago we had two dead girls with Ecstasy in their system, but they weren't overdoses. One was a hit-and-run and the other was a suicide. She jumped off the top of one of the beach hotels and caused quite a ruckus when she destroyed some rap star's tricked-out Suburban."

"Can I ask a weird question, John?"

"Fire away."

"Were both of your deaths two years ago blond girls?"

After a brief pause the detective said, "As a matter of fact they were. How'd you know that?"

Thirty-eight

Stallings took a few moments to assess the mood of his all-female audience. Sergeant Zuni, Patty Levine, and lieutenant Rita Hester sat staring at him. It was the first time he'd seen the lieutenant in the D-bureau since Sergeant Zuni had arrived.

As usual, based on rank and years of friendship, the lieutenant jumped straight to the point. "All right, Stall. You got two minutes to convince me why we need to put so much more manpower into an overdose case that I didn't want to take in the first place." She folded her formidable arms in front of her and gave him the glower that had made many a street thug cry.

Stallings wasted no time. He laid out the photographs of the three spring break deaths from Daytona the year before, then the two Panama City deaths from the year before that. All blond. He didn't have to state the obvious.

After a moment he said, "All five had Ecstasy in their systems at the times of the death. All five died during the traditional spring break period of March to April." He laid down the photographs of Kathleen Harding and Allie Marsh. "Two deaths with Ecstasy and residue from Durex condoms this year here in Jacksonville." Then he laid down the photograph of Chad Palmer and Gary Lauer. "Two viable suspects."

The sergeant and Patty knew where he was going, but the lieutenant took a moment to study all the photographs. She surveyed the others in the room quietly, then said, "What are you asking for, Stall?"

"We need a couple more detectives for surveillance. Maybe a tracker or two that we can slap on their vehicles. We need to take this seriously."

Rita Hester said to Patty and Sergeant Zuni, "Could you ladies give us a moment alone?" She waited until she and Stallings were alone in the small room and said, "Stall, you can't turn the death of every young girl into some kind of conspiracy. Sometimes kids overdose, or they drown, and sometimes they even run away. But not everything has some sinister meaning. Wrap up this overdose. Keep this girl's mother quiet. And move on. We have real homicides stacking up in the unit. They just found a girl in a parking garage who had been stabbed through her chin to the top of her head. We don't even have a case open on it yet." She looked down and shook her head. "I'm sorry, old friend, but I'm going to have to turn you down on this one."

Stallings drew in a long breath and said, "I can see your point, Rita. But with all due respect, that's bullshit."

"Just because I'm an administrator now doesn't mean I can't smack you, one old street cop to another."

"Then as an administrator, can you really risk the liability of ignoring something like this? Think of the financial shock to the city if there is a serial killer preying on spring breakers and we just let it slide."

He could see the lieutenant working over the problem in her head, the back of her jaw grinding. Her eyebrows furrowed. Finally, after almost a full minute, she faced him and said, "I'll tell you what, against my better judgment, I'll give you and Patty the leeway to check out your suspects. I don't want Lauer's reputation trashed if there's nothing there, and I don't want us facing a lawsuit from Mr. Palmer. You and Patty could have a little overtime and a little discretion, but I want this shit cleared up soon."

Tony Mazzetti cruised the streets at the site of the triple shooting. Life in the neighborhood had quickly gotten back to the usual ebb and flow of commerce, comedy, and connection. Because in this neighborhood if you weren't connected, you did very little commerce and saw very little comedy from day to day. He knew that when people saw a lone white guy in a Crown Vic, they assumed he was a cop. And that usually garnered extra attention from everyone, especially the crack dealers on the corner. But the crack dealers had to realize he wasn't a narcotics detective or he wouldn't be in such an obvious car and wearing a shirt and tie. The most courtesy extended to him was not offering to sell him drugs.

He'd passed Marie Brison's house several times, but there were no cars and no activity around the little clapboard house. The next time he met this white guy—and there would be a next time—there was no way he was gonna let him get away without a long talk. But now his goal was to find the only person who had spoken to him the night of the shooting. That was Pudge, the street prophet. A portly little man didn't stick out on the streets at all, and Mazzetti wanted to be subtle when he approached him. That ruled out rumbling into the bars or pool halls and asking a lot of questions.

Like a lot of police work, it involved time and patience. There was nothing for him to do around the office. Christina Hogrebe had a handle on the backgrounds of the victims and suspects. The little nerd Lonnie Freed from intelligence was trying to scrounge up a snitch who knew anything at all about the Hess Party.

Without saying a word or even knowing he possessed it, Patty had shamed him into submitting the suspected Ecstasy to the lab. The young female lab tech had muttered, "Seems like we're taking in a lot of Ecstasy lately."

Mazzetti just nodded, leaving her to work her magic. Not that he expected anything from the results, at least nothing that would help his murder investigation. But now he could look Patty in the eye and she couldn't say that he wasn't thorough.

After more than an hour of searching for Pudge, Mazzetti's stomach growled, so he pulled into a Church's Fried Chicken. There was no line this time of the day and the pretty young cashier looked surprised to see a large white man walking alone. He ordered a two-piece dinner and the Diet Coke, then plopped on the bench next to his car to enjoy the cool spring day. As he was about to take his first bite of a leg, he heard someone chuckle at the corner of the building. He turned as the short, squat figure emerged.

"That chicken sure does smell good."

"I hate eating alone, Pudge. If I bought you a dinner, you think we could chat?"

"A three-piece dinner?"

Mazzetti smiled. "With an extra order of okra if that's what you want."

Yvonne Zuni knew this would be the best time to come by the apartment. She had an ASP stashed in her waistline and her Glock Model 27 in her purse where it was easy to grab. This was tricky, but she'd weighed the pros and cons and decided to knock on the door.

She heard a chain on the inside slide across the bolt, and then the door opened wide. The pretty, well-endowed blond woman in her early twenties stood in a tight T-shirt and short, short jean cutoffs. Even with no bra on under the thin T-shirt the girl had more curves than almost any woman Yvonne knew.

The girl smiled, revealing straight white teeth that contrasted nicely with her deep tan, which, Sergeant Zuni suspected, had no tan lines. "I didn't think I'd see you again. I always felt like I should have thanked you more for what you did."

"This might be a chance." Yvonne stepped into the apartment without being invited and did a quick scan of the living room and hallway. "I know he still comes by sometimes."

"About once a week."

The sergeant tried hard not to say anything or show any disappointment. But the girl picked up on it immediately, embarrassed by her inability to give this guy the boot.

Sergeant Yvonne Zuni said, "You know he's never gonna get serious."

"That's not the problem. You saw just how serious he can get. But I know what you're saying. He's never gonna make a commitment to me." She sat down on the couch and put her face in her hands. "Everyone likes the idea of dating a stripper, but no one wants to bring one home to Mom."

"In your case you're probably better off not bringing that prick home to your mom."

The young woman smiled and said, "He's never even said anything about that night. Even with the ten stitches and the scar on his eyebrow, it's like he's blocked it out of his memory. He's never mentioned the fight, what caused it, what he made me do, or how you shut him up."

Yvonne sat next to the young woman and put her arm around her shoulder. "Right now he's got another problem, and I've got to ask you some really hard questions. But first I need to know if you owe me enough to keep from saying anything to him."

"You know how he is—I'm sure he'll get me to admit that I talked to you. But I'll do my best to keep the nature of our conversation secret."

"I won't put you in any danger."

"I've been in danger since I dropped out of high school and started hanging out with lowlifes like Gary Lauer."

Patty Levine sat in her county-issued Freestyle on the north side of West State Street. She could see Stallings's Impala three blocks up on the other side of the street. She brought up her binoculars so she could get a clear view of the driver in the blue Nissan 300ZX stopped on the side of the road. Behind the sporty little car Patrol Officer Gary Lauer dismounted from his heavy motorcycle, checked both ways for traffic, then strutted up along the driver's side of the vehicle.

She and Stallings had agreed that they needed to do surveillance on the two suspects. Unless something drastic happened this afternoon while they were following Lauer, they intended to pick up Chad Palmer as he left his office. Neither of them could clearly state what they hoped to gain by watching the suspects, but it was better than sitting around the office waiting for leads to come to them. That was one of the things she really admired about John Stallings. Despite his seniority and experience he was still interested and working every day.

It had been easy to find Lauer in the middle of his shift. All they had to do was monitor his zone's radio traffic and listen for a stop. Based on his record he was an industrious traffic enforcement cop. It was Stallings who had picked three different spots where he thought Lauer would be working. Stallings called them "game trails." Those were places where it was easy to hunt, because the game wandered along the trail. Lazy hunters and even lazy animals could find a comfortable spot to sit and wait for a target. In this case, Lauer sat west of the Arlington Expressway and waited for people to hit the slower speed on the on State Street. If traffic wasn't bad, drivers tended to keep moving along quickly. That was money in the bank for a traffic cop like Gary Lauer.

Patty could see the driver was a younger woman. Lauer crouched down to look at her eye to eye through the window, and the way both he and the woman were smiling made Patty believe the young woman was very attractive too.

This was a trend with the burly motorcycle cop. The first traffic stop that she and Stallings had pulled up on was a pretty young woman in a Volvo S60. The stop before this one was an attractive woman with a cowboy hat driving a Dodge pickup truck. Patty could almost guess the line he was feeding this woman now. How he liked his job even though it was dangerous. How he had to go to the gym to stay in shape in case he was in a life-and-death struggle. How it was hard to find a woman that understood the stress of police work. Christ, she heard enough guys feed that bullshit to waitresses, strippers, and nurses that she knew all the lines by heart.

She used her Nextel phone to call up Stallings on the direct connect. "Whatcha think?"

"Statistically I wonder how many women he pulls over compared to men."

"You think this is gonna get us anywhere?"

"I doubt it, but I did want to get a feel for how the guy worked. It looks like he uses the job as a way to meet women. It wouldn't be an issue except for what we suspect him of. I'm still hoping the cop in him wouldn't have any part of that."

"My female radar, which has been honed over the years, says that this guy is a creep who does not respect women. I don't think he's above giving Ecstasy to a girl to make her come home with him."

She kept watching Lauer as he stood up and patted the car with his left hand. He didn't write a ticket or even a warning to the young lady, but he did hold a piece of notepaper that she'd given him. Patty said into her phone, "Looks like he just scored a phone number."

"My guess is that this guy has volumes of phone numbers at home."

He let the Nissan pull away, then climbed back onto his motorcycle. He slowly pulled into traffic, shutting off his rear blue light once he was rolling west again. He passed Stallings without even giving him a glance. That was when two cars moving at once attracted Patty's attention. A silver Ford Taurus and a black Dodge Charger fell in behind Lauer on his motorcycle.

Then Stallings clicked her up on the phone. "Looks like we have company."

"You saw them too?"

"I'd lay money that it was Internal Affairs."

"How do you know that?"

"Because they're about as subtle as a sledgehammer and can't follow people for shit."

Thirty-nine

Tony Mazzetti sat with Pudge in front of the fried chicken place for more than an hour. If nothing else, the little guy was entertaining.

Pudge said, "The word on the street is the shooters you're looking for are, in fact, Caucasian. That would mean this could be the start of the race war I have foreseen for quite some time."

"You don't think it could just be a squabble over money or drugs?"

"You just assume that since young black men were shot they were involved in the drug trade. Is that what you're saying?"

Mazzetti stared at the corpulent little man. "Yeah, Pudge, that's exactly what I'm assuming. We did find a half a kilo of cocaine under one of the mattresses and thirty thousand dollars in cash."

"I see you are skilled in the lessons of rhetoric and are prepared to debate me on the subject."

"Actually I'm not prepared to debate you at all. I bought you dinner to see if you had any new information. Come on, Pudge, you see what's going on here.

No one benefits from an unsolved homicide. If you know something, now would be a good time to spill it."

Pudge took a moment and turned to look Mazzetti in the eyes. "In this case it might not hurt to think the killers came from outside the neighborhood. White men are a convenient excuse to avoid the truth. Also you found cocaine and money. Wouldn't successful drug dealers like those three dead boys have more cash than that?"

"What the fuck are you talking about?"

"Your search for the killers might be too wide. Perhaps you need to focus more on why those boys were shot than on who shot them. I don't know anything firsthand, I just hear rumors. I still think the lovely Miss Brison might help you if you caught her in the right mood."

Mazzetti was about to pull out a small notepad when he heard a sharp voice say, "Pudge, why you talkin' to the po-po?"

Mazzetti's head snapped up to see a thick young man in shorts riding low on his hips and no shirt standing a few feet away. Mazzetti stood up and faced the young man, his hand dropping to his right hip in case he needed to go for a gun. He wasn't sure what to say to the allegation. He turned to see what Pudge's reaction was, but the bench was empty and there was no sign of the street prophet.

A two-person surveillance team wasn't very effective against seasoned drug dealers or the slick white-collar fraud guys who expected cops to be following them. But Stallings hoped he and Patty would be enough to keep a loose tail on a dumb shit like Chad Palmer. They had done all right following Lauer but backed off when they realized IA had their own ideas. Stallings didn't care who solved the Ecstasy mystery as long as it was cleared up and out of his brain.

He'd slipped a portable tracker under the wheel well of Palmer's BMW, and Patty was using a laptop computer in her car to keep up with the signal. The tricky part was getting close enough to see what Palmer did once he was inside another building. They had followed him from his office and waited while he worked out at a high-end gym downtown near the river. Then waited while he had eaten at a Panera Bread.

Stallings was surprised when Palmer rolled into the parking lot of the dance club south of the city. It was still early for the dance club crowd, but maybe he tried to maintain some kind of schedule. They waited about twenty minutes. Patty was dressed very casually, in jeans and a cute blouse with her hair up in a ponytail, and was wearing glasses in an attempt to be harder to recognize. It sounded lame when she told Stallings what she was going to do until he saw her and realized a guy like Palmer might not even pick up on her in the club. She looked entirely different from the way she had on Monday morning when they interviewed him in his office. She never failed to surprise the veteran detective.

After about half an hour Patty came out from the club and slipped into the front seat with Stallings.

"He's in there talking to a very young blond girl at the end of the bar. It looked as if he knew her and she might've been expecting him. If we've got his car covered out here all we have to do is wait."

"I don't see any other choice. But if a girl gets in a car with him, I'm not sure I can let him drive away considering what we suspect him of."

Patty looked concerned and said, "We're probably not gonna have any PC. She was at least eighteen, and he wasn't forcing her into anything that I could see."

"I'll find the PC if I have to."

"I was afraid you might say that."

He checked for Ann as soon as he walked in the club. She knew that he'd be there early, and he hoped that would be enough incentive for her to show up alone. He'd gone so far as to tell her he'd only be there for about an hour and certainly be gone by nine.

The best he could do was try to develop a new target who had joined him at the end of the bar. But the girl had used her cell phone too many times in the hour that he had spent with her to try and separate her from the herd. If she couldn't sit there with him, downing Stolies on the rocks, and not have to chat with nine different friends, then there was no way he could slip away with her quietly.

She was pretty to look at and had a breezy manner, but it was mainly that light hair and pale blue eyes that held his attention.

Even the best predators went home hungry now and then.

Forty

Patty Levine wasn't used to starting her day at noon, but in an effort to use their time efficiently she and Stallings had decided to change schedules. She sat at her desk studying records when Yvonne Zuni approached.

The sergeant said, "Gary Lauer was in Daytona last year and Panama City the year before. The dates line up with the girls' deaths."

Patty said, "How'd you find out where he went on vacation?"

"Sometimes you have to work outside the box. I cleared up an ugly issue for a young woman who was romantically involved with Lauer last year. I asked her a simple question, and she gave me a straight answer."

"That creep has a girlfriend?"

"Several. You've seen him, and you know how young people can be. This is a nice girl who thought he was something he wasn't. The hell of it is she still sees him on and off."

"How ugly was the issue? Does it relate to this case at all?"

The sergeant slipped into the seat right next to Patty,

leaned in, and quietly said, "The son of a bitch knocked her up, then forced her to get an abortion. One night they had an argument that got out of control. He was on temporary assignment to narcotics, so when neighbors complained about the noise the responding patrolman called me to talk some sense into him. He started to get shitty with me, and I had to crack him in the head with my ASP."

"How'd you avoid an IA investigation?"

"Let's just say everyone agreed to keep their mouths shut. And don't tell your partner, but Ronald Bell in IA did a great job of smoothing everything over."

"I doubt Stall would believe you anyway. He hates Bell." Patty thought about it and said, "So, what do we do now, switch all surveillance over to Lauer? We told you we thought IA was on him already."

The sergeant smiled and said, "Again, I'm working outside the box on this. These are still serious but vague allegations. I'm going to brief Ronald Bell on what we're doing and see what kind of help they can give us. I think he likes to play his cards close. He never mentioned they were going to keep tabs on Lauer. In the meantime, I arranged for Officer Lauer to be offered one of the few overtime gigs still available. He's going to work the next three evenings at the big soup kitchen near the stadium. The mayor's office funds a uniformed officer to be there every night. That should keep him busy while we get our ducks in a row."

"So this guy makes extra cash for being a suspect in Ecstasy distribution?"

"I don't think it's right, Patty, but it's the best way to handle it right now. Don't forget we're still working on a wild theory, and he's not even the only suspect. You guys stay on Palmer tonight, and I want you to keep Stallings in check."

"What's that supposed to mean?"

"Everyone knows he can become irrational dealing with crimes against young women. He respects you and listens to you. You're on the list for sergeant—this is as good a time as any to learn the subtleties of supervision."

Stallings sat on a low wall in the sunshine, eating an Italian sub from Gino's. He had a can of soda resting perilously on the narrow wall. The Police Memorial Building was not exactly set up for casual dining outside. He liked the feel of the sun and he was hungry, so he plopped down to eat his favorite sub in the whole world. It used to be you could see the river from the spot, but now classless condos rose across the street, blocking the once-beautiful view. He intended to spend a couple of hours at his desk before he and Patty started their surveillance of Chad Palmer again. This was an odd case propelled by politics and his desire to satisfy Diane Marsh's perfectly reasonable parental expectation that anyone connected to her daughter's death be found. No matter why it was proceeding, Stallings was committed to see it through.

He reached down for his can of caffeine-free Diet Coke as a shadow fell across him. Stallings squinted into the sun to see who would bother him during lunch. In the bright spring sun all he saw was the outline of a large man in uniform with a holster on his right side and radio on the left. The patrolman said, "You're not man enough to come talk to me directly?"

Stallings immediately realized he was talking to Gary Lauer. In one quick motion he set down his sandwich and stood from his perch so he could face the motorman. "I did come talk to you face-to-face."

"Then why'd you talk to my girlfriend?"

Stallings shrugged. "Where do you get your girlfriends, middle school?" He couldn't resist baiting this asshole.

Lauer edged closer, an old intimidation trick that Stallings wasn't about to fall for. He casually brought up his hand in a fist with his thumb sticking out in front of his index finger. He held it in place so when the younger man moved closer it would strike him right in the solar plexus, knocking the wind out of him.

Lauer said, "I know someone was by my girlfriend's apartment asking questions about my vacations."

Stallings knew to play dumb even though he wasn't sure what the younger man was talking about. Besides, nothing provoked an irrational person like silence.

Lauer looked him in the face but stepped forward quickly, and Stallings felt his thumb mash into the uniform shirt. But the motorman was wearing a concealed ballistic with a steel shock plate vest over his heart and solar plexus. The move had no effect other than to hurt Stallings's thumb.

Lauer raised his voice. "You think you're better than everyone else because you put away a couple of big-time killers. But I got news for you, we all work hard around here, and I thought we all watched each other's asses. Guess I was wrong." Now he had Stallings's back against a hedge.

"Look, you douche bag, you brought this on yourself. You like to scare women, like to boss them around—I know your kind. Younger women are easier to intimi-

date. If I find out you gave Ecstasy to any spring breakers you won't know what hit you."

"You got no juice left around here, old man. No one
cares if you're looking at me or not. I even got a decent
overtime detail for a few nights. So you keep wasting
your time while real criminals run loose around the
city." He started to edge closer, forcing Stallings back
into the bush. Stallings let him push forward, then
slipped to the side, turned, and smirked as the big motorcycle patrolman stumbled hard into the bush. He shoved
his way back out and spun quickly to face Stallings.

Lauer said, "You better hope I don't see you away
from this building. Out on the street, your ass is mine.
I'll have another trophy to show off."

Stallings smiled and replied, "You mean like a matching scar on your right eyebrow?"

Patty Levine was better prepared for tonight's surveillance. She knew exactly what to wear to blend in at
the tiny club on the southeast side of Jacksonville. Today
she had on shorts and a nice shirt with her glasses
and a baseball cap changing the shape of her face. She
looked nothing like the professional detective who'd
spoken with Chad Palmer on Monday morning. As a result she was sitting a few stools away from him and was
even able to hear some of his conversation with the
young woman on the other side of him.

She didn't like watching Mr. Rich Kid, and she hated
to see a guy like him attract so many very young women.
He'd chatted with three different women in the short
time she'd been inside. Maybe he'd do something tonight to expose his role in Allie Marsh's death as well as
the others.

She kept a casual eye on Palmer from down the bar. Two young men took stools to the right of her. The overpowering odor of Axe Body Wash made her eyes water slightly. After only a minute, the guy closest to her turned her way and said, "You go to school around here?"

Patty laughed involuntarily. She said, "UF." Everyone in Florida understood that meant the University of Florida in Gainesville.

The young man smiled. "No shit, me too. What's your major?"

Patty wondered if the young man was blind or just so drunk he didn't notice the eight years' difference between them. She knew how to end this quickly. With a casual turn of her head she said, "Physics."

As she expected, the young man sort of nodded his head and turned back to his friend.

Her phone vibrated in her front pocket. She dug it out of the tight shorts, saw it was Stallings calling her, and flipped it open. She had to mash it to her ear to hear over the noise inside the bar. She knew to keep it very general on her side of the conversation and said, "Hey, what's going on?" Her partner had been very quiet this evening. He mentioned a quick run-in with the detestable Gary Lauer at the PMB earlier in the day but didn't go into any details. But she knew the confrontation had affected him. He didn't want to admit a cop might be involved in any kind of crime against a young woman. As much as she disliked the motorman she wanted him to be cleared in this too.

Stallings said over the phone line, "You doing okay in there by yourself?"

Patty glanced over at the boy to her right, laughed,

and said, "You'd be surprised how well I could do in here if I wanted to."

"What about our boy?"

Patty turned slowly to see what Palmer and the young woman were up to. As soon as she faced his way he laid a twenty-dollar bill on the bar, took the young woman's elbow, and they both started heading out the door. All Patty had time to say was, "He's on the move now. He'll be through the front door in about five seconds." Now came the tricky part.

Forty-one

Tony Mazzetti sat in the dark office alone, wishing he'd become a fireman instead of a cop. No one expected anything of firemen except the obvious: spray water on a fire. The rest of the time they could work out, train, and sleep. Three things he liked to do anyway.

Instead he hunched at his desk, puzzling over the cryptic comment Pudge, the street prophet, had made. When the odd fat man said to look closer rather than farther, did he mean the neighborhood? The drug trade? The fucking Hess Party? He hated riddles like this. Good investigations were logical, direct, and straightforward. That's why he was in homicide and not narcotics. Shit, he'd rather be in fraud than narcotics. At least he could still identify scumbags and know exactly what the crime was with fraud. In narcotics, victims were other scumbags and the targets were more scumbags trying to make a buck off dope. Usually in his homicide investigations he had forensic information to corroborate witness testimony. It was simple: Someone saw Joe Blow shoot Sam Citizen and the medical examiner pulls a thirty-eight slug out of Sam Citizen. Case fucking closed. But all he had in this triple shooting were nine-millimeter slugs inside bodies and a lot of holes outside the small house. Sure, the forensic weenies could tell that the killers used at least two guns and one of them had to be some kind of automatic weapon. They had fired from the front door and hit all three victims immediately. The only wounds in common were a single nine-millimeter shot to the head. They'd all been riddled with body shots, but each had a bullet in the head. Probably after this occurred, the outside of the house and a Lincoln Navigator parked in the driveway were hit a total of nineteen times. The crime scene guys counted thirty-four shots fired. None by the victims.

Now, for some reason, Mazzetti was concerned about something some crazy street guy had to say. The rumors on the street had all been conflicting. Some people saw a Camaro before the shooting; others saw a Cadillac Escalade with dark windows. Once the rumor about white men started, everyone jumped on board.

Mazzetti stared at his desk hoping some kind of answer would pop into his head. It wasn't as if he had anything to do other than work right now anyway. Patty was stuck on some kind of bullshit surveillance with Stallings. He didn't count on seeing her again until late. They said they would eat a very late dinner at her condo. It was kind of nice to look forward to spending time with someone for a change.

Mazzetti muttered a few curse words as he fixed his eyes on the file and thought, *I hate open cases.*

As soon as Patty told him their subject was on the move, Stallings sat tall in his seat to get a good view of the front door to the club. The parking lot had some cars in it but was by no means packed. He'd already identified Palmer's BMW and could see both the front door and the car. There was no way the pharmaceutical rep would spot him sitting a couple of rows away in his nondescript Impala.

The door opened, and Palmer, dressed in jeans and an untucked oxford button-down long-sleeved shirt, strolled out arm in arm with a cute, and possibly drunk, young woman. Stallings was good at estimating ages and he put this girl at nineteen, twenty at the most. About right for the college students in this area of town and the clientele of this little club. Now he was faced with the real question of what these surveillances were trying to accomplish. The girl was over eighteen and obviously walking with Palmer voluntarily.

Stallings considered the situation. Had he let the crime against a young woman affect his judgment? What was his plan? Wait for her to turn up dead tomorrow and then try and pin it on the pharmaceutical rep?

Stallings watched as the couple paused on the passenger side of the BMW. He had a clear view straight down the row of cars. Somehow the image of this girl reaching to kiss Palmer made him think of his own daughters. He hated the idea that they would ever have to deal with a slimy, manipulative prick like this. The idea of a man who was nearly thirty trolling for teenagers at bars made his stomach turn.

Then the movement caught his eye. It was the experience of sixteen years of police work in every unit from road patrol to homicide. The handoff. It happened every day in every city in America. Something changed hands, someone passes something off to someone else—whether it was a package, money, or drugs, it always had a certain look to it. In this case Palmer turned his head in each direction, reached in his pocket, pulled out a small plastic bag, then placed it in the palm of the girl's hand. She smiled, plucked something from the baggie, then popped it in her mouth. Had he really seen something so overt, or was he looking for a reason to intervene?

As he watched, he saw the girl hesitate as she swallowed, then look up and kiss Palmer again on the lips. The pharmaceutical rep's hand slid down her body and rested on her butt. Something inside Stallings snapped.

He was out of the car and moving without conscious thought. Palmer's head jerked up in surprise, recognition hitting his face an instant before Stallings's closed fist. The girl squealed as Palmer made an odd sound and dropped straight back onto the hard parking lot with a thud.

Palmer shook his head and started to scoot to a sitting position, but Stallings kicked him hard in the chest, knocking him flat again.

Palmer moaned, "What the hell is going on?"

Stallings saw how frightened the girl was. All he could say was, "What did he give you?"

The young girl stared at him with her mouth open.

He raised his voice to a shout. "What did you just swallow? I saw you—don't try and hide it." He shoved Palmer back flat on the ground, only this time left his foot on the man's chest.

The girl started to cry.

Stallings crouched down next to the bloody pharmaceutical rep and started to pat his front pockets, reaching in the last one and pulling out a baggie. He opened it and spilled the five pills into his open hand. Each of them appeared professionally made, and they were all a solid color.

Now the girl started to sob loudly. She was able to moan, "Who are you, and why are you doing this?"

Stallings realized his shirt covered his badge and gun. Still squatting next to Palmer, he reached in his pocket, and pulled out his ID so the girl could see the badge. All he said was, "JSO."

The girl clutched her stomach and said, "Oh my God, are you going to arrest me?

Now Stallings took a moment. Palmer was quiet, lying flat on the ground trying to keep the blood flowing from his lip and nose to the minimum. Stallings said calmly to the girl, "I saw him give you something and you put it in your mouth. What was it?"

The girl pointed at the pills in the palm of his hand and said, "Just one of those Percocets. I'm sorry—I won't do it again. Please don't tell my parents."

He looked down at the five commercially produced painkillers in his hand and then at the bloodied, whimpering pharmaceutical rep and quietly said to himself, "You have got to be fucking kidding me."

Patty raced up. "John, what are you doing?"

Stallings took a moment to look at the bloody man, then at the very young girl, and decided he didn't regret anything he'd done.

Forty-two

The sun had just risen as Stallings woke. For a few moments, as he lay still in the small bed of his rented house, he had the slightest of hopes everything had been a dream. The irrational beating of Chad Palmer. The discovery that he wasn't distributing X. The expression on Sergeant Zuni's face. His right hand throbbed slightly, and he saw the cuts on his knuckles where they had dug into Chad Palmer's teeth and knew it had been no dream. He'd fucked up in a big way this time. And there was no one to blame but himself.

As soon as Yvonne Zuni had arrived at the hospital where Chad Palmer was getting stitched up, she looked at Stallings and said, "Go home until I call you." She had taken charge, but it didn't sound as if she cared about his reasons. The sergeant was looking at facts, and the fact was he had no right to hit Chad Palmer in the face. It didn't matter now. He doubted he'd be working for her or anyone else at the sheriff's office. A flood of thoughts rushed through his head. How do I tell Maria and the kids? How do I explain my behavior?

Do I need to retain an attorney? Why didn't I kill the son of a bitch once I'd started?

He rolled over and stared at the ceiling, realizing for the first time he was still in his clothes from the night before. The whole evening was a blur for him, but he knew he'd had a late dinner, and after a brief ride near Market Street, looking for his dad, he'd come home and collapsed, the weight of the last few weeks catching up with him.

Incredibly, his cell phone hadn't rung all night, and now he wondered if he should call the sergeant and see what kind of shit he was in. He'd never had a complaint filed against him. Most cops suffered numerous frivolous claims of brutality and excessive force. The funny thing was Stallings used his fists much more than most cops. But he knew when to hit and what to say afterward. That was the gift God had given him to carry into his chosen profession: the ability to make people like him even after he kicked their asses. But now he'd finally gone too far with the wrong guy at the wrong time.

Patty Levine didn't like the expression on her boyfriend's face as they shared a cup of coffee at Dunkin' Donuts near the PMB.

Tony Mazzetti almost beamed when he said, "How much blood was there? I mean, was it from several wounds or just one massive head wound?"

"Mainly from his lips. Stall really only punched him the one time."

"Holy shit, the nut job finally went over the edge. I knew it was just a matter of time before Mr. Squeaky Clean cracked."

"You don't have to be happy about it. I mean we all

work on the same squad and it wasn't like he went postal and shot someone indiscriminately. He punched a guy giving drugs to a nineteen-year-old girl. Given his history, it didn't seem outrageous at all."

Mazzetti waved off her criticism. "I'm not happy about it. It's just he tends to be a little self-righteous."

"Why? Because he's had to go back and rework two of your cases?"

Mazzetti looked hurt but focused on his coffee for a moment. "I'm glad you're not in trouble with him."

Patty didn't know if she was in trouble or not. The whole thing had been handled very quietly. Yvonne Zuni stepped right in and was on the phone to IA immediately. Patty only caught snippets of the conversation, but it sounded as if this was how Yvonne the Terrible had gotten her nickname. She had wasted no time sending Stallings home and bringing in investigators from the internal affairs unit to handle the questioning of Chad Palmer and his young friend.

Patty had protested she should be there, but the sergeant told her she was a witness, and now all she had left to do was go home and wait till she was called back. But Patty hadn't exactly waited. She was headed back in at nine sharp, and she didn't intend to keep her mouth shut. Not only did she owe a lot to John Stallings, but the guy had been through too much to get crushed over something like this. She didn't know what she could do, but she knew she couldn't just sit at home.

He'd come by his sister's house to say hello and maybe grab one of her really good grilled-cheese sandwiches for lunch. But he also enjoyed spending time with his nephew even if it was only watching him watch

TV. He could see their shared genetics in the boy's keen eyes and quick movements.

But now, sitting at the counter with his sister, he faced one of the many barrages of questions she fired at him from time to time. It wasn't an inquisition, like when his mother would clearly be worried about his outside activities. He finally realized what his mother had suspected, and he'd had no real contact with her in several years. He figured dear old mom was just as happy with that arrangement.

"I'm not saying you *have* to settle down, I was just wondering why you don't," his sister started. "I mean you spend most nights away from here anyway, but you never give me any clear idea of whether it's with one girl or a hundred different ones."

He didn't answer directly, but he had to smile about keeping his apartment secret for so long. He'd met his landlord, Lester, at the Wildside when Lester was delivering alcohol from his beverage truck. He'd struck up a mild friendship, and Lester had offered him the detached apartment behind his house for a few hundred dollars a month. He wasn't nosy and asked no questions, which made him a great landlord.

His sister said, "Mom worries because you live with me. I have no idea why. What happened with you two?"

"Same stuff that happens in all families. She doesn't approve of some things I do, and I don't give a shit."

"She said she had a psychiatrist she wanted me to take him to"—she lowered her voice and nodded toward his nephew watching TV in the next room—"to see about expanding his vocabulary."

He looked over at the boy and nodded his head. He didn't talk much either when he was a kid.

His sister continued. "Of course she doesn't have any money to help with the evaluation."

"I got some cash if you need it."

"You already do too much for us now. Let's see what happens with him in the next few months, and then I'll decide if we need to be more proactive." She patted his hand, stood from the stool, and turned to finish making their lunch.

He sat on his stool at the kitchen counter and gazed at his nephew. The sound on the cartoon his nephew was watching was turned down to almost nothing as usual. The boy didn't like to crowd his senses with unnecessary sights and sounds. It was quiet enough to hear the heavy trucks behind the commercial buildings on Cleveland Street. He saw a movement through the sliding glass door in the backyard. The neighbor's cat was strolling through as if he owned the place.

He caught his nephew's eyes tracking the cat. He didn't move his head or show any interest other than his sharp eyes assessing the cat and the terrain.

The boy was a predator himself.

Forty-three

Yvonne Zuni was utterly exhausted. She'd been called out from her home shortly after Stallings had been involved in a fight outside a club in southeast Jacksonville. At least that's how she was phrasing it to anyone she talked to today. She grabbed a few hours of sleep in her office because she wanted to head off the inevitable Internal Affairs investigation into the incident. Now, still at the PMB, she sat across from the senior IA investigator, Ronald Bell, in the small snack bar near the main entrance.

The sergeant wanted to stress the point one more time that Stallings had observed what he believed to be a serious crime and acted in the safety of himself and the female with Chad Palmer. She knew Stallings and Bell had a history and realized it had something to do with the disappearance of Stallings's daughter a few years ago. Personally, she liked the handsome, older detective because he'd never filed an official report when she had to crack Gary Lauer in the head with an ASP. It'd been a stressful time and a stressful night. When Lauer started to scream at his pregnant girlfriend, Yvonne

Zuni had snapped. Although she liked to think she'd given him a warning, in reality she popped the ASP and swung it before she or Lauer knew it was coming.

If it hadn't been for the nine stitches and the hospital visit, she doubted anyone at the sheriff's office would have ever heard about the incident. Lauer was embarrassed he'd lost control, and he was embarrassed a woman half his size had knocked him off his feet and sent him to the hospital. But cops being cops, stories were told, and rumors ran rampant through the department. Finally Ronald Bell had knocked on her door and asked a few simple questions. He could've made it into a big deal but instead wrote it off as a personal conflict and had Lauer moved from his temporary duty assignment in narcotics back to the motor unit where he figured everyone would forget about it and Lauer would have no chance to bother anyone else while he wrote tickets on the expressways headed east from the city or any other direction to somewhere nicer.

Bell looked over his coffee at Yvonne Zuni and said, "We can probably write this whole thing off. Mr. Palmer is not interested in losing his job over distributing samples of a narcotic. We searched his house pretty carefully and all we found were other manufactured pharmaceutical samples. We found no homemade Ecstasy or any signs he ever tried to make it. This incident could be a notch in my belt, but I'm willing to let the whole thing slide for the sake of that crazy son of a bitch you call a detective."

Yvonne knew not to say anything, but a smile crept over her face.

Bell continued, "I strongly recommend you send that unstable moron home for a few days to cool off. We can't have him think he can get away with this kind of shit all the time." He rubbed his eyes and looked at Sergeant Zuni. "Even though he's been doing it for years."

She casually reached across and placed her small hand on Bell's, and said, "You know he's a hell of a cop and has done a lot of good. He just has some issues."

"We all have issues."

"Ain't that the truth."

Stallings was restless as he contemplated his life at the small, quiet house he'd rented in Lakewood. It was odd being home in the middle of the day. The fact there was no one here gave him a sense of emptiness almost as deep as he felt after Jeanie disappeared. But there was nothing for him to do at this little house. No yard to cut. No dishes to do. He barely lived here except to use the bed every night.

He jumped in his car, not sure what his status was as a police officer, but since no one had told him not to, he decided to use the county car as he always did. He cruised by his mother's house to make sure she didn't have any chores he needed to do. He found her as he usually did, sitting on her back porch reading a novel.

"Hey, Mom."

As usual he had to wait a second until she finished the paragraph she was reading. Finally she looked up and smiled. "What are you doing here in the middle of the day?"

"I, 'um, took a day off."

His mother chuckled. "Sometimes you remind me of your father. For all his faults he was a poor liar too." She closed the hardbound book on her lap and smiled at her son. "I heard you ran into him on Sunday."

"I figured one of the kids would blab it or Helen would hear about it and tell you."

"Actually, I heard it from your father."

Yvonne Zuni had to admit to herself she enjoyed Ronald Bell's company, and for the second time he'd proven he was a stand-up guy. She realized she was looking for reasons to keep talking to the dapper detective. The red tinge to his face, coupled with his casual but expensive sport coat, made it seem as if he was windburned from sailing, but she realized that in fact, as it was with most cops, it probably had a lot more to do with alcohol. Finally she said, "What about your people's surveillance of Lauer? I haven't shared with my detectives that we had split the case. I did tell them we'd given Lauer an overtime detail at a soup kitchen near the stadium."

"Well, it's partially true he is working the detail at the kitchen, but I've had two people keeping tabs on him until we think he's down for the night. The problem is he knows the roads and the traffic enforcement better than anyone else and drives like a NASCAR champion. The only time he obeys any traffic laws and signals is when he's in uniform, on that big bike of his. He went by his girlfriend's apartment, the one where you had the incident last year, but was only inside about ten minutes. It seems like all the guy does is lift weights and eat giant subs. Last night he went straight home from the overtime detail at eleven o'clock and had not left his condo by two when my detectives shut down their surveillance."

"Seems like you guys have it covered pretty well. Is there anything I can do to help?"

Bell took a moment to consider it, then said, "I'd be happy if you could just keep the muzzle on Stallings. I have no problem with letting the whole thing drop, but he needs to go at least a day without clocking someone."

"Some of it has to do with stress. And he's been under a tremendous strain for a long time now."

Bell said, "I've heard that before, but it doesn't excuse his behavior."

The sergeant said, "To me it does. I have a good idea what he's been going through."

Bell didn't say anything, but she knew he expected an explanation. For the first time in two years she decided to talk about it.

Yvonne started slowly, finally working up to the source of her own stress and frustration. "You know I'm divorced now?"

"Every male cop at the SO knows when someone like you is no longer married." He laid that charming smile on her.

"It's hard to keep secrets in a place like this, but the reason we broke up was the stress on our relationship when our one-year-old son died of leukemia."

Bell said, "I'm sorry. I didn't realize that."

"The first day I started to feel alive again, the day I felt like I had a purpose and a connection to the world after months and months of breathing was the day I popped that asshole, Gary Lauer, in the head. So I really feel like I have an idea of what Stallings is going through."

"You talked to Dad?" He tried to keep it under a shout, but this was about the most astounding thing he had ever heard his mother say.

"Yes, dear, I speak to your father. I even meet him occasionally. You can't spend so much of your life with someone and not feel something for them."

"But he was such a . . ." Stallings search for the right word.

His mother said, "Asshole?"

He nodded, still trying to absorb this information. "The way he treated Helen and me growing up. Her running away and you throwing him out. I always assumed he'd ruined your life and you were bitter toward him."

"No, dear, I got over it a long time ago. Life's far too short to hold a grudge. Once he stopped drinking, he reverted to something like the man I married forty-five years ago."

"Was our encounter an accident?"

"You would have to ask your father. I might've mentioned you were taking the kids out for pizza on Sunday."

"Were you ever going to tell me Dad was back in the picture or that he was looking for me?"

His mother shook her head and said, "It wouldn't have done any good. You're as stubborn as he is, and you would've avoided him no matter what he said."

"So what do you expect me to do now, go look for him?"

His mother smiled. "I could never tell you what to do or how to do it. Just like your father."

Forty-four

It had taken John Stallings longer than he'd anticipated to track down his father later in the afternoon. He'd been hoping he could walk into the rooming house and his father would be in the lobby with some of the other old drunks, playing cards or backgammon or watching the ancient TV in the ornate walnut cabinet. Instead, the nice lady who ran the place had explained James Stallings had gone to get something to eat. She gave him three possibilities: a bar near the stadium that had cheap hamburgers on Wednesday nights, a hot dog stand that had one-dollar hot dogs, or a soup kitchen off Market Street where his father often worked and ate what was left over.

Now it was seven o'clock, and as soon as Stallings walked through the doors of the "community restaurant" he could see the main body of diners had already cleared out and in the corner, where young men were stacking chairs, there was one table filled with an older crowd and a few plates of food. At the head of the table he saw his father. It was as if he was holding court, and it reminded Stallings of his childhood, when his father

would entertain many of the other fathers in the neighborhood with stories of the Korean War, the changing
Navy, and how the goddamned Democrats would turn
the country to socialism. It took Stallings a moment to
realize this was the first time he had ever seen his father
entertaining a group like this without a beer in his
hand.

He hesitated near the door and even thought about
turning around and going back another time, but he
caught his father's eye and the old man did something
he'd never done before in Stallings's life. He excused
himself from the table to come talk to his son.

It'd been an awkward twenty minutes while they sat
across from each other over the long table. He didn't
know what to say after all the years of hating this guy.
But he quickly discovered the hate had faded but not
disappeared altogether. He held him responsible for
his sister, Helen, running away from home, and in some
odd way for Jeanie disappearing as well. He could never
explain it. He'd never talk to anyone about it, and he
certainly wasn't about to discuss it with his father. Not
after all these years.

His father's voice was hoarse but lacked the harsh
edge it had when he'd been younger. The old man said,
"Your mom has kept me up to date on you and the kids
over the years. Charlie looks like a real athlete. And
Lauren is as pretty as her mother."

"You missed out completely on Jeanie. She was special."

The old man hesitated. "I followed the story and
even tried to do my part, helping with some of the community searches and asking everyone I knew on the

streets if they'd seen or heard anything. It was the same time I was coming out of my haze."

Stallings shook his head, looked at his father, and said, "Dad, why're you like this now, after all these years?"

His father smiled, rubbing his hand over his gray buzz cut, the wrinkles around his eyes filling out. "If I were to put it in one word it would have to be 'sober.' "

Stallings assessed the older man, trying to understand what he'd gone through. He'd never realized his father had been fighting with alcohol, not just guzzling it. This was a lot to process after a stressful day. He had five messages on his phone. Three from Yvonne the Terrible, one from Patty Levine, and one from Maria. He couldn't imagine any of them was good news. Maybe his father could give him some good tips for living out on the street.

As he was about to start asking his father important questions like how his health was or what he did for money, he heard someone step up directly behind him and say, "Well, well, well. I knew you'd end up in a shit-hole like this. I just didn't expect it to happen so fast."

Stallings twisted in his seat and was shocked to see the strapping figure of Gary Lauer in full uniform.

Patty knew the administrative officer at the medical examiner's office was anxious to leave. He'd mentioned dinner, his wife, his kids, exhaustion, and anything else he could without saying, "you have to close your files and leave." She'd been distracted by her concern for John Stallings. The new sergeant had worked a miracle and gotten Stallings off the hot seat, but she'd been unable to reach him. Sergeant Zuni told Patty all Stallings needed to do was lay low for a day or two and try not to smack anyone. Only Patty realized how hard it might be for her partner. The sergeant was also concerned she'd been unable to tell Stallings so she'd had Patty leave him a message too. That was one of the reasons it'd taken so long at the medical examiner's office.

She'd been studying photographs and all the reports from Allie Marsh and Kathleen Harding, the suicide from the University of South Carolina. It was no surprise they shared X in their system and the chemical residue of Durex condoms. Tony Mazzetti had already explained to her these were not uncommon traits for spring breakers to share. But she wanted more. She had studied both files and made copies of the entire written report. The medical examiner had been very thorough, and she knew he was as sharp as they came. There had to be something else.

She noticed Kathleen Harding had been missing her left earring. A straight post diamond stud. No one made much of a fuss about it and there was no explanation for it in the report. Allie Marsh had both earrings and one in the cartilage of her left ear. But both in the photos and in the report Patty noticed she had been missing a belly-button ring. The report noted the discoloration in the shape of a small flower where the ring had sat a millimeter below her belly button. And on the autopsy photos, when she checked closely, she saw the same discoloration. It happened with a lot of jewelry when someone got a tan—whatever was underneath stayed pale. It was a curious and tenuous connection between the bodies.

But it was a lead worth following.

*   *   *

Stallings stood and faced the cocky young motorman. "What are you doing here, Lauer?"

"I'm working off-duty. I'm supposed to be here. What are you doing?"

"I'm not going waste my time talking to you."

"I heard you went crazy and hit some poor dude in the head. I figured you'd be out of a job."

That's what Stallings figured too, and he didn't want to give this dick any reason to hassle him.

Lauer's eyes cut over to Stallings's father. "Who's your friend here, Stall?"

He saw the rage in Lauer's face and didn't want to drag his father into any personal feud he had with the big, uniformed cop. He knew how hard life was for older men on the street. Stallings's father, no matter what had happened in the past, didn't deserve this bully following him around.

Stallings forced his voice to be even and calm and said, "Let's discuss this outside, Gary."

"Love to." Lauer turned quickly on his polished boot and banged out the rear door with Stallings close on his heels.

As Stallings glanced over Lauer's broad shoulders and a uniform with the big Glock forty on his right hip and an ASP in a holster on his left hip, the idea of this guy mingling with college kids or bullying old street people started to eat at him. Suddenly Lauer stopped in the gravel lot outside the ratty white building. He turned without warning and immediately poked Stallings in the chest with his index finger.

"I'd like to know why you have a hard-on for me."

Stallings poked him back in the chest and said, "I'd like to know why you have such issues with women."

"You need to mind your own business, old man. If

you don't shut your mouth, I'm gonna have to shut it for you.

Stallings couldn't help himself and said, "I'd like to see you try." He knew it was too late. He was too far gone to control himself, so he waited for the right opportunity.

Lauer balled his right fist, and Stallings, with years of street experience, simply twisted his body hard to the left and brought his right elbow across Lauer's thick chin, knocking the young man virtually unconscious on his feet. He didn't bother trying to catch Lauer when he fell backward.

Stallings's phone rang as he stared down at the groggy, uniformed police officer. He pulled it out of his pocket and flipped it open. "Stallings."

Patty Levine said, "John, I've been trying to reach you. I found a couple of interesting connections between Kathleen Harding and Allie Marsh."

"Shit, Patty, I don't even know if I have a job anymore."

Patty said, "The sergeant straightened it all out. You're in the clear."

"Yvonne the Terrible got me out of the trick bag?"

"She said all you have to do is go a day without smacking anyone."

Stallings hesitated, looked down at the dazed Gary Lauer, and said, "That may be an issue."

It'd been a long night, and he was tired and sore for several different reasons. The music in the Wildside failed to lift his spirits, and even the sight of all these pretty girls did nothing for him in his current state. Usually a night in the excitement and noise of a club would cheer him. His season as a predator was coming to an end. At least for this year. He still had one prize he was hoping for, and that's why he was here so late. This wasn't where the pretty, young Ann tended to hang out, but he'd told her he'd be here tonight. If she showed, he had her in his trap. The only question was whether he would take her tonight or try to prolong the excitement and take her later in the week.

Normally he wouldn't worry about details like this, and he'd go on the hunt again immediately, but he was starting to feel the heat. He'd used up this hunting ground and wouldn't try it again for a long time. He hoped no one figured out his traveling pattern. Maybe in a few more years he could come back here.

He scanned the crowd filled with blond heads bobbing all over the dance floor. He nodded greetings to every few people as they walked past. Mostly faces he knew from the clubs, very few names came to mind. None of them were potential prey. The males were a lot of guys he'd met who were doing their own kind of hunting. But he was the King Predator, and he knew it. The thrill of the kill kept him going. Then someone caught his eye near the front door and he had to stand on his tiptoes to see her face. It was Ann, and she was hot in tight jeans and a simple T-shirt. He felt the rumble of excitement grow from his toes to his head. It wasn't only the sexual excitement of seeing her dressed like that; it was the excitement of the season's last kill.

Instead of going over to see her, he held his place, wanting her to have to search him out. It would reinforce whatever he told her later. If he said to meet him the next day or night, she'd be more inclined to do it if she had to look for him now. He waited patiently like a big cat on the African plain.

He heard someone's voice to his right, but he was so

focused on Ann it didn't register, and he kept staring in the young girl's direction. Then someone tapped him on the right shoulder, making him flinch as he turned to see who'd interrupted his hunt.

The young man with greasy brown hair said, "Yo, dude, I didn't think I'd ever see you again."

He looked at the young man and recognized him but couldn't immediately place him.

The young man said, "Got any more cars we need to push into the water? I sure could use more X."

A chill ran down his back as he realized his past had come back to haunt him

Forty-five

Yvonne Zuni knew to listen and maybe throw in a smile as Ronald Bell shook his head in exasperation.

The IA investigator said, "Didn't we have this conversation yesterday? I said all he had to do was go twenty-four hours without smacking somebody."

"I think even you'll agree under the circumstances he was probably provoked. We can't have a suspect dictating who's involved in an investigation and who's not."

"I'm afraid we can when the suspect is a cop and the lead detective on the case punches him in the face. I know it's all bullshit. I know a muscle-bound motorman like Gary Lauer could handle himself and the only reason he's making the complaint is to screw up the case. What can I say, he knows how to manipulate the system."

"This doesn't mean I have to take Stallings off the case completely, does it?"

Ronald Bell wiped his face with his hand and let out a long breath. "He can work the case, but he cannot have contact with Lauer. That's about the only thing we can do at this point. But it does make me think Officer Lauer has something to hide."

Yvonne took a quick look around the hallway on the third floor of the PMB, then stepped toward the tall, attractive detective and gave him a hug and quick peck on the cheek. "Ron, I really appreciate how understanding you've been through this whole thing."

Bell chuckled and said, "I guess we better make the waiting time a lot shorter for Stallings. Tell him if he can go ten minutes today without smacking someone, he can come back to work."

It had been a bit of a wild night, and he'd slept good and late. But despite seeing several decent prospects and all the other craziness, he'd been able to tell Ann to meet him at the beach this evening. He'd been very subtle about his desire to spend a few moments alone and away from loud bands and noisy bars. She had volunteered she'd be able to borrow one of her friend's cars near dusk and meet him at the quiet beach between Atlantic and Neptune.

That left the question of the kid who'd helped him push Lisa's car in the water. All he'd said was hello and then wandered off, but it was one more link he didn't need. He had the kid's name and could figure out where he lived easily enough, but he didn't want to be rash. That was not entirely true. He was holding off taking action on the kid because he thought it might help pass the time until the next spring break and hunting season.

Now he raced around his apartment in wild anticipation of what would happen tonight. He'd given her one hit of Ecstasy last night and was saving the last one to cover his tracks. This would be so simple and straight-forward it wouldn't matter how many cops were interested in spring break deaths—they'd never figure out what happened to Ann. It was so diabolically simple he couldn't believe he had never used it before. It offered him everything from exciting sex to the power he'd earned and deserved as the King Predator on the spring break plain.

He paused for a moment to gaze at his collage of past conquests. That was the one thing he'd need from Ann. He needed her to pose for a decent photograph, preferably in a skimpy bikini. This might be so phenomenal he'd rearrange the photographs with the lovely girl from Central Georgia at the center.

He opened his souvenir box sitting on the desk. Nothing matched in style or metal, but he knew the story behind each piece. He'd find a prize on Ann's body somewhere, even if it had to be just a simple earring.

He closed the box and clapped his hands together, rubbing them back and forth as if he was trying to get warm, but in fact he was trying to dissipate some of the energy building in him. Clearly he couldn't hunt back here for a couple years now that there was so much interest in Allie Marsh's death.

He didn't see any reason why he couldn't keep doing it other places.

John Stallings stared at the sergeant, shook his head, and said, "You mean he suckered me into the confrontation just to get me off the investigation?"

"Looks that way."

Stallings shook his head, amazed at how he had un-
derestimated Gary Lauer and how this kind of ploy had
reinforced his growing belief the motorcycle cop had
not only provided Ecstasy to college girls, but may have
been systematically murdering them. The whole idea
turned his stomach.

Sergeant Zuni said, "This doesn't excuse your behavior. You got some temper issues, and you and I have to
deal with them. But right now I need you to do whatever needs to be done on the Allie Marsh case."

Stallings nodded. "I know I let you guys down like I
let down Diane Marsh. I also know you went out on a
limb for me, and I appreciate it."

"While you're handing out thank-yous, you might
want to give one to Ronald Bell. He bent the rules quite
a bit to avoid having you suspended like he should've in
both incidents."

"You're kidding me. Ron Bell helped me? I'm not
sure if that's better than being suspended, but I'll make
sure I say something the next time I see him."

Patty Levine appeared at the sergeant's doorway and
said, "We need to talk."

They sat around a small conference table in the
room next to Sergeant Zuni's office, and Patty explained
what she had learned from the medical examiner. The
missing jewelry might not be a big issue, but the fact
that the two girls looked so similar, had Ecstasy in their
systems, had had sex using Durex condoms, and had
died within a week of each other made her think a deliberate, cunning killer was another commonality between the girls.

Sergeant Zuni said, "I wonder how common missing jewelry on the corpse is. I've never really considered the issue before."

Patty said, "Funny you should ask, because I checked with the medical examiner last night and he said it was one of those things they always check but wasn't too common. The scary thing is there's a homicide victim in the morgue right now who's missing a nose stud. She's also blond with blue eyes."

Sergeant Zuni said, "Is that the body they found over in the parking garage who'd been stabbed through the chin into her brainpan?"

Patty just nodded.

Stallings said, "We need to focus on the two girls we've linked. The photos and information from Daytona and Panama City may be interesting and may even be of use later, but right now they're only distractions. We need to put a full-court press on Gary Lauer."

The sergeant said, "What if he's not the killer?"

"He's the only decent suspect we have left. We have narcotics talking to ex-dealers, and we've been looking for Jason Ferrell ourselves. It may be a long shot, but it also would set his mother's mind at ease. I didn't want to call her until I've actually talked to her son."

The sergeant stood, nodded, and said, "Get to work."

Forty-six

Tony Mazzetti turned to his partner, Christina Ho-grebe, and said, "For a little fat guy, Pudge can be hard to find on the street. I just want to make sure he's still okay and see if he could be clearer on his tip."

Christina said, "He said to look closer rather than farther. Why don't we go by the scene of the shooting and check around the house itself?"

"Good call. It's not like we have a ton of other leads to follow up right now. I don't want to be around the office anyway. Not with all the shit Stallings has stirred up. We probably have IA detectives all over the place."

"Patty told me he's all clear and back in the office."

"What? He unloads on the wrong suspect and hits a cop and gets a pass on the whole thing? That's craziness."

"You sound like you're disappointed."

"I like Stall and everything, but there are certain rules we should all have to follow. That guy steps out of bounds more than a white NBA player, but he skates on any possible punishment. It's more an issue of fairness with me."

"You mean like how overtime is divided fairly as long as you get twice as much as anyone else? Where you get to choose most of your assignments? That kind of fairness?"

"Don't be a smart-ass. It makes you seem petty."

Christina Hogrebe was still laughing when they pulled in the driveway of the house near Market Street.

John Stallings was an interviewer. Every detective had strengths and weaknesses, and clearly his strength was talking to people. All those *CSI* TV shows had convinced the general public forensics solved all the problems. That was bullshit. Witnesses talked, and detectives still had to interpret results out of the crime lab. So sitting here in the Jacksonville Sheriff's Office crime lab, listening to one of the techs who specialized in chemical analysis, went against Stallings's nature. Thank God he had Patty with him to interpret everything this geek said. It also seemed to him as if the young scientist had a fairly obvious crush on his partner.

The young man, in his late twenties, had a lean build and thick glasses. The glasses didn't help any attempt the young tech made at looking cool. Right now he seemed like one of a dozen other crime lab techs wanting to show off how smart they were.

The tech said, "There has been a lot of X run through the lab recently. The one pill from the suicide victim, Kathleen Harding, matches exactly the three pills you submitted."

Stallings nodded—this comfirmed his suspicion Jason Ferrell had made the Ecstasy Kathleen Harding used and the three pills the redneck meth manufacturer, Leonard

Walsh, had provided Stallings. So far he could follow the young crime lab tech easily.

"All four of these pills were from the same batch. Chemically, they matched perfectly and were made by someone with some skill and training."

Patty said, "Does the marking *J2A* mean anything to you?"

"I've done some research, and it appeared on a number of X tabs, but it has no chemical or pharmacological significance." The young man flipped several pages on a clipboard. "The Ecstasy pill Detective Mazzetti submitted looks exactly like these on the outside, but chemically it's much different."

There was silence as Stallings and Patty stared at one another. Patty slowly turned to the crime tech and said, "What pill did Mazzetti submit?"

"The other day Detective Mazzetti turned in an Ecstasy tab under the case number for his triple shooting. I assumed you were all working together on it."

"Do you know where Detective Mazzetti found the pill?" He had to work hard to steady his voice. So many years of dealing with the wily detective had made him skeptical of any coincidences.

The lab tech shook his head.

"How is it different chemically from the other pills?"

"It has about one tenth the potency of the other pills. Still has the same marking and colorations. It's just very weak."

Stallings turned toward his partner and said, "We need to talk to Mazzetti right now."

Tony Mazzetti stood in the backyard of the house where the triple shooting had occurred the week before. A typical tiny backyard, bordered by a rotting wooden fence and fruit trees that hadn't been pruned in years. He was trying to get a feel for the yard and where someone would stash drugs or other contraband if they had to. His partner, Christina Hogrebe, had a steel rod she was using as a probe in the soft dirt on the side of the house. They had agreed Pudge's tip might mean they would have to search the house and grounds more closely. Until they found the street prophet, they had to cover every possibility.

Mazzetti walked over to the back door, sat on the small stoop, and gazed out over the yard, trying to imagine where he might stash something in an emergency. When he stepped to the yard he noticed an area of disturbed weeds and grass under a scraggly orange tree. He kneeled down and used his finger to dig into the dirt. His cell phone rang, making him stand, reach in his pocket, and pull it out.

It was Patty and she didn't even bother greeting him. All she said was, "Tony, where'd you get the Ecstasy pill you submitted to the lab?"

He had to think what she was talking about, but before he could give her a straight answer his instincts asked, "Why?"

"What do you mean, why?"

He could hear the frustration in her voice and tried to explain it as best he could. "Jesus, Patty, you yell at me when I don't submit stuff to the lab, and now you yell at me when I do submit stuff to lab. I'm just curious why you want to know about some nasty homemade Ecstasy tablet."

"Because we may have found a link to our case."

"You can link a triple shooting with a drug overdose of a spring breaker?"

"Tony, where'd you get the pill?"

"From the lady in the house across the street from the triple shooting."

"Based on the neighborhood, I'm assuming she's African American?" She sounded disappointed.

"She is, but she claimed her white boyfriend gave it to her."

"Did you see this guy?"

"Just for a split second. A white guy about thirty with brown hair."

"That guy is probably Jason Ferrell. He made the Ecstasy you found in Kathleen Harding's purse."

Mazzetti had walked into the carport of the house while Patty had yelled at him, but now he jerked his head up and stared at Miss Brison's house across the street. Could her boyfriend—she'd called him Chuck, but she admitted that wasn't his name—know something that could help him on this case? It didn't really matter, because a fellow detective who happened to be his girlfriend was asking him for help. Finally Mazzetti said, "I think I know where we can find your X dealer."

He loved to feel the cool breeze off the ocean and had already surveyed the park and surrounding beach. There were a few people around but not enough to interfere with any plans he might have with the beautiful Ann. He watched as she pulled the big Buick into the parking space closest to the beach walkway. He parked his Jeep in the corner of the lot so it was obvious when she drove in. He hustled down the sidewalk to greet her.

She surprised him with a full embrace and a kiss on the lips. He let the kiss linger and felt her tongue probe

into his mouth and her hips grind into him. He'd definitely waited long enough for this one. Power surged
through his body as he started to realize his potential as
a predator.

Ann said, "You're right—this place is perfect." She
opened the rear door of the Buick and pulled out a
blanket. "And it's nice and private down the beach a
ways."

He held out his palm, offering the last hit of Ecstasy.
"Just for you."

She plucked it out of his hand, held it up to the dim-
ming light of the setting sun, turned to him, and asked,
"What does J2A mean?"

"I have no idea, but it's on every pill my buddy Jason
has ever given me."

She stuffed the pill in the front pocket of her tight
shorts and said, "Thanks. I might do it later, but right
now I need to concentrate."

As long as she took the tab before he invited her out
for a swim. That was his plan, and it excited him so
much there was no way he was going to vary from it.

Forty-seven

Stallings felt comfortable with the way they'd set up the surveillance. For a change it felt as if they had enough people to accomplish their mission. Mazzetti and Christina Hogrebe were watching the front of the house from the carport of the house where the triple shooting had occurred. Stallings and Patty sat in his Impala a few blocks down the street with a view of the approach to the house. He wasn't worried about being spotted, because everyone knew the cops were working a triple homicide and he didn't think it would be unusual to have cops at the house or down the street. He doubted anyone suspected they were interested in a white chemist shacked up with a woman across the street.

Patty said, "What do you think about going in and talking to this Miss Brison?"

Stallings shook his head. "Mazzetti already said she covered for him once. If he's still driving the blue Mustang we'll see him pull up."

Patty said, "You know you're lucky."

"How so?"

"With all the shit that's happened in the last few days and the way you reacted to it, you should be sitting at home on suspension, if not under full criminal investigation."

He just nodded, because he knew she was right. That was the beauty of a steady partner; they were allowed to say anything they wanted and you had to listen. He was lucky his partner was smart and insightful and had some common sense.

She said, "The sarge really saved your ass."

Again he nodded.

"That's frustrating."

"What is? Agreeing with everything you say?" He thought about it and added, "I gotta find a way to make it up to her. She proved her value, and now I have to prove mine."

"If we catch Jason Ferrell and close out the Allie Marsh case, that should do it. I think Ferrell can point us in the right direction, and if it was Gary Lauer, then he's all done as a cop. But if it was someone else, we should be able to clear Lauer completely."

He didn't answer, because the way he felt right now he didn't want Gary Lauer working as a cop no matter what the outcome of this case. It had been a slow evolution of thought for him to recognize some people should not be police officers. They didn't have the right temperament. It was easy to lose your police certification. Unlike a lawyer who could commit a felony, spend time in prison, and still go back to practicing law, or a fireman who could claim a chemical dependence to slip out of virtually any problem, a cop had to go by policy as well as the code of the street. Two sets of rules that didn't always coincide. That was one of the reasons he'd been reluctant to believe a cop would do something as stupid as distributing X to meet women.

Stallings started to dream about catching the guy responsible for at least two girls' deaths. "I can't wait to catch Ferrell." He saw the expression on Patty's face and had to say, "Don't worry, I'm not gonna beat his ass. First thing I'm going to do is make him call his mom so she won't be worried anymore."

He saw Patty squinting through the windshield and followed her gaze in time to see the blue Mustang pull in the driveway.

Ann wasn't lying when she told him she liked the spot. It was a beautiful beach with the Atlantic gently rolling onto the deserted shore. She hadn't even noticed anyone in the parking lot when they pulled in. But there was something wrong with the whole situation. Ann was smart. Not just book smart, but, as her dad always said, she had a good head on her shoulders too. She liked always being the voice of reason among her girlfriends and keeping everyone out of trouble. But now she felt ashamed. That was not one of the emotions she was used to. She should've ignored this guy after finding him dancing with the loudmouth from Georgia. That whole confrontation had shaken her a little with the cute, chubby girl right up in her face at the bar. She'd done nothing to deserve it. And she hadn't seen the girl again. Thank God.

She felt she was too smart to be fooling around with this guy at all. He was way too good looking, and she knew guys like that viewed sex as a sport with a scorecard. She didn't know if she was an early-inning hit or a late-inning hit, but she knew he was looking to knock her out of the park. And she felt slutty, because the only reason she was doing it was for more of those Ecstasy tablets with the funny *J2A* mark on them. She'd smoked some pot and drank now and then, but she could take it or leave it. The homemade drug was a different story. This Ecstasy seemed to supercharge her and put her on another plane of existence. She didn't want to waste that on this guy. That's why she had saved the X tab for later. And she knew she'd probably hit him up for more before she left Jacksonville. That's why she was going to sleep with him today. Like any good former Girl Scout she was prepared. She'd packed a blanket and had been drinking steadily for hours so she could always use the excuse she was drunk. Besides that, he was awfully hot, in a very superficial kind of way.

She'd told her boyfriend, Derek, that during spring break he was free to see anyone he wanted just like she was. At the time she said it, with him looking like a puppy in front of her, she only halfway meant it. By halfway she meant she should be able to see people on break and he shouldn't. It was funny when she'd told her girlfriends, but now she felt guilty thinking about him at his parents' house in Pensacola. He was probably playing Nintendo Wii with his little brother and a couple of the buddies he grew up with. She doubted he was at the clubs looking at other girls. Right now she knew she couldn't say much about it if he was. This was definitely one of those incidents she'd never bring up. She knew it was wrong. She hadn't even told her girlfriends where she was going or who she was seeing. It felt dirty but in a sexy kind of way.

She even briefly thought about her parents and how she was certain her father still thought she was a virgin.

She'd made sure he kept that idealized vision of her and only brought home the best possible husband candidates. Deep down she doubted Derek would make the cut. He was cute and funny, but he was getting his degree in psychology and her father would say that is a waste of time and not much of a potential income earner. She viewed it much the same way. If she played her cards right, she knew she could see Derek for the rest of the semester and maybe start over again with an engineering student or maybe even an accounting student in the fall.

She had to stop linking sex to getting the Ecstasy tabs; it made her feel too much like a prostitute.

The beach was so deserted no one even noticed them on the blanket Ann had brought. He tried to get her to take the X before they went into the water, but she said she had to drive and didn't think it was safe. He knew that was the least of her worries. He thought about it and decided the Ecstasy in her system wasn't necessary because she'd just be another drowning victim not used to the riptides of the Atlantic Ocean.

He rolled off her with a grunt and started to peel off his condom, saying, "That was great."

She stayed flat on her back, mashed into the sand, with no real expression on her face, but her eyes cut to him and she suddenly sat up, wiping grains of sand from her lopsided breasts while checking up and down the beach to make sure no one surprised them. She mumbled, "Yeah, great. I'm going for a swim." With that she struggled to her feet in the soft sand and trotted into the water alone.

This was exactly what he wanted, even if it wasn't

with the enthusiasm he'd expected. Now it was time to feel the real power of life and death. It was time to bring down his last antelope of the season. As he stepped into the cool surf he had an odd feeling. Usually he enjoyed being a big cat prowling the open plain, but now, with the water gently rolling over his feet and seeing Ann's blond head bobbing in the ocean, he suddenly felt like a great, South American crocodile. He slipped into the water accordingly with his head up, arms at his side and feet pushing along the bottom. He envisioned wrapping her in a giant death hug and spinning in the water like a crocodile until she had drowned. In fact, he had to make it appear completely accidental. He'd drawn too much attention with Allie Marsh already. He'd figure out a way to get her underwater and leave her there.

He gauged their distance, then plunged underwater, racing toward her like a crocodile on the hunt.

Tony Mazzetti liked clearing homicides in and around Jacksonville. He liked piecing together the puzzles each case presented. Some cases needed a lot of interviews and had witnesses coming out the wazoo. Some cases needed help from forensics, and the nerds in the lab made him look good on a regular basis. In some cases, a few precious cases, there was media coverage with a spotlight that made him shine. He liked those the best and always tried to send the news clips to his mother.

But this was one aspect of police work wasn't crazy about. He didn't like tactical situations. He never enjoyed kicking in doors or even drawing his gun if he didn't have to. That's what the goddamn SWAT team was for. This was not a fact he had ever shared with anyone else for fear of being labeled a coward. Cops were paid to risk their lives sometimes. And he did—he just didn't enjoy it like some screwballs did. He had no idea if this guy, Jason Ferrell, was dangerous or not. But now was not the time to voice those concerns.

As he crept up the driveway of Miss Brison's house, he crouched down and stuck a folding knife in the Mustang's front tire. He looked over his shoulder as the air hissed out of the tire and said to Christina Hogrebe, "A little insurance." A moment later he was at the front door of the clapboard house with his partner right behind him. Patty Levine and Stallings were covering the rear of the house. This time when they asked to speak to the white man of the house he'd have nowhere to flee.

He pounded on the front door, not caring if he startled anyone inside and frankly hoping to scare their target out the back door. It only took a moment for the front door to open a crack and Miss Brison's pretty face to appear.

"Whatchu making all that racket for? This house ain't so big I can't hear a knock at the front door."

She sounded much sharper tonight than she had the last time they had spoken. Mazzetti didn't want to risk losing this guy, so he wasted no time stepping through the front door and forcing Miss Brison backward as he did. He scanned the room quickly as his partner stepped past him and did a quick scan of each room down the hallway on her way to the kitchen. Mazzetti heard her open the back door in the kitchen, and Stallings appeared with her at the end of the hallway.

Mazzetti turned to Miss Brison. "Okay, where is he?"

"Who?"

"Jason Ferrell."

Her eyebrows arched. "Who?"

"Jason Ferrell, the man we saw walking in here from the blue Mustang."

"Oh, you mean Chuck. I like to call him Chuck."

"You can cut the shit. We're not leaving here unless we have Chuck with us. Now where is he?" The house wasn't that big and certainly wouldn't be considered cluttered, but he knew their fugitive had to be in here somewhere.

Calmly, Miss Brison pointed over Mazzetti's shoulder toward the front door and said, "No need to fuss, sugar. He's right there."

Mazzetti turned to see a man slip from the curtains and out the front door in a heartbeat. He called back to Stallings and Christina and raced after him. He cleared the front door and took a second to scan each side of the house, then heard the engine to his Crown Vic rumble to life.

"Oh shit." He sprang across the porch and down the three steps, pulling his pistol as the car squealed away from the curb and headed down the street. Mazzetti considered squeezing off a few rounds even though his life was not in danger. He wished it was with the embarrassment he was about to suffer.

From behind him he heard Stallings say, "Tony, you dumb shit, did you leave your keys in the car?" Stallings didn't wait for an answer as he darted for his Impala. A few seconds later they were racing after Mazzetti's car.

Forty-eight

Ann seemed distant as they floated in the water, but it didn't really matter now. He knew exactly what had to happen. He swam next to her, his toes barely touching the sandy bottom while Ann had to tread water. He tried to kiss her, but she turned her head. He started to feel the power of the predator surge through him as he approached her from behind, wrapped his arms around her, sucked in a deep breath, then, in one quick motion, squeezed the air out of her and pulled her under the surface.

For a moment he thought she'd offer no resistance. Then she struggled and started to flail her arms and legs, but he kept up his pressure and dragged her to the ocean floor. He couldn't spin like he wanted to. Like a crocodile would. But he knew in a second, as her struggling grew weaker, he'd absorb her life force as it leaked out of her.

Then, he didn't know if it was by accident or on purpose, the back of her head struck him hard in the face. He loosened his grip for a second, and one of her feet came up between his legs. He felt the air knocked out of his lungs, and he had nowhere to suck in new oxygen.

When he floated to the surface a moment later, he could hear her kicking away toward shore, screaming, "What the fuck is wrong with you? Horsing around is one thing, but you almost drowned me!"

He started to regain his composure and slowly swam toward her into the shallow water and then matched her step for step as she marched toward the blanket that held their clothes.

"I'm sorry. Come back into the water, and let's swim."

"Are you crazy? You're an asshole." Her voice cracked with a sob.

"Come on, baby, I did you a favor by fucking you on the beach. Now I want to swim with you."

She turned, her naked body clearly visible in the moonlight, her eyes wide. "I know you didn't say that." But before he could respond, she swung her mean right hand and struck him in the eye, following it up immediately with a hard kick into his exposed genitals. He dropped to the wet sand gasping for air.

Almost a minute later, when he had the strength to raise his head, all he could see was an empty beach. Ann was gone and had taken all of their clothes with her.

Ann still gasped for breath, even though she was away from him and only standing in waist-deep water. Now she felt vulnerable standing naked on a public beach even if there was no one around. She didn't know why guys thought shit like that was funny, but she really couldn't breathe. He may not have realized it. Maybe it had something to do with all she had to drink that afternoon. But that didn't change the fact that this guy was an asshole. She couldn't believe some of the things he'd just said to her. She realized she shouldn't be naked on the beach with a guy she barely knew, so far from home, but that didn't excuse the fact that he had no class and was no gentleman.

She was furious. As he came back toward her again she swung hard with her right fist, then threw her left leg up to catch him solidly in the groin. Her karate instructor she'd had for one year when she was eleven would have been proud of her form. She felt a deep satisfaction as he tumbled onto the sand as if he was about to spit up.

Then a new thought hit her. What if he was into that auto-asphyxiation crap? He could've done that on purpose and really gone too far. She didn't know if he'd been drinking too. The cocky son of a bitch could've drowned her and wouldn't even have realized it.

Now, among the alcohol, stress, and adrenaline dump, she suddenly felt very tired. For some reason that exhaustion made her think about the Ecstasy tab in the front pocket of her jeans. It would give her energy and put her into a good mood. But she wanted to get away from this jerk first.

She felt a little guilty leaving him gasping for air and naked in the surf. She looked up and down the beach. Still empty. Serves him right. She quickly slipped on her clothes, not even bothering to dry her hair. As she walked up, bundling up her towel, she wondered how bad her craving for Ecstasy would be once this last pill was gone. She hoped she never had to see this guy again.

* * *

Stallings ignored Mazzetti's incessant chatter and concentrated on where he would turn, searching for the stolen police car. He left Christina and Patty at the house to see if they could find out anything from the very odd Miss Brison. Stallings was pretty sure he didn't want Patty to be a witness to what might happen if they caught the elusive Jason Ferrell.

Stallings reached for his radio, but before he could mash the button, Mazzetti put his hand on Stallings's arm and said, "Let's leave this off the air for now."

"Tony, what are you talking about? It's a fucking pursuit."

Mazzetti used a low tone and said, "Come on, Stall, if this gets out, I'll never live it down."

Stallings hesitated, then tossed the radio back onto the seat. It wasn't smart, but he understood what a veteran detective like Mazzetti was thinking. As he was about to suggest a different area to search, the Crown Vic rolled through an intersection, almost striking them. Stallings spun the wheel of the Impala hard, cutting through someone's front yard, and squealed the tires on the pavement as the Impala came up behind Jason Ferrell and Mazzetti's Crown Vic.

Now the chase was on.

This was humiliating. Ann had left him naked, bruised, and with no car keys. They were in the front pocket of the shorts that had been sitting on the blanket. Now he huddled in the bushes of the park, trying to figure out a way home. He already had devised new ways this bitch would pay for her treachery. Instead of feeling the power of the predator he was scared, sore, and twitching to get revenge.

Then he saw an opportunity. A teenage couple sitting on a low wall around the parking lot. He couldn't risk violence with them because his Jeep would identify him as the culprit. But he did think he could talk them into helping by explaining he'd been robbed. All he needed was a ride back to his apartment. It wasn't too far.

He called from the bushes, "Hey guys, can you help me out?"

The heavyset young man and his pretty dark-haired girlfriend looked around to see where the voice was coming from.

He stood, letting the bushes cover him partially. "You guys. I've been robbed and I need a little help."

This time the young man turned completely around and saw him. He left his girlfriend on the wall and stepped over toward the bushes. "Man, you naked or what?"

"Yeah, I'm naked, and I can't get into my Jeep." He pointed across the lot. "I'll make it worth your while if you give me a ride back to my apartment."

"I don't know, man. My girl and me like the beach." He glanced back over at the pretty girl and added, "Hang on for me to see what she says."

He waited a moment while the two conferred. They stood together and walked across the lot, ignoring him as they approached his Jeep. The young man turned, and shouted, "I can get into your Jeep."

He called back to the young man, "Really?"

The man didn't answer. Instead he bent over, picked up a large rock off the ground and smashed the passenger side window of his Jeep. He had the door open in a second and was rummaging around inside. The girl kept watch on him, giggling the whole time.

They couldn't do this to a predator. He darted out of the bushes, letting his natural athlete's body drop into full long strides. He was so fast that by the time the girl could turn around to warn her boyfriend he was on top of him.

The fat young man stepped out of the Jeep to meet him but instead was greeted with a full-body block into the side of the Jeep that snapped his head so hard he fell to the ground semiconscious. The girl screamed, but he turned and with the long arc of his left hand smacked her in the face, sending her to the ground next to the boy. Her body twisted on the impact, knocking her brown bikini top askew. She didn't cry as she glared back at him, the wide red splotch of the strike across her cheek.

"Don't explain what you could do to make up for the broken window. First, you can give me a shirt and pants."

The young man just stared at him, not moving.

"I mean right now." He snarled each word carefully.

The young man slipped off his T-shirt and tossed it to him.

"The pants too," he said snapping his fingers to speed things.

The young man scurried to stand and slip off his baggy shorts and tossed them over.

He reached in the pocket and pulled out a set of keys. "These belong to that piece a shit Toyota over there?"

The young man nodded furiously.

The young woman gazed at him, rubbing her cheek.

He said, "This is what we're gonna do. We are gonna walk back to your car. You're gonna let me borrow it. Then I'll it bring back to you while you wait over there in the bushes." He paused for effect, then added, "naked."

The girl stood.

"Both of you naked starting right now, and you really don't want to piss me off again." He had regained his stature as a predator and watched as the young man slipped off the multicolored underwear he wore and the girl first peeled off her cockeyed bikini top, then shimmied out of shorts, displaying a very attractive ass.

He led them both back to the same bushes where they'd found him.

"Not a peep out of you until I get back." He could tell by the look in their eyes they understood how serious he really was.

Forty-nine

Stallings didn't like being in a pursuit that wasn't authorized and in an area decidedly unfriendly to police officers, next to a cop he would prefer not to be in the same car with. But that didn't stop him from doing his best to close in on the stolen Crown Vic. He, like most cops, didn't get in many chases, and the Impalas they issued the detectives weren't designed for high-speed chases and cornering the way some of the patrol cars were. But luckily Jason Ferrell wasn't much of a driver and he clearly had no idea of where he wanted to go. That was the case with most people fleeing the police.

They were very close to the house where the pursuit had started, but Stallings wanted to wait until they were in an area with wider streets. He didn't want to risk this moron losing control of the Crown Vic and driving through someone's bedroom wall. Instead, he gave the young man space and backed off several car lengths.

After another few minutes on the main road, Stallings saw a baseball diamond on the left, turned to

Mazzetti, and said, "This is our one chance, Tony. If we miss him here we're gonna have to call in."

Mazzetti nodded solemnly, understanding his fate.

Stallings mashed the gas, closed in on the Crown Vic, and pulled to the left. Now he could see the scared driver was definitely Jason Ferrell. His hair was shaggier than in the photos, but he was basically an easy spot. As they reached the edge of the baseball field, Stallings swerved toward the Crown Vic and watched as Ferrell instinctively swerved away from him, caught the curb, and spun the Crown Vic out on the wide infield of the first baseball diamond.

Both detectives were out of the car with their guns drawn and in Jason Ferrell's face before he recovered enough to try to pull away.

Mazzetti said, "Now you're in one shit pot of trouble."

He had left the shitty Toyota running while he ran into his apartment, changed clothes, grabbed his spare keys, and, to be on the safe side, picked up a long, razor-sharp combat knife he had bought at a gun show last year. His mind was still swirling as he thought about Ann and her despicable behavior.

The drive back to the beach was fast, and he pulled up next to his Jeep. No one was visible, but he knew the two naked people were in the bushes and yelled over to them. "Come and get your car and clothes."

At first there was no movement, but after a few seconds the girl stood tall and walked across the lot as if she was in a beauty contest, not ashamed of one inch of her lean body. She had real grace and some indescribable quality, which radiated beauty. Then the fat schlump popped up and scurried after her like a frightened dog. How had these two ended up together?

He had the knife tucked under his shirt as he casually leaned against his Jeep.

The girl stopped in front of him, making no attempt to cover herself. The fat guy bumped up next to her with his hands over his genitals. She looked at him for a moment. "Now what?"

He took the key to the Toyota, slid it into the car's door lock, and snapped it off in the lock. He smiled at the girl. "Now, I'll give you a ride anywhere you want, and he can fend for himself."

Without hesitation, the girl accepted her bundled clothes, slipped them on, and climbed into the Jeep, ignoring all comments from her boyfriend.

He didn't offer the boyfriend his clothes. He drove off with the pretty girl and left the chubby naked man whimpering by his disabled car.

Back at Miss Brison's house, Stallings sat directly in front of Jason Ferrell as the young man trembled and his eyes darted around the room to the other detectives. The first thing Stallings said to him was, "Your mom is worried sick about you."

"Huh?"

"You disappeared, you idiot, and your mom hasn't heard from you in three weeks." Looking at the scared, meek man, Stallings lost a lot of his anger. He decided it might not be a bad idea to listen to him before jumping to any conclusions.

Understanding slowly dawned on the young chemical engineer. "You mean the only reason you were looking for me was my mom was worried?"

From across a room, Mazzetti said, "I got a few questions about the shooting across the street."

Stallings added, "And I have a few questions about the Ecstasy you made and who you sold it to."

"So I'm not really in trouble?"

Mazzetti stomped across the room shouting as he came closer. "Oh no, you're in trouble, dipshit. You can't steal a police car and drive around Jacksonville without being in trouble. In fact, you ran from me twice." Mazzetti balled a fist when he was right next to him. "I oughta kick your ass."

Stallings snapped his finger to get the young man's attention. "There's only one way to keep this madman from killing you. You have to help us out with a few things."

Ferrell glanced around the room and said, "When did my mom call?"

Stallings thought about it and said, "Two weeks ago last Monday."

"What day is it now?"

"Thursday."

"Is it still February?" Ferrell's red eyes scanned the room again, and the shakes that had been confined to his hand spread through his whole body. "I kinda lost track of time. But I'll help out any way you want. Just tell my mom I'm okay."

Her name was Sharee, and her light brown hair flowed behind her as the wind whipped in from the missing window. She had not said one word about the fat guy they'd left at the beach.

"You got any weed?" she asked after a few minutes of driving west.

"Bad for you. You look too fit to smoke grass."

"Got anything?"

He thought about his final X tab leaving with Ann. He shook his head. "Sorry, I'm dry."

"Somehow you seemed like a guy who would have something. You were pretty cool back there. You weren't really robbed, were you?"

He smiled and shook his head.

"A girl?"

He nodded.

"Your girlfriend?"

"Not even close."

She reached across and rubbed his shoulder, then let her hand drift down his body until it rested in his lap. After a few seconds of massaging, she looked at him with those big, dark eyes and said, "What's a matter? You a fag?"

He shook his head. "You're not my type."

He dropped her at her father's house a few miles later.

It had taken a few minutes to calm Tony Mazzetti down and keep him from physically assaulting the bewildered Jason Ferrell. But now John Stallings had the young chemical engineer in the kitchen alone. He didn't seem like a jerk or uncooperative in any way; he was just sort of out of it. He had moments when he was lucid, but more often than not he stared off in space and mumbled long, incoherent sentences.

Stallings scooted a chair directly in front of him and sat down so he could look at the young man eye to eye. He noticed Patty Levine slip in from the other room and lean against the kitchen counter. A standard practice the partners used. When one person interviewed a subject, the other hung back and took notes. That allowed the interviewer to focus on the subtle nonverbal cues given off by a witness or suspect.

Stallings said, "We know about Leonard Walsh and the meth recipe you were making for him."

"Who's Leonard Walsh?"

"You don't know a guy with a meth lab over in Baker County?"

Jason's eyes focused for a moment as he looked at Stallings and said, "You mean the guy by the national forest? Redneck with all the trailers?"

"Yeah, that's him. He says you were going to use your abilities as a chemical engineer to create a new meth recipe. He said you tried to get him to sell Ecstasy instead. He gave us the Ecstasy tabs you gave him."

Jason was nodding slowly in agreement with everything Stallings said. "I really hadn't started on his meth recipe. I don't think meth is good for all of the rednecks west of Jacksonville. X is much safer."

"Tell me about the X. Who did you sell it to?" Stallings couldn't control his impatience to know which of the suspects was a client of the chemical engineer.

"I sold to a whole bunch of people. Mostly the people I met in bars. It's not like I handed it out like candy. I sold bigger lots so I only had to deal with twenty people or so. Nothing serious, I liked the extra income."

"You didn't make enough from your regular job?"

"I had a lot of expenses."

"Like what?"

Jason just looked around at the kitchen.

Stallings said, "You finance Miss Brison's life here, don't you?"

"Everything was for her. I started making the X as a way to get her off heroin. Then she got hooked on the X. So I had to start making special batches for her that were less and less potent. Now I've got her almost back to reality."

From the other side of the kitchen, Patty said, "That explains why the Ecstasy tab Tony sent to the lab was so much weaker than the others."

Jason twisted in his seat, nodding. "Exactly. She's hardly even noticed, and soon she'll be able to deal with the world drug-free."

The young chemical engineer had answered a lot of questions in Stallings's mind, but he still had the most important one yet to ask. "Did you ever sell any Ecstasy to a guy named Chad Palmer or Gary Lauer?" Stallings truly didn't know if he wanted Palmer to be the man or Lauer.

Jason scratched his head, concentrating hard on the question. He looked back at Stallings and said, "Dude, I don't keep track of names. I'm a strictly first-name-and-short-description kind of guy. Like Joe, the truck driver, or Tom, the garbageman."

"Then it would be Chad, the pharmaceutical rep, or Gary, the cop."

Jason perked up and said, "A cop? I sold to an undercover cop?"

"Don't worry about that. All I need is information. Do either of those guys sound familiar? They're both about your age, athletic, dark hair."

Slowly Jason shook his head. "I think a pharmaceuti-

cal rep would have access to a lot better shit than my Ecstasy. And I'd know if I was dealing with a cop. I'm pretty
smart that way."

Stallings looked over at Patty, knowing they'd hit another dead end in the case. Now the question was what
to do with the spacey adult runaway.

Fifty

It was dawn, and Patty Levine felt herself dozing in a comfortable chair in the corner of the hotel room where they'd stashed Jason Ferrell for the night. It was Sergeant Zuni's idea to keep track of the wily chemical engineer without booking him in case narcotics could use him as a snitch. It was her background in narcotics that gave her the idea, and it seemed reasonable last night. Patty had volunteered to take the first shift of watching him because she knew she wouldn't sleep much anyway.

Listening to the lovesick chemical engineer talk about how he changed his whole life to help Marie Brison, including making his own Ecstasy with decreasing potency, had brought Patty's own drug use into the light. She always had some excuse to keep using her regular regimen of Xanax, painkillers, and Ambien. For several years she'd used the excuse of being a female in a male-dominated profession as a way to keep taking the anxiety drug. But she knew she was more capable than most cops and more physical than most cops. Now she had to analyze why she should keep taking the Xanax.

The Ambien was a more obvious issue. She couldn't sleep at night. The fact that she stayed awake the entire night while Jason Ferrell snored on the bed across the room showed that her insomnia was still going strong. Sure, she nodded off, but it was only for a few minutes.

The final leg of her pharmaceutical trinity was the various painkillers she'd been prescribed for numerous injuries and strains she had received while involved in competitive gymnastics. Now she wasn't sure the scholarship to the University of Florida had been worth the years of discomfort. This seemed to be the easiest habit to kick of the three kinds of drugs she took. Today would be her test. She would tough out any pain she felt. It didn't matter if her hip throbbed like a bass speaker at a rap concert or her back radiated pain all day. She would not pop a Vicodin or Percocet no matter how badly the pain affected her.

Her experience in police work taught her not to try to kick all three drugs at once. She'd focus on the pain pills first. Then deal with her anxiety and insomnia as her life started to adjust.

As close as Patty was to John Stallings and as serious as she was getting about Tony Mazzetti, she'd never told either of them anything about her drug use. She was pretty sure neither of them had any idea.

Jason stirred and sat up quickly in the bed. He was still in the clothes he'd been wearing when they found him. He stared at Patty for a moment, shook his head, and blinked his eyes. "Where am I, jail?"

Patty had to smile. "Do you remember anything about last night?"

"I know you're a cop named Patty, even if you don't look like it. And you work with a scary guy named Stallings. I may do X at night, but it clears out pretty quick."

"You ever wonder if you're wasting your talent as a chemical engineer?"

"You mean by finding ways of getting rid of the Maxwell House waste products? Because I think I helped at least one person by making the Ecstasy."

Patty shook her head. "We've got two dead girls with Ecstasy in their systems. One of them overdosed on it, and her heart exploded in her chest."

The color drained out of Jason's face. He clutched his stomach and scooted to the edge of the bed, looking over at Patty in the chair. "You think it was my Ecstasy that killed her? I never meant for anything like that to happen. That's why I was making such weak tablets." He paused, gathered his thoughts, and took several deep breaths. "What can I do to help? I have the recipe on my computer."

"I don't know what good the recipe will do. What we really needed was who you sold it to. And not just first names and job descriptions. Besides, you could only remember three or four clients last night."

"But I have a full list on my computer."

That caught Patty's attention. "You really are more lucid this morning. Where's your computer?"

"I don't have any idea."

The phone startled John Stallings first thing in the morning. He'd already tossed and turned most of the night, worried about Patty at the hotel room with Jason Ferrell. Not that he didn't think his partner could handle herself—she was tougher than any cop he knew. He just hated when someone got stuck on a shitty detail.

He fumbled with his cell phone as he glanced at the clock and saw that it was seven in the morning. He popped it open and mumbled, "Stallings."

Yvonne Zuni said, "John, there's a possible break in the case. Meet me down at the PMB as quick as you can. Come up to the third floor."

Stallings sat up in bed trying to clear his mind. "The third floor? Where on the third floor?"

"Internal Affairs. Gary Lauer is being questioned there right now, and we might have an opportunity to break him on the Allie Marsh case."

"What's he at IA for?"

"Apparently he got drunk last night, said it was all the pressure he was under, then got into a big fight with his girlfriend. The neighbors called the cops, but he'd already left her apartment." There was silence on the line for a moment. Sergeant Zuni added, "A neighbor found the girlfriend this morning with her wrists slashed. She's at the medical examiner's now."

"You think Gary Lauer tried to hide her death as a suicide?"

"Whether he did or didn't, this might be the time to question him. Because with the two dead spring break girls someone could've tried to hide a murder behind a suicide and an overdose."

Instantly Stallings thought of the string of girls from Daytona and Panama City.

Tony Mazzetti knocked on the hotel room door three times, balancing Dunkin' Donuts coffee and a mixed dozen donuts in one hand. He was a little earlier than his scheduled eight o'clock arrival, but he didn't know how well Patty was doing. On the few occasions he spent the whole night at her house she either tossed and turned or slept like a log. No one considered Jason Ferrell any kind of a threat, and Patty really knew how to take care of herself, so that wasn't a concern. They'd already broken all kinds of official rules by holding the chemical engineer in a hotel overnight, but if he really was going to be of any use as a drug informant it'd be hard to keep it quiet that he'd spent the night in jail. This was an old trick, not officially sanctioned by the sheriff's office or especially the state attorney's office, but it was used on occasion not only to give someone a break but to take a shot at the big case cops always wanted to make. The guy had been too screwed up on God knows what for Mazzetti to get any straight answers out of him. Today he planned to ask him about his own case, the triple shooting near Market Street.

Patty had a bright smile on her face when she opened the door, and Mazzetti was surprised to see Jason Ferrell sitting at the cheap table in the corner of the hotel room. His eyes seemed clearer this morning, but he still had the disheveled appearance of an absent-minded professor or street person.

He resisted giving Patty a kiss on the cheek as he entered the hotel room but did make a show out of presenting her with the donuts and coffee. She accepted them with a nod that sent her pretty hair across her face.

Mazzetti said, "Anything new with your car thief here?"

Jason said, "I'm sorry I took your car. I guess I panicked." He grabbed two donuts from the box and devoured one in a single bite. "When can I get back to see Marie? She doesn't do well on her own."

Mazzetti shook his head as he plopped in the chair across the table from Jason. "We've been cutting you a break so you could get a decent night's sleep here, but you're not free to go yet."

"Why?" He looked at Patty with big puppy-dog eyes.

Mazzetti kept talking. "You got until five o'clock today to come up with something good. Someone had better go to jail based on information you provide or at five o'clock you get booked for making your Ecstasy."

"But I thought you guys liked me. Patty and I bonded."

"You're not our fucking mascot. Make a case, or you'll have a new permanent address."

"I already told you guys I have the list of my clients on my laptop."

Mazzetti opened his notepad he carried everywhere with him. "I'm much more interested in a bigger crime. One that happened very close to your love nest."

"I don't know what you're talking about."

"The triple shooting right across the street. You were there at Marie Brison's house. I know because that was the first night you ran from me. You had to have seen something."

"You mean that was real?"

Now he had Mazzetti's attention. "You did see something. I knew it."

"It was during a time when the X was still pretty strong, and I might've been using a homemade sleeping pill as well. I couldn't tell you what day it was, and I thought I had dreamed it, but I did see someone shooting up the house across the street." He slapped his forehead and added, "That's why all the police were there afterward. Of course it had to be real."

"Yes, it was all real. Three dope dealers are dead. I've

got a mother and her two terrified daughters stashed at a hotel for safety. Now what exactly did you see?"

Jason stared off into space, his eyes not clearly focused on anything as he slowly and carefully said, "I cannot believe it was real. The way the girl with the red highlights in her hair stepped out of the front door with the gun in her hand. I thought I'd heard a few firecrackers, so I had looked out the window and I saw her step out and pull the trigger. She wasn't aiming at anything. She held the gun and let it stitch the windows and one of the cars in the driveway."

"Then what happened?"

"She sort of strolled back into the house. I think I might've dozed back off on the couch in the living room, and when I woke up I had assumed I dreamed the whole thing. I mean, I had seen the girl before. She lives there. Why would she shoot up her own house?"

Mazzetti wrote notes furiously as a lot of things started to make sense now. It was weird that this spaced-out druggie had been able to put all of the pieces of the puzzle into place for him.

Jason watched Mazzetti and said, "Does that help you at all, Detective?"

Mazzetti cut his eyes to Jason, then over to Patty sitting on the edge of the bed. "Think about what you just told me. Go over it in your head carefully. I want you to make sure this is exactly what you saw. Take your time." Mazzetti knew how crucial this testimony would be. He also knew the slim chances of keeping an X-head like this lucid, let alone alive, until this case could go to trial in a year or more. He was glad Patty was here to witness the testimony, and he intended to get it on video later in the day. But first he wanted to make sure this airhead had it right and clear in his mind. Mazzetti was patient;

all good homicide detectives were. He could wait for an hour while this guy sorted out what he had seen. But after about a minute and a half, once Mazzetti stood up again, he realized Jason Ferrell had dozed off with a donut's powdered sugar trailing down his chin to his chest.

Mazzetti looked over at Patty. "Oh, he'll make a bang-up witness."

"Does what he says make any sense?"

"Perfect sense. The girl with the red highlights in her hair is one of the victim's sisters. She was the only witness, and her statement has changed a couple of times."

"You don't think she shot her own brother, do you?"

"One thing homicide has taught me is never be surprised." He stood and said, "Are you doing okay? Because I really need to grab Hoagie and haul ass over to the hotel where we put the mother and daughters from the shooting. I need to talk to the girl right now."

Patty looked over at the snoozing Jason Ferrell. "I think I'll be safe until someone else can come relieve me."

This time Mazzetti did give her a kiss and darted out the door to take a shot at closing this homicide.

Fifty-one

Stallings had never been comfortable in the IA division, at least not since he'd been questioned after Jeanie's disappearance. He understood the concerns about why he and Maria had waited so long to report their oldest daughter missing, and he'd been elusive in many of his answers, but it was only to protect Maria and the fact that she'd been whacked out of her head on prescription painkillers at the time. Now he was watching his chief tormentor, Ronald Bell, talk to a clearly agitated Gary Lauer. Mazzetti, Yvonne Zuni, and Ronald Bell's partner were all in a small chamber attached to the interview room watching the proceedings through thick, mirrored glass.

Lauer fidgeted in his hard seat, repeatedly cracked his knuckles, and twisted his head to crack his neck too. He blurted out curt answers to any questions and made comments on the uselessness of IA.

As much as he hated to admit it, even to himself, Stallings had been very impressed with Ronald Bell's hardball tactics. He knew what the crimes/persons unit wanted to pin on the motorcycle patrolman, and he was asking all the right questions to try and trip him up. First he covered Gary Lauer's relationship with his girl-friend who had slit her wrists. Then he masterfully walked the conversation toward his habit of visiting dance clubs and his efforts to meet women there. Now the senior IA investigator was asking him about his girl-friend's drug habits.

Ron Bell said, "Was she a drug user of any kind?"

"Not around me. She knew I couldn't tolerate that kind of activity."

"Cut the shit, Lauer. I know you have no problem with drug use, and I know you stepped out on her all the time. Why don't you take this opportunity to come clean and maybe save yourself from going crazy?"

"I don't even know what you're talking about. She was a casual thing on the side and knew I hit the clubs. And I don't know where you get the idea I'm okay with drug use."

"I heard you don't mind handing out the X now and then."

Lauer stood sharply, kicking the chair behind him across a small interview room. "Bullshit. That asshole Stallings has got it in for me. You know I had to file a complaint to keep him away from me."

"Why did you file a complaint? Because he was get-ting too close to the truth?"

Lauer started to pace back and forth, turning his back on Ronald Bell and wiping his face a couple of times. He didn't turn toward the mirrored glass in the interview room, and Stallings figured he knew there was an observation area next door.

Ronald Bell calmly and deliberately stood from the table and said, "Hang on one sec." He stepped out of the interview room and five seconds later entered the observation chamber. He spoke in a low voice. "You guys see I keep hitting him from all sides. He claims the girl really didn't mean much to him and she was fine when he left. Which we all know is true. She had a long history of drug use, so suicide isn't that far out of the realm of possibility."

Yvonne Zuni leaned in toward Ronald Bell and Stallings and said, "She was terrified of him. I think she'd be happy he'd left for good. Can I talk to him?"

"Be my guest."

Stallings stood, staring at Lauer through the one-way glass, aware Ronald Bell and he were on the same side in this case. The idea he could stand next to the IA investigator and not want to punch him disturbed Stallings. So he remained silent and focused on the small interview room as Yvonne Zuni entered.

As soon as the door opened, Gary Lauer turned around. "What, are you gonna hit me again?" He reached up and touched his left eyebrow.

"It's probably what you need. But I don't want you to have to go around telling people how a chick kicked your ass two different times." She smiled as she sat down at the table. "Come on, Gary, you and I both know you have issues with women."

"I have issues with certain women. And you're one of them."

"But we worked together for a while. I figured you might have an easier time talking to me."

"Sure, the supervisor of the guy who's trying to wreck my career. That's who I'm gonna talk to." He wiped his face with a shaky hand as perspiration stains blossomed around his underarms and down the middle of his simple gray T-shirt. He sat down and immediately stood again and slowly pulled out the chair and tried to sit down and act casual. "You guys got nothing on me. Why treat me like this?"

"We're not trying to treat you badly. We're just trying to get at the truth."

Stallings continued to watch the window, noticing Lauer's jerky movements and flop sweat. As much as he hated the idea of a cop doing some of the things he thought Lauer had done, he had to be honest with himself and admit this guy looked like a loser right now. This guy was a bully and didn't respond to anything but bullying.

Stallings looked across at Ronald Bell as he watched the interview too. "You think if one of us gave him a heart-to-heart as cops, he might see the error of his ways?"

"Can't be you, because you let that dumb-ass goad you into punching him. So no matter what happens, I can't officially let you into the interview room. It would only bolster his argument that we're all out to get him, and you're behind the entire conspiracy. Besides I don't think we've reached the point where we need to beat a confession out of him."

Stallings was about to respond when he heard Lauer say, "Am I under arrest?"

Every cop knew that question could be the end of the interview right there. It was a delicate time that had to be handled carefully. The defendant could walk out of an interview or invoke his right to an attorney; then any chance they had of getting a confession would end abruptly.

Yvonne Zuni didn't answer. Sometimes that was the right move.

Lauer said again, "Am I under arrest? Or am I free to go? Please answer the question right now."

Yvonne Zuni mumbled, "You're not under arrest."

Without another word Gary Lauer stood, turned, and banged the door open, marching out of the room.

Stallings didn't hesitate or ask permission. He darted out of the observation room and walked quickly to catch up to Lauer before he reached the elevator at the end of the hallway. He placed a hand on Lauer's shoulder and turned him. He didn't waste time on a greeting or any other preamble. Stallings said, "There was a time when you swore to protect people. It had to mean something to you. It means something to all of us. For some reason now you're a danger to people. I don't know what went screwy in your brain, but you lost perspective. If nothing else, think about the girl who lost her life because of you today. You may not have killed her. But she's dead and you're sure as shit the reason. You need to come clean or find a way to stop yourself somehow before you hurt anyone else."

The smirk never left Lauer's face as he said, "You give that same kind of pep talk to your daughter before she split?" He waited, inviting Stallings to punch him.

Stallings had to swallow hard, take a deep breath, and let this asshole walk away from him.

Patty Levine, not sure what to do with her prisoner or whatever she was supposed to call Jason Ferrell, checked out of the room, and now he sat in the front seat of her county car. She'd taken him to McDonald's, where he wolfed down two Big Macs. The only place she was certain she shouldn't take him was the PMB. At least not if the narcotics unit might use him as a snitch.

Sometime before Tony Mazzetti had dropped by, Jason Ferrell had recalled that he stored a lot of information on his laptop computer. The problem with a smart guy who did a lot of drugs was he couldn't recall where he'd left the computer. They'd made a run by his apartment building and couldn't find any hint of the computer. Then, against Patty's better judgment, he checked Marie Brison's house and again had come up empty. But Patty noted how much more lucid Miss Brison seemed than her boyfriend nowadays. Maybe his idea of decreasing dosage had helped her clear her head and get off drugs. Tony Mazzetti had described how spacey the beautiful black woman was the first night he'd met her.

But now Patty felt like a mother running errands with their child. He did pretty much whatever she said, asked a lot of stupid questions, and contributed almost nothing to her efforts to find his computer.

"You have to buy gas for this car?" asked Jason.

She shook her head.

"Have you ever had to shoot anyone?"

"No, I never had to, but I did anyway." Patty smiled at the confused and worried expression on Jason's face. Maybe if she gave him something to think about he'd shut up for a few minutes. But Patty thought of a question for the chemical engineer. "What does the *J2A* marking on your Ecstasy mean?"

He looked out the window and mumbled, "Nothing, just something I put on the tabs."

"Come on, it has to mean something. I can tell by your reaction."

"It means Jason to Alyssa."

"Who's Alyssa?"

"An old girlfriend I had in college. I thought she'd come down here to Florida when I got my first decent job, but she decided the life of schoolteacher in suburban Chicago was too exciting to leave. And when I told her I would stay, she clarified it was the life of a *single* schoolteacher that she wanted to live."

"If she knew how romantic you were, using the markings on your Ecstasy tabs, maybe she'd change her mind." Patty didn't know what else to say, and she didn't mean it as a joke, although she knew when she told Mazzetti about it later he'd laugh his head off.

"It's not really romantic. It just means that the pills fuck with your head almost as much as she did. When I figured out I could help Marie with the tabs it took on another meaning. Sort of like 'screw you, Alyssa. I got a beautiful new girlfriend.' "

Patty nodded, knowing he sounded like every scorned boyfriend she'd ever met. As she was thinking about where they could land for the next few hours until someone told her what they wanted to do with Jason, she started to feel the effects of no sleep and the constant activity of the last two days. She sighed.

Jason said, "You've got to be tired."

"I didn't realize how tired until now."

"I think I have the ingredients to make you some decent speed at my apartment. You want to swing by and see what I can do?"

"That's sweet, Jason. But I think I can last until I can grab a nap." The sad thing was she'd been thinking some good amphetamine would perk her right up. She hadn't realized the frame of mind she was in about prescription drugs until the last few days. Now she'd gone more than thirty-six hours without pain pills or sleeping pills and almost three hours since she'd taken a Xanax. It wasn't perfect, but at least she was making progress.

Then Jason snapped his fingers and said, "I think I know where the computer is."

"Where?"

"The company owned the laptop, so I probably took it by there and left it."

"You mean the company in the Maxwell House building?"

Jason Ferrell nodded his head.

Patty thought back to how she and Stallings had tricked the manager the last time they were there, thinking they'd never see the man again.

Patty swallowed hard and said, "Uh oh."

Tony Mazzetti and Christina Hogrebe sat in the front room of the Residence Inn suite where the shooting victim's family had been held as a precaution. Now things were looking less obvious, and Mazzetti had focused his attention on the seventeen-year-old daughter of the woman he'd moved from the house. At the moment, the mother and the younger daughter were at a meeting with county social workers. The social workers were not allowed to discuss their case with the police, but Mazzetti figured the woman had to explain why none of her children had ever attended a public school and why the only one under sixteen still wasn't in school. She might be smart enough to claim she had homeschooled them, but he doubted it.

Both he and Christina had agreed they didn't want to make this confrontational unless they had to. So now he sat back while Christina led the girl through a series of questions.

Christina brushed her blond hair from her face, leaned toward the scrawny girl, and said, "Tosha, now you're saying you did see a carload of white men shoot your brother and his friends?"

The girl had a sleepy quality to her voice. "I seen on the news the police was looking for white boys and it make me think, and I remembered."

"Your first statement said it was an SUV and you couldn't see who was inside."

"I started remembering I seen a white arm holding one of those big black guns." She lifted a hand to play with the same piece of hair she always did. The red highlights swirled to make one red spoke out of her unruly head.

"Would you mind coming back to the house with us?"

"Why?"

"So we can see which window you looked out of and what you saw."

The girl said, "Can you protect me from the white people?"

Mazzetti thought, *We're the only white people you need to worry about now.*

Fifty-two

John Stallings met Patty Levine and a surprisingly co-
herent Jason Ferrell at the office where he used to work
deep inside the Maxwell House complex. They'd been
met by the same manager with the same attitude from
their last visit, during which they'd said they were going
to get a subpoena but never actually bothered after the
man told them what they needed to know and let
Stallings glance through Jason's address book.

The manager pointed at Jason and said, "That man
no longer works here and has no right to be here." He
looked at Stallings, adjusted his gaze for the height difference, smiled, and added, "I'd be happy to talk to
you, Detective, once you got a subpoena."

Stallings said, "I'm sorry about the misunderstanding
last time we met."

"It wasn't a misunderstanding. You lied to me. I have
since been in close contact with our legal department
and know I need a subpoena from the state attorney's
office, compelling me to talk to you, before I say anything else."

"We don't actually need to talk to you. We just need

to let Jason get some information from his laptop computer."

"That computer is the property of this company. Neither you nor Mr. Ferrell can have access to it." The manager picked up a single sheet of paper with typewritten instructions printed on. "For something of that nature I would require a court order or search warrant. I'm sorry it has to be this way, Detective, but you left me with no alternative after our last encounter."

Stallings knew pricks like him got off on the minor power that occasionally came their way, and everyone loved telling the cops to go to hell when they were in no danger of going to jail. He knew better than to waste time arguing with the man and instead grabbed his cell phone and explained the situation to Yvonne Zuni. He knew she'd get someone right to work on a search warrant. He gave a description of the building and what they were looking for.

The manager said, "I'll be happy to talk to you when you have the appropriate legal documents." His smile was his version of a bitch slap. He started to turn to walk back to his office, obviously expecting Stallings to leave.

"Hold on, cowboy."

The man turned back slowly to face Stallings.

"Based on the importance of the information we're looking for and the ability for you or anyone else in this office to erase data from the laptop computer, I'm afraid I'm going to have to secure your office to keep anyone from fooling around with the computer."

"You can't be serious."

Stallings leveled a stare at him and said, "Do I look like I'm joking?"

*　　*　　*

Tony Mazzetti knew this girl was about to break. His partner, Christina Hogrebe, had masterfully pushed her into changing her statement several times and now was closing the deal by getting her to see the inconsistencies. It had taken almost the entire ride from the downtown hotel back into this shitty neighborhood west of the stadium.

Now the girl was getting a look at her house for the first time in daylight. Christina paused and let the girl see the random bullet holes in the front of the house, but that wasn't what they were counting on. They opened the front door and ducked under the crime scene tape still secured across the entrance. He flicked on the light, and immediately the dank, musty smell of blood mixed with marijuana smoke assaulted his system. The house was clearly no palace even before more than a gallon of blood was spilled on the old cement floor. No one had been back in to clean the house, and he doubted the place was valuable enough to pay the exorbitant fees professional cleaners required for messy crime scenes like this.

Christina was a pro, so she waited while the girl got a good whiff of the smell and had a moment to study the bloodstains on the floor with one bloody handprint on the wall where a young man apparently tried to sit upright.

Christina said, "So your mama and your baby sister were two houses away at your auntie's house?"

The skinny girl nodded her head as her eyes continued to focus on the bloody corner in the room.

"And you never saw the men when they entered the house?"

This time she shook her head, still staring at the blood.

"Why didn't your brother or his friends try to defend themselves?"

The girl shook her head.

Christina let out a long, audible sigh. This was sort of her telegraph to Mazzetti she was about to spring a trap, or at least ask a hard question. She said, "Tosha, we know what happened. We've got too much evidence not to come up with a clear picture of how things went down. All I need to know is why. You tell us why, and I'm sure you had your reasons, it can really help me out. Haven't we treated you real well this whole week?"

The young girl slowly nodded her head.

Christina knew not to interrupt or hit her with another question just yet. She wanted to let what she said sink in and the girl think about it. In fact, the forensics analysis had been very contradictory. The only thing she knew was the three men were shot in the head. It had to be three quick shots because there were no signs of resistance or defensive wounds. The theory was the shooter then walked outside and sprayed the house as he left.

Now the girl shifted her gaze first to Mazzetti, then to Christina. In a very low voice she said, "It wasn't right how they treated me. Then they started looking at my baby sister the same way. I couldn't let that happen to her. She's a sweet girl and she ain't never given it up for nobody. At least I wasn't no virgin the first time they did it to me."

Christina looked over to Mazzetti slowly and then back to the girl. "Did they rape you?"

She shook her head. "I never told them no or nothing like that. But I didn't want to do it either. It's been going on three years. Since I was fourteen. And nobody done nothing about it. They didn't even think anything about it. If one of them got horny they jus come looking for me. Even my own brother."

Mazzetti knew they had to get her on tape and video as soon as possible. But he also wanted to let her tell the whole story and maybe even lead them to the guns.

Christina wrapped an arm around her shoulder as the girl started to sob. "It's okay. They were wrong doing that to you." Then Christina showed why she deserved to be in the homicide unit. Without missing a beat, still in the tone of a concerned parent, she said, "Where'd you hide the gun? We gotta find it before some kid gets hurt by accident." She kept her arm around the girl, murmuring, "It's okay, it's okay."

After a minute of crying and wiping her face on Christina's pretty blouse, the girl looked up and said, "I buried two guns and some cash in the backyard."

In the office of the small waste-management company housed in the Maxwell House building, John Stallings looked across at Patty Levine and Jason Ferrell sitting quietly in the corner of the reception area. He and the manager had come to an agreement that no one would enter Ferrell's former office until the search warrant arrived. Sergeant Zuni had grabbed a couple of detectives, written a quick warrant, and was getting it signed by a judge now. The delay annoyed Stallings, but he didn't think he'd get much more information than he already had.

Ferrell was a complete space cadet and said he never knew any customer's last name. If it weren't for the information he'd provided on Mazzetti's triple shooting they'd probably be booking him into the county jail right now. But the laptop was evidence, and Stallings

didn't want to risk losing anything that might help to
determine if a serial killer was working the spring break
crowd. And he still thought the killer might be Gary
Lauer. It'd take him a long time to get past his idea cops
were above crimes like that. Most people based their
perception of police on news reports of bad cops usually in distant cities. No one ever took into account what
a small percentage of the total profession that repre-
sented. Stallings knew it took a certain calling and attitude to make it through the police academy, let alone
your first few years on the road. It was inconceivable to
him that a cop could stray so far from his pledge to
serve and protect.

Patty quietly nodded off next to Jason, and Stallings
realized she had not really been to sleep since yesterday. Jason Ferrell sat quietly as he looked around the
room, his eyes a little clearer than the day before.

Stallings's phone rang, and he dug it out of his pocket.
"John Stallings."

Yvonne Zuni's voice was clear. "We're on the way with
the warrant.

"Good. We need to get Patty home for some rest."

The sergeant's tone changed. "John . . ." She was
very measured and careful as she continued. "I just got
a call from Ronald Bell."

Stallings didn't like the sound of that. He wondered
what had happened now and if he was about to be pun-
ished for one of his many steps outside the policy book.
Cautiously he said, "Yes?"

"He's at the scene of a suicide." She paused again.

Stallings's heartbeat increased and he felt sick to his
stomach. Immediately he thought of Maria and the
stress she'd been under with the separation and her

fight to stay clean. It felt like an hour before Yvonne Zuni said anything else.

"Gary Lauer put a bullet in his brain at his girlfriend's apartment. No note, no last phone calls. I think all the guilt was starting to get to him."

Stallings muttered, "Thanks," and absently closed the phone and tucked it back into his pocket. He looked across at Patty and Jason. It wasn't worth waking Patty, and Jason wouldn't know who he was talking about. So he didn't say a word. He wasn't sure how he felt about it either. This did seem to point to the fact that Lauer was involved with the other girls' deaths as well as feeling responsible for his girlfriend's suicide. Maybe Stallings's little pep talk had gotten through to him. Some part of Stallings felt relief at the news, and that made him feel guilty. Cops had a hard enough life and committed suicide too often for him to feel satisfied he'd pushed someone to do it instead of making a case on him. It was a complex situation about which no one would have any good feelings. Even if Lauer had distributed X and was responsible for the spring breakers' deaths. This would leave a bad taste in everyone's mouths.

Fifty-three

By the time the search warrant arrived at the small office it was dark outside and Patty Levine felt as if she were in a dream. She caught a quick nap sitting upright in the lobby, but now, with the sergeant and Stallings watching Jason Ferrell access his computer, she couldn't even consider going home. She'd been shocked when Stallings told her about Gary Lauer's suicide. She was so tired she didn't know how she felt about it

Jason tapped away on the keyboard, and, like a teenager whose parents were amazed by his skill, he couldn't help but show off some of his security measures to Stallings. After a minute, the formula to the Ecstasy appeared on the wide screen.

Stallings said, "You can show me that stuff later, Jason—we're seizing the whole computer. I just want to make sure we're not missing something on your client list."

Jason nodded as if that sounded good to him and opened the client list.

Stallings, staring over his shoulder, gave a visible start and said, "Jesus Christ, that's your list?"

Jason nodded pleasantly.

Patty walked from the side to take a position behind Jason and see what Stallings's excitement was about. It only took a second to see what had grabbed his interest.

Stallings said, "Jason, you didn't tell us you had each of their cell phone numbers next to their names."

"I didn't know it mattered."

"We can find out the last name if we have their cell phone number."

"Really? You can do that kind of stuff?"

That's when Stallings didn't answer and Patty knew why. He lifted his hand and put his finger under the third name on the list. He leaned in close to see the name again and said to Jason, "Describe this man to me."

"He's a nice fella. Kinda lean, dark hair, real athletic looking. He bought a pretty big lot of the tabs. I don't know why."

Stallings looked as if he was about to be sick to his stomach. He stared at Patty and said the name on the computer out loud. "Larry, the bartender at the Wild-side."

Suddenly it all made sense.

Stallings shook his head and said, "The fucking bartender had access to all the spring breakers he wanted. Larry knew the slang for spring breakers from Daytona and Panama City. He knew how to avoid the video in the Wildside, and that's why Allie Marsh was seen with everyone except him." Then he muttered, "Oh my God."

"What is it, John?"

"Gary Lauer killed himself and he really didn't have anything to do with Allie Marsh." Stallings looked like he might vomit.

Patty said, "It was a choice he made and it didn't have anything to do with our investigation. Don't drive yourself crazy over Gary Lauer."

"Should I drive myself crazy over talking to a killer and never realizing it?"

She was already thinking of the fastest way to find Larry Kinard.

It was early for a bar like the Wildside, but Larry Kinard was already done with his half shift. The manager was trying an afternoon happy hour bash that had started at four o'clock. Larry came in the late afternoon to help set up and now, before the place started kicking for the night, he was all ready to head back to his apartment and grab some sleep.

As he wiped down his end of the bar, he was about to turn his duties over to the new, young female bartender when he heard someone call his name from the high-top table a few feet away. He was shocked to see Ann standing there with a plastic bag in her hands.

"I know you must be mad. I was all messed up from a week of partying. I thought you might want your clothes back." She held up a plastic bag. "I have your car keys too."

He stared at her, setting the rag down to the side. Although she looked beautiful with her blond hair hanging loose around her shoulders, he still wanted to stab her in the throat with something sharp. He didn't say anything.

Ann said, "What could I do to make this up to you? I am so sorry I left you stranded with no clothes."

"So am I."

She stepped closer, setting the bag on the table.

He could smell her scent. She was back to being prey. He quickly scanned the rest of the bar to see if anyone noticed her speaking to him.

Ann said, "Do you have any more X?"

"I have some back at my apartment."

"When do you get off?" She gave him a sly smile as if she was in charge in setting the agenda.

"I could take you over there right now. Where's your car?"

"I parked my friend's car down the street at the public lot. In case you weren't here, I was going to look for you at one of the other nearby clubs."

He smiled, knowing what a perfect opportunity this was. "I'll meet you out front in a couple of minutes." He nodded as she smiled and turned away. This was gonna be sweet.

Ann was not happy about approaching him and giving his clothes back, but all she really needed was a few more hits of X to get through the break and back to school. Besides, now that she had some time to think about it, she realized he was just roughhousing and had an inflated view of himself like any guy. The only thing that threw her for a loop was when he said he had some of the tabs back at his apartment. She hadn't really planned to go anywhere private with him. The club, even though it wasn't crowded, had plenty of people around, and she felt safer there.

She had a choice to make. Was getting some more X that important? It didn't take her long to realize it was. She'd already had sex with the guy—what else could happen?

* * *

Yvonne Zuni was feeling the pressures of command as she scrambled to get help for both Tony Mazzetti and John Stallings, as their cases seemed to come to a head at the same time. She had sent Stallings and Patty to the Wildside to find Larry Kinard. She and another detective were still with Jason Ferrell.

Now she had Tony Mazzetti on the phone. He'd developed a good suspect who had confessed to the shooting. She was surprised it turned out to be one of the residents of the house. She asked Tony, "You found both of the guns?"

"She pointed out where she had buried two guns. I'd risk my entire career the ballistics will match those guns to the shooting. Plus there was about thirty-five thousand dollars in cash stuffed in Ziploc bags."

"What other resources do you need over there?"

"Crime scene is here now processing the guns and checking out the rest of the yard. Christina and I are going to book this girl on first-degree murder. The media is gonna go crazy as soon as they hear about it. I'm gonna need to get home and change before I talk to the reporters."

"Why are you going to talk to the media?"

"Because that's what I've been doing for the past few years in homicide."

"If they need a comment they can call the lieutenant. That's her job. We've got a lot going on right now, and I might need you on Stallings's case." She had everything handled, but she didn't want the detective to think he could call the shots and decide who would or would not talk to the media.

She just hoped Stallings and Patty could grab Larry Kinard without too much trouble.

Fifty-four

This was the second time he'd had prey to this apartment. Lester wasn't home, and the neighborhood was very quiet tonight. He also had the advantage of not having the victim's car in his driveway. It was a simple plan. Fuck her, then kill her. He still wasn't sure if he was going to leave her back in her own car or find a place to hide her body completely. Considering the interest of the Jacksonville Sheriff's Office, he tended to think he'd leave her somewhere damp and swampy.

She wandered through his little place ahead of him, looking for signs of a female roommate. Then she stopped in the hallway, noticing his collage of other prey. She said, "Larry, who are all these women?"

"Just girls I thought were pretty."

She stepped forward and brushed the corkboard with her fingertips. A couple of loose photos on the frame moved at her touch. "You sure do have a one-track mind. These girls could all be sisters."

He gazed at her as she stared at his work of art and wondered if it wouldn't be as much fun to kill her fast and not even worry about the sex. His erection told him that would be fine. He felt the power start to build and surge through his arms and legs. He flexed all over like a big cat ready to pounce. He joined her at the same table where he'd mounted Lisa, then broken her neck. The same sharp letter opener was still in the drawer. He leaned in close to her, sniffing to make sure he still had her scent right, and kissed her on the neck to hide what he was really doing. He slid the drawer open and took a quick look down at the letter opener.

"That poster is kinda creepy." Ann stepped away from him quickly. "If you have any Ecstasy I'll take it with me."

She had no idea it was already too late. He was now completely in predator mode.

Fifty-five

Stallings and Patty raced from the Wildside dance club. The manager had told them Larry Kinard had just left after having worked the early shift. He gave them Kinard's address, and now Stallings had the gas pedal pressed hard against the floor. Patty was on the cell phone advising the sergeant where they were going and asking for as much help as they could send.

Patty said, "John, slow down. If we're killed on our way there it won't do anyone any good, and my mom will be pissed at you."

"Sorry, we gotta grab this guy, and it's a way to keep my mind off of Gary Lauer."

"I understand, but Kinard has no idea were looking for him. He may not even be home yet. We have a better chance of T-boning someone than we do of losing him."

Stallings slowed down but still managed to pass one of the many buses running between downtown and all points east. He turned to his partner and said, "Who else is coming?"

"The sarge says she and Mazzetti are on their way,

and Hoagie is coming from the crime scene near Market Street. Should we wait for the whole posse?"

"Let's do a drive-by and check the place out. I promise I won't do anything stupid." He appreciated the fact that Patty knew not to tease him right now.

Not only did he feel the power as a predator, he vividly recalled how he felt when Ann had left him naked and bruised at the beach. That was why he wanted to throw a good scare into her first. He could've just attacked her as she gazed out the window or hidden the deadly weapon, but instead he turned around slowly, smiling with the letter opener in his right hand and touching the point of it with his left index finger.

Ann said, "You look like something out of a stupid horror movie. Stop fooling around and find me the X."

He stepped closer to her and reached out to take her hand. Tentatively, she reached out to his and let out a giggle.

He said, "What'll you give me for the X?"

Now she gave him a broader smile, came closer, and said in a soft voice, "What would you like?"

He glanced over his shoulder and said, "I'd like to put your photo on that board too." He slashed upward quickly with the letter opener, making a deep gouge in her chest and cheek. He liked the stunned expression on her face and decided he'd wait to let what was happening sink in completely.

Her shriek only heightened his excitement.

As soon as Ann entered the little bungalow she got a weird vibe. She wasn't sure if it was from the building or from Larry, but one way or the other all of her internal alarms were telling her to get out fast. She took a good look around and saw no indication of anything unusual. She wasn't sure what she was looking for. Maybe child pornography or a bottle of ether. Her mind was starting to cook up crazy ideas about this guy. But she had to admit he'd been a perfect gentleman since she'd talked to him at the club, then followed him back here in her friend's car.

She noticed a nice, framed corkboard bulletin board crammed with photos of young women. It took her a moment to realize every single one of the girls had blond hair and blue eyes. They were all shapes and sizes—some with big boobs, some without; some shaped like pears, others tremendously athletic. But every single one of them had blond hair and blue eyes. Immediately she thought of her own blond hair and light blue eyes and felt a chill run down her spine.

She couldn't help herself as she turned around and told him how creepy bulletin board looked. She said, "If you have any Ecstasy, I'll take it with me." When she turned around he was standing there with some kind of a letter opener or knife in his hand by his side. He looked so goofy with that grin, she thought it was a joke.

Ann said, "You look like something out of a stupid horror movie. Stop fooling around and find me the X."

He said, "What'll you give me for the X?"

Ann tried to make her voice sexy and gave him a little smile and said, "What would you like?" But she had no intention of giving him anything other than a quick hug or kiss. Right now she was thinking that if she could just get her hands on the X, she'd grab it and head out the door and never have to see this jerk again. Then he did the one thing she really didn't expect.

He swung the letter opener up, catching her in the chest and face. She was stunned more than anything else for a moment until she felt the blood dripping down her face and imagined what it must look like.

Then her screaming drowned out any other thought she had.

Patty looked out at the dark house and said, "Are you sure this is it?"

Stallings had pulled his Impala to the curb, checked the notes he'd made at the Wildside, and said, "It's the right address, but it's awfully dark." He looked around at the other houses. "I wonder if the neighbors would know anything." He slowly pulled the car ahead and noticed the driveway slipped away to the back of the house. He saw light at the end of the driveway. "Is that an apartment in the back?"

Patty rolled down the window for better view and saw at least one vehicle and a couple of lights on at the much smaller structure. "It's gotta be. A lot of these places on the east side have little attached apartments."

As Stallings was deciding which neighbor to talk to, they heard a female scream from inside the back apartment. There was no time to wait for help or talk to the neighbors. They both sprang out of the car.

He watched as Ann stumbled back, touching the thick, sticky blood, pouring out of the gash on her face. She started to hyperventilate, and he thought it was gonna cause him to ejaculate in his pants.

"You're not so smart now that you can't surprise me."

He stepped toward her, keeping the sharp letter opener well within her view. "Strip down."

Between crying and gasping for air she managed to spit out a "What?"

"You heard me. I said take off all your clothes, and I want you to do it right this second."

Her eyes darted around the room quickly, and she jerked her shirt over her head and unhooked her bra with amazing speed. She wasted no time kicking off her sandals and sliding down her jeans. She stood straight up, perfectly still, only her belly sucking in and out with each strangled cry.

He took a moment to study her and decide what he might take as a souvenir. He had a photo of her from one night at the bar. For right now he was satisfied to watch her beautiful body tremble in front of him, knowing that when he decided it would all be over. He had to savor this one because it would be months and months before he had another chance.

Ann sniffled and managed to say, "What are you going to do with me?"

He let his smile spread slowly. "I thought it would've been obvious by now. I'm going to gut you like a fish, then dump your body somewhere between here and downtown Jacksonville."

"I said I was sorry and I shouldn't have left you at the beach."

"And you will be sorry, I promise." He stepped forward, knowing she couldn't retreat far into the room.

When she bumped into the rear wall he paused a moment, reasserted his grip on the letter opener, and prepared to step forward hard and thrust at first directly into her heart. Then he was going to swing it up under her chin like he did with Holly.

A noise distracted him. At first it was a creak on the small porch; then it sounded like an explosion.

For a moment she couldn't breathe; when she started to suck in oxygen, it didn't feel like enough as her heart raced like she'd never felt before. She was afraid even to try it, but she forced herself to lift her fingers to touch the warm sticky blood on the side of her face. She'd stopped screaming and started to sob instead.

She looked up, and Larry still had the weapon in his hand. The idea that her own blood was splashed along the side made her stomach turn. Just out of instinct she backed away, shuffling her feet slowly on the wooden floor. She murmured apologies, but she wasn't sure who they were to. She kept saying, "I'm sorry. I'm sorry." Somehow she thought it was more an apology to God or her parents or anyone but this guy who kept advancing toward her with the knife still in his hand. But he wasn't closing the distance between them. Maybe he was just trying to scare her. Her mind raced as she realized that everyone who had ever been in a situation like this tried to rationalize it. She tried to make it seem like it wasn't really happening. But she knew right now that her life was in danger and if she didn't do something, this man in front of her, whom she had seen naked, whom she had had sex with, who had supplied her with drugs, was going to stab her to death.

Somehow she felt as if she was coming to grips with it until she bumped into the back wall of his apartment. Now she had nowhere to go. And he kept coming toward her.

* * *

Stallings had his big Glock duty pistol in his hand as he crashed through the door. Patty was on the porch covering the inside of the small detached apartment with her Glock through the window. The door wasn't thick, but it was well made and was harder to get through than he'd thought. He took a moment to let his eyes adjust inside and get over the shock of crashing through the pressboard door.

Patty came in directly behind him as he scanned the hallway in front of him. It was empty. As he stepped forward and turned toward what had to be a bedroom, there was a flash of movement in the dim light and a loud noise. He jumped to the side of the door, scanned it with his gun out in front of him as Patty took a position on the other side of the door. Immediately he noticed a nude woman standing perfectly still against the rear wall. He held his position.

"Where did he go?"

The woman dropped straight forward onto her knees, sobbing uncontrollably.

He entered the room followed by Patty. They scanned each corner, and Patty ducked into the attached bathroom.

Stallings went down on one knee to hold the woman by her arm, giving her a gentle shake. "We're the police. Are you okay?" But when she looked up he saw for the first time the wound on her face and upper chest.

From inside the bathroom Patty yelled, "Clear," and stepped back out into the bedroom, joining Stallings with the hysterical young woman.

The girl sniffled. "He was going to kill me."

"Who?" asked Stallings.

"Larry."

Stallings scanned the room quickly and noticed the

screen out of the main bedroom window. As he stood and stepped toward it he said, "Did he go this way?"

She just nodded.

He stared out into the pitch-black backyard and realized it would be useless to chase after him. He didn't know what direction he went. But Stallings knew he could call in a lot of cops real quick and get this whole area sealed off. He looked out the back window as he opened his phone. There was no trail or trace of where Larry Kinard had fled. As soon as the dispatcher came on the line Stallings started feeding her information for the arriving units to set up a perimeter.

Larry Kinard acted on instinct when he saw his front door disintegrate. Before he even knew how many cops had busted in, he twisted and dove out the window in his bedroom. Landing on his feet, he kept his balance and ran directly into the bushes behind his house and kept running onto the main highway. He knew he had to get back into Jacksonville, where there were crowds and places he could disappear. His biggest stroke of luck was a bus stopping outside the convenience store about a mile west of the beach.

He was fully clothed and still had his wallet in his pocket. Thank God he hadn't had sex with Ann and found himself running naked once again. Instead, he calmly stepped onto the bus, dug in his pocket for his wallet, and gave the driver five dollars. Change automatically dropped out of the dispenser, and he walked past two derelicts to sit in the seat opposite the rear door as the bus picked up speed.

There was only one more stop before they hit the

wide swampy area and then the St. Johns River. No one got on at the second stop, and he noticed two police cruisers racing east.

A smile crept over his face when he realized he'd have another season to hunt.

Stallings and Patty wrapped the girl in a blanket and kept talking to her until paramedics took her away. One of them had told Stallings the wound was superficial and would require stitches. He said the same thing every fireman had ever said about a facial injury: "All head wounds bleed a lot worse than they really are."

Sergeant Zuni had arrived and taken over control of the perimeter, sending patrol cars a mile or more in each direction to block any route of escape. It was a slow night, and every cop in the city seemed to have come out to help. Even though Larry Kinard was obviously the man they sought and was a lot more than an everyday Ecstasy dealer, Stallings couldn't help but think about Gary Lauer and what had happened. Stallings's instincts might have been right about a cop not killing young college girls, but Lauer had other issues. Maybe he couldn't work out how he felt about his girlfriend. Stallings didn't want to think how responsible Lauer felt for the girl's suicide, because right now he knew how responsible he felt for Lauer's.

Stallings and Patty were waiting for Crime Scene to come and process the apartment as well as for Mazzetti to run a search warrant past the judge. But it hadn't taken long for them to notice the collage of blond girls in the hallway. And Allie Marsh's photo was in the corner of the corkboard.

Patty stared at the framed collage and said, "Do you think these could all be victims?" Her voice was hushed, and it showed the dread she had at asking the question

"God, I hope not." It was all Stallings had for the moment.

Fifty-six

To John Stallings this is what police work really meant. They might've missed the killer, and Larry Kinard was loose on the street, but with the right people in the detective bureau they had accomplished a lot in a couple of hours. He listened to a patrol sergeant's radio as they sat on the porch of Larry Kinard's house. He could visualize the wide perimeter that had been set up to catch the fleeing suspect. A patrolman had been smart enough to question a bus driver coming back from downtown, and he said he'd picked up a man matching Kinard's description an hour before and dropped him off downtown. It hadn't been enough verifiable information to cancel the perimeter, but it had caused another dozen patrolman to flood downtown looking for the fugitive.

Stallings had roughed out a probable-cause affidavit on someone's laptop computer, and Sergeant Zuni had assigned another detective to run it through the duty judge so they could search the house. The days of just tossing someone's house were long over, and the procedures and details of search warrants and subpoenas had taken a firm hold in most large police departments in the country. Although Stallings was anxious to search the house, he was actually more concerned with the capture of Larry Kinard.

The girl the paramedics had taken said Kinard had given her Ecstasy and he was acting weird. Everyone seemed weird when they tried to stab you. She admitted to having sex with him at Neptune Beach and that they got involved in rough horseplay in the water. The horseplay had upset her, so she had left him at a park near Neptune Beach without clothes or keys. She'd really thought that's why he had gotten upset and attacked her with a knife. Patty had done an outstanding job of keeping her calm and getting the pertinent information out of her. But now Stallings thought about the photo collage of blond girls and felt sick to his stomach at the idea that these girls could be murder victims.

He'd been very impressed with Yvonne Zuni's grasp of command and how she'd organized the search for Kinard as well as getting a search warrant and pulling in Crime Scene. Now she was on her phone. She quickly looked at the porch where Stallings, Patty, and a uniformed sergeant sat on a wide bench and said, "Warrant signed. Stall, you direct Crime Scene and get this show on the road."

After the preliminaries, which included a videotape of the premises, sketches of how the searches took place, and an evidence tech on a computer near the front door, Stallings and Patty went immediately to the collage. He pulled it off the wall and set it on the desk. He found Allie Marsh's and Kathleen Harding's photos. Stallings identified the two girls from Daytona. That left twenty more photos.

The crime scene techs found a box of Durex condoms, which they took into evidence. Patty discovered the small box of odd pieces of jewelry. While Stallings looked over her shoulder, she turned and said, "Trophies."

"What's that?"

"These are trophies. Something from each of his victims."

"How do you know?"

"It seems clear to me. Right here under the photographs, I can picture him digging through this box, recalling each of his victims.

"How many pieces are there?"

Patty counted slowly and said, "Thirteen pieces."

They were single earrings, belly-button rings, and a nose stud, as well as rings and bracelets. Stallings leaned in closer, feeling as if he might vomit, praying to God he didn't find any of Jeanie's jewelry in the box. He thought hard about his daughter's choices in jewelry, and nothing in the box seemed familiar, but it didn't make him rest easy. This guy was a monster and would have no defense other than insanity. And he might pull it off. He could convince a jury he'd been abused as a kid or neglected or had some seen traumatic event that pushed him to this unthinkable violence. There'd be legal motions, which would drag on for years. Maybe he'd even end up at Raiford with the last serial killer Stallings had caught, William Dremmel. He'd acted so crazy that the case barely even made it to court. Stallings had shown great restraint and captured the man who'd drugged girls until they slipped into death. He had wanted to kill the bastard, but in deference to Patty's efforts to reform him he'd risked his own life to capture the killer alive. But that effort had been mooted by the lenient treatment Dremmel had received in the media and court.

Much of it was based on Dremmel's childhood abuse by his mother. But the result had still been Dremmel skating on the most serious punishment after taking the lives of several girls and shattering the lives of their families. Stallings had known one of the girls and her family.

Stallings thought of something even more disturbing. What if Kinard cooperated and traded information about the victims to avoid the death penalty? It was a common enough tactic, and sometimes parents of missing children welcomed the closure. The media fed on it, and often that media attention only bolstered the killers. The whole concept made Stallings ill.

Of course all of that nonsense was contingent on catching him.

Patty Levine stretched in her bed, turned, and checked her alarm clock. It was ten o'clock in the morning. She'd slept five hours after being awake almost forty. But she had slept without the aid of any pharmaceutical drug even if it was on the edge of extreme exhaustion. She checked in at the office, and nothing was new on the search for Larry Kinard. She took a few minutes to clean her condo, grab a decent breakfast, and reconnect with her cat, Cornelia.

An eleven o'clock news teaser for the noon broadcast said, "Jacksonville police search for possible killer." Patty knew things were not going well if the sheriff's office had gone to the media for help. Then a photo of Larry Kinard provided by the Wildside popped on the screen.

Patty noted they didn't use a name. She and Stallings had learned during their investigation, which had lasted much of the night, that Larry Kinard was a fictitious name, and everything he'd given the bar except his address and cell phone number were from various other people both living and dead. Somehow Stallings had even gotten a security rep at the cell phone company to go through some records, but there were more than two hundred different numbers called from Kinard's phone, and it would take some time to figure out where he was hiding and whom he'd contacted. Kinard had left the cell phone in his haste to escape, so they couldn't try and triangulate where he was from the cell phone or see whom he called after he fled. All the easiest ways to find fugitives were out.

As Patty got into her county car, Stallings called her and said to meet him at the Wildside. They had a lead.

It didn't take long for her to shoot across the river and rumble into the empty lot of the Wildside dance club. Stallings was out front with the manager who'd helped them before and a young man with long greasy hair, whom she didn't know.

As she approached she heard the young man say to Stallings, "No lie, man. I helped him push a Mazda into the water at a park east of the river. Then I gave him a ride."

Stallings gave the young man a hard look and said, "Where'd you give him a ride to?"

"Over west of the river. On Cleveland Street past Edgewood. You know, where there's a mix of houses and crappy strip malls."

"You didn't know this guy at all?"

The kid shook his head and said, "I saw him working here the other night. Otherwise I wouldn't have known anything about him. I wasn't sure what to do—that's why I came by here. I swear I would've called the cops."

The manager laughed. "He tried to shake me down for cash to keep the club's name out of the news."

Stallings had a half grin when he said to the kid, "And you helped this guy push a car into the river and gave him a ride for no reason?"

The kid said, "Just a good Samaritan."

Stallings looked at Patty, and she knew, as any good partner would, that he was asking her what she thought without saying a word. She said, "He's full of shit. He knows we're looking for this guy as a suspect in a murder and he's trying to shake money out of the bar. I say we charge him as an accessory." She contained her smile, but it had the effect she wanted. The young man started to talk fast with details they could use.

At least now they had a decent lead.

Larry Kinard didn't have time to feel sluggish. He only got a few hours' sleep, but now he was up and around in his neat bedroom at his sister's house, figuring out what he could take with him and what he'd have to leave. His sister had no connection to him on paper. He'd told her he was avoiding a mortgage fraud charge and that's why he had a new name and Social Security number. She'd gone along with the story for more than three years now. For his part, he'd stuck by her through a number of dicey relationships and once had to knock a man unconscious in the living room after he'd spanked Kinard's nephew.

As he hurried through the living room his sister said, "What's going on? Are you going to have to leave again?"

"Yeah, there's not enough work to keep me going here. But I'll still come by and see you guys, and I should be able to send you money every month too."

She followed him into the kitchen. "But I need a good male role model for Justin."

He looked at her and thought about his near-silent nephew. Briefly he considered taking them with him, but he could never share a house with them, at least not during spring break.

His sister turned and silently stalked back into the living room, plopping down on the couch to watch TV. She got like this sometimes. These feelings of abandonment had never left her after their parents had divorced. They had seen their father once in almost twenty years. The parade of men in and out of her bed had not helped the situation. Kinard was the one constant in her life besides Justin.

Then he heard his sister say, "Oh my God."

He hurried out the living room and saw she was staring at the TV. It only took a second for him to notice his employee photograph from the Wildside was on the screen, and he knew things were going bad fast.

Fifty-seven

John Stallings and Patty Levine drove slowly down Cleveland Street in the area where the young stoner said he'd dropped off Larry Kinard. The sheriff's office's marine unit had divers in the water at the park where the kid claimed to have shoved a car in the water.

Patty said, "You think this kid is full of shit?"

"He seems sincere, but how many of these crazy-assed tips do we get when we go public on a case? I can't believe the sarge got the marine unit to dive for the car already. But before we call out the cavalry, we need to do our homework."

"Hoagie says they've identified at least five dead girls from the collage. Kathleen Harding and Allie Marsh, plus two from Daytona and one from Panama City. Looks like you found another serial killer."

"I believe you were with me the whole time, and we haven't found anyone yet."

"I know you're beating yourself up about Gary Lauer. But think about all the good we're doing by stopping a creep like Larry Kinard."

Stallings nodded, looking down the streets as they drove slowly. "I've got the analyst running utilities and searching tax records in the area, but I doubt we'll find anything that matches Kinard. He had to have a friend or maybe even a family member over here."

Patty said, "We know he doesn't have a car and he left his wallet at the apartment. He may do something desperate and stupid."

Stallings pulled up to a corner with a small strip mall and a row of houses behind it. This was where the young man had dropped him off. There were too many variables. Was it really Larry Kinard? Was the kid too stoned to know exactly where he dropped him off? Was the story even true?

Patty rolled down the window and said, "I'm waiting on a call from the sarge to see if there's anything new. Otherwise, I'd say let's go to the park and see if there really is a car in the water."

Stallings opened his window too, figuring it was a nice day and there were worse things than watching divers jump in the water while they waited for some clue as to Larry Kinard's whereabouts.

Larry Kinard froze in the kitchen doorway as his sister slowly turned her head and said, "That was you. They're looking for you in connection to a murder. Is that true?"

"I didn't murder anyone."

"Then we can explain it to the police. And you won't have to leave."

"I don't think that would work very well."

His sister stared at him silently, slowly stood, and

called out for her son. A couple of seconds later, Justin came hustling in from his bedroom. "C'mon, sweetheart, we need to get out for a few minutes."

Kinard said, "Where are you going?"

"We need food. And Justin needs to get out. Is that okay with you?" Her tone had turned confrontational.

He'd seen his sister's attitude with other men, but never had it directed at him. He took a breath and said, "No, it's not a good idea to leave right now."

"You can't tell me what to do in my own house." As she started to walk past, he grabbed her by the arm. Instinctively she jerked away. This time she screamed, "Keep your fucking hands off me!"

He wondered if the neighbors were used to her screeching, but he couldn't have her draw attention to them right now. He snatched her arm again and jerked her into the kitchen away from Justin.

Before he could say a word she started to wail. A combination of curse words and screams.

He raised his voice enough for her to hear him, shouting, "Stop it! Keep your voice down and we'll discuss it." But she kept screaming, wiggled her arm free, and swung at him with a closed fist.

Without thinking he ducked the fist and snatched a long butcher's knife from a stand on the counter. When she swung again he ducked the punch, spun her away from him, and plunged the knife deep into her back just to the left of her spine. As he felt the knife skip off a rib, he realized what he had done.

Without another sound, she stumbled forward, grabbing at the refrigerator handle, then tumbled flat on the kitchen's hard floor. She tried to say something as blood quickly pooled under her body. She lay perfectly still.

Kinard stared at her, knowing he'd lost all control. He heard a sound behind him and turned to face his nephew. He had to think clearly now and figure out what steps to take.

Across the street from Stallings's Impala, the garbage truck lifted a wide, battered green Dumpster and tilted it upside down into the back of the truck, causing a series of thunderous crashes. Stallings had started to roll up his window when between the crashes he heard something else. He paused and listened carefully and realized it was a very loud, agitated woman's voice. Then all he could hear was the Dumpster again. Before he could figure out if he had actually heard it, Patty turned to him and said, "Stall, that was a scream."

This was close enough to their experience the night before that they couldn't hesitate now. Stallings still dwelled on the fact that if he had been a little quicker, Kinard would be in custody or dead right now. They both popped out of the car quickly, trying to get a fix on the direction of the scream. Behind him Cleveland Street had light traffic. The few businesses in the strip mall didn't attract any crowds, so he was pretty sure the scream had come from the residential neighborhood in front of them. He walked to the hedge that separated the parking lot from the first house. Patty ran faster and turned toward the first house, cut through the yard, and started checking each house from the backyards. They started to move at the same pace with Patty behind the houses and Stallings along the cracked and warped sidewalk.

The first house had all of its windows closed and he doubted they would've heard a sound so clearly coming from inside. He wondered if it'd been a loud TV. The second house had a beat-up Pontiac in the driveway and all the windows open in the front. A short, covered porch ran the length of the house. He turned onto the walkway and slowly climbed the three steps to the porch, still listening. He paused, motionless for almost a full minute. He took another few steps, feeling the wooden deck bend and creak. Still nothing. He stood silently, listening.

Then his phone rang.

Kinard eased through the small living room. He turned around once and put his fingers to his lips to make sure his nephew didn't make any noise. He'd already motioned for the boy to stay put in the family room and not to go into the kitchen. Kinard still didn't know how he was going to explain this mess to the boy.

He held the bloody knife in his right hand next to his face. He could see a shadow on the porch, but he wasn't sure if it was a person or a tree in the front yard. Kinard paused by the open jalousies that let in the cool breeze but didn't allow anyone to see in or out. Some diffused light broke through the glass.

Just as he was about to convince himself no one was on the porch he heard a cell phone and it was close.

Now he had to take action

Fifty-eight

Stallings whipped open the phone quickly, whispering to Patty, "What've you got?"

Patty obviously wasn't hiding from anyone. She spoke in a clear voice but realized instantly what Stallings was doing. "Do you need me to come to you?"

Stallings let out a short, quiet, "Not yet."

"I trotted through all eight yards and didn't see or hear anything suspicious. A couple of the houses have people home, but there was no one screaming. I'm on the next street ready to meet you."

Stallings didn't say anything, because something told him to listen. A board creaked in the living room, but there was no sign of anyone at the door. The jalousie glass didn't allow him a decent view into the room. All he could see was a crack between two of the open slats. There was a china cabinet with clear glass panes. He crouched to get a better view through the open jalousies and saw a reflection of something metal in the glass of the china cabinet. Just as his brain processed that it was a knife, the reflection moved with blinding speed.

* * *

The phone had given away the position of the intruder. Kinard tried to close the distance silently and figured whoever was on the porch was next to the front door; then he saw a shadow cross the window. This time there was no doubt it was a man.

Kinard committed to action, stepped forward, and plunged the knife between the jalousie slats, hoping to catch someone by surprise. He felt the knife nick someone and heard him yelp.

The crashing of the glass and thump of a gunshot shocked him, forcing him to stumble back a few feet.

Stallings didn't even hear the screen rip as a knife darted out between the jalousie slats, striking his left hand. He stumbled back, making a quick assessment of the gash on his left hand and drawing his gun with the right. From the ground he kicked the last few slats, sending them crashing down in a cascade of glass. He also fired two rounds through the next set of slats, knowing they'd end up in the china cabinet. He needed to force back his attacker. He also knew the shots would bring Patty Levine running.

He scampered back to a low crouch, did a quick peek into the house from the broken glass, and saw a man halfway across a room with a knife in his hand. Stallings lowered his head and ducked into the house, standing as soon as he was inside, holding his gun on the man.

Instinctively Stallings yelled out, "Police, don't move!" He took a second to assess the man and realized it was Larry Kinard. Then he shouted, "Drop the knife, Larry."

Kinard dropped the knife onto the hard floor, held

out his hands in front of him to show he was unarmed, and slowly started to back toward the next room.

"Hold it right there, Larry. It's all over." He crept toward the retreating man and froze when he saw a little boy behind him.

Kinard took advantage of the surprised hesitation and darted with incredible speed into the room.

Stallings raced forward to see Kinard disappear through a sliding glass door into the backyard. As he started to give chase he glanced to his left and saw a woman's body on the floor of the kitchen, blood spreading in a wide, dark pool. He couldn't just leave the body. Not with a little kid in the next room. It took all of his will, but he turned into the kitchen to check the body for a pulse and let Kinard run. There was nothing else he could do.

He also had to keep the boy from coming in and seeing the blood on the floor. He holstered his gun and grabbed his phone as he turned toward the terrified boy. "It's okay, buddy." Before he could get Patty on the line she burst through the opening he'd made in the glass. She didn't hesitate to come right to her partner's aid.

Stallings immediately stood and started toward a sliding glass door. He pointed into the kitchen but held his finger up to his mouth so she wouldn't say anything. As he ran out the door he said, "It's definitely him. Call in the cavalry."

Fifty-nine

Larry Kinard didn't bother to look behind him. This cop had proved how sharp he was, and he appeared to be in pretty good shape. He ran as hard as he could, leaping over the low wall and hedge that led to the back of the strip mall on Cleveland Street. He glanced both ways down the parking lot and didn't see anyone. He turned left and broke into an all-out sprint, but as he approached the next block he could hear a distant siren and wondered if Stallings had been able to call in other cops so quickly. He skidded to a stop, scanned the area, and decided a tall industrial Dumpster might be his best bet.

He opened the plastic lid, then hesitated. The smell of filth and thought of bacteria kept him in place for a moment. He wasn't sure he could do it until he heard the siren clearly coming closer. He scaled the Dumpster easily, tumbling onto plastic bags of garbage and soggy cardboard boxes. He worked his way into the bags and boxes, covering himself as he settled lower in the Dumpster. A shiver ran through him at the thought of this much contact with other people's discarded waste.

The odors that attacked him were monstrous. Old coffee grounds, ashtrays, half-eaten sandwiches, and really disgusting stuff tumbled down on top of him. Something alive squirmed past his foot as a cockroach ran up the sleeve of his T-shirt. But now the lid was closed and he slammed his eyes shut in the dark, smelly Dumpster.

Patty Levine had glanced in the kitchen and knew there was a bloody body on the floor. She also knew she was a lot less intimidating to the scared little boy trembling in the family room than Stallings had been. She had quietly set him up on the couch and sat next to him, trying to coax a name from him.

She had already raised dispatch on her phone, saying she needed immediate help at this address and they had a suspect with a weapon. That would get every cop in the district rolling to her in a few minutes.

The fact that Stallings had raced off after Kinard had not thrown her at all. She knew they couldn't leave the young boy in the house with the body and she was better suited to keeping him calm. But there was still part of her that wished she could be looking for the killer as well. That's where duty and responsibility took over from adrenaline and desire. She'd break free as soon as she could and help her partner search for Larry Kinard.

Stallings had left the yard and run behind the other houses to the end of the street, but he saw no sign of Larry Kinard. The adrenaline dump and discharging of his weapon had sapped him of energy, so he took a second to breathe and slow his heart rate. The pistol felt like it weighed twenty pounds in his hand. He started to jog behind the houses in the other direction, passing the house Kinard had run from and then clumsily sliding over a low wall and hedge into the rear nasty parking lot of the strip mall.

Again he checked each direction. He saw no sign of the fleeing killer, but he did hear the approaching sirens of help. He made sure his badge was clearly visible on his belt and pulled out his wallet ID as well. He didn't want some excitable rookie shooting him by mistake.

There was no one in the lot, and the only movement he could see was a garbage truck on the next block, the same one that had nearly drowned out the screams that led him to the house in the first place.

The cruiser raced past the lot and screeched to a stop, and roared in reverse until he was level with the lot again. A round-faced young man shouted out an open window at Stallings. "Where do you need me?"

"Set up a perimeter of a few blocks in each direction and maybe we'll bottle this guy up. He's a white male, about thirty, with dark hair and a blue T-shirt. He left a homicide scene two houses away. Be careful."

The young man nodded, jumping on his radio as he sped away in the new cruiser.

Stallings still wanted to be the one who caught this guy.

Larry Kinard heard a car's engine and some shouting, but no one checked the Dumpster. He settled even lower and could see a beam of light from the rusted-out lower corner of the square garbage container. He even adapted to some of the smells, but the thought of bacteria kept him near panic. Now he needed a weapon. He wished he hadn't dropped the knife, but he could tell by the look in the cop's eyes he would've been shot if he didn't.

He felt around with his free right hand, gripping the rubber handle of a broken golf club. It rose about two feet to a sharp metal end. All it was good for was jabbing, but that might be all he needed if someone checked the Dumpster. Just enough of a diversion so he could run away. That was his only goal now. It still hadn't sunk in he'd killed his sister and left his nephew with no one in the whole world but his unstable grandmother. There was no way he could take the boy with him, not at the speed he had to travel. He saw himself in Seattle, where the street population was welcomed and no one asked many questions. After a few months under the radar he could find another identity and set up shop somewhere else. There were always spring break vacationers. And predators like him always found a place to hunt.

Stallings held his position as more cruisers sped past, following the instructions of the first officer on the scene. As soon as someone pulled into the parking lot, Stallings would team up with a uniform and monitor a radio. He checked in with Patty to make sure she was all right. She said the boy was not responsive and she expected the paramedics at any moment.

Stallings saw the garbage truck cross the street into the lot and walked toward it, his badge in his hand, ready to direct the man out of the area. But the driver was intent on his job and lined up the battered steel arms of his giant truck with the sides of the Dumpster. He moved in quickly without hesitation, sliding the arms into the sturdy metal sleeves quickly and pulling the Dumpster into the air smoothly and steadily. The swinging Dumpster and moving arms made an outrageous racket, and the driver couldn't hear Stallings shouting to him.

He watched as the arms twisted and the Dumpster flipped upside down. The load of garbage tumbled out into the rear of the truck and Stallings clearly saw Larry Kinard's arms flail as he fell in the back of the full dump truck.

Stallings picked up his pace toward the truck, his gun in his hand. He thought about calling in the patrol cars for backup. He froze as he heard the truck's compactor engage. His first instinct was to race to the driver and have him shut off the compactor. But then he thought about the collage of victims. Of Allie Marsh's bright face and her mother's anguish. He even thought of the silent little boy and the dead woman in the house a few hundred feet away. He considered the endless legal proceedings and media coverage. He made a conscious decision to wait while the compactor finished its job.

The crushing and snapping sounds made him flinch as he wondered if any of the noises could be Larry Kinard's bones. He thought, for just a moment, he heard a muffled scream from inside the solid metal truck.

The giant arms slapped the empty Dumpster back into the same spot on the scarred asphalt while the compactor retracted. Now the driver looked over and saw Stallings. He raised his hand with his badge, and the driver waved, pushing the truck into neutral and then swinging down out of the high cab.

The middle-aged black man smiled as he wiped his brow with a dirty bandana. "What's up?" he shouted from the perpetual noise of his truck in his ears.

"We might have a problem," was all Stallings said.

Sixty

Patty Levine stood in the skanky parking lot behind the strip mall where Stallings had seen their suspect, Larry Kinard, get dumped into the back of a garbage truck. That had been over an hour before. Fire Rescue and Crime Scene had been searching the compactor trash for more than forty minutes now.

A social worker and psychologist were on the scene, taking custody of the boy found in the house. A tentative identification had his name as Justin Small and the dead woman was his mother. Right now they didn't know anything else about her or why Larry Kinard would be in her house, but based on the statement from the stoner kid who had led them here they had some sort of longer-term connection. She prayed to God the little boy was not that monster's son.

Tony Mazzetti and Yvonne Zuni had joined them in a grim vigil. Occasionally a fireman would look up with excitement on his face, but so far they had not found the killer's body. Then one of the firemen turned and vomited over the side of the garbage truck. All four of the detectives jumped back as the vomit made a re-sounding splat on the asphalt.

The young crime scene tech looked over at the sergeant and said, "We only found part of him."

Mazzetti clapped his hands together and smiled. "Two big cases closed in two days. Not bad at all." He looked over at Stallings, who showed no emotion, and said, "The compactor works quick. You didn't even get a chance to say anything to the driver."

Patty glared at her boyfriend. No one wanted to ask how long the interval was between when Stallings saw the suspect fall into the garbage truck and when he stopped the driver. But in a sick way Mazzetti was right. At least this creep couldn't kill any more girls.

Patty draped her arm over her partner's shoulder. "It is good to be lucky sometimes, but you were always prepared when we got a lucky break." She patted him on the back and noticed her boyfriend's look.

Patty didn't know why, but just the little glance from Mazzetti pissed her off. She'd been on edge for several days and knew that part of it was a form of withdrawal from the prescription drugs she'd been using for so long. She also knew things would get worse. When she didn't have a big case like this staring her right in the face, drawing her away from her life and problems, she'd probably start to think about the relief the drugs had given her. She knew she was in for a fight. She just hoped she didn't screw anything else up while she concentrated on it. Mainly she didn't want to screw anything up with Tony Mazzetti. But somehow she had a cold feeling in the pit of her stomach that said she was in for a lot more trouble than she thought from just taking a few pills.

It'd been almost two days since she'd used any prescription drugs at all. It may not be much, but it was more of a step than she'd taken in almost five years. Right now the question was did she feel like shit because she wasn't using her meds or did she feel like shit because she just did more in three days than most people did in a year? She looked around at the other cops on the scene, people she respected, people she admired. It didn't matter what her parents thought or how they viewed her occupation; she liked being a cop.

She was tired, sore, and hungry and had a headache, but a satisfied feeling reached much deeper. Patty would enjoy it for now because she knew harder times were on their way.

Yvonne Zuni settled into her desk in the Land That Time Forgot at about six. The two evening detectives in the office didn't report to her and so barely acknowledged her. This had probably been the busiest two weeks of her career, and if it was any indication of life in the detective bureau she might not last. She had briefed the sheriff and command staff on both cases and proudly stood on the sideline while the sheriff explained the details of the investigation to a crowded news conference at about four that afternoon. Tony Mazzetti and Christina Hogrebe stood next to her, but Patty Levine and John Stallings said they had better things to do.

There was still a lot to do in the Larry Kinard case. It was clear now that Allie Marsh and Kathleen Harding had been murdered, and that he had used Ecstasy as a way of covering his crimes. They also confirmed some of the photographs were of dead girls from Daytona and Panama City. Neither department was overjoyed at the aspect of reopening cases that had been closed as either suicides or accidents. It didn't look good for the detectives and did nothing for the tourism industry. But Sergeant Zuni didn't care as long as all the girls in the collage were identified and their parents notified. It would be a long, brutal job to track down each girl's identity. It was one of the few things they could've used Larry Kinard for, had he lived, but even then he would've used it as a bargaining chip in court. Florida's most famous serial killer, Ted Bundy, had tried to use the same kind of information to delay his execution years before.

They were still working on Larry Kinard's real identity. They also wanted to find out his association with the dead woman from Cleveland Street. The young boy had not spoken and was in the care of County Welfare. Every time Yvonne Zuni saw a young boy like him she thought of her own son and what he might look like now.

As much she hated to admit it, Tony Mazzetti had done a bang-up job identifying the sister of one of the shooting victims as the killer in his case. She'd reviewed one of the videotapes that showed the young girl sobbing one minute, then coolly explaining how she had put the gun to her brother's head first, before shooting his two friends quickly so they couldn't react. She'd also admitted to planning the killing weeks before it occurred. That meant the crime was premeditated and she was eligible for the death penalty. It wouldn't come to that because of the extenuating circumstances of the sexual abuse and the fact that the three men were actively involved in the drug trade. Regardless, the girl's life was shattered.

There was a tap on her door, and she looked up as Lieutenant Rita Hester leaned into the office. "Good job all around. It's funny your concern before taking the job was that there wouldn't be enough excitement. That still bother you?"

The sergeant smiled. "I promise I'll never say anything like that again."

Now, in a more serious tone, the lieutenant said, "I don't want anyone going after Stall for any of his foolishness this week. You can see he always has a purpose."

The sergeant shook her head. "You were right. He's got a way of doing things he shouldn't and not getting in trouble."

Rita Hester smiled. "It's about the best skill a cop could have. He's always a good ace in the hole."

After the lieutenant left, Yvonne Zuni finished the last of her briefing sheets for the night. She was satisfied command staff would have no more questions about either case. With any luck she could get a feel for how the unit worked on a regular basis next week. She left her office door open as she slipped a light coat over her shoulders and took her purse. Nodding good-bye to the detectives, she went to the main elevator and down to the lobby instead of going to the parking lot as she usually did.

She heard a male voice say, "There you are. Right on time."

A smile spread across her face as she turned and saw Ronald Bell in a spectacular suit and tie leaning on a column. He casually straightened up, adjusted his silk tie, and stepped toward her.

He reached for her hand and said, "Any thought as to where we might have dinner?"

Yvonne Zuni shook her head and couldn't keep

from smiling as she realized she'd turned a corner in her life.

It was the first Saturday John Stallings had hosted a dinner at his little rental house in Lakewood since he'd moved in.

He'd spent the morning in his regular Saturday routine. Perhaps it was more of a ritual. He sat at his desk and wrote more than thirty e-mails to different detectives across the country. He never sent a mass e-mail; he made each one personal. But each essentially said one of two things: it either introduced him and his situation with Jeanie, or it was a follow-up to someone he'd already introduced himself to. There was virtually no department too small for him to ignore. And he'd use his skills in organization that the sheriff's office had spent a small fortune teaching him through classes and conferences to make his nationwide search for Jeanie as efficient and systematic as possible. He had a spreadsheet, which he updated weekly with who he'd contacted, what he'd said, what response he'd gotten back, and a date when he should contact them again.

Although he concentrated more of his efforts in the Southeast because he believed the greatest chance of finding Jeanie, if she was still alive, was in the Southeast, he also made a point to reach out to the other regions of the country. In the spring he focused more effort on the Pacific Northwest. In the winter he wrote to detectives in the Northeast and upper Midwest. Part of that was the theory he used based on his own work. He felt that detectives who were possibly snowed in or avoiding bad weather outside would spend a little more time with his e-mail and checking their records. That was also why he always sent extra e-mails on Saturday mornings. That way detectives saw the e-mails first thing Monday morning when they came into the office. It gave them a full week to think of ways to help him.

He definitely used his position as a police officer not only to elicit sympathy but also to emphasize the brotherhood that existed between most cops. He knew it was wrong to use his position, but as a father he could justify anything he had to do just to know what happened to Jeanie. He had even flirted with the JSO forensic artist so she would create a series of images that aged Jeanie with different hair styles. He used the images with his e-mails. He'd never done more than take the artist out to lunch, even though she had dropped strong hints she was interested in a more intimate relationship.

He tried to do a good chunk of this work on Saturdays so no one would ever accuse him of using county time for his personal crusade. Sure, there were times when he couldn't avoid making a phone call or checking e-mail while he was at work, but no one would really fault him for that. If anyone ever asked, he knew he could look them in the eye and say that he did most of his work looking for his lost daughter sitting in his own house. It didn't matter if that was the house he once shared with his wife and kids or this lonely little rental a few miles away.

Thursday nights he always checked certain websites like the National Center for Missing and Exploited Children and other resources designed to help parents who were looking for their children. It gave him a focus and stability in his week when he knew what he was doing one night and one day, week in and week out. Sometimes he wondered if that was what kept him going, and it definitely helped him understand Maria's obsession with helping other parents of missing children.

The events of the week had receded in his mind, and he'd slept well the night before. Physically, he felt better than he had in a long time.

Emotionally he'd come to realize he and Maria would not be getting back together. It was a hard thing to accept when his heart rate still raced every time he saw her. But they'd come to a consensus on Lauren's interest in nightlife, and that was what was important: the kids. His youngest daughter had bridled under the new control her parents had put on her, but she was adapting. The fact that she was here at his house with Charlie on a Saturday night was all the evidence he needed things were changing.

He had avoided the TV news for two days after he heard the term "repeat heroes" used to describe Patty and him. He didn't feel like a hero. Sometimes, when he closed his eyes, all he saw was Larry Kinard tumbling into the back of a garbage truck and the sound of the compactor crushing him in with the rest of the trash. Not only had the pressure killed him, but a broken seven iron had been shoved through his midsection, and a busted bottle had slit his neck in the compactor.

Now he plopped down next to Charlie on the couch that was in the house when he rented it and watched a soccer match being broadcast in some Eastern European language.

Lauren had assumed the role as caretaker at the new house and had carefully arranged the dining room table even though the main course was a bucket of extra-crispy fried chicken from KFC. But she had shown her excitement and Charlie had shown his by vacuuming the living room and dining room without being asked. The four chairs at the table were all pulled back exactly five inches, and now Lauren circled the table, making sure no invisible force had changed that formula.

The doorbell chimed with the middle tone missing, giving it an Addams Family quality. Charlie turned excitedly on the couch. "Is that him? Is that him?"

Stallings laughed, patting the boy on the shoulder. "One of you open the door and see." As Charlie and Stallings crossed the room, Lauren fell in behind them, just as excited as her little brother.

Stallings took a moment, then opened the door. He looked out at the clean, neatly dressed man, smiled, and said, "Hello, Dad. I'm glad you could join us for dinner."

More Books From Your Favorite Thriller Authors